Raves for the novels of Darkover:

"This is the best Darkover novel in a long time.... It's a tale of culture clash, in classic Darkover style, a delightful return to a fascinating world, and a great read."
— *Locus* (for *Exile's Song*)

"The events in this particular book can be read as a stand-alone volume, but there are so many threads that are interconnected that it would be enriching to read some of the fascinating stories that predate the events of this one. I enjoyed many of the twists that are presented and was intrigued by the revelations about those enigmatic beings called the chieri ... Ms Ross very expertly continues to expound upon the impressive universe created by her friend and mentor, the great Marion Zimmer Bradley."
— Night Owl Reviews (for *The Children of Kings*)

"[*The Alton Gift*] is a must for fans of the series, and reads as if Deborah has been channeling Marion's spirit."
— *Center City Weekly Press*

"Bradley's consummate skill at presenting complex political intrigue side-by-side with acute personal drama makes her Darkover series both involving and intricate."
— *Library Journal* (for *Traitor's Sun*)

"Ms. Bradley spins a mesmerizing tale with masterful craftsmanship. Filled with rousing adventure, intriguing possibilities and fascinating characters."
— *Romantic Times* (for *The Shadow Matrix*)

"For sheer skill in storytelling and world building, for wit, for strikingly intelligent development of the concept of telepathy, above all, for continuous concern for people, Bradley has put some more famous sagas in the shade."
— *Chicago Sun-Times*

THUNDERLORD

A DARKOVER® NOVEL

MARION ZIMMER BRADLEY

AND

DEBORAH J. ROSS

DAW BOOKS, INC.

DONALD A. WOLLHEIM, FOUNDER

375 Hudson Street, New York, NY 10014

ELIZABETH R. WOLLHEIM
SHEILA E. GILBERT
PUBLISHERS

www.dawbooks.com

First mass market printing, August 2017
1 2 3 4 5 6 7 8 9

DEDICATION

For the best sister in the world!

AUTHOR'S NOTE

Thunderlord takes place about a generation after the events of *Stormqueen*. Each book can be read on its own, without any knowledge of the other.

1

Beyond the jagged western peaks of the Hellers, the most massive of Darkover's mountain ranges, a storm was gathering. As yet, only a few clouds marred the skies and the winds had not quickened. Sunlight filled the meadow under its blanket of snow, warming the air with the promise of approaching spring, but the stands of conifers cast shadows as deep and chill as Zandru's Hells.

Kyria Rockraven pushed back the fur-lined hood of her jacket and tilted her face to the sky. Even at this distance, she could feel the storm on her skin and taste the lightning to come. She did not know *how* she knew that a day as mild as this would quickly turn to killing cold, but she could not remember a time when she could not do so. She had never spoken of it, not even to her father or her younger sister, never sure if it were a good thing or a sign of the Rockraven curse.

Behind her, the aged chervine jerked on its lead line and snorted as if it, too, sensed the shift in the weather. It had come to a halt when Kyria paused and now it pawed determinedly at the ice-crusted snow. It uncovered a patch of grass, still bearing occasional seed-heads, which it nipped off neatly.

Kyria patted the pony-sized animal affectionately. It had

carried her through many a childhood adventure, although it was too small for her to ride now. "At least one of us has something to eat."

Her gaze flickered upward again as she judged how long she'd have before the storm swept down from the heights. If she hurried, she could finish her circuit, checking the traps that had supplied a significant portion of the cook pots this winter. With luck, there would be another rabbit-horn or two, enough for a stew when eked out with the dwindling store of root vegetables. She wondered what it would be like to pass a winter without being hungry. When she'd tagged along when her younger brother Rakhal was first taught trapping, an enterprise suitable for boys too young to hunt, her father had scowled at her but had not forbidden it. He might have suspected how many family dinners her traps would supply once Rakhal had joined the army of the Hastur king, but he'd refrained from comment. That way, he didn't need to insist she behave in a more womanly way, she wouldn't have to openly defy him. So the fact that for two years now, she'd gone out in all weather, dressed in Rakhal's much-patched castoff jackets and breeches, had never become an occasion for a public quarrel.

Kyria tightened her hold on the chervine's halter rope. "Come on, then. The sooner we finish, the sooner we'll get home."

She picked up her pace, angling across the meadow toward the edge of the conifers. Here at the edge of the stand, weedy bushes formed a thicket. Kyria led the chervine through a gap. The light dimmed, cut off by the masses of blue-black needles, and the temperature fell. She shivered, as if the storm were already upon her, then forced herself to concentrate on finishing her task.

She continued checking the traps but had not gone far when, with a familiar, wordless intuition, she sensed the distant rumble of thunder. The sky was no longer clear, but scudded over with clouds. Wind whipped over her skin, so cold it burned. As she watched, the clouds darkened. The first flurries of snow whirled around her, thickening with every passing moment.

Moving briskly, she started back across the meadow. The snow made speed difficult, but she pushed forward with each stride. As best she could, she placed each foot in the impressions she'd left on the way out. The chervine came along without protest, as if it too sensed how close the storm was.

Within a quarter of an hour, snow fell so heavily, Kyria could see only a few feet in front of her. The gusting winds blew every which way. She paused, wiping away the snow that clung to her eyebrows and lashes. Already her cheeks and the tip of her nose were going numb. With one hand, she loosened her knitted scarf and pulled the edge over the lower part of her face.

In that brief moment, the newly fallen snow had almost obliterated her footsteps. The nearest trees, only a few paces away, appeared as shadows. Try as she might, she could make out nothing more distant. The danger of her situation—how easily she could become lost—settled on her like a second blanket of ice. She'd known the storm was coming and that it would be bad, but she had not imagined the suddenness of its descent.

Her body was still warm but she could no longer feel her toes and fingers. Her muscles felt thick and sluggish, and a number of times she fell but caught her balance against the chervine. The beast plodded on, apparently unconcerned by the weather.

Soon Kyria felt as if she'd been struggling through the snow for hours, half a day certainly, far longer than it had taken her on the outward journey. Surely she should have seen some sign of the castle or its outbuildings by now. The light was fading, although that could be the darkness of the overhead clouds. She tried her best not to think of a fire blazing in the main hearth. Her younger sister, Alayna, would smother her in a down comforter and bring her hot spiced wine.

No, imagining that won't help at all.

She lowered her head, putting all her strength into pushing her way through the snow. A change in the smell of the air, sensed as much with her mind as with her nose, made her lift her head. The snowfall lessened for a moment, and she made out the curve of hill that led to the great stone-walled house. Below, she glimpsed a warm orange light.

The sight of home infused Kyria with renewed energy. She knew this stretch between two low hills, for it was the only approach to the front gates. The path was wide enough for two horses or a cart, but smoothed over by many feet over the centuries. The next thing she knew, the stable master burst from the stables, lantern in hand.

"*Damisela* Kyria! Bless Aldones, you're safe!"

He drew her into the dark shelter of the barn, where the wind no longer blew snow in her face. One of the stable boys took the chervine's lead rope, saying he'd bring the rabbit-horns to the kitchen, and the stable master was half-carrying, half-leading her up to the house.

The door flew open before Kyria had climbed the last step. Her adolescent nephew, Gwillim, stuck his head out and exclaimed loudly, "I told you she would come!"

"Get out of the way, child!" His mother, Lady Ellimira pulled his arm. "Don't block the door!"

Kyria found herself swept up into a very different sort of blizzard, one whirling with color and light, familiar faces, and voices exclaiming. Her sister-in-law, Lady Ellimira, took charge of the proceedings. She was a big-boned woman, too long in the jaw to be handsome, but her dowry of cattle and pastureland had made her an excellent match. Although visibly pregnant with her third child, she was energetic and robust; she dragged Kyria through the chilly entrance hall and into the more intimate, well-heated family parlor. All the while, she issued one order after another as if she were a general in King Allart's army, keeping anyone without useful work away from interfering with those with. Within a surprisingly short time, Kyria's sodden outer clothing had been stripped off and a thick warm shawl wrapped around her.

Ellimira seated Kyria in a chair before the fireplace and placed a goblet of spiced hot wine into her hands. "Drink!"

The men of the family kept their distance while Ellimira gave orders. Kyria's eldest brother, Valdir, Ellimira's husband and heir to the estate, was not present, although he would undoubtedly have a thing or two to say privately to Kyria later.

Lord Pietro Rockraven watched the proceedings from his throne-like chair of age-darkened wood, on the other side of the hearth. Living in the mountains had aged him beyond his middle years, turning his hair the gray of granite and paring his features into feral leanness. Painfully aware of his silent regard, Kyria could not bring herself to meet his gaze. Valdir would berate her because young women like herself, of good breeding and reputation, were not supposed to wander the countryside, but the worry in Lord Rockraven's eyes was born of his love for her, and that made it far more difficult to endure. No matter how Kyria had misbehaved as a child, he had never railed and shouted at her as he had at her brothers.

At last, Ellimira decided that Kyria was not likely to perish from exposure, or perhaps she saw that it would soon be impossible to hold the curiosity of the household at bay. She opened the door. "You may visit with Kyria," she announced, "but only for a few minutes. Don't overwhelm her with your chatter!"

"Kyria! I'm so glad you're safe!" Alayna, Kyria's youngest sister, entered first, in a swirl of lavender scent. She threw her arms around Kyria. "I was so terribly worried— we all were!—when the storm hit. At first, nobody realized you were still out there, and then Gwillim discovered that one of the chervines was missing—" Alayna had a flair for the expressive telling of tales, and as usual had taken a few details and spun an adventure straight out of a winter's night ballad.

As dearly as she loved her baby sister, Kyria had no wish to become the heroine in such a tale. "Enough, please! I'm home now, with nothing worse than a bit of a chill, and Lady Ellimira has seen to that. The storm came up faster than I expected, that was all."

"Indeed, we must not overtire you after your ordeal." Ellimira stood over Kyria, elderly Aunt Siobhan at her shoulder, and Gwillim and his younger brother behind her, politely waiting their turn. They all had things to say, the boys about how exciting it was to be lost in a blizzard, and the old lady about how when she had been a child, it was said that the Rockravens could summon winter storms from Zandru's Seventh Hell. Ellimira clucked in disapproval and hustled everyone out of the room, except for Lord Rockraven and Kyria herself. As Alayna departed, she cast a conspiratorial glance over her shoulder and mouthed the words, *Talk later!*

"Come here, child."

Leaving the shawl in a heap on the chair, Kyria

approached her father. This was the moment she'd dreaded, when she must face the consequences of her adventure.

"I'm not going to scold you, so stop looking like a rabbit-horn caught out of its burrow," he said. "I'm not entirely displeased with you for tending the traps in Rakhal's place, although some would call it improper for a young woman of your rank to enjoy such freedom."

Some do not have so many mouths to feed, Kyria thought.

"Papa, I only sought to—"

"We will discuss the matter shortly." Lord Rockraven took Kyria's hands in his, his fingers warm although knotted with joint troubles. The gentleness of his touch broke her depressing train of thought. "What I want to hear first is how you came to be caught by the storm."

"It came upon me suddenly, sir."

Pale eyes glinted beneath jagged brows. "And you had no warning, no sign of it?"

Kyria hesitated. She *had* felt the storm, even when the day was mild and the skies clear. "I . . . I could feel it."

"I have long suspected as much, ever since you were a little girl and would wake in the middle of the night, crying that lightning was coming. I would show you the skies, so clear you could count a thousand stars, but the next day, your thunderstorm would be upon us." He sighed. "It distressed your poor mother, who thought the tales were mere superstition."

Kyria summoned her courage to ask, "Are they *mere superstition*, Papa? Or—or is the Rockraven curse real?" *And do I have it?*

"I do not believe that any Gift must necessarily be a curse." His eyes flickered away from hers, as if his thoughts strayed to darker matters. "Like everything else, it can be used for good or ill. Some say that psychic talents were deliberately bred into our bloodlines, either by carefully selected marriages or direct manipulation of the cell-seeds that carry the trait. Others question that such a thing is even possible, although I have heard of even stranger experiments carried out in the Towers. This is why I have never allowed you or any of my children to be tested for *laran*, lest those folk use their findings as an excuse to turn you into a broodmare for their own purposes. Fortunately, only you and Rakhal experienced threshold sickness, and in neither case was it severe enough to threaten your lives, so there was no need to send for a *leronis.*"

Kyria's head was spinning. She had never heard her father speak of such matters, not the Towers and how they cultivated *laran*, nor his fears for her and her siblings. She remembered a time, shortly after her breasts had begun to grow, when she'd felt dizzy for no reason she could tell, and certain foods had tasted peculiar and sometimes nauseating, but she had thought it was because she was growing so fast. She'd overheard the cook say something about growing pains to the scullery maid. Alayna had never complained of such symptoms, but Alayna had never had a single pimple, either.

But—"Gift?" The word escaped her mouth without her conscious thought. "You said this storm sense is a Gift?"

"It saved your life this day, did it not, by prompting you to turn back before the storm was fully upon you?"

Kyria lowered her eyes.

"Ah, my brave little Kyria. I did not mean to frighten you with what might have happened. You are back with us, safe and whole. In the future, should you ever receive a similar warning, I urge you to heed it. Look on it not as a curse but as a strength."

"Feeling a storm even before it can be seen must surely be a good thing, especially here in the Hellers. But, Papa, why is it called a curse? Why would people think such a thing?"

Lord Rockraven's gray eyes darkened and his brows drew together. Kyria had never seen him look so somber. "In generations past, those of our blood who possessed this storm sense were prone to unusually severe threshold sickness. Their *laran* awoke early, at the earliest sign of adolescence. Many did not survive."

Kyria had heard such stories, but thought them tales to frighten disobedient children.

"Then there was the affair of your great-aunt, Aliciane. I was never certain what happened—she was my father's sister, you know, and he refused to say anything beyond that she had gotten herself mixed up in the appalling business at Aldaran. I think he must have gotten the story confused, as that war happened about the same time King Allart and his own brother came to blows over the Hastur throne. We know that Aliciane became singing-woman and then *barragana* to Lord Mikhail Aldaran, but she was never his wife. It caused a scandal here at home. Her father—your great-grandfather, that is—called her names not suitable for a *damisela's* hearing, when he referred to her at all, which is probably why we know so little of her story."

Kyria had heard whispers about her kinswoman, but had always considered them idle gossip. It was always easier to make up wild tales about someone who wasn't present to contradict them. "That doesn't sound so bad, what she did," she said when her father paused.

"If the story were indeed true, then she would be guilty of nothing more than what many other women have done. I believe she was widowed young and had a son to provide for." He made a helpless gesture. "Rockraven was no richer then than it is now. Perhaps it was the best she could manage for herself and her child. No, the stories about the Rockraven curse say that she carried the genetic ability to *control* those storms. To call lightning from the sky and use it to blast her enemies."

Kyria shuddered, recalling the power of the storm she herself had so narrowly escaped and that had been a *natural* storm. "Such an ability would be a dreadful weapon."

"Yes," Lord Rockraven responded, "it would indeed. Now we will say no more of this, for we have another matter to discuss."

The traps.

"I was concerned when you followed your brother, Rakhal," he said, "but in the end, I decided it did no harm. You tagged after him like an adoring puppy, but you did not drag Alayna into mischief. Rakhal was always a trustworthy lad. I knew he would look after you. Then when he left us, I expected that would be the end of it. I admit that at first I did not suspect you were going out alone. You must have timed your outings so that you would not be missed."

"I—yes, sir. I wanted to do my share, what little a daughter can do for her house." *An unmarried and unmarriageable daughter*, she added silently, struck with an unexpected pang of sympathy for Great-Aunt Aliciane. What would she, Kyria, have done under those circumstances?

"I fear I have been overly permissive as a father," Lord Rockraven continued as if he had not heard. "I allowed you greater freedom than was safe or prudent for a gently reared young woman. Such lenience might put your well-being at risk, were it not for your storm sense. Looking at you now, I see that you are no longer a child playing at adventures in your brother's clothes."

Kyria glanced down at her shirt of heavy, use-softened linex and worn leather breeches. The thick knitted vest, made to her brother's shape, stretched across her breasts, even though it was too large across the shoulders. She flushed at how unseemly it was to appear before her father dressed like this, and wished she had had a chance to change into a proper woman's tunic over full skirts.

"I have neglected your future for too long," her father was saying. "Perhaps in some fashion, I have indulged in a selfish desire to keep you with me. Now I cannot ignore the passage of years. You are a woman grown. I must not neglect your happiness for my own pleasure in your company."

"Papa, you must not call yourself selfish! And I *am* happy!"

"You are a good child and a credit to your family, but consider what is to come. Eventually I will die, and Rockraven will go to Valdir. Ellimira is not the most affectionate of women, but she will be a strong chatelaine, strict and orderly. Your sister, Alayna, is so sweet-tempered and biddable, and she does her share of the household chores, so she can make a home anywhere. But you, Kyria, will not be content to live as an unmarried spinster under Ellimira's rule."

Reluctantly, Kyria agreed. That fate had occurred to her, but there was nothing she could do about it except to stay out of Ellimira's way. "I must try harder, then."

"You mistake my meaning. I was not chastising you for failing to come up to Ellimira's standards of deportment."

"I don't understand. What choice do I have? The neighboring estates are hardly overflowing with husbands."

At that, her father chuckled. "The shortage of men in need of good wives is not yet upon us. The roads will soon be open again, and we will see what they bring."

What man would want a wife whose only skill was trapping rabbit-horns? She was useless, penniless, and not nearly as beautiful as Alayna.

"Until then, I expect you to comport yourself like a properly raised young lady of your rank. There is to be no more sneaking out, dressed like a ragamuffin in Rakhal's old clothes. I will not have you behaving as if you had never been taught better."

Kyria had expected such a speech from Ellimira but not from her father. Secretly she'd hoped that he would continue to ignore her forays, but now that he had spoken so directly to her, she had no choice but to obey. "In this and all things, I will try to please you."

— ◆ —

"I knew you'd get into trouble sooner or later," Alayna said. She was sitting on the bed she and Kyria shared, legs crossed under her full skirts, when Kyria closed the bedroom door behind her. The room was small and dark, the windows narrow, and the few pieces of old-fashioned furniture almost black with age, but it did possess a small fireplace, and a soothing warmth spread from the newly lit flames. "Did I not say so?"

"You did, and you were right," Kyria responded with an apologetic smile. Alayna had teased her, but she'd never betrayed Kyria's secret. "Sort of. I'm not *exactly* in trouble. Nothing like bread and water or being confined to my room for a tenday. You will be delighted to hear that he instructed me to behave like a proper, marriageable young woman."

"Marriageable?" Alayna's eyes brightened. "Where will he find a husband for either of us?"

"I don't know. Maybe suitors will drop like snowflakes from the sky."

Alayna gave an unladylike snort. "Or sprout like cabbages in the spring. But as long as there are two of them— twin brothers, of course, so we will never be parted—oh, and they must be handsome and gallant and rich, too, so neither of us will have to do a stick of work—then I suppose they'll do."

With a satisfied grin, Alayna bounced off the bed to help Kyria take off her wet boots. At least the heavy winter socks had stayed dry, or mostly dry. Alayna *tsk*ed in disapproval, very much like Ellimira did, as Kyria struggled out of the vest and breeches. "Those things must be older than the mountains! Look at these seams—they're falling apart! It was just as well you got caught now, or you'd soon be running around bare-arsed."

Alayna helped Kyria into the warmest of her nightgowns and wrapped her in a comforter. She brought out a basin and coaxed Kyria to put her feet into it.

Now that the interview with her father was over, and words said that could not be unsaid, Kyria felt shivery all over. She touched her toes to the water. "Ouch!"

"What's the matter?" Alayna glanced over her shoulder, away from plumping pillows and arranging a warming pan under the covers. "Scared of a little water? Whatever shall you do when it comes to soap?"

"It's hot! What are you trying to do, scald me?"

"It is *not* hot. It only feels that way because your toes are nearly frostbitten." Alayna dipped her fingers in the basin. "See? It's barely lukewarm."

"I say it's too hot."

"And I say you're acting like a hoyden who's allergic to bathing."

"Now *you're* sounding like Ellimira's evil twin sister!"

"Am not!"

"Are too!"

Alayna's expression softened. "I'm sorry, dearest. Here you are, half-frozen, bossed around by our sister-in-law and then by Papa—I'm dying to hear what more he had to say to you—and now I'm being wretched to you! Can you ever forgive me?"

"Well," Kyria admitted, "I've been rather a grouch, too."

"Then we're even and shall pardon each other."

As Kyria sank first one foot and then the other into the basin, the heat seeped into her bones as proper sensation returned to her toes. She murmured in contentment as Alayna brushed her hair, braided it with the ribbons, and tied the ends together neatly. When Kyria's feet were warm, she toweled them off and burrowed under the covers like a wild creature in its nest. Her eyes drifted closed. The mattress shifted as Alayna, now in her own nightgown, slipped under the covers. Kyria felt her sister's delicate touch on her temple, brushing back a stray tendril of hair.

"You're going to sleep before finishing the story, aren't you?"

"What? No!" Kyria tried to stifle a yawn, and failed.

"Yes, you were, and it would be very mean for me to insist, even if I have to pinch you every five minutes to keep you awake."

"Yes, it would. I'll tell you, Layna. Tomorrow morning."

"All right, then." Alayna propped herself up on one elbow to plant a kiss on Kyria's forehead. "I'll remind you if you forget. A promise is a promise."

2

The sound of the door creaking on its hinges woke Kyria. By the angle of the sunlight streaming between the half-closed drapes, it was well past midday. Alayna peeked in. "Oh, good. You're finally awake."

Alayna nudged the door open with one elbow and backed into the room, carrying a folding table laden with covered dishes. "Am I not a devoted sister? I have brought you breakfast." She began uncovering dishes. "Potted plums—which you might want to skip as last summer was not the best harvest and cook burned an entire batch—toast, and boiled onions. I think those are potatoes, but I'm not sure. And an entire pot of *jaco*!"

Sitting up, Kyria lifted the covers. "Yes, I think those are potatoes."

"And I shall help you eat them." Alayna took some onions and a piece of toast, and settled herself next to Kyria. The two sisters occupied themselves for next few minutes.

"Pass the plums, if you please," said Kyria.

"You don't want them."

"I do."

"They're scorched, I told you."

"Layna, I am the best judge of whether or not I want plums for my breakfast."

Alayna passed the pot of stewed plums and waited while Kyria tasted them and wrinkled her nose in disgust. "I told you so."

Kyria refused to take offense. Papa might forbid her the small amount of freedom she had managed, Ellimira would certainly scold and nag, but Alayna's sunny disposition would always make the burden easier.

"What else do you want to know about my last day of trapping?" Kyria asked, brushing the crumbs of the toast from her fingers. "Beyond that I got very cold."

"It must have been dreadful to get caught in a sudden snowstorm." Alayna's eyes pleaded for the tale of a desperate struggle through terrifying obstacles. A handsome rescuer who appeared and then mysteriously went on his way would be an agreeable embellishment.

"It did come up quickly," Kyria agreed. Had Papa told Alayna about the Rockraven Gift? "I . . . had a feeling it was coming on, and fast. Know what I mean?"

"I know when a seam is going to turn out crooked, even when it still looks all right." Alayna's brow wrinkled. "I suppose it's a matter of experience. I've stitched ten times more dresses than you, but I probably wouldn't recognize a fast-approaching storm until I was knee deep in a snowfall."

"You were born and bred in these mountains. Of course you would see the signs." But maybe no more than any other person. Papa had also said that Alayna never suffered from threshold sickness, so perhaps she lacked any trace of storm sense.

Kyria reached out to take her sister's hand. "Then we must be certain you are never out alone where such a storm might come upon you."

"Don't be a goose. *I'd* never go traipsing off by myself."

"Oh, Mistress Prim and Proper."

"No, Mistress Likes-To-Keep-Her-Skirts-Clean." Alayna sighed. "It seems that neither of us has any choice beyond which to do first, darn socks or mend torn linens. They both have to be done, and there are not enough hands to go around."

Kyria pushed the last plum around her bowl. Alayna had been right: it was too burned to be palatable. *Like so many things we must endure.* When they were children, she and Alayna had pored over the few story books the household possessed, fanciful tales of adventure and heroism. Kyria had exchanged those stories for Rakhal's traps, for in her estimation it was better to be the trapper than the prey. Alayna's romantic yearnings no longer seemed foolish, but a way of making life bearable.

— ◆ —

Kyria's storm proved to be the last of the winter season, for no sooner had it passed than spring arrived in earnest. Snow still fell every night, as it did in these mountainous realms, but so lightly that roads became passable again. Each tenday, more of it melted than fell. Freshets of melt-water poured into streams and then into rivers. Buds swelled on the branches of deciduous trees, and from the cold frames in kitchen gardens came the first, very welcome, harvests of rhubarb, leafy greens, and slender-stalked, tangy onions.

As the days lengthened, Kyria could not bear to be confined indoors. She walked in the kitchen garden, and then the grounds around the house, slowly widening her circles. Eventually she saddled her old chervine and went riding outside the gates.

"Come with me," she pleaded with Alayna, and on one occasion, Alayna agreed.

Kyria mounted her on the chervine and walked alongside. Although an icy chill still lingered in the shadowed groves, the open spaces were sunlit and pleasant.

"Blessed Evanda, that sun feels good. I've been cooped up for an age," Alayna said. "I feel like a child on Midsummer Festival Day, only instead of sweets and games, I get an hour's freedom."

Kyria smiled as she walked along, one hand on the chervine's neck, still fuzzy with its winter coat.

When she spoke again, Alayna had turned serious. "I'm sorry I teased you about running wild. I thought you didn't . . . I love you, but we're not the same."

"I've known that since we were children, Layna. You always wanted to be the princess, and I wanted to be the banshee-slayer and rescue you."

Alayna jumped down from the chervine's back, ran to pick a star lily, and held it out to Kyria. "For my heroic sister."

Smiling, Kyria stuck the flower in her hair. "Now we can both be princesses."

They talked and laughed until, all too soon, it was time to return. Alayna was late coming to bed that night. She refused to explain, but Kyria suspected that Ellimira hadn't given her a half-day off but had expected her to make up the day's household tasks like any servant.

Ellimira always found work for Kyria to do, as well, one disagreeable domestic chore after another, until Kyria felt she had all the responsibility of running a household with none of the authority to actually make decisions. To make matters worse, Lord Rockraven took advantage of the milder weather to send out riders, sometimes Valdir, on various missions to the small kingdoms surrounding their own, so there were always people coming and going and tracking mud across the floor.

Kyria came across Alayna, standing at the front doors, which had been opened to air out the entrance hall, waving to Valdir as he trotted out of the courtyard. Kyria slipped her arm around her sister's slender waist and they exchanged silent, knowing glances. Lord Rockraven was making good on his intention to search out husbands for them.

When Alayna moved away, Kyria caught an expression of sadness in her sister's lovely face, an anticipation of their eventual parting. She closed the distance in one determined stride and took Alayna's hand.

"We are safe, dearest. Where will Papa find a husband for either of us, unless it be some poor soul who has even less to live on than we do?"

"I would marry such a man if I truly loved him and he loved me."

"Be serious. Could you live without a new hair ribbon at Midsummer Festival?" Kyria said, forcing a tone of levity.

"I may act like a goose, all romantic dreams and happy endings, but we do not live in such a world." Alayna turned back to Kyria, tears glittering in her eyes. "I know there are no rich twin brothers waiting for us, even ugly ones. One or the other of us must surely go to an arranged marriage, and as I can bear our sister-in-law's temper far better, you will be the one who leaves." Her voice dropped. "I would give up a thousand ribbons to have it not so. But the world goes as it will, not as you or I would have it."

No words of comfort rose to Kyria's mind. Expressions of reassurance seemed hollow. She stood there, unwilling to give voice to false hope, as Alayna hurried back into the house.

One afternoon, after returning from a ride, Kyria was half-way to the house when Gwillim raced up to her. "There's a party of men on the road—a rich lord and his guards, it looks like, with a cart and fine horses—they're coming here. Mamma says you must put on your best gown. Hurry! They'll be here soon!" Fairly dancing with excitement, the boy tugged her toward the house.

A rich lord? Was it possible her father's efforts to find her a husband had been successful? Yet she could think of no other reason for such a party to visit Rockraven.

As Kyria allowed herself to be drawn along, she tried to see the great house as a stranger might. It had been built in a modest style, the stone walls well-crafted and the proportions pleasing, but that had been a long time ago. Generations of harsh weather and no money to spare for upkeep had taken their toll.

Once past the main doors, Kyria was surrounded by a flurry of activity. From the top of the central stairs came Ellimira's voice, issuing commands. Kyria drew Gwillim aside, out of the way of one of the house servants, a girl from the nearest village.

"Tell your mother I am making ready as quickly as I can." Not waiting for Gwillim's assent, Kyria hurried through the kitchen—in even more uproar than the rest of the house—and up the back passage of stairs.

Alayna was just coming out of their room when Kyria hurried down the corridor. Alayna had dressed in her best gown, soft blue wool that set off her ivory skin and brightened the gold of her hair. She was so excited, her words tumbled over each other and her hands moved constantly. Kyria had never seen her sister so keyed up.

"Blessed Cassilda, you're back. What a day to go out riding!" Alayna darted back into the bedroom and opened Kyria's clothes chest. "Don't stand there. We must get you properly attired."

When Alayna reached for Kyria's single good dress,

cream-pale linex with darker green embroidery in the pattern of a trailing vine, Kyria shook her head. She'd worn the gown only a few times, for Midwinter and Midsummer Festivals, and last year on her eighteenth birthday.

"Don't you want to look your best?" Alayna said, dancing from one foot to the other.

"This tunic will do very well."

"But it's so *plain*."

"It's not plain, it's subtle." Bands of embroidery in the same shade of dark green ran along the hemline and side seams. "I will disgrace no one by wearing it, especially if you help me with my hair."

Alayna relented, taking up a long-toothed wooden comb. The familiar task calmed her. "How do you get your hair so tangled?"

"I stay up all night knotting it—ouch!"

"Sit still."

"Well, if you wouldn't jerk the comb through it—Ow! Ow!"

"Do your own hair, then."

Kyria craned her neck to scowl at her sister. "I could always go down as I am."

"What, with that rat's nest of curls?" Alayna sounded as if her own reputation would be irreparably damaged by Kyria's lack of a proper coiffure. She returned to her task, only more gently, and within a short time, had reduced the wild tangle to a neat braid, coiled low on the neck.

Kyria took a last moment to glance in the tiny, age-spotted hand mirror. She hardly recognized her own reflection, a woman with bright cheeks and dark-lashed eyes set in a perfect oval face.

"You've made me look all grown up."

— ◆ —

The rest of the family had gathered in the usual parlor, all except for Lord Rockraven and Valdir. When Kyria and Alayna entered, Ellimira and the nursemaid were making an effort to keep the two younger children in order. Alayna perched in her usual spot, a backless stool next to a wicker stand that held needlework supplies. She picked up her latest project, a sock that needed darning, and set to work. Kyria selected a chair cushion cover she'd been embroidering.

"Who are they, these men Papa is meeting with?" Kyria asked Ellimira.

"We'll be informed at the proper time." Ellimira sounded too distracted to be annoyed. From the downward turn of her mouth, Kyria suspected that the unborn babe was pressing on her back. For the first time, Kyria felt a twinge of sympathy for her sister-in-law, who did not have even an hour's respite from supervising the servants, keeping track of the stores of food and the holes in the linens, and all her other duties.

At the sound of a man's heavy tread in the hallway, everyone came alert. Ellimira paused in mid-stride, Gwillim jumped to his feet, and his younger brother, Esteban, let out a yelp. Kyria felt as if her heart had just doubled in size, so that her chest could no longer contain its beating. Something akin to storm sense tingled along her nerves. The fine hairs on her arms stood up.

Once, she'd overheard her father say that one of the Tower breeding experiments had resulted in a form of *laran* that allowed a person to see the future, but it had proven so unreliable that the poor wretches eventually went mad, beset by visions of catastrophes they had no power to prevent. She did not know whether such a power would be a blessing or a curse, but at the moment, she would have risked much for a hint of what was to come.

Valdir entered the room. Although both his sons were on their feet now, his formal bearing and stern expression held them back from rushing to him. Alayna's half-darned sock slid to the floor, but she made no attempt to pick it up. For a moment, the room fell utterly silent.

"What news, my husband?" Ellimira asked.

"We have received an emissary from the realm of Scathfell. I may not speak of his business here. *Damisela* Kyria is to accompany me for the rest of the interview."

Kyria had to jog to keep up with Valdir as he strode down the hallway. The strip of carpet was so worn that it hardly cushioned the sound of his bootheels. They soon arrived at the presence chamber. Valdir opened the door and indicated she should precede him.

Inside, candelabra of their most expensive beeswax candles pushed back the gloom. Her father sat in his usual high-backed chair. A strange man, also seated, faced him.

Kyria had only a moment to study him and the two others who stood at attention behind him. Even at a glance, she noticed the armor under their travel cloaks. Their hands rested on the hilts of their sheathed swords.

Wear no sword at kinsman's board, she recalled the old proverb. But these men were not kin.

"Come here, daughter," Lord Rockraven said, gesturing to her.

Kyria drew a breath, determined that no matter what happened, she would not embarrass her family. She kept her gaze slightly lowered as befitted a gently reared young woman of her caste. Her mouth went dry, however, and her heart pounded in her ears. She felt the gaze of the Scathfell lord upon her, a prickling and a heat on her skin, as if she stood too close to a fire.

Then her father was speaking again. "I present to you Kyria Marilys Rockraven, the eldest unmarried daughter of my house."

"*Damisela*, I greet you in the name of Gwynn-Alar, Lord of Scathfell. I am Ruyven Castamir, his proxy in these negotiations."

Kyria curtsied gracefully enough to satisfy even Ellimira's standards, and looked up. Her gaze passed over *Dom* Ruyven's fur-trimmed cloak with its silver clasps, and his robe of fine wool, belted with links of the same metal. These were only the trappings of his rank. She wanted to know what kind of man he was. He looked surprisingly ordinary, older than Valdir and younger than her father, with a neatly trimmed beard and a receding hairline. The look he gave her in return was measuring but not offensive.

Dom Ruyven returned his gaze to Lord Rockraven. "You did not mention that she was a beauty."

Kyria almost glanced over her shoulder to see who he was talking about. She was not accustomed to being described in such terms. Alayna was far prettier and more ladylike.

"My lord will be well pleased," *Dom* Ruyven said.

Lord Rockraven lifted a finger and stilled whatever Dom Ruyven was going to say next. "We have not yet accepted the offer. *She* has not yet accepted it."

"Papa," Kyria said, "has *Dom* Ruyven come to make a

marriage proposal with me and one of Lord Scathfell's sons?"

"Indeed not," their visitor said gravely, "for he has no sons. My mission is to negotiate a betrothal to Lord Scathfell himself."

Kyria's knees wobbled, threatening to give way under her. How could this be possible, that she should be wed to such a powerful lord? Thoughts tumbled around in her mind like pebbles in a storm-lashed stream. What could he want with someone like her, a penniless country-bred girl, when he could have a great lady and all the lands and herds she would bring him?

Maybe he had no need of such wealth, maybe he was rich enough for twenty men, but why send his agent all this way to ask for her hand? He didn't know her nor she, him— what if they hated one another on sight? She knew a wife's duty; she would be obliged to lie with him, no matter how odious she found him. What if she displeased him and he beat her? She had heard of such things, although no man under her father's roof would ever treat a woman so.

If she said yes, it would mean a place of her own, away from Ellimira's scolding—but she would be alone, friendless except for her husband. Worst of all, she would have to leave Alayna.

But she would not blurt out any of these things, lest she embarrass not only herself but her father. She lifted her chin with as much dignity as she could muster, given the turmoil inside. "I am honored by Lord Scathfell's offer."

Dom Ruyven nodded, looking pleased, although not for his own sake but for his master's, or so Kyria thought. The devotion, clearly born of love, spoke well for Lord Scathfell's character.

"Now as to the betrothal contract—"

"My daughter has not yet agreed," her father repeated. "What say you, Kyria? Shall it please you to pledge yourself to Lord Scathfell through his proxy and then journey to Scathfell Castle where you will be wed in person in the formal manner, *di catenas*?"

Kyria gulped down a protest that this was all too sudden. She needed time—she hardly knew how to think about the proposal. "I—I would like to know the terms, sir. If I may."

She caught the twinkle in her father's eye, as if he were saying, *I told you she has a good head on her shoulders. No silly flibbertigibbet this, with no more brains than a banshee, but a young woman of sense.*

"I see no reason to involve the *damisela* in such matters," *Dom* Ruyven responded, "but neither have I been instructed to keep them secret. She seems like a sensible girl, cognizant of the honor of such an offer." He went on to describe, in terms simple enough for even Gwillim to understand, that Lord Scathfell sought an alliance with the Rockraven family, and what better way to accomplish that than by the bonds of marriage? He had learned that there were two daughters of marriageable age, and so determined to make an offer for the oldest, as was proper. It was never good when a younger sister married first, especially when the match was so, "if I may speak plainly, *advantageous.*"

"You, Lady Kyria, are exactly the young woman he had in mind. You are comely, modest, and not without sense, or you would not have inquired. In yourself and in the alliance with your family, you are sufficient. Lord Scathfell requires no dowry. To the contrary, he has offered your father a bride-price." He then named a sum, in gold and silver coins, that left Kyria speechless. She knew the expense of running Rockraven Castle, how much linex and oats cost, even how much a stable boy must be paid. Her bride-price would be enough to make all the necessary repairs, and dower not only Alayna but any daughters Ellimira might bear.

I could do all this for my family. For Alayna. She will be able to marry for love.

"What say you, Lady Kyria?" *Dom* Ruyven said. He kept calling her *Lady Kyria,* as if she were already wed. "Do these terms meet with your approval?"

"They are very generous. But Papa—do *you* wish for me to accept?"

"I wish for you to be happy, *chiya.* Nothing more than that. My marriage to your mother was arranged by our families in just such a fashion, and two people could not have been more content with one another. Romance is a thing of the moment, but a union begun with good will and the approval of both families will endure even the harshest winter storms. Lord Scathfell is by all accounts an honorable man. His generosity is proven beyond question. Clearly, he is greatly desirous of this match, and that bodes well for his treating you with respect. I believe you will have as good a prospect of a happy marriage as anyone."

"Then I—I accept. But with one condition. Or a request, if you will." Kyria glanced from her father to *Dom* Ruyven. "I have never been parted from my younger sister, not even for a night. I ask—I beg you that she be allowed to accompany me until I am settled in my new home."

"That favor I can grant, and do so with joy. The *damisela* will be cared for as yourself and be welcome in Scathfell Castle for as long as it pleases her to remain our guest."

— ◆ —

Lord Rockraven dismissed Kyria shortly thereafter, the two men to deliberate further.

Kyria flew down the stairs and into the family parlor. "The man is an emissary from Lord Scathfell! He's made me a marriage offer. With an enormous bride-price, enough to secure Rockraven's future. And Papa has accepted. And Alayna is to accompany me."

Ellimira clapped her hands to her cheeks. Alayna jumped up from where she had been sitting and ran to Kyria. She gazed into Kyria's eyes, blinking hard, clearly too overwhelmed to speak. Kyria took Alayna in her arms and held her tight.

When at last Alayna had calmed and the embrace ended, Kyria became aware that her sister-in-law had lowered herself to a chair, sitting right on the edge. Ellimira normally held herself erect, but now she hunched over as much as her swollen belly would allow.

Kyria dropped Alayna's hands and ran to Ellimira. "I am so thoughtless—are you well, *domna*?" *Is the babe well?*

Ellimira lifted her face from her hands, her cheeks wet with tears. She tried to speak, gave a hiccoughing sound, and nodded her head.

I had no idea how very worried she was or what a relief this new wealth would be.

"Layna, bring a cool cloth for our sister's forehead—"

"You will do no such thing," Ellimira said in her usual brisk way as she stood and brushed her skirts into order. "'Twas a momentary reaction, nothing more, hardly worth fussing over. Now off with you. Good news is all very well, but it won't get noses wiped, linens mended, or a dinner suitable for our noble guest prepared."

Alayna rolled her eyes at Kyria. Clearly, nothing had changed in the running of the Rockraven household. They escaped before Ellimira could assign them tasks.

Once in their bedroom, Alayna took Kyria's hand in her own. "You are truly to be married? And I am to come with you?"

"I would not have it otherwise, sweetheart," Kyria replied. "How could I go so far away and not have you with me? And listen, for this is the best part: you will have a good dowry out of my bride-price. I will make sure of it. You need not live in sufferance under our sister-in-law's roof but may choose to marry where your heart chooses. Perhaps one of my husband's handsome courtiers will fall in love with you."

"As long as *you* are happy. What did *Dom* Ruyven say about Lord Scathfell?" Alayna asked, a dreamy expression in her eyes. "Is he tall? Handsome? A mighty warrior? A divine dancer?"

"I assume he can dance, like every other grown man. As for the rest . . ." Kyria sighed.

"You don't care? That's the most unromantic thing I've ever heard. Kyria, he could be as hideous as a toad, or have a squeaky voice *like this*, or—or be a coward, or a lover of men."

"Doubtless, you believe I should have questioned his agent thoroughly on these and other essential matters, like the color of his bed sheets and what he calls his favorite hound." Kyria heard the fear in her own voice. Her marriage was to be a business arrangement that would save her family from poverty. Marrying for love was out of the question for someone in her circumstances.

"You will find out all those things and more, soon enough," Alayna conceded. "I truly hope he is everything you dream of."

"Papa gave me the right of refusal, but how can I judge wisely, never having met my prospective husband? He might be all those things you mentioned, adored by his entire court, and yet be someone I cannot love—and who cannot love me. What if we can't stand each other?"

"There, there," Alayna murmured, drawing Kyria into an

embrace. "You may not fall in love the instant you behold one another. Even I know that is not always possible. Yet if Evanda smiles, you and your husband will come to care for one another. When you bear him a son and heir, he will cherish you beyond words. All will be well, I promise it."

If only I had your confidence in the future, Kyria thought, and vowed to try her best to share her sister's hope.

3

Now that negotiations had been completed, the formal betrothal ceremony would take place, to be followed by the marriage itself at Scathfell. It took several days to prepare for the festivities, during which the entire household thought about very little else. Lord Scathfell's men must be housed and fed, their mounts likewise, and the largest chamber in the castle cleaned and decorated as elaborately as if it were Midsummer Festival. Kyria's holiday gown was not sufficiently grand for the occasion, according to Ellimira, so Ellimira herself altered her own second-best gown to fit Kyria. Its cut was old-fashioned by even Rockraven standards, having been her grandmother's, but the emerald-hued spidersilk panels had survived the decades undimmed. It was by far the most beautiful thing Kyria had ever worn. She balanced on a stool in Ellimira's parlor, arms slightly away from her sides, while Ellimira, Alayna, and the maidservant who was most skillful with the needle basted the hems of her sleeves and skirt.

"This is so beautiful!" Alayna breathed, "Kyria will be able to wear it for her wedding gown as well, won't she?"

Ellimira furrowed her brow. "Mind your stitches, child. The gown will do well enough for a betrothal ceremony here, but it's hardly suitable for a wedding *di catenas* to a man of Lord Scathfell's standing."

"How do you know what is appropriate for the wives of great men?" Kyria asked.

"I have not always lived at Rockraven. Now, enough chatter. Kyria, stand still. Cease waving your arms about like a scarecrow."

"I'm not waving—" Kyria halted herself in mid-protest. In that moment, she saw her sister-in-law not as the sharp-tongued chatelaine of Rockraven Castle or the mother of two rambunctious boys, but as a woman with her own family, a family she had not seen and only rarely mentioned since coming here as a bride.

She could be me.

———◆———

The dress was finished in time, and the bodice fitted so snugly that Kyria could hardly draw a deep breath. Ellimira adjusted the laces even tighter, so that Kyria's small breasts were half bared by the low neckline. It took several hours to arrange her hair, coiled low on her neck, with a few tendrils curling gracefully to frame her face. Ellimira brought out her precious store of cosmetics, carefully applying rouge to brighten Kyria's cheeks, a hint of color on her eyelids and lips, and a touch of perfume on the pulse point at the base of her neck. Kyria knew better than to protest. In this mood, Ellimira was like the storm, sweeping over everything in her path. At last, she finished, and handed Kyria her own hand mirror. Kyria could not decide if it the face was that of an elegant lady, a terrified child, or a porcelain doll.

The entire family gathered in the presence hall, where the betrothal was to take place. Valdir and Ellimira escorted Kyria, one to either side. Alayna was already there, looking as radiantly happy as if this were her own betrothal, as were the two boys and their nurse, standing to either side of a central aisle that led to where Lord Rockraven sat in his usual chair. *Dom* Ruyven and two of his men, arrayed in the same colors, waited beside Lord Rockraven. Valdir and Ellimira brought Kyria to stand facing the Scathfell lord and then withdrew, leaving her alone.

Dom Ruyven wore a chain of precious copper around his neck. A sash of crimson and black crossed his chest, pinned by a brooch set with glittering stones. Kyria took this to mean that in these proceedings, he acted as the proxy for

Lord Scathfell. She would promise herself to him through
this man, and his oath would be as binding as if his master
made it.

The next moment, her father was by her side, announc-
ing his intention to offer his daughter in betrothal to
Gwynn-Alar, Lord Scathfell, and calling upon everyone
present to witness the binding contract. The phrases were
formal and old-fashioned. She hardly heard the recitation
of the obligations, the various declarations—that neither
party was already married or promised, that she was the
legitimate daughter of her parents, that *Dom* Ruyven was
fully empowered to make this commitment for his lord, and
so forth. At one point, her father asked if she freely con-
sented to the betrothal, and she answered as Ellimira had
schooled her. Then came the signing of the contract by her
father and *Dom* Ruyven. Apparently women were not supposed to be able to even write their own names, although
Kyria and all her siblings could read and write. She startled
when *Dom* Ruyven embraced her and kissed her on the
lips. His touch was so lacking in feeling, he might have been
kissing a doorpost.

Of course, she thought, *he isn't kissing me for himself.
Lord Scathfell—I've got to stop thinking of him as* Lord
Scathfell *and as* Gwynn-Alar, *my promised husband—
would not deputize a man to act in his place who might take
advantage of his position.*

She came back to herself at the sound of applause. *Dom*
Ruyven gestured to one of his men, who brought out a chest
as long as a man's forearm and half that distance high, and
held it out for her to open.

"Gifts from Lord Scathfell to his betrothed," *Dom*
Ruyven said, "a few small tokens of his regard, in promise
of the richness of the life they are to share together."

The chest itself was beautifully crafted of rich, red-tinted
wood, the lid inlaid with silver wire. Pouches of brocade and
velvet filled the interior, which was also lined with velvet.
She tipped open the top pouch and slid out a necklace of
river pearls set with tiny rubies. Alayna gasped aloud. Kyria
did not know exactly how much it was worth, but it was far
more than all the jewelry the entire household possessed.
Numbly, she placed the necklace back in the chest and
opened the next pouch, heavier than the first. At first she

thought it was a brooch like the one worn by *Dom* Ruyven, but when she turned it over, she saw that it was a miniature portrait.

A smile lit *Dom* Ruyven's face. "My lord is handsome, is he not?"

Kyria peered at the painted image. If the artist had been at all faithful to his subject, her promised husband was not handsome, he was *beautiful*. His face was perfectly proportioned, set in a mane of red-brown hair. Such a man, and one with Scathfell's wealth, could have any woman he wanted for a wife.

"My daughter is stunned into speechlessness by the image of her promised husband," Lord Rockraven said.

There was a smattering of laughter. Kyria flushed and murmured something about Lord Scathfell being a very comely man. Gratefully, she surrendered the chest to Ellimira, who would take charge of displaying the valuables and then safeguarding them until they could be transported to Scathfell along with their new owner.

Kyria took her seat next to *Dom* Ruyven at the dinner following the betrothal ceremony. He greeted her formally and then proceeded to eat his dinner, slowly and silently. Having discharged his duty, he apparently had no further interest in her. She swallowed her food without tasting and could not have sworn whether she'd eaten rabbit-horn or dead leaves. The wine warmed her belly and eventually she was able to draw an easy breath. At a sharp glance from Ellimira, she pushed away her goblet. It was one thing to become pleasantly relaxed at such a gathering and entirely another to drink more than was seemly. She glanced at her father's pensive face as he sat isolated at the head of the table, then at Valdir on his right and Ellimira opposite her husband.

One more day, and then I will never sit at this table again.

The thought sent a pang through her breast. To distract herself, she turned to *Dom* Ruyven. "Thank you for the portrait of Lord Scathfell."

"It was my duty, *damisela. Gratitude belongs to my lord, who commanded its creation.*"

"Tell me, what manner of man is he, beyond his appearance?"

"He is Lord of Scathfell."

"I understand that. But as we have never met, and I hope to please my husband, will you not help me by telling me something of what I am to expect? Is he a hunter? A musician? A—" She could not think what else a great lord might do with his time, what interests or concerns he might have. Surely, he need not worry about how to feed his family and household, or where to get the materials to patch this wall or that window.

Dom Ruyven set down his eating knife, leaving only a few crumbs on his plate. For a long moment, he seemed to be considering his answer, and Kyria's stomach clenched. If his own agent, so clearly devoted to him, could not think of anything good to say, what kind of monster was she betrothed to?

"You must understand that my lord has never known a time of true peace. He was but a child when the Witch-Child of Aldaran blasted all the lands around. His brother had perished some years before, also at the hands of Aldaran, and his father died not long afterward, leaving him alone to defend Scathfell. Everything he has done, everything he has hoped for, has been not for himself but to keep his people safe."

The Witch-Child of Aldaran?

"He loves Scathfell above all other things," *Dom* Ruyven went on, "excepting of course his newly betrothed lady. He would do anything and make any sacrifice to prevent Aldaran from perpetuating a second such outrage."

4

"Wake up! Oh, Kyria, wake!"

Kyria reluctantly opened her eyes, squinting at the candle flame not two inches from her nose. The rest of the bedchamber lay dark and still. "Gods," she murmured, pulling the bedcovers over her head, "it's the middle of the night. Go back to sleep, Layna."

Alayna yanked the covers back. "It's an hour before dawn, Ellimira's been up for hours, and breakfast's waiting for us downstairs. How can you *stand* to stay in bed one instant longer?"

There was no help for the situation. Kyria knew all too well how determined her sister could be. Sighing, she sat up.

The night before, Ellimira had chosen traveling clothes for both Kyria and Alayna, and these were now spread atop their packed chests. Everything else was at hand, such as warm cloaks and saddlebags containing small items they might need during the day. The chest containing Kyria's new jewels and her gifts for her bridegroom would remain in Ellimira's keeping until their departure.

When Kyria came downstairs, Ellimira had laid out breakfast in the family parlor. Gwillim and Esteban were nowhere in sight, presumably still in bed under their nurse's watchful care. Gwillim might remember her in years to come, but she'd be no more than a name to Esteban and the next baby: "Auntie Kyria," who went away to be Lady Scathfell.

Alayna consumed her breakfast with a healthy appetite, chattering away the entire time. Kyria forced herself to chew and swallow, beset with visions of starvation on the road if she did not fill her stomach before setting out. The meal ended and she had no memory of having eaten, only an empty plate to prove that she had. All too soon, Ellimira herded her and Alayna toward the front door.

Dawn brightened the sky. In the paved area outside, *Dom* Ruyven and his men were already mounted. Their horses pawed and snorted plumes of water vapor, for night's chill still clung to the morning air.

Lord Rockraven and Valdir waited on the steps, over-looking the leave-taking. Alayna paused to kiss her father on the cheek before hurrying down to the cortege, but Kyria paused, irresolute. Now that it was time to say fare-well, there was so much she wished she had done or not done, said or not said. Now she had run out of time. Until that moment, she had not realized how dearly she loved her father.

"Go with my blessing," he said. He had done his best to secure her future, and now there was nothing more to say or do. With a nod he looked away, over the heads of the men and horses. It seemed to her that he was blinking too fast.

"Lady Kyria, here is your horse, another gift from Lord Scathfell." *Dom* Ruyven indicated a pretty gray mare with gentle eyes, a mount suitable for a lady. Kyria went to the mare and stroked her neck. She had never ridden such a fine animal.

Alayna was already sitting on a tall, strong-looking bay, arranging her split skirts to ride astride. Kyria thought the horse more appropriate for one of the guards, and a second glance told her she was right, for one of the Scathfell men looked very unhappy as he sat on what surely must have been a pack horse. It was a pity that air-cars, powered by *laran*-charged batteries and piloted by those skilled in their use, were prohibitively expensive, and at any rate could not manage the treacherous currents of the Hellers range.

Alayna would have loved the luxury of riding in one instead of on a horse.

Kyria felt a touch on her sleeve and turned to face Ellimira. As usual, her sister-in-law's face bore a harried expression. "We have never been on affectionate terms, as sisters ought," Ellimira said, turning to put the gray mare between the two of them and the rest of the party. "If I have been unkind, I am sorry for it. I will not burden you with excuses. But I will offer this word of advice: be careful. Rockraven is set apart from the sorrows and strife of the world, and nothing out there is as it seems. We have never taken sides in the war between Aldaran and Scathfell. King Allart's Peace may hold sway in the Lowlands, but I fear that any respect it commands in the mountains is no more than a gesture. Never forget that your bridegroom's father was one of the parties in that war." She finished by giving Kyria a long, searching look.

"I will remember," Kyria said. It was on the tip of her tongue to ask about Great-Aunt Aliciane, but *Dom* Ruyven was summoning them all to depart. The Rockraven stable master took hold of the mare's reins and led her to the mounting block.

— ◆ —

While they were still on Rockraven lands, the day felt like a pleasure outing. The sky was fair and bright, the horses fresh, and Kyria found herself eager to get on with the adventure. Alayna chattered away happily, drawing more than a few smiles from the guards. Kyria was too busy taking note of how the captain managed the party, with men in front and to the rear, and she and her sister, whenever possible, surrounded by armed horsemen. There were no horse boys, no servants, just a band of men who acted as if they'd had plenty of experience wielding their swords, certainly sufficient to protect one lord and two young women.

The first night on the road passed pleasantly enough. The guards set up a tent for Kyria and Alayna, and a second for *Dom* Ruyven. They had fresh provisions from Rockraven, and one of the guards, a stocky older man named Timas, had a gift for cooking, for he prepared a meal at least as good as what Kyria was accustomed to at home. She was stiff from riding all day. If Alayna was uncomfortable, she gave no sign. She was probably too excited to complain.

Night fell swiftly, a hush sweeping down from the east and across the sky, leaving a web of stars in its wake. Alayna withdrew into the tent and very shortly commenced dainty, lady-like snoring. *Dom* Ruyven had retired, too. Kyria sat by the fire and sipped the tisane that Timas assured her would ease her sleep.

The captain, whose name was Francisco Alvarez, hunkered down beside her. "*Damisela*, you should follow your sister's example and take your rest."

Kyria studied the man responsible for her safety. Other than a formal greeting when they'd set off, they had not exchanged more than a few sentences. The firelight shone on his strong, regular features. She judged him to be akin to Valdir in age, a man accustomed to hard work and constant vigilance. His day would not end until he'd seen her safely to her tent. It would be churlish to delay his own rest simply because she wanted to savor a few moments of quiet.

She handed him the nearly empty cup. "Then I shall see you in the morning."

— ◆ —

The next day passed, and the one after that, until Kyria lost track. Twice they came across little villages, where Captain Francisco paid in coin for whatever was to be had—bread and bean soup, and once a goat, slaughtered and dressed, and a little grain for the horses, which were showing the effects of hard travel.

The road dwindled into a trail, winding through steepening mountains, often the party forced to go single-file. One afternoon, they followed a path that clung to the side of a mountain as clouds darkened overhead. Kyria sensed the approaching storm as a leaden weight, pressing down on her. The gathering clouds were dense and sodden, but without the taste she'd come to associate with lightning. But that did not mean they were harmless.

Before long, a wind whipped down from higher up in the pass, carrying an edge like ice. Kyra pulled on her mittens and drew her hood snug around her head. Alayna, riding behind her, let out a yelp as her horse jigged sideways. The nearest guard leaned out from his own saddle to grab her reins.

Then snow began, at first only a few flakes flying every which way, then more and more. The wind turned gusty, sometimes blowing the thickening snow sideways. It came in blasts, so loud that Kyria could hear nothing else. The snow blew into her hood and caught in the folds of her cloak. Within the hour, it was impossible to make out the terrain beyond the ears of her mount. She prayed the mare had the sense to follow the other animals or at least stay on the trail. Suddenly, her horse halted, head lowered and tail clamped to her rump. Kyria twisted around in the saddle but could not make out more than the dark blur that was the head and shoulders of Alayna's horse. She called out, as loudly as she could, "What's happening?"

"We cannot go on," the captain called through the whirling snow in front of her. "We must find shelter."

"Where?"

Kyria could not make out his response, for the wind picked up again, howling through the gap between the mountains. Her mittens were already soaked through, and her fingers and the tip of her nose were so cold they went numb.

I could die out here. Alayna *could die!*

If only she could command the storm to disperse. Or move off and dump its load of snow somewhere else. She concentrated, imagining the clouds thinning and the wind dying down. For a moment, it felt as if she were pushing against a mountainside with her mind. Then the feeling vanished, leaving her panting with exertion. She tried again, seeking a way to the heart of the storm, but it was no use. She must trust to the trail knowledge of the Scathfell men.

A moment later, one of those men emerged from the flurry, carrying a long rope. He made a loop and slipped it through the mare's headstall, then continued on down the line. They were being tied together, so that they would not become separated in the storm. When he came back along the line of riders, Kyria raised her voice. "Where are we going?"

"Traveler's shelter!" He gestured toward the trail ahead. "Trail branches a few miles ahead. Should cut the wind some. Stay close, though. We're skirting banshee hunting grounds." Then he turned and disappeared behind the curtain of blowing snow.

"Kyria!" came Alayna's voice from behind. "What is it?"

"They're taking us to a shelter!" Kyria shouted back.

The horses began to move off, so slowly it felt as if they were shuffling through the snow. Kyria shivered in her tightly wrapped cloak. With every howling gust, she imagined the screech of a banshee, the hunters of the heights. The giant birds had neither wings nor eyes, tracking down their prey by body heat, and they were said to be able to disembowel a horse with a single slash of their talons. Unable to see more than a few feet, she and all the other people in her party would never realize they were being attacked until it was too late. Once she had regarded such tales as amusing ways to pass a winter's evening, but now she wished she'd paid better attention to the various ways the hero had escaped being killed. Alayna, she thought ruefully, would be of no use whatsoever in such a struggle.

Kyria scarcely noticed the moment when the winds blew less strongly and the path was no longer bordered on one side by steep rock but by a more gentle slope where the leafless skeletons of trees grew thickly, acting as a windbreak. She caught glimpses not only of the rider in front of her, but also of the one in front of him. She turned around to see how Alayna fared and saw she rode huddled over, her hood and cloak pulled so snugly around her that the only things showing were a pink nose and a few stray locks of blonde hair.

"Have courage, dearest," Kyria called over her shoulder. "We haven't far to go."

Alayna bobbed her head in response. At least that was what Kyria thought. Then Kyria went back to holding her cloak tight around her body while steadying herself on the pommel of the saddle.

They trudged on beneath a white-gray sky. The snow flurries eased up and then worsened so many times that Kyria lost count. During the lighter spells, she made out the ridge of dark gray stone to one side, as steep as the face of a cliff. When she glimpsed it again, the slope was more shallow, and snow clung to the crevices At last the trail curved around a rock fall and they came out into a glen. Here the trail widened enough so that two or three of them could have ridden abreast without being crowded. To either side, fallen snow draped the gently rising shoulder.

With a start, Kyria realized that the snow in front of them was not smooth. A set of tracks marked the center of trail, although the edges were blurred with new snow and the whipping of the wind. Even so, she thought they had been made by one animal or several, traveling single file.

The captain, who had been riding point, called out, "There it is!"

Kyria looked up from the blurred tracks to see a dwelling of sorts at the end of the glen. The roof slanted sharply, extending to form the top of a livestock paddock. Two animals moved in the shadows there—horses, she thought, for they looked too large to be chervines. Smoke arose from the chimney on the opposite side.

The smoke terrified Kyria. *I'm in the middle of nowhere, and I have no idea who that is in the shelter. He might be a perfectly innocent fellow traveler. Or a vicious outlaw who would think nothing of disposing of anyone who got in his way.*

Then she reminded herself: *I'm surrounded by armed men, sworn to protect me.*

"Why have we stopped?" came Alayna's plaintive voice. She sounded as chilled, hungry, and exhausted as Kyria felt.

"There's someone already there!" Kyria called back. Then she saw the captain coming toward them.

"Is it safe?" *Dom* Ruyven shouted.

If it weren't, Kyria had no idea what they would do. Whoever was in the shelter might not have noticed their approach yet. They could still turn back—and go where? Alayna could not withstand the cold much longer.

"Rest assured, my lord, my ladies, no harm will come to us from our fellow traveler," said Captain Francisco. "Trail truce holds in these mountains, as it does everywhere. Even the most bitter enemies lay down their swords within those walls. However, these accommodations may be rougher than you are accustomed to. We will of course make every effort to ensure your privacy, but these shelters were not intended for comfort. *Damisela* Kyria, you and your sister should prepare yourselves."

"I assure you, we do not expect a bower filled with silken couches and hothouse blossoms. Merely getting out of this storm, having a dry place and perhaps a fire, will suit us very nicely." Kyria sounded braver than she felt, for her teeth were beginning to chatter.

Captain Francisco smiled, not unkindly. "Wait here while I make our presence known to our fellow traveler."

"I don't like this," *Dom* Ruyven said as the captain rode off toward the shelter. "The risk . . ."

"It is the captain's job to keep us safe on the trail," Kyria said, a bit snappishly. "Surely we can trust his judgment in this matter. And none of us, least of all my sister and myself, could survive a night in the open."

In the pause that followed, she could almost read his thoughts, that her life and welfare must be safeguarded at all costs. Certainly, a man would want to protect the bride he'd paid such a price for, but something about *Dom* Ruyven's intensity puzzled her. Was there more to this marriage than met the eye?

A few minutes later, the captain and the guard who had ridden out with him returned partway and gestured for the rest of the party to approach. When Kyria slid to the ground in front of the shelter, her knees threatened to give way beneath her. She caught the mare's stirrup and steadied herself. Timas eased Alayna from her saddle, lifted her, and carried her to the door as it swung open.

"Here, let me take her," a man inside said in a smooth, even baritone. "She's chilled through."

The Scathfell guards set about unsaddling the horses, taking them to the paddock lean-to, and bringing their belongings inside. *Dom* Ruyven offered Kyria his arm, and she took it, acutely aware of her fatigue.

Inside the shelter, she found a fire burning in the soot-streaked fireplace. Appetizing smells arose from the travel-sized pot hanging from a hook, and if she was not mistaken, hearth-cakes were baking on a flat stone set on a bank of embers. She almost fainted at the sight.

Then *Dom* Ruyven eased her into a wooden chair, well within the circle of the fire's warmth. One of the other men offered her a pottery mug, twin to one her sister already sipped from. It was *jaco*, strong and laced with honey. Normally, Kyria didn't care for overly sweet things, but the first taste sent a rush of energy through her body. If the drink had not been scaldingly hot, she would have downed it without pausing for breath. She pulled off her mittens and cradled the mug as the warmth eased the cold from her fingers.

Their host—if a fellow traveler who'd had the fortune to arrive before they did could be called so—stood with his back to her, gesturing as he spoke to the captain and *Dom* Ruyven about how to divide the single chamber and ensure a degree of privacy for the women. She saw then how an open doorway beside the fireplace led to what looked like a pantry where closed bins were stacked on the other side. The remaining two walls, facing one another, bore built-in beds, three high. The lowest on one side had been made up with blankets. *Dom* Ruyven seemed to be arguing that he would not share a room with a stranger, and the captain was insisting that the women must have the best the shelter had to offer and that the sides of the room could most easily be cordoned off. The stranger interrupted in soothing tones, saying that he was happy to give up his place and sleep on the floor with the other men. *Dom* Ruyven accepted the offer with grudging grace.

The stranger turned back to Kyria with a perfectly straight face, but she caught a flash of merriment in his eyes. Those eyes were set under arched brows that, like his shoulder-length hair, were burnished with copper lights.

"Yes, I'm feeling much better," Alayna was saying in a stronger voice. "It's terribly rude of me, I know, but is the stew ready?"

The red-haired stranger chuckled as he straightened up. "Not quite, *damisela*, but when it is, you shall have the first serving." A single stride took him to stand before Kyria. "You're looking better, as well. However, looks can be deceiving. Ladies, please understand that I mean no insult, and certainly you may have your guardian," with a glance at *Dom* Ruyven, "right to hand. But I would be remiss if I did not ascertain you have taken no greater hurt than a healthy appetite. May I examine your feet?"

Alayna looked surprised, but Kyria understood immediately. Rakhal had lectured her more than once about the dangers of frostbite. "Most certainly," Kyria said. "And there is no need to ask anyone's consent when it comes to our well-being."

Kyria leaned over and fumbled with her boots. The outer

leather was damp where the snow had melted and soaked in, but her thick wool socks were still dry. She glanced up to see the stranger kneeling before Alayna. A high color had risen to Alayna's cheeks, and she giggled as the stranger touched her bare toes.

She's always prattled about meeting a handsome stranger, and now she has. Kyria knew she ought to be happy for her sister, even if the flirtation must be limited to a few days at most, under circumstances hardly conducive to romance, and yet she felt a vague sense of disappointment. She chided herself for resenting her sister's moment of happiness; after all, she herself was betrothed. Even if she hadn't yet laid eyes on her promised husband.

"My sister and I seem to be quite well, foot-wise," she said in a voice that rang with forced cheer.

"Nevertheless," the stranger said, coming to kneel before her. His touch on her foot was gentle, his fingers smooth of calluses and surprisingly warm. "You are quite right. I can see that you have little need for my diagnostic skills." Again, she caught the twinkle of mischief in his gray eyes, as if he were sharing a secret with her.

She cleared her throat. "May I know the person to whom we are indebted for such expert care?"

He looked startled. "You are unfamiliar with the customs of the trail, *damisela.* We do not offer our full names when in the shelter. In this way, even the worst enemies may sleep securely under the same roof. Cold is no respecter of politics."

"I thought there was a truce in the shelters."

"Indeed there is. By keeping our names and our purposes to ourselves, enemies remain unknown to each other, and we strengthen the truce."

Kyria nodded. That made sense.

"However, I don't expect you to call me *Hey there!* or *You pickle-brain!* My friends call me Edric."

Edric. She turned the name over in her mind, finding it simple and strong. "I'm Kyria, and you have already met my sister, Alayna."

"*Damisela!* What are you thinking, to put yourself on such terms of familiarity with a stranger?" *Dom* Ruyven burst into their conversation, his face reddened with more than the closeness of the fire.

He was perfectly correct, but Kyria bristled at the strict, confining rules of propriety. She might be forced to adjust, assuming her promised husband demanded it of her. Meanwhile, she refused to renounce the ease and friendliness she had been enjoying with Edric. "What am I thinking?" she said to *Dom* Ruyven. "Why, merely ensuring that no one gets called *pickle-brain* by mistake."

Edric's composure never faltered, but she could *feel* him laughing with her.

5

The young woman who glanced at him with such merriment in her eyes was like a fresh spring breeze in his mind. She was lovely, too, with the clear, bright skin and vitality of someone who'd spent a great deal of time outdoors. Also an active, self-reliant person by the way she managed her own boots without waiting for help.

And she had *laran*, unfocused and untrained as it was. It rang through Edric's mind like a silver bell before he slammed his own psychic barriers shut. A moment, a breath, and he severed all contact. The first oath he'd taken at Tramontana Tower, the fundamental promise of all telepaths, was *never to enter the mind of another without consent.*

In that brief moment, however, she'd become aware of his gaze. The color in her face heightened, and she lowered her eyes. Her guardian looked to be on the verge of losing his temper.

"Your pardons, *vai domyn*," Kyria said without a hint of subservience. "I must tend to my sister. Traveling through the storm has fatigued her greatly."

Without waiting for a response from either Edric or *Dom* Ruyven, Kyria began arranging one end of the room for women's quarters, and in short order, a rope had been strung, several mouse-chewed blankets from the shelter's store had been draped over it, and the two sisters disappeared behind their rudimentary privacy screen. Edric found himself mildly disappointed to lose their company. The younger one, Alayna, was pretty in a conventionally feminine way, but he'd been subject to too much attention from such *damiselas*, urged on by their ambitious parents to make such an advantageous match. Even if the pretty blonde didn't know who he was, she had undoubtedly spun some romantic nonsense in her mind about him. That much was clear from the way she gazed at him with doe-like eyes. He needed no *laran* to imagine her thoughts: *the handsome, mysterious stranger*.

The older sister, *Kyria*, appeared to harbor no such delusions, at least none he could detect. He would have liked to speak further with her, but they would likely be snowbound together for several days, so it was best not to court trouble. Edric intended to be on his way as soon as possible after the storm cleared.

My mother's health is failing . . . No, that was an exaggeration. Many who suffered a bout of lung fever made a complete recovery. But the news had shaken him badly. *What if she became an invalid, no longer able to act as Regent? What if she succumbed to the fever while I was so far away?* And if she died or become incapacitated, their estranged kin would seize upon that weakness.

The thought of the mountainous region at war, as had not been seen in a generation, sobered him. He no longer had the luxury of remaining in his Tower sanctuary. It was time to assume the responsibilities of his birth. He had departed Tramontana the day after learning of her illness, and forged on even when his mother's messenger fell ill and could not continue the journey. *Blessed Evanda, keep my mother in health until I return.*

"*Vai dom.*" The captain of the armed escort interrupted Edric's thoughts.

"No title, please. Just Edric. We travelers need not be so formal."

The captain's face softened in a brief smile. He was of middle years, keen-eyed but pleasant of countenance, if somewhat weathered from much time outdoors. "And I am Francisco, captain of this party. It seems we have displaced you from your bed. Will you partake of our spacious accommodations?"

Edric pretended to inspect the rough wooden planks. "You are most generous, for I see it is as well-padded as any granite shelf."

"An expert on granite shelves, are you?"

"None but the finest."

Francisco chuckled. "And for that, you shall share the fine repast prepared by Timas, as well. You seem to have some skill in healing, my friend. May I presume upon you further to make sure none of our horses has taken hurt? One of them was moving stiffly for the last hour."

Edric answered that he would be glad to help and followed Francisco to the lean-to. The body heat of the animals had already warmed the air, and the place smelled of the grain that had been stored there as fodder. Star, his blue roan mare, whickered a greeting, but his dun pack horse only flicked an ear in his direction and then went back to dozing. Francisco's glance lingered on the mare, clearly assessing her quality, but made no remark.

As he examined the horses, Edric relaxed his *laran* barriers. He had no special empathy with animals, as the Ridenow and MacArans were said to possess, but his early training as a monitor allowed him to sense disruptions in the energy flow of living things. When he bent to inspect the legs and feet of the horse that Francisco indicated, the one ridden by the pompous lordling called Ruyven, he reached out with his psychic senses as well, probing for deeper injuries that might not yet manifest, even to a trained horseman. The horse flinched when he pressed along its back muscles. If he had been alone or with a group of *leroni* trained in Tower ways, Edric would have used his starstone to amplify the power of his mind, but he didn't know these people or their purposes. While trail truce might hold while they were snowbound, it did not compel their silence after. A single, ordinary traveler might pass with little remark, but a trained telepath, wielding a matrix with skill . . . no, he dared not draw that kind of attention to himself. Home was still a long way off, and Francisco had keen eyes.

"I think this fellow's a bit saddle-sore," Edric remarked, giving the horse a pat on the neck. The horse swung its bony head around, regarding him as if to say, *You can't fool me. I know what you are.*

"There's a supply of herbs in the shelter," Edric went on.

"I'll make up a heating mixture and massage it in every couple of hours."

"Surely one of my men can do that . . . sir." Francisco protested.

"I'll move my gear out here and sleep above the hay rick. It'll be warm enough." Edric kept his tone light. The less time he spent in the company of strangers, the less chance his identity might be revealed. It was a pity he would not get to speak further with Kyria, but safer this way.

Alone in the lean-to, Edric slipped his starstone from the pouch of triple-layered insulating silk that hung by a cord around his neck. Like all Tower workers, he had trained in the basics of healing. A breath, another breath, and then he slipped effortlessly into a state of heightened psychic awareness. As Edric massaged the prepared mixture of herbs into the horse's back, he reached out psychically as well. Sluggish brown energy permeated the ligaments and muscles where the weight of rider and saddle had pressed. He untangled the knots and eased the flow along the horse's energon channels.

The work, although taxing, was a joy to perform. After so many years living among other telepaths, his mind open to theirs, it was a relief to not have to maintain his mental barriers. He had not drawn a free breath since he'd realized that Kyria, too, was sensitive.

Kyria. Why must his thoughts keep returning to her?

He pressed his cheek against the horse's neck, feeling the solidity and warmth of the animal. Through the physical contact, he sensed the horse's contentment. How much simpler were the lives of animals, who had no need for deceit, for schemes and envy. Or for feuds that ran like poison through the generations.

The hayrick proved not nearly as comfortable as Edric had hoped, and a thread of icy air wound its way through gaps in the outer wall. At last, he was able to burrow under sufficient hay to be reasonably warm. He had to use the body temperature regulating meditations he'd learned at Tramontana, necessary during the long, bitter winters there, but in the end, his body relaxed and his mind drifted.

In that liminal state between awake and asleep, the

storm sang to him. At first its voice sounded faint, the distant wailing of the wind through the mountain passes, the sounds that any traveler might hear. Then its tone turned sweet, a lover calling to him. In the back of his mind, he sensed the massing clouds, the pressure of the air fronts, the shift and play of temperatures, and most of all, the slowly building electrical forces. He could taste the tension in the air, the release of moisture high in the atmosphere, as seductive as wine. As the minute droplets froze, turning into crystals of ice, they sang through his senses like a vast chorus of siren voices.

The storm elements formed a symphony, and he longed to be one with it. With a thought, he could send the snow in cascading falls *here* or drive it *there*, gather it up in a blinding sheet, call the winds to whip it into a blizzard ... and break his most secret, solemn vow. He was treading close enough to betrayal as it was, indulging himself in the rapture of the storm. But to control it outright was another matter. Since the awakening of his *laran*, he had believed that if he ever used his storm talent—ever summoned lightning and hurled it where he directed—that it would destroy not only himself but everyone around him.

He had not always been able to summon lightning and command winds with his mind. The talent had come upon him with the equally tempestuous onset of puberty. He had lain abed, ravaged with fever and so disoriented he could not tell if he were awake or dreaming. He remembered his mother, Lady Renata Aldaran, sitting beside him, singing wordlessly, her face bathed in the blue light of her starstone. Afterward, the servants told him that she had not left his side for more than a few minutes all the three days of his crisis.

"At least your *laran* came upon you at the usual time," she had said once he was past danger, although it was years before she explained what she meant. Only when it was clear that his Gift involved controlling thunderstorms did she take him aside.

"Dorilys had such a talent, but hers manifested before she was born, poor thing," Lady Renata told him, alone in her bower with the door firmly bolted. "Had her pregnant mother, Aliciane of Rockraven, been in the care of a Tower healer, we might have delayed or modified the baby's *laran*.

But as Aliciane did not have our help . . . 'Twas said the babe killed her own mother in her birthing. I do not know the truth of that, for I did not come to Aldaran until Dorilys was on the brink of womanhood." She turned pensive, and that sad look Edric knew so well passed over her still-beautiful face. "Donal believed it."

"You mean to warn me," Edric had said after a long pause, "that the same taint runs in my own blood. From my father, you mean."

"From your father, yes." And here, Renata had looked away, her eyes too bright. "But not from Lord Aldaran. *That* blood is safe enough."

"I don't understand." Edric had felt as if the foundations of his life, his lineage as Lord Aldaran's only son, his very identity, had been shaken. "Are you saying that Lord Aldaran was not my real father?"

"That is exactly what I mean. Your father was Donal Delleray, the legitimate son of Aliciane and her late husband. He came to Aldaran as a child, and she as a widow. When she became Lord Aldaran's *barragana*, she bore him a daughter, Dorilys. Dorilys manifested the full-blown storm *laran*, but Donal had only the genetic potential. He in turn passed that potential to you."

Edric had been incensed. "Then I am a—a—" He did not know how to accuse his mother, whom he dearly loved, of being unfaithful to the man he'd always considered his father.

Gently his mother had taken his hand. "Your father—your real father—died shortly after the battle between Aldaran and Scathfell. It was then that Dorilys used her power to summon lightning storms and worse, so that her brain became so overloaded that she lost all control. She became a danger to herself and to the people who loved her." A pause, a pulse of grief, and then Renata continued, "Lord Aldaran knew that I carried Donal's child. He loved Donal as a son, and so he married me."

"Why didn't you tell me?"

"I am sorry to have kept your parentage secret. I suppose I hoped that you would be spared the storm Gift and there would be no need. As long as Lord Aldaran lived, such a revelation would only cause him more sorrow, and the gods know he had suffered enough. We all had, from this dreadful war with Scathfell. Lord Scathfell had lost Dorilys and Donal, and his kinsmen at Scathfell. You may not like the reasons I kept silent, but you must allow that I had them."

Grudgingly, Edric had nodded. Remembering the conversation now, he thought more kindly of his mother's decision. But even then he had understood the fear behind her words—fear for him and even greater fear for them all, should his Gift be as powerful and as uncontrollable as that of Dorilys.

He swore then to never call upon that Gift, no matter how dire the circumstances. To that end, he had left his home for the arduous mental training of a Tower.

Now, as the winds coaxed with their alluring song, and the snow-laden clouds pleaded for him to join with them, Edric fled into the disciplined meditation he had learned at Tramontana Tower: *let all things be as nature intends, and grant me the strength to remain apart from them.*

Thunderheads glowered in his mind, taut with unspent lightning. The storm built and built, no longer cajoling but commanding, a vast, impersonal force. His heart quailed at the magnitude of its power and the frailty of human flesh. It would take but a thought to send the storm elsewhere. To shift the winds, to dissipate the clouds . . .

Grant me the strength to remain apart.

——— ✦ ———

Cold woke him, and a wail like a banshee's keening, and grayness. Below, the horses moved restlessly, even Edric's roan mare and his otherwise imperturbable pack horse. Edric soothed them with word and touch, and then threw down more hay. Someone would have to muck out the floor, one duty he would happily turn over to Francisco's men.

The horse with the sore back blew contentedly through its nostrils as Edric ran his hand over the affected area. He suspected that the horse would be ready to travel before the storm cleared. Giving the horse a final pat, he ducked outside, heading for the door to the main shelter.

Ice-laced wind slammed into him, almost knocking him off his feet. It cut through his woolen cloak and jacket. The fallen snow, which had been knee-high in places, was now piled as high as his chest against the stone walls. A channel of sorts ran from the stable door to the main shelter, where the snow was not so thick. As it was, he staggered and fell twice in the short distance.

The room felt like an oven after the brief exposure outside. The center had already been cleared, the blankets rolled and neatly stacked, and the men sat or stood at their ease. Blankets still curtained off the two sets of bunks.

"Your pardons," Edric said, stamping and shaking off snow. "I seem to have brought the storm with me. Is that porridge I smell?"

"It will be, once it's proper cooked," Timas answered with a friendly grin. He handed Edric a mug of *jaco*, steaming hot. "Those groats must have been stored here at the beginning of time, they were so hard, even with soaking overnight."

"How fare the horses?" Francisco asked.

"They're snug enough. I fed them, but they'll need water and mucking out." Edric blew across the surface of the *jaco* and took a sip.

"I'll see to it," Francisco said, nodding to two of his men. "You and you, come with me."

"Edric, I thought I heard your voice." Kyria poked her head out from behind the blanket curtain. The next moment, she slipped out, clearly trying to avoid wakening her sister. "Was it wild out there? Or peaceful, because horses don't snore?"

Why does she make me want to laugh?

"The accommodations were adequate, *damisela*. Thank you for your concern." Not even *Dom* Ruyven could find fault with *that* reply. "I hope you rested well."

She cocked her head, as if contemplating further mischief. "As you see." Then, perhaps relenting her lightheartedness, she glanced back at the curtained bunks.

"Your sister—she has taken no hurt from the cold?"

"Nothing that sleep in a warm place will not cure." She went over to the hearth, stepping around the seated men. It wasn't possible to take more than a stride in any direction, the central room was so crowded. The shelter hadn't been designed to hold so many. She stirred the porridge, examining the bits that clung to the spoon. "Hmmm. Not ready yet."

"Could have told you that, *damisela*," said Timas.

"I have some nuts and dried fruit—just trail food, you

know—in my saddlebags," said Edric. "If you're hungry, that is." Too late, he recalled his resolve to keep his distance.

She gave him another of those enchanting half-smiles. "I was hoping there would be something useful to do. I heard the captain say we were going to be snowbound, although he couldn't say for how long."

"Yes, the snow is already too deep to travel, and more is coming down."

Kyria turned back to the porridge. "It would taste better with a bit of dried fruit, if you can spare it. Unless . . . if we might be here longer than our food supply, and we can't hunt or trap in the snow, then it might make better sense to save it."

"We won't use all of it," Edric replied, going to where he'd left his saddlebags. "And your sister and your kinsman look as if they could use the extra nutrition."

"My kinsman? Oh, you mean *Dom* Ruyven. He isn't—" She broke off as the man himself emerged from behind his own hanging blanket. As usual, he was scowling.

"*Vai damisela*, I have warned you of the inappropriateness of speaking to strangers."

Kyria's expression turned mutinous, but she answered in an even voice, "We're going to be cooped up together in this confined space for gods-know-how-long. It would be downright rude to refuse to speak to one another. Besides, *Dom* Edric has just offered his supply of fruit and nuts to make the porridge more palatable. Shall I pretend I didn't hear him?"

With each phrase, *Dom* Ruyven's face turned redder. Edric jumped in before the older man could respond. "Not *Dom*. Just Edric."

Francisco and his two men came back in, bringing gusts of icy wind. *Dom* Ruyven made a grumbling sound and disappeared back behind his blanket.

Edric and Francisco settled down to discuss the weather and trail conditions, and when the storm was likely to pass. Edric knew it would be several days at least, but he agreed with Francisco's assessment that the storm showed no signs of abating any time soon. Kyria listened from the other side of the room, her expression thoughtful and intelligent.

By the end of the morning, Francisco's men had inventoried the shelter's food and animal feed stores, and inspected the tack and personal gear for damage. They went over every stitch and buckle, and every place leather might have been rubbed thin or a button about to come loose. Kyria set to work with them, clearly knowledgeable about sewing leather. Edric, working on his own equipment, watched her, trying to not be obvious. He smothered the impulse to grin when she handed Francisco a headstall, throatlatch impeccably re-stitched, and said, "What else needs doing?"

"Lady, perhaps you might attend your sister," Francisco replied, "since it would be improper for any of us to intrude on her."

Kyria pushed her way into the makeshift sleeping alcove. A moment later, feminine murmurs could be heard from behind the blanket. A short time after that, both girls emerged. Alayna's hair was mussed and her face rosy with sleep, but she looked well enough. Kyria wrapped her in both their cloaks and took her outside, presumably to the latrine.

Timas prepared a fresh pot of *jaco*. Just as it was ready, the girls returned, filling the shelter with their bright chatter. The men seated on the floor looked up, and a couple of them smiled. Comb in hand, Kyria sat Alayna down on one of the few chairs and proceeded to tease out the wind tangles from her hair, until the result was a shimmering golden cascade. Edric found himself staring, along with the other men. He was an only child, so he'd never watched women do this, and normally such an intimate task would never be witnessed, even by kinsmen.

Kyria braided Alayna's hair, and then coiled the plaits low on her sister's neck, deftly preserving modesty by keeping the nape covered. A few tendrils curled prettily around Alayna's face. "There! You look very nice."

"There's no mirror—how can I trust what you say?" Alayna replied, but her voice was light and teasing.

"Oh, I've made you look horrible, just to play a trick on you," Kyria said. "Ask anyone you like."

Every one of Francisco's men was captivated. As for Edric, he had always known he must ensure an heir for Aldaran, but he had never imagined what a pleasure it could be to see that gloomy old castle brightened by such love as he saw between the two sisters. At Tramontana, he'd had close women friends, sometimes lovers, but never one single

woman who had reached into his heart. He had thought it
was not possible, that somehow he was so flawed as to be
incapable of it.

He had never realized how deeply he longed for it.

His reflective mood lifted as Alayna leapt up, dove behind the blanket, and emerged a moment later with a
wooden flute, which she handed to Kyria. While Kyria
played a simple melody, Alayna sang. Alayna's voice was
sweet, her manner vivacious. Her skirts swayed as she sang,
so that she seemed to be dancing. A few of the men clapped
their hands on their knees or tapped the wooden floor in
time to the music.

Next, Alayna sang a lively courting song and then a lullaby that Edric didn't recognize. If she were not of good
birth, as she so clearly was, she might make an excellent
singing-woman. He wondered what Kyria's voice was like,
for her speech was melodious without pretense, but she
showed no sign of setting aside her flute.

Midway through the singing, *Dom* Ruyven joined them.
He listened with a measuring expression, as if he were noticing Alayna for the first time. So Kyria was the one he was
responsible for, Edric thought, and not her sister. Whatever
the arrangement, neither young woman seemed to object,
and at any rate, it was none of Edric's business.

6

Early on the third day, the winds died down, as Edric had anticipated, and that evening, the sky was so clear, the swathe of stars filled the heavens with light. By the following morning, he accepted the logic of joining the other party. They were traveling in the same direction, over the only pass through these mountains, and he could not deny the safety to be found in numbers. As much as he disliked *Dom* Ruyven and mistrusted his own motives where Kyria was concerned, he got along well with Francisco. The captain was efficient but considerate, and he clearly had earned the loyalty of his men. Any party under his protection would be properly cared for.

Edric woke early and helped Francisco and his men put the shelter and stable to rights. They'd intended to let the two women sleep as long as possible, but Kyria pulled her blanket curtain aside and proceeded to pack hers and her sister's belongings. Edric smiled at the sight of Alayna, curled up on the bunk like a kitten, covered by her cloak and fully dressed, even to her boots. Kyria helped Timas to fry the last of the porridge, doling it out to the men and then scrubbing the griddle stone clean.

They set out while shadows still lay blue and chill across the glen. Although the drifts of snow reached the height of a man's chest against the buildings, it was not nearly so thick along the trail. The men took turns forging a path through the shallowest parts, changing positions to spare their horses. When Kyria expressed the opinion that she ought to be allowed to do her part, *Dom* Ruyven scowled at her, at which Kyria looked so fierce that Edric restrained himself from laughing aloud.

"*Vai damisela*," Francisco intervened, "my men and I are charged with the safety of this party, and the snow is not our only obstacle. These mountains are home to fierce beasts, snow leopards and banshees, as well as lawless men. Should we be attacked, we must place ourselves between you ladies and the oncoming danger."

Kyria opened her mouth, but then clearly thought better of it. "Good Captain, I thank you for your dedication to our welfare. I would in no way make your task any more difficult."

"That was well said," Edric commented once they were on their way again, riding directly behind her.

"I did not say it to please *you*, only because it was the truth."

Oddly, that comment pleased Edric. "Are you always so forthright?"

"I have never mastered my sister's pretty speech. I suppose that must be deemed a fault."

"No man of sense would prefer artifice over honesty."

A pause, then: "I pray you are right."

———— ◆ ————

By midafternoon, the sun shone brightly in a cloudless sky and the air grew noticeably warmer. The horses' hooves turned the snow to slush, but it would freeze again overnight. The trail began to rise, and in the lengthening shadows, Edric could make out the pass above them. It was well above the tree line, like a canyon between the barren mountainsides.

"We'll make camp here," Francisco announced.

"What?" *Dom* Ruyven protested. "There's no shelter."

"There is a little," the captain replied, indicating a ledge of rock, "and none whatsoever up there."

The space beneath the ledge could hardly be considered a cave, but its floor slanted upward from the trail, so very little snow had accumulated inside. By placing the horses on the outside and by sharing blankets and body warmth, a party might pass the night without freezing. It wouldn't be comfortable for the women and there would be little privacy, but it was their only option. Cold made no distinction between lord and commoner, men and women, even the most fierce enemies.

Francisco and his men set about preparing the cavity, gathering what downed wood might be found within a short distance, and heating a meal. Edric did his share of tending the animals, giving them an extra measure of grain because there was no hope of forage.

He approached the two women as Kyria, sitting beside her sister on a flat rock, tried to arrange her cloak to cover them both. Healthy color bloomed on Kyria's cheeks, but Alayna's face was pale, and her lips were starting to turn blue. Edric smoothed the unruly folds and drew the heavy wool snugly around their shoulders. "The camp will be ready shortly. Is there anything else I can do for your comfort?"

"Not unless you can conjure up an inn with a hot bath and a feather bed," was Kyria's reply.

Almost all the light had seeped from the western sky, and across the east, a scattering of stars burned cold and blue. The temperature had begun to fall, but at least Edric's storm sense gave no warning of another snowfall.

"Best use the latrine and get within," Francisco announced. A wind came down from the pass, quickly gaining in strength.

Edric took one last look at the stars, now brighter than before. His cheeks and nose were already going numb with cold. It was going to be a miserable night.

One of Francisco's men had tethered the horses in such a way that their bodies would keep off the worst of the wind, and the others were arranging themselves with the two women in the center, to make the best use of the combined heat of their bodies. Kyria lay curled around her sister.

Edric lowered himself to his place, careful to not jostle his neighbors. It wasn't easy, for by this time, the fire had gone out and no starlight penetrated the overhanging ledge. Beside him, he heard the sound of blankets being gently moved and a murmured, "Hush, Alayna's already asleep."

"I'll try not to snore," he whispered back.

The others settled into their places. Although his body craved sleep, Edric silently went through the drills to maintain his *laran* shields while he slept, one of the fundamental skills in a community of telepaths who lived and worked so closely together. He changed his mind about the night being miserable. None of them would be truly warm, but neither would they risk freezing. His joints would ache the next morning, but that would pass quickly, between the work of breaking camp, saddling the horses, and setting forth. No, the threat to his rest was the young woman, so close to him that he imagined he could feel her warmth. She faced away from him, wrapping her sister in that same warmth. Even so, he felt her softness on his own body as she relaxed into sleep. Against all sense and prudence, he allowed himself to drift on the sensation.

Images formed in his mind. He seemed to be floating on his back in a sun-warmed stream, watching the patterns of dappled sunlight through the branches overhead.

—— ✦ ——

More snow had fallen during the night, as was to be expected at this altitude. Francisco roused them all as the first hint of crimson light stained the line of peaks to the east. They would need every hour of travel time to make it over the pass. Breakfast was eaten cold, except for a pot of heavily sweetened *jaco*.

Edric set about doing his share of the morning chores, which included bringing a cup of *jaco* to each of the young women. Alayna was still within the cavity, but Kyria was standing beside her horse.

"How fares your sister?"

"We must get her to a warm place as soon as possible." She looked pensive. "She should never have come on such an arduous journey. She chose it for my sake, so that we would not be parted so soon. Well, and the adventure. I've done a terribly selfish thing in bringing her into such risk. She's always been more delicate than me. I've been told I should be more like her, a gently reared *damisela*, but now I am glad to be strong and accustomed to the outdoors, for how else would I be able to take care of her?"

She took a swallow of *jaco* and made a face. "This is too sweet. I cannot drink it."

"You must. You will need the energy, for today's travel will be long and hard. Make sure your sister drinks hers as well."

Her chin lifted and for a moment, he thought she might refuse. Then her expression softened. "You are right, and I would be a fool to disregard the advice of one who speaks only out of concern for our welfare."

They set off, setting an easy pace for the long climb. As the trail rose, the snow thinned, as if it had found no purchase on the wind-smoothed rock. The wind, which had not been so fierce in the shelter of the overhang, came rushing down the pass, so cold that it burned exposed skin. The party wrapped their faces in scarves and pulled their cloaks around them. The horses plodded on, heads down, tails clamped to their rumps.

The trail did not run in a straight line, but curved back on itself and around rocky shoulders. They paused now and again, mostly to give the horses a rest after a steep climb. Past midday, Francisco called for the men, Edric included, to dismount to ease the strain on the horses. Although the captain pointedly excluded the women, Kyria got off and insisted she was strong enough to lead her horse.

"That way," she explained to Francisco, as if it were the most reasonable thing in the world, "if Alayna's horse needs a rest, she can ride mine." With those words, she took the reins and headed uphill, taking her place behind Timas.

Edric led Star beside her when the trail was wide enough for two animals to walk abreast. "That was a kind thought, but unnecessary. Neither you nor your sister are stout enough to pose a burden."

"That is hardly the point."

"What is the point, then?"

"I have not been waited on and pampered all my life, and I do not intend to begin now."

My promised husband—Edric, caught off his guard, heard her thought in his mind—*will doubtless try to turn me into a beribboned ornament, but he will not succeed.*

— ◆ —

They climbed and climbed, moving more slowly as they gained in altitude. From time to time, Edric glanced upward, although the crest of the pass seemed no closer than

before. The wind, cold and shockingly dry, carried away his
sweat and turned his throat raw. His lungs burned. He lost
all sense of time, focusing on taking one step and then another, and tried not to think of what Kyria must be feeling.
He felt certain that Francisco would call a halt and insist
that she ride, but whenever he glanced back, there she was,
her skin rosy with the cold and exertion, holding on to her
horse's stirrup.

Shadows lengthened as the afternoon wore on, and the
sky seemed darker than before. The narrow trail forced
them to go single file. The horse and man just in front of
Edric came to a halt so suddenly, he almost collided with
the horse's rump. From behind, he heard Kyria call out,
"Captain Francisco, what is it?"

"Made it—the summit." It was difficult to hear above the
wind, blustery and fierce, but the sense was clear. "—rest—
a little ways below—out of the wind—"

They mounted up and moved at a more rapid pace over
the high point of the pass. Not only were they going downhill, they were now out of the worst of the wind. The trail
ran straight for only a little way before it twisted again,
winding through narrow passages that forced them to go
single-file. The weary horses slipped and slid over loose
stones. From time to time, Francisco, who rode at the head
of the party, let out a sharp whistle and gestured for them
to slow down. Once or twice, he halted them and sent back
orders, passed from one to the other, to drink as much water as they could. Edric understood the wisdom in this, and
his estimation of the captain increased even more. They
would most likely find running water or even snow down
below, but it would not do any of them good if they became
ill from dehydration and altitude.

Dusk was nearing and shadows deepened as the party
passed below the tree line, descending from wind-scoured
cliffsides to clumps of forest. The thin, dry wind of the
heights gave way to air laden with the smells of greenery.
Edric inhaled more freely than he had for the last few days.
The headache he had been ignoring disappeared, and his
stomach rumbled with renewed appetite. The others
seemed to be feeling better as well, even Alayna. They were
through the worst part of the journey, through the highest
of the passes, and they had made it without serious injury.

The trail flattened, turning as it passed between huge rocky shoulders that made it impossible to see either the front or the rear of their caravan. Star stumbled on loose stones and caught herself. Edric patted her neck, crusted with dried sweat.

"Just a little farther," he murmured.

From the head of the column came the call, "Hoy, there!"

"Ai—yi—yi!"

Edric jerked alert at the sound of shouting. For a moment, he felt disoriented, because the cries seemed to be coming from more than one direction, or else they echoed weirdly against the rocky slopes to either side. No, they were coming from in front of him—

A woman screamed—*behind him.*

Ambush!

The next instant, frenzied skirmishing surrounded him. Men on foot came swarming from the front and rear, rushing toward the mounted party. One jumped down from above, landing on the guard in front of Edric and pulling him to the ground. Shouting rose above the whine and clash of steel, and the whinnying of terrified horses.

A voice rose above the clamor, a woman's—*Kyria, her voice muffled as if a hand were clamped over her mouth*—

"Protect the women!" Francisco's voice slashed through the uproar.

"To me! To me!"—*Dom* Ruyven?

Edric slid his sword from its scabbard. A man, eyes white-rimmed in a face darkened by weather and grime, rushed at him. Battle-trained, Star responded to the shift in his weight, positioning Edric for the blow. He had not fought, not physically, since his arrival at Tramontana Tower, but as a boy and then a youth he had been trained as the heir to a great kingdom, and now his muscles and nerves remembered. He drove down, using his height and the power of the horse beneath him. The edge of his sword barely slowed in its course as it sliced through flesh. He heard a scream, a man's this time, and then another, further away. A sudden weight, a falling away, and the blade came free. Star was already pivoting on her hindquarters to face the next attacker. He caught sight of Alayna, golden hair gleaming in the failing light, as she struggled to control her panic-stricken horse. The bay whirled around, wringing its tail and threatening to buck, but by Evanda's blessing had not yet unseated her.

Francisco was shouting, a rhythmic cry that was echoed by his men. Edric could not understand the words, but it sounded like a war cry.

An unfamiliar man in mountain-style skins, riding a horse that was little more than a pony, emerged from the mass of men and horses. Star settled her weight on her hindquarters, poised to rear on command. Edric braced himself in the saddle just as the other man wheeled his mount in the opposite direction.

"Retreat! Retreat!" Yelling, the man brandished a blade, short and curved on one side. The fighting ceased immediately as the attackers, those still able to fight, disappeared as rapidly as they'd come.

"Look out!" one of Francisco's men cried, just as a handful of rocks, some barely the size of gravel but others as long as a horse's head, slid and bounced down from the highest slope.

There was no place to run in the narrow gap. A handful of pebbles rained down on Edric. Star flinched, but her courage did not fail. A yelp or two marked where larger rocks had struck flesh. Then it was over, the dust of the fall already settling to earth.

Men uncovered their heads and rose from where they crouched. One of the horses was down, thrashing and giving out weird, chilling screams. Francisco, already on foot, rushed to the beast and slit its throat. A man groaned, and another bent over, breathing so hoarsely that Edric suspected he'd taken a blow to his solar plexus. Over these sounds came Alayna's frantic cries.

"My sister—she's gone! They've taken her!"

7

One of the men helped Alayna from her horse and held her while she subsided into near-hysterical weeping. Francisco strode up and down, shouting a string of commands, some to search the area, others to evaluate the condition of the party, including their animals. Kyria's gray mare and the pack horse carrying the two women's personal belongings were missing.

"We must go after her!" Edric cried, wheeling Star about. "There's no time to lose!"

"Go rushing off when you don't even know which way they went?" Francisco grabbed the reins and wrestled the roan mare to a standstill. "Think, man! Did you see who took the lady? Was it one, or many? Did they go back up the trail or down?"

For a moment, Edric could make no sense of the captain's questions. His heart was beating too hard, and a sickness shot through his veins. *Battle-fever . . . and fear.* He brushed his fingers across the front of his jacket, over the place where his starstone lay, shrouded in insulating spidersilk. Even without his touching it directly, the stone acted as a talisman, reminding him that he was a trained *laranzu*, in command of his body and his mind. "You are right," he said, although the words felt bitter on his tongue. "What can I do?"

"You have skill as a healer, yes? Then see to those who are in need, man and beast."

"Captain! Over here!" called Geraldo. "We've got one of them—he's still alive!"

"Excellent," Francisco replied in a tone that sent a chill through Edric. "Let us see what we can learn of this ambush and where the scoundrels have taken *Damisela* Kyria."

Edric swung down from the saddle and started toward where two men crouched over the writhing body of one of the bandits. He could barely make out their forms in the failing light.

"Not you." Francisco grabbed Edric's arm and held him fast. Edric, who like all Tower telepaths avoided all but the most careful physical contact, was shocked into immobility.

"But he—if he knows where—" Edric did not have the Alton Gift of forced telepathic rapport, but in that moment, he wished he did. The next heartbeat, he was horrified at the thought of ripping apart the mind of another person, no matter how dire the circumstances. Such a thing was not unheard of when Towers served their liege lords in warfare. Instead of using their *laran* for healing, or the manufacture of fire-fighting chemicals, or the transmission of messages across distances through matrix relays, *laran* workers created *clingfire* that burned through flesh and bone, or bonewater dust that left the land itself poisoned for generations, and spells that drove men mad.

Francisco's iron grip did not slacken. "My men need you. Would you have them needlessly bleed out their lives or sicken with wound-fever?"

Stung, Edric hung his head.

"If this man knows anything, I will find it out," Francisco continued in a more sympathetic tone. "The *damisela* was under *my* protection, and I will do everything in my power to get her back. I will need every man capable of riding and fighting." Releasing Edric, Francisco strode away to the captured ambusher.

Edric began assessing the wounded. The work steadied him, for he did not examine the men with his physical senses only. As he had been taught at Tramontana, he used his *laran* to probe more deeply into their bodies, searching for internal bleeding and fractures. It would have been easy if he had been able to take out his starstone and use it to amplify his natural gift, but he did the best he could.

From the other side of the improvised camp came a man's shriek, then incoherent babbling. Edric paused in his examination, wanting desperately to know what was going on. If he could read the brigand's unguarded thoughts, plumb his emotions—but then the gibbering broke off. Another man spoke, his voice low but commanding: Francisco. And then there was no more. Edric, his *laran* open for monitoring, felt the rogue's life force waver and then go out.

"I'm well enough," said the man under Edric's hands, "but please see to my friend."

"I'm sorry, my thoughts wandered for a moment. You're sure this doesn't hurt? All right, I'll go check on your friend now."

To Edric's relief, no one was seriously injured, nothing beyond a couple of sword cuts and bruises from the rock fall. The ambushers hadn't aimed at killing. Yet there were only three of the guards fit to ride hard or fight, plus the captain, who looked determined enough for any ten men. And Edric himself.

Dom Ruyven took Alayna into his care, speaking to her in a soothing manner and wrapping her in his own fur-lined cloak.

Edric approached Francisco. "Did he"—meaning the dead outlaw—"tell you anything?"

"Just some unimaginative cursing." Francisco sounded as if he wished he'd kept the prisoner alive just to wring out a morsel of revenge.

By the time Edric had finished dressing the men's injuries, full dark had fallen. The uninjured guards took torches and searched the trail in both directions. Edric, his nerves as taut as the strings of a *rryl* lap harp, checked the remaining horses. They seemed unhurt, beyond the excitement and smell of blood coming after an exhausting day. None of them, not even his own Star, was capable of a hard, fast chase, and they could not afford to lose even a single horse to lameness.

"I'm so worried," came Alayna's sweet voice through the darkness.

"As are we all, poppet, and the good captain is doing all he can," *Dom* Ruyven answered. They were sitting on a folded blanket, close to one of the torches. "At least, *you* are safe. We must take heart from that."

"You've got to *do* something! You can't just *leave her*—" Alayna broke off, gulping down sobs.

Edric crouched down beside the girl. "Are you well, *vai damisela*? You have taken no hurt?"

"She has no need of your tending," *Dom* Ruyven said, drawing his cloak more tightly around both of them.

"I—I am all right," Alayna said in a trembling voice. Her eyes were red and tears clung to her lashes. "I am well cared for, as you see. I thank you for your kind concern."

Edric was just straightening up when Francisco and his men returned. "What's the news?"

"We might as well make camp here," Francisco said. "The bandits followed the downward trail, but not for long."

"You're giving up?"

"There is no point breaking our necks in the dark when we're injured and exhausted. There's only one place they could have come from—Sain Erach."

"Sain Erach?" Edric repeated. "I've heard of Sain Scarp, as foul a nest of villains as any. But not Sain Erach."

"From the tales, Scarp is far worse. They're said to kill for the joy of it, but these folk are more practical or greedier, which amounts to the same thing. If I'm right, they won't harm the *damisela* if she can bring them a fat ransom. They'll find out who she is and send word to her people." Although Francisco sounded confident, Edric sensed his weariness and frustration at his own failure to protect his charge.

"Ransom? That's a good thing, yes? Her people will pay it?"

"Let's hope so."

Although this stretch of trail was not nearly as exposed as their last two encampments, and although Edric's muscles ached with fatigue and his body craved food to make up for the energy used in *laran* monitoring, he lay awake after the others had started snoring. His thoughts kept going to Kyria. Even if he dared to use his starstone, he could not reach her mind at such a distance, but that did not stop him from thinking about it. He told himself that Francisco had experience with the people of these mountains, and therefore must be right—the men of Sain Erach would not harm Kyria for fear of losing their ransom. But she was alone, a gently reared young woman in the hands of rough, lawless men.

The more he thought such things, the more his fears fed on themselves, the more tightly wound his nerves, and the farther away sleep receded. At last, however, the demands of his body overrode the anxieties of his mind, and he drifted off. Once or twice he startled awake, heart pounding. The camp lay still and silent, except for the snoring of the men and the restless movement of the horses. Once, however, he heard a voice, low and indistinct: *Dom* Ruyven.

"... will not harm her ... what the good captain said."

After a pause, Alayna's voice answered, but Edric could not make out her words. Then she began sobbing. *Dom* Ruyven made hushing noises but said no more.

— ✦ —

Light flooded the eastern sky, although a handful of stars still glimmered just above the tops of the western peaks. Scrubbing the dregs of sleep from his eyes, Edric checked on his patients. They all fared well, or as well as could be expected, given the nature of trail medicine and the coldness of the night. At least, they need not contend with the sickness of the mountain altitudes. The supply of downed, dry wood was plentiful here, so a hot breakfast with plenty of *jaco* awaited him when he finished.

"Should we not make haste after the outlaws?" he asked Francisco.

"Sit down, lad," the captain replied, just as *Dom* Ruyven joined them. When the three men and Alayna—for she clung to *Dom* Ruyven—had settled, Francisco said, "We face a difficult decision, and it is not mine to make. I can only advise. This is our situation: we are too small a party to divide up, not in these parts. We must be able to care for our wounded and to defend ourselves against another attack, whether by men or wild animals. Banshees, wolves, perhaps even catmen, if they have ventured this far."

Alayna turned even more white, as if carved from alabaster. She did not respond when *Dom* Ruyven patted her shoulder.

"Yes," Francisco said. "I see you understand the risks, *damisela*. Even with an intact party, we might be hard-pressed to protect you. With a divided force . . ." He spread his hands out to indicate the futility of such a prospect.

"Therefore," he went on, "whatever we determine as our course of action, it must be a united one. We can either all go on to—" He hesitated, glancing at *Dom* Ruyven, who shook his head minutely, warning him to keep silent on where they were headed. "We can go on to our destination, presuming the ransom demand will be sent there, or we can all go in search of *Damisela* Kyria. But we cannot do *both*."

Edric sat back on his heels. *Not even* try *to rescue Kyria? Depend on the bandits to send word to her family? Zandru's hells, what are they thinking?*

Alayna sat through the discussion, her face white and her eyes glazed, as if she had no more tears to shed. "My sister . . . we cannot leave her in the hands of those—those *ruffians*."

"And we will not, little lady," *Dom* Ruyven said. "But we cannot help her by rushing about blindly. That would risk provoking her captors into a rash action, perhaps even retaliation against the *damisela* herself. Her best chance is to be exchanged for a ransom in the proper way. That is how things are done in the world. Trust me, things will not appear so terrible once you are safe amid the comforts proper to a lady of your station. And in a short time, your sister will be restored to you. All of this will seem as a bad dream, nothing more."

While Dom Ruyven was talking, Edric could not bear to look at him. Francisco might command the other men, but he took his orders from *Dom* Ruyven. And *Dom* Ruyven was clearly determined to await a ransom demand from the comfort of his master's castle.

But he has no authority over me.

Edric met Francisco's gaze and realized they were thinking the same thing: *a single man might penetrate such a fortress, undetected.* Francisco nodded, almost imperceptibly. He would not defy his master's agent, but that did not mean he approved of *Dom* Ruyven's decision.

— ✦ —

Francisco, in the lead, pointed out to Edric where the tracks had led last night. Although no tracker, Edric could follow the smaller trail leading north, up into a region of jagged hillsides, the perfect setting for a nest of outlaws.

Dom Ruyven, who was behind them, called out, "What are we stopping for?"

"Just taking my bearings, my lord," Francisco said over his shoulder. He clucked to his horse and moved off.

They went slowly, for the horses were still fatigued from the long, hard climb the day before. The trail dipped, less steeply now, winding as it followed the contour of the mountainside. The land here was still rugged, but from time to time, glimpses revealed hills covered with forest and meadows that marked the sites of fires from years ago. The trail widened, but did not branch. Edric began to worry that they would have gone too far before he found a credible excuse for leaving the company. He was relieved when Francisco called a halt in a little open space, a crossroads of sorts. To each side, patches of hardy grasses grew between clumps of low, wind-twisted brush. Two smaller paths diverged from the main road, but neither showed any sign of recent traffic.

"We'll rest here and let the horses forage." After dismounting, Francisco set about loosening his girth and slipping off the bridle so his horse could graze.

Edric, having seen to Star's comfort, walked over to where Alayna had spread her cloak on a flat stone. Francisco had set up a rotation of sentry duty, taking one of the first positions himself, and *Dom* Ruyven was nowhere to be seen, presumably attending to private matters behind one of the taller bushes.

"How fare you, *damisela*?" Edric asked.

"In body, much better now that we are over the pass," she answered. "In mind . . . there is no help for it, is there? I cannot rescue my sister, although *she* certainly would come after *me*, were our positions reversed."

"Indeed, I believe she would."

"Will you sit beside me?" Alayna said after a moment. She sounded forlorn, in need of comfort. "The sun is very pleasant, although tonight is likely to be just as cold as before."

Edric could not restrain himself from smiling. "I hardly think your guardian would approve." Therefore, he sat down next to her.

"He is *not*—well, not in any legal sense. He's only our escort, or rather Kyria's. Before Kyria was taken, he'd hardly said two words at a time to me. I'm just along for company. My sister and I have never been separated, you know. Or you would know, if you were a girl and had a sister."

"As you can see, I am not, and I have neither sisters nor brothers. She must love you very much."

"Aye." Tears glittered on Alayna's long lashes. She lowered her voice and spoke rapidly, the words tumbling over one another. "Evanda grant that *Dom* Ruyven is right about the bandits wanting a ransom, but what if he is wrong? I will endure the waiting, of course. I have no choice. But if I knew *someone* was searching for her—you owe us nothing, but please, by everything you love—I beg of you— help her—"

Before Edric could promise her that he meant to do so, Dom Ruyven hurried up to them. Under other circumstances, it would have been unseemly for an unmarried man to sit so close to a young woman not his kin, but the journey and the dangers they had survived created a sense of fellowship. Alayna had no need of cosseting from a pompous lording. She needed a friend. She needed to know that someone was going to rescue her beloved sister.

Edric rose and offered Alayna a courtly bow. "And so, *vai damisela*, I take my leave of you. And of you as well, *vai dom*. Here our ways must part. You continue on to your destination, and I to mine. Lady Alayna, I wish you a speedy reunion with your sister. You are in *Dom* Ruyven's care now. I will bid farewell to Captain Francisco and be on my way."

As he turned away, Edric heard Alayna's sweet, light voice calling after him, *"Adelandeyo!"*

Go with the gods!

8

Edric followed one of the smaller trails, which ran straight for a short distance then curved between jagged out-croppings. Rock formations created coves where patches of grass and low-growing, broad-leafed plants flourished. He slipped off Star's bridle, loosened the girths, hobbled both the mare and his pack horse, and let them forage.

Dom Ruyven had been confident of Kyria's safety, sure that the bandits who had taken her would contact her people—her *promised husband*, Edric reminded himself—and return her, unharmed. Edric understood that such transactions took place, but he also knew that the successful conclusion of the bargain was by no means assured. A dozen—a dozen dozen—things could go wrong. Messages could go awry, horses lamed or riders lost in the mountains, the ransom could be more than Kyria's *promised husband* was willing to pay ... or *Dom* Ruyven might be mistaken to begin with. The bandits might have some other use for Kyria.

No, do not think of that. Think only of her safe ... untouched.

Hurry! Hurry!

Let me not be too late.

He was going to drive himself mad at this rate.

Kyria would not languish in captivity during drawn-out, uncertain demands and negotiations. He would rescue her first.

Edric reckoned that enough time had elapsed so the rest of the party had gone on. Pausing now and again to listen in case his estimate of the time had been wrong, he retraced his path to the encampment. Not only was it empty, but the ashes of the breakfast fire were cold and scattered. He headed back up the trail at a brisker pace, to where Francisco had indicated he'd tracked the outlaws.

In the dirt, Edric easily made out the prints left by several horses. He was not a skilled enough tracker to tell how many but knew there were more than one. He searched the ground and the wind-twisted brush to either side, hoping to find a sign that Kyria had passed this way, that she had been awake and able to drop a button or catch her skirt on a branch and leave threads entangled there, but there was nothing. Such things happened only in ballads, he supposed. But she *had* come this way. He had only to discover where she was taken.

The surrounding terrain grew rougher, but the trail led on and on, still wide enough to easily accommodate a laden horse, still smooth enough for rapid passage. The men of Sain Erach evidently came this way often enough to keep the way open. The trail descended into a gully cut by a swiftly flowing stream.

Edric halted and let the horses drink while he filled his water skins. The water was icy cold and had the slightly metallic taste of melted snow that has passed over rock. It didn't look deep, and if the bandits used this ford, so could he. Star went forward willingly enough, but the pack horse, snorting and rolling his eyes, took a sudden dislike to getting his feet wet. In the end, rather than forcing the poor beast and risking a broken leg from a panic-driven misstep, Edric got down and led both horses across.

The midday sun was bright enough, but a tension in the air, in the sky, made Edric uneasy. He did not sense a storm gathering. Not yet. The air currents could easily disperse. And if they did not, he would do what everyone else — everyone *ordinary* — did: he would wait out the storm. Suddenly aware that he was clenching his teeth, Edric forced himself to relax. By his promise to himself, by the oath he had sworn to his mother and on his father's grave, he had made himself one of those *ordinary* people. Yes, he could sense an oncoming storm, even one as tentative and unformed as this one, and yes, he knew he had the power to control it—divert it, gather it, *use it*. But he would never use that power, so it might as well not exist.

The trail passed near a stand of scrubby trees, climbed for a short stretch, and reached a crest. From there, Edric looked down on a shallow, rock-strewn valley that rose sharply on the far side to a promontory. The trail crossed the valley where it intersected another, broader track, almost a proper road. Edric made out what looked like a ruined fortress near the top. Smoke rose from an unseen source. A chimney?

Retreating to the trees, he let the horses graze and sat down to contemplate a strategy. Sain Erach was well-situated, where any lookout with half a brain could spot a rider crossing the valley. There might be another, less exposed approach from the other side, but it would take him the rest of the day to circle the promontory, with no assurance of success. After surveying the route again, Edric decided that his best chance was to wait for dusk.

Now that he was alone, there was no need for secrecy regarding his *laran*. Edric removed his starstone from its pouch. The gem, already warm from being carried close to his body, immediately brightened on contact with his skin. The pale blue color intensified, and twists of light glimmered in its interior. The stone possessed no intrinsic psychic power, only the quality of enhancing what was already in his mind. The moment he first held it, his mind had keyed into the crystalline structure. The stone had become a mirror to his talent, such a part of himself that he could not imagine himself without it.

Now he cradled his stone, focusing his thoughts on it, *through it* . . . He closed his eyes and reached out with his enhanced psychic senses. One aspect of the Gift of storm sense was an exceptional sensitivity to electrical tension in air and in other elements as well. Human minds generated faint currents, which made controlling storms risky, for flesh was not made to channel the immense power of lightning.

Edric pictured the bowl of the valley and the rising promontory beyond it, searching for flickers of energy.

There were many, for animals seemed to give off the same bright sparks, but these were tiny pinpoints, not the larger, more complex patterns of humans. At last he withdrew, satisfied that there was no traffic on the road or sentries patrolling beyond the fortress walls.

But if he could sweep the valley with his mind, how much farther might he reach? The fortress itself? Kyria had *laran*, he was sure of it. She might be untrained, and he dared not hope she could answer him, but he might ascertain that she was alive . . . and what she was feeling.

Once more, Edric focused on his starstone. This time, instead of imagining the valley, he shaped his mental probe like a spear aimed at the top of the promontory. For a long moment, he felt nothing. He might as well be trying to contact a star on the other side of the galaxy. Then he felt— heard—something, low and monotone, rough-textured but straight—*stone. Shaped stones*.

From time to time, Edric had taken his place in matrix circles tasked with mining metals and other minerals. He knew how to penetrate layers of rock for what lay beneath, although he had always been part of a team, minds joined through the skill of their Keeper, bodies safeguarded by their monitor. His mind had passed through rock as if it were water, moving *between* the tiny particles.

Gently, gently now, he cautioned himself.

The next instant, he was through. Instead of the density and mineral taste of stone, he touched the diffuse lightness of air, punctuated by the tangled nets of brightness that marked living people. Were it not for the distance and his own imperfect skill, he might have been able to determine their numbers and locations within the fortress.

Elation blurred his senses for a moment before he wrestled his emotions back under control. *Pride, stupid pride* had all but destroyed not only his own Aldaran but Scathfell as well, only a generation ago. He must never forget that.

Once more calm, he shifted ever so slightly, shaping a mental call: *Kyria!*

At first, there was no answer, only the near-emptiness of air, the anonymous knots of brightness. And then he felt a glimmer of something more, the imprint of her personality like a spill of candlelight in a moonless night. He'd sensed her *laran* before, uncertain and untrained. This contact resembled gazing into a distant, oblique mirror of his own mind, yet she was distinctly feminine, strong-willed, and clinging to both strength and will to fend off the terror that coiled tighter and tighter around her.

I'm here! You're not alone!

He waited, listening, turned himself into nothing but listening, but he detected no change except a deepening of the fear.

I'm coming, he wanted to tell her, but she could not hear him, or if she sensed his mental sending, she might well interpret it as her own wish for deliverance.

Still, she was there, she was alive, and she had not yet abandoned hope. He prayed to whichever god might be listening that she would be able to think clearly and act decisively once he'd made his way to her.

— ✦ —

Edric woke as the eastern horizon was darkening, although brightness still colored the west. He came alert as he had been taught, smoothly and with no hint of disorientation. The horses had been drowsing as well; the pack animal snorted and rolled his eyes as Edric got to his feet. He'd already decided to leave the dun here, ready to go in a moment but tied loosely, so that if things went wrong and he did not return, the animal could pull free. Star braced herself as he tightened the girth, then exhaled with what he assumed was a resigned expression.

"Sorry the rest wasn't longer, or the grass deeper," he murmured as he swung into the saddle.

With eyes and *laran* senses alert, he left the grove and began the descent. All the while, he watched the fortress for signs of life. He arrived at the bottom of the slope and still saw neither movement nor lights. The trail swung north, where it intersected the broader road. By now, light was fading from the western horizon. To the east, the sweep of the galactic arm glittered. Again, he glanced up at the fortress, and this time, because he saw it from a different angle, he caught the flare of orange-tinted light. It seemed to come from the lowest level, although he saw square patches of dimmer light above.

The slope here was steep, so Edric attempted a series of

switchbacks. He'd lost track of the trail and after the first curve, he couldn't see the lights, either. The mare stumbled on loose rock. Halting, he considered the risk of a fall and resulting lameness, maybe a broken leg. No matter how difficult the rescue was, it would be nigh impossible without a sound horse.

Idriel, largest and brightest of Darkover's moons, rose behind the western crest. Edric felt his heart rise with it. He was not an especially devout man, adhering to the form of worship rather than its spirit. At times like this, however, he felt the nearness of something he had no words for, something inexplicable and wondrous.

Star lifted her head and, unasked, began to climb again, up and up, through moonlight now almost bright enough to cast shadows. A night hawk cried overhead, wheeling away on the air currents.

When he was almost to the top, Edric caught a noise so faint, he could not be sure he'd heard it. He brought the mare to a standstill, listening hard. There it came—men's voices, but faint and echoing, most likely from the side leading to the main road.

Edric dismounted and used touch more than sight to locate a stone to anchor the reins. His sword banged against his legs, yet it would be his best defense in an armed fight.

He collided with the wall so suddenly, he almost lost his balance. The stone ran on, straight-sided although roughened by wind and the seasons, for the length of a man's body . . . and then another length. And then he no longer touched stone but wood. As he hoped, the wood proved to be a door, weathered but clearly still in use. The fortress had at least two entrances—a front gate that led to the main road, and this. He would have wagered a substantial fortune that it was by the lesser road and through this, the lesser door, that the men of Sain Erach had brought Kyria.

Although the hinges creaked, the door opened wide enough to slip inside. He found himself at the end of a short hallway. At the far end, a lighted torch set in a wall sconce cast enough light to get a look at the hallway. Openings to one side showed chambers either empty or with piles of jumble too ill-lit to distinguish. The doors had either rotted or been removed.

Reaching the end, he found stone stairs leading both up and down. He took the torch from its holder and moved it from side to side, aloft and then low, searching for clues that anyone had passed this way and in which direction they had gone. Cobwebs clung to the corners. The stairs leading upward dipped in the middle, where the stone had been worn glossy, and only a little dust covered the outer edges, whereas it lay thickly across those leading down except for a clear, central swath. With as much stealth as he could summon, he went down.

The stairs ended in a landing, then descended again. Edric paused, willing his heart to slow while he listened. He thought he heard a sound coming from below—*a woman's whimper?*—but it might have been the passage of wind through a chink in the wall.

He passed a second landing on the way to the bottom. The air smelled dank, and the torch guttered. The thought of Kyria, alone and frightened in such a place, tore at his heart.

The stairs debouched onto another opening, this one bearing bits of wooden framing. The torch illuminated only the first yard or so of floor, but it was enough to make out a trio of doorways, two to one side and one to the other. Like the others, their doors had long since disintegrated or been taken away for firewood.

Edric paused at the first doorway and lifted his torch. The room was empty, bare except for a pile of what might have been straw before time and nesting rats had turned it to powder. Moisture gleamed on the walls. The walls were solid, as to be expected this far below ground, except for a heavy staple of metal—iron, he guessed, from the rust stains running down like pale, bloody ribbons. It must have been set so deeply in the wall that even the most resourceful of scavengers could not pry it loose.

When he stepped across the central corridor toward the single room, his boots made a scuffing sound. The whimper came again; he had not imagined it. He reached the farthest opening in three long strides. The interior resembled the one he'd inspected, except for the woman on the floor. She'd been blindfolded, and her wrists bound together and pulled overhead by the rope looped through a similar iron staple. He rushed to her side and, setting the torch on the bare wood, eased off the blindfold.

"Edric?" she asked in a hesitant, roughened voice. "Am I d-d-dreaming? What are you d-d-doing here?"

"You're awake, Kyria." Edric began working the knots tying her wrists loose. "And I'm here to rescue you."

9

"R-rescue m-me? Are y-you mad?" Kyria was shivering so hard her teeth chattered. Both her jacket and cloak were missing, and the cell was as frigid as the near-frozen ground outside.

"Should I go away and leave you here?" Edric said, trying to keep his voice light.

"N-n-no! I mean—w-why would *you*—?" Kyria broke off, gasping and then gritting her teeth as Edric's efforts to loosen the knots only jerked the loops tighter around her wrists.

"Why would I go to the trouble of saving you when the men who should have been responsible for you refused?" He could not possibly say such cruel words to her.

Edric gave up on the knot, removed the eating knife from the top of his boot, and applied it as carefully as he could. Kyria stifled a cry as her arms fell to her sides. She tried to rub her upper arms, but the movement was clumsy. She must have been left in that position for hours.

Edric held out his hands to help her to her feet. She flinched, then made a visible effort to control herself and nodded. As he lifted her, he felt the chill of her skin through the sleeve of her bodice. He pulled off his jacket and wrapped it around her, then added the gloves tucked into his belt. Both were too large, but far better than nothing.

She fumbled with the gloves, then held out her hands for him to put them on her. "My sister—?"

"Safe with Francisco and his men."

"But *you* came after me."

He bent to scoop up the torch. "There's no time to explain. We need to move quickly and quietly. Can you manage stairs and then a steep downhill slope?" He didn't know what he'd do if she couldn't. Carry her across his shoulders and pray he didn't slip?

"Mmm."

He took that for a *yes* and led the way down the corridor. She followed on his heels. He heard the swishing of her skirts, then a pause at the bottom of the stairs as she gathered them up. She managed to keep pace with him, although toward the top, she was breathing hard. At the outer door, he lifted the torch, casting a feeble light down the rugged slope.

"I don't know this place," she whispered. "This isn't the way they brought me in."

"But it's how I came," he said. "Listen, the first part will be rough, even if we dare use the torch. But I've got a horse waiting in a little ways and then my pack horse across the valley. You'll be able to ride once we get there." He meant to sound encouraging, but the prospect sounded bleak to his own ears.

"We mustn't use the torch," she said, her voice steadier. "When they find I'm gone, they'll follow us by its light. With any luck they'll think I've retraced my steps through the other gate."

Even shaken by her captivity, she was able to think clearly, to plan. Edric dared hope that together they stood a chance.

Their progress, while slow, was steady. Edric fell into a rhythm of testing the ground with the foot on the downhill side, stepping, joining his other foot, and reaching down again. The terrain was rougher and steeper than he remembered. He quelled his fear of getting lost by reminding himself that *down* meant *away from the fortress,* and that sooner or later, he would come to the uphill slope.

The roan mare nickered a greeting even before he could

see her, and he used the sound as a guide. Kyria gave a little cry of relief as they reached the horse. Without meaning to open his mind to hers, Edric caught her fear that something would go wrong and both of them would be dragged back to the fortress. He donned his second jacket from his saddlebags, swung into the saddle, and pulled Kyria up behind him. With a little maneuvering, they were able to arrange his cloak around both of them.

Trusting to the horse's superior night vision, he let Star pick her way down the hill. Although Idriel shone ahead as brightly as ever, he could not make out anything resembling a trail. Star seemed to know where she was going.

Kyria wrapped her arms around Edric's waist. A moment later, he felt the gentle weight of her head on his shoulder. The air around them felt warmer under the draped cloak. His heart beat faster. He said nothing, only pressed her arms closer to his body with one hand while he held the reins in the other.

Still there was no sign of alarm from the fortress.

Star reached the flat bottom of the valley, then slowed again as the land grew steeper. She struggled up the slope under the weight of two riders. Edric lifted the reins, and she halted, head lowered, sides heaving. Just as he debated dismounting, he heard shouting behind them.

Distance distorted the sound, as it echoed off the rocky sides of the valley. Behind him, Kyria tensed. Edric swung his leg over Star's neck and dropped to the ground.

"We'll go faster this way," he explained, "and we'll spare the horse. With any luck, we'll be over the crest before they realize which way we've gone." Taking hold of the reins, he headed up the hill.

"I should walk, too," Kyria protested.

"Save your strength." Edric concentrated on climbing, pushing himself with the thought of the Sain Erach men rushing down the trail on fresh horses.

"Edric?"

He kept going, trying his best to keep sight of the trail. "Yes?"

"Edric! Pay attention!" She sounded so very much like the mistress of novices at Tramontana that Edric's feet rooted into the rock. "Look!"

Turning back to the valley, Edric spotted a line of torches, three or four of them, moving rapidly away from the fortress, but angled away from their own position. He made out the shapes of mounted riders.

"They're following the main road," he murmured, hardly daring to believe in this stroke of luck.

"That's how they brought me in," Kyria reminded him. "This isn't good."

"No, it's great. We can make it back to our original route without those brigands on our tails."

"That's exactly the problem. They took me down that trail and then along there." She indicated the road from the fortress. "When they attacked our party, they came at us from two directions—from up the trail *and down*. If we continue the way Francisco was taking us, we'll head straight into them. Even if we don't, they'll know every deer path and rabbit-horn den for miles around."

Kyria was right. The Sain Erach riders would know this territory like the insides of their own bedrooms. They'd search the trail in both directions, and if they didn't find their quarry, they'd launch a daylight search, combing the area.

"What are we to do?" Kyria said. "We can't go back over the pass, not without warm clothing and food, and we can't continue down the trail."

"I'll think of something." Edric remembered the crossroads and the track he'd taken his horses up, hiding until *Dom* Ruyven and the others had gone. It might lead to one of the main passages through this part of the Hellers. Unless the Sain Erach riders were extraordinary trackers, they would not realize which trails Edric and Kyria had taken, for the stony ground was already crossed by the prints of other horses.

Edric explained his plan, trying to sound confident. "At the worst, if we have to come back down the trail, the hunt may well have disbanded. The two of us should be able to slip through their territory without drawing the attention of a larger party."

Kyria turned silent, her doubt like a gray miasma, so he gave up his attempts to buoy her spirits.

Idriel had set, and clouds obscured the stars by the time they arrived at the crest where Edric had left the pack horse. From here, just past the crest, they were out of the line of sight from the valley. Kyria sat hunched in the saddle, as if she could not summon the strength to dismount.

Edric held out his hands, and she fell into his arms. Her skin felt like half-frozen silk. She drew a shuddering breath and when she let it go, he felt her warmth on his cheek. Not daring to linger in the moment, he eased her to the ground.

"I'll bring you water and a little food," he said in a voice he scarcely recognized as his own. "You must rest while you can."

She nodded, a movement of shadow upon shadow. Searching by touch as well as sight, he found a water skin and the saddlebag in which he carried trail food. He unfolded the oiled cloth wrapping and took out a flat cake of dried fruit and nuts, pressed together with honey. He also had jerked meat, but that required softening; the sweetness of the confection would give Kyria energy more quickly.

She accepted the cake and bit off a piece. Edric took a portion for himself and soon felt the lift as his body responded to the concentrated nourishment. He was tired, but that could not be helped. At Tramontana, he had worked all night and thus learned the limits of his strength. He could go on for some time.

At the memory of his Tower work, something brushed his mind. His storm sense woke, nudging him. The sensation was not an outright warning, not yet, only an awareness of the shifting atmospheric currents. The storm he had sensed earlier as only a possibility was gaining strength.

He unloaded the pack horse and redistributed the bags, taking into account that each horse now must carry a rider. Francisco would have accomplished the task more efficiently, but in the end, Edric was satisfied he'd done the best he could.

The red sun had not yet cleared the eastern ridge of mountains, but dawn had given rise to day. Dark-bellied clouds condensed across the north, heading in their direction.

"Kyria? It's time to go. Are—are you all right?"

Kyria lifted her face to the north, her gaze fixed on the clouds. A wind sprang up, pulling at the loose strands of her hair and bringing color to her cheeks. "Yes, I'm fine. Just ashamed that you have done all the work while I sat here like a lump." Waving off his offer of assistance, she clambered to her feet and brushed dirt and bits of dried grass roots off her skirts.

Edric boosted her onto Star, for the mare was weary and she was the lighter rider. Then he mounted the pack horse. The pack saddle wasn't nearly as comfortable, and he knew from experience the dun's gaits were rough and his mouth like leather. He tapped the pack horse with his heels and sent the beast into a trot. They had to get well beyond the crossroads before the Sain Erach men reached it. More than that, they must find shelter before the storm hit. When he glanced over his shoulder, he saw how Kyria's mouth was set in a fierce, determined expression, and her eyes were wild.

Her promised husband lacks the sense of a moon-blind rabbit-horn to let such a woman slip through his hands.

Luck rode with them, and when they reached the main track, they saw no sign of their pursuers. Without any need for speech, as if they had one thought, they urged their horses onward. Edric had already traveled this section of trail twice before, but now he counted every minute, every hoof beat. The wind fell away, and the air, which had been growing progressively more chill, turned milder, but he was not lulled into believing the clouds would dissipate.

"There!" Edric broke his silence to indicate the crossroads, now only a short distance away. The side trail was but minutes away.

Clouds darkened the sky. The air tasted of lightning to come.

He could see the flat place where they'd camped and the main road leading down and away, curving around the shoulder of the hill—

Two riders emerged from behind the hill, followed by three more.

Behind him, Kyria let out a cry of dismay. Edric hauled on the reins. The pack horse resisted, dipping his head. Kyria's horse crowded his rump, and he threatened to kick. Edric jerked the horse's head up, trying to see a way out. They had enough room to turn around, but this trail would only lead them back to the fortress.

They hadn't been spotted, not yet.

He glanced up at the clouds, denser now and laden with promise. The wind picked up again.

Use me, pleaded the storm. *I am yours for the taking, all the power of wind and lightning . . .*

Something inside Edric yearned to answer the storm, to seize control of it. He had the power to save both of them, to save *Kyria*, and all he had to do was reach out with his mind. Use his Gift, as he had been born to do.

In memory, he heard Lady Renata relating how his kinswoman Dorilys had killed her own mother with such a Gift, how the lightning had overwhelmed and then consumed her. Stripped of self-control, she'd become a deadly menace to herself and to the people who loved her.

I dare not use the Gift. I will not use it.

Half in horror, half in desperation, Edric kicked the dun so hard, the beast leaped forward. Within a few strides, they reached a full-out gallop. Down the trail they sped, each moment bringing them closer to the crossroads.

The lead rider must have seen them, for he lifted one arm in signal to the others. Edric could not hear the other man's words, only the shout of exultation.

Faster! Edric clapped his heels to the pack horse's sides.

Edric and Kyria reached the crossroads, and Edric wrestled the pack horse under enough control to send him down the same branch they'd used before. They had no hope of outstripping their pursuers, he thought with a spasm of sick despair. They had only a short lead, they'd been sighted, and the hunt was on in earnest now.

The trail twisted so that he could no longer see the crossroads. Maybe they could find a place to hide while the bandits rode past. To either side, the ground looked treacherous, the slope to one side so steep that only a mountain chervine could find footing there. From what he could see of the trail ahead, it ran along a sheer rock face, while smaller boulders strewed the other side.

Above and before him, lightning flickered, closely followed by sullen rumbling, as if the clouds were holding back their full power, saving it.

The pack horse did not flinch, stolid beast that he was. Pinning ears to neck, he raced on at a pace that would have been foolhardy over such a terrain under any other circumstances. Edric hazarded a glance over one shoulder and saw Kyria on Star, gallant Star, only a couple of lengths behind.

The trail dipped suddenly and became so steep that the

horses slipped and scrambled for balance. By an amazing stroke of luck, neither of them put a foot wrong. The pack horse slid on a patch of loose, gravel-fine stones, and almost sat down on his hindquarters. The descent ended in a stream that was swift and foamed with white, but narrow enough for a horse to jump.

The pack horse, unused to such obstacles, came to a prancing, snorting halt at the water's edge. Kyria caught up with Edric the next moment, her gaze fixed on the far bank. Star gathered herself in a smooth, powerful motion, and sailed over the stream. Edric watched her disappear from view around a dense, willowy thicket. He circled the pack horse, trying to get as good a run-up to the jump as possible. At the last moment, the horse set his feet and refused. Cursing the beast for obstinacy, Edric tried again. He felt every passing moment as a death knell. The Sain Erach riders would be upon him any moment now.

The pack horse bent his head, sniffed at the water, ruffled his nostrils, and began to wade across. It seemed to take forever to cross, until finally they climbed onto the far bank.

Shouting from the top of gorge reached Edric's ears. He twisted in the saddle to see the riders from Sain Erach begin their descent, single file. The overhead clouds and the steep sides cast the riverbanks into shadow, so he could not see their expressions, but he *felt* their surge of triumph.

This was the place, he thought. Here, where they must come at him one by one, he would make his stand. They were too many for him to kill. He would die here, in any event, but he might delay them long enough for Kyria to get away.

If she kept her wits about her—if she realized she'd have to get off the trail—if she used what hiding places presented themselves—

She was intelligent and resourceful. She would realize she must not tarry, must not turn back for him.

Run, Kyria. Keep running, and live.

10

Drawing his sword, Edric turned the dun to face the on-coming riders. His breath came light and fast, and his pulse hammered in his ears. He'd done his best to keep fit during his years at Tramontana, but he could not equal the skill of a trained sword master.

The storm condensed overhead, a blanket of darkness over the river gorge. Edric tasted lightning in the air. The faces of the oncoming riders shone like pale ovals. The second man rode a spotted horse, and the white patches stood out against the gloom.

Closer now ... closer ...

The lead rider reached the far bank and let out a howl like a wolf that has scented its prey.

Lord of Light, be with me.

Brightness laced the sky and, a moment later, thunder sounded above him. A second flash followed almost on the heels of the first and then a roll of riotous sound. The pack horse flattened his ears and reared, threatening to hurl him-self backward. Edric managed to keep his seat as he wres-tled the animal under control. For a moment, he seemed to be succeeding. Then the dun arched his spine and launched into a series of spinning bucks. Edric lost his seat. The horse lost its footing and went down, hurling Edric through the air.

By luck, he landed in a deeper part of the river. Water rushed over him, filling his mouth and nose. The sword jerked out of his grasp and was gone. The current tossed him this way and that, so that he could not tell up from down. The water looked black in all directions, laced with bubbles. He kicked but found no solid surface. For all he knew, he might be thrusting himself deeper.

Edric hit a rock with his elbow, then another with his back. The next moment, he slammed up against a hard, flat surface. He tried to push his head above water, but the current was too strong. It pinned him against the rock, his own strength too feeble to overcome it. His lungs, half-emptied to begin with, burned.

Then the current shifted, dragging him across the rock. The next moment, he was free. His head broke the surface. He drew in a lungful of air, gasped and choked, and almost went under again. By another stroke of luck, he grabbed hold of a rock that stuck up above the water like a tabletop, and was able to haul himself on top of it. He saw then that the river had carried him only a short distance. The horse was thrashing and squealing, struggling to rise. One of its legs was almost certainly broken.

There was no time to end the horse's suffering or salvage the supplies. The Sain Erach riders were gathering on the far bank. One pointed to the horse, and another to Edric himself. They hesitated, fearful of risking their own mounts to a similar fate.

In that moment, Edric's *laran* came alive. His mind opened to the storm. He felt it as intensely as if he'd peeled off his skin. His nerves shrieked with the electrical tension between cloud and land, that needed only an infinitesimal shift to ignite.

The rock face on the far bank, a treeless promontory, jutted high above the surrounding trees, and energy gathered at its topmost point. Edric sensed the path the discharge would take from the cloud, a clear, branching channel through the air.

Use us! The roiling storm overhead and the equally charged rock sang through his veins. All he had to do was to reach out, to shift that open channel, and he could send the next lightning strike wherever he wished; tree or rock, or into the body of the Sain Erach leader.

Temptation rocked him, as fierce as any natural cataclysm. He would char the bodies of his pursuers and then be free to ride after Kyria. Together they would escape to safety.

He glanced up at the promontory. The next moment, a third round of lightning burst across the sky, brighter than before. Burning white light blanketed the gorge. An instant later, there was a loud crack, as if the world itself had split open.

Lightning struck the highest point of the promontory. A fissure appeared in the solid rock, and then an enormous section broke free. It crashed into the lower portion of the rock face, splintering off more debris as it fell. Huge sheets of rock pummeled the riverbed. Chunks smashed into trees on either bank. The earth shook with the impact. Water shot up in all directions. Shards of rock, many of them bigger than Edric, slid into the gorge.

Edric scrambled to his feet, for the moment unable to feel his injuries, and raced up the trail. It was so steep, he had to use his hands, grabbing at trunks of the willowy bushes and anything else he could find. One knee gave out under him and he fell, sliding back down the slope for a terrifying moment.

He scrambled to his feet and kept going, slipping and struggling back up, again and again, until he could no longer move. He lay on a patch of sloping earth, panting, his pulse hammering in his ears. He had no idea how far he'd come. He thought there had been more lightning strikes, but he could not be sure. The thunder had subsided into a distant rumble. Rock was still coming down somewhere behind him, or so he thought. He might have been hearing the echoes in his skull.

He should get up, find shelter.

He wasn't shivering, and it was a bad sign that he no longer felt cold. He managed to draw one knee up and then the other, to push his body away from the earth. If he could not run, he could walk, and if he could not walk, he must crawl.

He crawled.

He was in shock, that much was sure, and shock was why

it was so difficult to think. He could not tell how badly injured he was. He had no weapon except for the eating knife in his boot. The lack of food or water didn't bother him, although later it would. The biggest problem was that his clothes were drenched. Loss of body heat would kill him as surely as the rockslide or the Sain Erach riders. At least, he didn't have to worry about them at this moment. If he got out of his clothes, buried himself under dry leaves . . .

Sitting back on his heels, he fumbled with the fastenings of his jacket. His fingers didn't work right. He couldn't remember what he was doing. It was getting darker . . . Night must be near.

He looked up at the sound of hoof beats and a horse's nicker. A rider appeared on the trail above him, faced shadowed by the hood of a cloak. The white markings on the horse's forehead glimmered in the gloom beneath the trees. He fumbled at his belt, but his sword was not there. He'd lost it, although he could not remember where.

The rider jumped lightly to the ground and rushed toward him. "Blessed Cassilda, you're half frozen!"

Kyria? No, she couldn't be here . . . she'd gone ahead.

But it *was* Kyria, pulling off the cloak he'd given her and wrapping it around him. "I heard the crash," she murmured as she tucked the thick wool around him. "It sounded as if an entire mountainside had come down. I was so afraid for you!"

"Horse. Gone."

"And those horrible men from Sain Erach?"

"Gone, too. Maybe buried."

"Here, lean on me." She slipped her shoulder under his arm and hauled him upright.

"Can't—"

"Yes, you can, and yes, you will. We can't stay here; it's too exposed. The rain's held off this long, but it's sure to start soon. We must trust to the blessings of Evanda that we'll find shelter further along."

They struggled the short distance uphill to where Star stood, quiet and alert. The mare nuzzled Edric, her nostrils flaring as she inhaled the smell of the river. Kyria turned Star around to the downhill side so it was easier to mount. She got on first, then reached down to help Edric on behind her.

"No argument now," she said, again reminding Edric of the mistress of novices at Tramontana Tower. He took her hand and mounted, thinking of the irony of riding pillion behind her. Their roles seemed to have reversed.

They went slowly, letting the mare set her own pace. There was no more lightning, but the sky overhead was so dark, it might as well have been twilight.

The temperature fell as the clouds blocked the feeble light of the red sun. Edric felt it on his face. It wasn't going to rain, as Kyria had feared. If it was this cold, the clouds would be freezing. They had been climbing steadily and the surrounding trees had become more twisted and spindly. The ground, what he could see of it, looked flinty, marked in places with piles of pea-sized gravel, over soil so thin and poor, it barely covered the rock beneath.

Kyria halted the mare just as they left the last thin copse. The trail ahead wound along the side of a sharply rising, barren slope. The wind, which had been blowing fitfully, died down as the first snowflake landed on Edric's bare hand. It melted so quickly that he could not be sure he had really seen it. More flakes drifted down, at first singly, then in patches.

They would find only the flimsiest of protections if they retraced their steps. Try as he might, Edric could not recall any patch of forest dense enough to keep off the snow, and the trail was blocked at the river gorge.

"I don't know how common those shelters are in this section of mountains," he said. "It may be that too few travelers use this trail to be worth maintaining them."

Kyria inhaled, the breath hissing between her lips. "I don't like the idea of going back, either, but it may be our only choice. Let's go on until that far crest."

With a sigh, the mare moved off, picking her way along the pebble-strewn terrain. Fortunately, the trail did not rise much, but ran along the side of the slope.

We've got to find food, he thought. *Water will be no problem if we can make a fire.*

With a startle, he came awake. The mare had halted. Looking ahead, he saw they'd come to the crest Kyria had mentioned. There was no sign of any habitation or travelers' hut, but the trail dipped into a valley of sorts. A grove of thickly growing trees filled the bottom. Beyond, the mountainside was bare, although from this distance it looked as if there might be rocky overhangs and maybe even caves.

The snow was coming down more heavily now, and it was no longer melting where it landed. It dusted the mare's mane and formed a delicate lace over Kyria's shoulders and bare head.

"We'll try the trees first," Kyria said, nudging the weary mare with her heels.

Although not tall, the trees grew close together, as if huddled for warmth. Like all their kind at this elevation, they were conifers, a variety of fir. Their lowest branches hung down to form a curtain, and the debris of many seasons piled around their roots. The scent of their needles filled the air.

To one side, several of the trees had fallen or snapped off midway up their trunks. Edric noticed charred areas here and there. The largest downward sloping branches formed a tent, and Kyria found her way through. They dismounted and led the horse into the confined gloom. Layers of dried needles cushioned their steps. Very little snow penetrated the branches, only a thin patch here and there.

"Unsaddle the horse while I set up camp," Kyria said. "I don't suppose there's anything she can eat here."

Edric replied as he loosened the girth, noticing that Kyria had thought first to care for their mount. She set to work immediately, moving away the fallen branches to expose a thick bed of soft needles. As soon as he'd removed the saddle, before he'd even unbridled the mare, she held out her hand for the blanket and unfolded it over half the needles. Wiping her hands on her skirt, she straightened up. "Do you have any dry clothes—socks, an extra shirt—in those saddlebags?"

"Socks. And a shirt." He forbore mentioning that she was wearing his extra jacket.

With hands still clumsy from cold, he fumbled at the clasp of the cloak. Kyria helped him, then carefully spread the folded cloak over the saddle blanket. Immediately, his skin felt as if it were being encased in ice. His teeth began chattering. Gently but firmly, she pushed him to the ground, and pulled off his boots and socks.

"Take off the rest and put on your dry clothes," she told

him. "Then wrap yourself up in the cloak as best you can. I'm going to look for firestones, but I'll be back in a short while."

Edric was too cold to argue, too cold to think. He didn't wait for her to leave before dragging off his wet clothing. Taking his dry socks with him, because he didn't think he could get them on without help, he crawled between the folds of the cloak and pulled the edge over his head. The inner layer of wool was still damp from contact with his river-drenched clothing. Hugging his body with his arms, he curled into a fetal position.

A time later, how long he could not tell, he became aware that he was no longer shivering. His top shoulder and hip still felt cold, but the bedding beneath him was surprisingly warm. Drowsiness weighed him down. He remembered that was a sign of freezing to death, as was confusion. Despite a resolution to remain awake, he found himself drifting.

Someone was moving about near him, or so he thought, from the rustling of cloth and the faint cracking of twigs. He forced his eyelids open, but could make out only the suggestion of a form, a shadow in the dim light.

Hello? he tried to say. *Who's there?*

"It's just me," a feminine voice responded. "Go back to sleep." He rolled over and drifted off again.

Edric roused again as a thick comforter came to rest on top of the cloak. How thoughtful of the servants. How much warmer he felt—but was that a good thing? He couldn't remember. Then the mattress settled, giving off a fragrance like musty fir. A length of cold, smooth silk touched his back—no, it was solid, legs spooning his, a soft belly against his buttocks, the press of breasts to either side of his spine. Breath over his shoulder, an arm reaching to cover his. He shuddered at the touch of icy fingers and even colder toes.

"Sorry," came that same female voice, next to his ear. "My feet and hands are cold."

Kyria?

"Not exactly seemly, is it, being naked together?" she murmured. "We can debate the proprieties once we've survived this night, and I honestly think this is the only way."

"Must be dreaming . . ."

"Yes, that's it. Mmm, such a good dream, too. Soon you'll be lovely and warm."

———	✦	———

When Edric woke the next morning, he did feel warm. He was wrapped in his cloak, sandwiched in between layers of dried needles. Except for the mare, whose body heat filled the space, he was alone. Through the hushed silence, he could hear nothing except his own breathing and the horse's. A small fire near the open side of the shelter burned within a circle of rocks. The carcass of an animal, perhaps a variety of mountain hare, hung from sticks over the fire and gave off a savory aroma.

Responding to pressure from his bladder, he looked around for his clothes. He found one sock between his knees and the other in the crease of the folded cloak. His boots, a second pair of socks, pants, shirt, and underwear had been spread out just beyond the fire circle. They were dry. Edric dressed, wrapped himself in the cloak, and went outside to find a private spot.

He paused at the entrance to the tree shelter to look around. Snow had fallen overnight, draping a thick layer over the branches. The other trees were as heavily laden, like cones of white. Yesterday's storm had passed, leaving clear skies and only the faintest stir of air. Footprints marked a track toward the rest of the grove.

"There you are! Good morning!" Kyria emerged from behind one of the larger trees. She'd bound her skirts to her legs with strips of cloth, and she moved with assurance. She carried an armful of sticks of various lengths and thicknesses.

"You're looking better." She shoved the wood into Edric's hands and bent to inspect the roasting meat.

A short time later, both of them were sitting on the insulated ground, contentedly chewing on the bones. Kyria had packed the water skins with snow the night before, and it had melted, leaving delicious water.

"How did you do all this?" Edric gestured at the fire and the remains of their meal. "And how did you know how to make a shelter?"

"My younger brother Rakhal taught me trapping, and I

picked up the rest along the way. I used to trap game in the winter, when food supplies ran thin."

By her accent, she was well-born. "That wasn't a problem with your family?"

"For a long time, Father pretended not to notice, so long as I was careful. Alayna kept teasing me that I was going to get into trouble, running all over the mountains in my brother's cast-off clothes. Really, why should it make a difference if I wear skirts or breeches at home? The traps work just as well and people have to eat. Eventually, I had to reconcile myself to the fate of women everywhere. At least my father was able to arrange an *advantageous*" — she put a slight, derisive twist on the word— "match for me."

"I, for one, am glad of your skills," Edric said, licking a drop of fat off his fingers.

"I'd rather not have needed them." She glanced skyward. "At least, my sister is well cared for."

Edric heard the longing in her voice and yearned to ease it. "Soon you will be reunited and all this will be no more than a fireside tale."

For a moment, she was silent. Then: "I borrowed your knife, the one in your boot." She slipped it out from the top of her own boot and offered it, hilt first, to him.

"You'd best keep it for the time being."

After a little silence, they discussed how to proceed. Without the supplies carried by the pack horse, they'd have to stop every day with enough time to trap more game, slowing their progress and keeping them in the heights longer, which increased their risk from weather and other hazards. They were still below the tree line, but banshees had been known to hunt at lower altitudes if the snow was deep enough. The mare needed to forage, and there was little grass here, even if she could reach it through the snow. In the end, they decided to remain in their shelter long enough to trap and cook enough meat for a day or two.

The next morning brought a catch of two more hares and a rabbit-horn. They ate the fattest portion of the rabbit-horn and set another portion aside in the snow for dinner, then sliced the lean meat and hung it on a primitive tripod over a small, smoky fire to preserve it. The process took an entire day. As they worked, they talked of inconsequential things or of the work. Once they had finished preserving the last of the meat strips, however, the issue of their destination would have to be faced.

Edric found his opening as they finished their evening meal. Everything had been made ready for an early start the next morning, and night had fallen. The only light was the cook fire at the entrance to their shelter, but he would not need to see Kyria's expression to know her feelings.

"We cannot go back the way we came," he began. "The rock fall made that trail impassable. So we must trust that this trail leads to a settlement—a village or small estate—and then to a road that will take us to one of the passages through these mountains. It's clearly in use, although not by large numbers of travelers." Although he did not say so aloud, the trail had been leading in the approximate direction of Aldaran.

"When we were strangers, sharing a traveler's shelter together, we observed shelter-truce," he went on when she did not comment. "We refrained from asking or offering our full names and destinations. If I am to escort you to your promised husband, I must know who he is."

"He will not want me now."

Even in the dim light of the dying fire, Edric caught the heated color as it swept across her cheeks. "I was in the hands of the lawless men of Sain Erach, and then alone, unescorted, with a man not my kin. I may be countrified and unsophisticated, but even I know what everyone will assume. And a man like my," she paused, took a deep breath, "like my promised husband will not take to wife any woman who is not—who has—"

Feeling Kyria's distress as sharply as if it had been his own, Edric reached out his hand and took hers. The touch of her skin sent a ripple of awareness all through him. A look, a movement, a breath would catapult that awareness into love.

Edric had forgotten the sexual prudery of the world outside Tower walls. In a matrix circle, minds and hearts knew no barriers, and matters such as physical intimacy were discussed openly. No one could hide attraction, nor was it healthy to do so. Because sexual energy flowed through the same channels as *laran*, pent-up frustration could cause dangerous blockages. In his time at Tramontana, Edric had enjoyed several lovers, mostly women. Their only promises to one another had been honesty. All had parted on affectionate, respectful terms.

"Surely your promised husband knew you to be a woman of virtue when he chose you? He will believe you, rather than appearances."

"Would that were so." Kyria shook her head. "He has never laid eyes on me, nor me on him." The light from the coals glittered on her unshed tears. "My father never insisted on an arranged marriage, but they offered such a large bride-price, how could I refuse? Oh, Edric, I have not the words for what that meant to us! Our future secure— and a dowry for Alayna! I never dreamed I would be able to save my entire family. How could I not agree? But that hope is gone now that my virtue has been tarnished. I am of no value to my promised husband. He will think himself well rid of me."

So wrought up was Edric with the aftermath of their escape, the psychic closeness catalyzed by physical touch, and by Kyria's plight that he acted without thinking. He took her face between his hands, holding her with all the tenderness he could pour into the gesture. She closed her eyes, lashes dark against the rose blush of her cheeks, and lifted her face to his. The next moment, his mouth pressed to hers.

He had kissed women before, and lain with them, but never before had he done so with his heart so open, utterly without reservation. In that kiss, he offered himself to her, everything he was or could ever hope to be. He had no expectation that she might return his feelings, he knew only that they flowed from him without hesitation.

"Sweet Cassilda, who is this fool of a lord?" he asked once he could draw breath. "Tell me his name that I might challenge him for your hand." Insofar as he was capable of rational thought, he meant the words as romantic nonsense, but she took them seriously.

"My betrothed is Gwynn-Alar, Lord of Scathfell, and I believe he will relinquish his claim on me for a mere blade of grass. As for my own consent, you have had my heart since the first moment I saw you."

Scathfell! Of all the Zandru-cursed lords on the face of Darkover, why did it have to be Scathfell?

He pulled away, his heart aching under the weight of the world.

"What's wrong?"

For a wild moment, he considered denying anything was the matter, rather than attempting to list the ways his brief moment of happiness had been shattered. His mind churned with old history and present realities. What had he been thinking? He could not marry the daughter of an impoverished lordling, without power or strategic alliances, not even to spite his most bitter enemy. Not even to follow the dictates of his heart.

Before he could draw breath, an ululating cry broke the silence outside. It lifted and fell in a long, eerie wail, echoing off the mountainside so that Edric could not tell from which direction it had come. But he knew what it was. Only one creature hunted by night in these mountains, its cry terrifying its prey into immobility.

11

When Kyria clasped her hands over her ears, Edric's instincts urged him to do the same, to shut out the banshee's cry. It was said to drive men mad, but he had never before understood why. The sound pulsed, throbbing, until it vibrated his eardrums and seemed to fill his skull, driving out all rational thought. And then it subsided. But he had learned discipline at Tramontana, how to overcome physical discomforts and to master his fears. In a working matrix circle, a lapse on the part of any one worker might have disastrous consequences for them all. Now he drew Kyria to him, held her close against his body, and forced himself to *listen*.

The banshee wailed again, louder now. The cry rose and swelled, shrill and eerie, cresting and dying down, only to begin again. The mare snorted and tossed her head; the whites of her eyes showed as gleaming crescents. Yes, the banshee's cry was definitely louder. The thing must be coming closer.

"The fire!" Kyria started toward the opening to the shelter, where the embers still glowed red. "It'll draw the banshee. They hunt by warmth. We have to put it out!"

He grabbed her arm and stopped her before she could scatter the remains of the fire. "Listen to me! The banshee will come to the fire, yes, but it will seek out the hottest object *first*. That will give us a chance to get away. Or find a way to kill it."

"Kill a banshee? Are you insane?"

Edric wanted to laugh, but there was no time to point out that she'd asked the same question when he'd rescued her from Sain Erach.

"We have no weapons, unless you count that little cooking knife," she went on. "Or do you propose to bring it down with your bare hands?"

"I don't know. I'll think of something." He spun her around toward the fire. "Build it up! Hurry!"

He rushed to the flimsiest portion of their shelter, the place where the snow-covered branches were thinnest. He seized the nearest branch, and by luck it was thin enough to snap. One after another, he broke the ones he could and bent back others. Some were sturdy as trunks and refused to yield. He left them. The draped shelter shook under the force of his assault. Bits of bark flew up and the roughness of the wood bit into his gloves, but he kept on. In the corner of his vision, the fire flared up. Bless all the gods, Kyria was so competent.

Clumps of snow slid down on top of him, and the wind coming through the opening felt just as cold. The opening was now big enough for a person to slip through, if they didn't mind splinters, but not the horse. And Star's speed was their only hope of getting away while the banshee occupied itself with the fire.

"The mare!" Edric shouted over his shoulder. "Saddle her! And hurry!"

He kept pulling and shoving, grabbing one branch after another. Then the banshee let out another wail. Its nerve-rending, unearthly cry sounded even louder now. Closer. The mare whinnied, on the edge of terror, and he heard Kyria's voice, soothing the horse as she wrestled with the last buckles.

"Done!" she exclaimed.

Edric left the opening, hoping that a determined effort would be enough to pass an unmounted horse. Lather now covered the mare's neck. Her sweat smelled acrid. She threw her head back as he grabbed the reins. Through his gloved touch, he felt the tension in her body and how close she was to breaking.

"Easy, easy." Edric reached out for the horse with his mind as well as his words. Star lowered her head just a fraction.

"Hold her," Edric said, thrusting the reins into Kyria's hands. "Stay under the branches. The snow will mask the heat from your bodies. If the banshee gets past me, you'll have to push your way through the opening. Wait until you're outside to mount up. Promise me that this time, you'll keep going."

"And you? What will you be doing?" Kyria said as she led the mare to the opening. "You're going to make an idiotic stand, the way you did back at the river?"

"Promise me."

She glared at him, mutinous. The blaze burnished her cheeks like sunrise.

"Star can't carry both of us, not at the speed you'll need to outpace that thing," he said. "At least one of us will get away."

"I won't—there must be another way—"

Her protest was overpowered by another wail, so loud it shook the branches of the shelter. A horse-sized shape emerged from the darkness. Edric caught a blurred glimpse of a stormcloud-gray body that tapered to a naked neck and head, like that of an enormous *kyorebni*, the vulture of the heights. Fleshy discs took the place of eyes. The firelight gleamed on its sharp, hooked beak. The banshee paced back and forth on the far side of the fire, snaking its head down toward the flames. It was searching . . . hunting.

"Go!" Edric shouted at Kyria, who stared at the banshee as if ensnared, her expression one of horror.

The mare tried to rear, slamming the back of her head into the branches. She plunged back to earth, trembling. The banshee wailed, in full hunting mode now. The movement of the horse must have engaged its tracking instincts.

Desperate to distract the banshee, Edric lunged to one side of the fire. "Hey!" he yelled, waving his arms. "Here I am! Come get me!"

Quicker than Edric would have thought possible, the banshee darted toward him. The fire was still too high for the enormous bird to scale, assuming it could jump at all, but it moved around the fire with terrifying speed. Edric sprinted to the other side of the fire. The banshee changed direction. Again he swerved, and again the gigantic bird followed him. It was fast, almost supernaturally so, and the lack of eyes didn't hamper it.

From the far end, Edric heard the shuffling of hoofs and Kyria's voice as she tried to soothe the mare. Momentarily distracted, he stumbled, on what he couldn't see, and barely avoided sprawling on the ground. Before he'd gotten back to his feet, the banshee had come most of the way around the fire.

"Edric, watch out!" Kyria screamed.

No longer separated by the fire, the banshee was almost on him. Its bulky body loomed over him. He noticed for the first time the thick webs between the toes, toes that ended in curved, talon-sharp claws. This close, the carrion stench of the creature almost overpowered him. His muscles refused to obey him. He watched with horrified fascination as the banshee tipped its head, preparing for a disemboweling strike with its beak.

A fist-sized knot of wood sailed past Edric and smacked into the banshee's skull, striking near the beak. The banshee skittered to a halt, hissing and swinging its head from side to side, trying to make out the direction of the attack.

Edric kicked the edge of the fire. His boot toe lodged underneath one of the larger sticks and sent it hurling into the air. Cinders flew up in a fountain of burning debris. With a squawk of frustration, the banshee recoiled, giving Edric enough to time to make it to the other side of the fire.

The banshee recovered more quickly than Edric thought possible, and he found himself darting and weaving again, trying to keep the fire between himself and the banshee.

This game couldn't go on for long. Eventually the fire would die down, or he would tire or lose his footing again. Either way, the banshee would be on him in a moment. Kyria had gotten in a lucky shot, but chunks of wood made a poor defense. He had to find a way to slow the banshee down or interfere with its ability to sense movement. He had no weapons except his bare hands, not that they'd be any use against that wickedly hooked beak.

Think! He could not tell if the interior voice was his own or that of his Keeper back at Tramontana Tower, who had berated him so many times for acting on impulse.

The banshee sensed heat and movement—how? Those

flat, fleshy discs on either side of its head? Nervous systems carried tiny electrical currents. Perhaps the banshees used those same currents to detect changes in their surroundings.

Electrical currents. The same energy as lightning, lightning that he could control. It wouldn't be the same as calling a storm or sending bolt after bolt smashing into an army. He needed only to confuse the banshee, blind it until he and Kyria could get away.

To buy a morsel of time, he danced back and forth, forcing the banshee to change direction several times in succession. As fast as it was, he was more nimble. He reached for his *laran,* for that place within his mind that could not only detect but manipulate electrical energy. Normally, he'd use his starstone, but there was no time to take it out and focus through it.

As his vision shifted, the banshee's body appeared doubled, one an opaque gray shape, the other a network of luminous threads that condensed into nodes of brightness. The brightest lay in the center of the bird's skull, attached by glowing ribbons to the fleshy discs.

Again the banshee's wail filled the shelter. With doubled sight, Edric watched as the banshee gathered itself and charged straight through the fire. It crouched and pulled back its neck to strike, but before that hooked beak shot out, Kyria leaped at it from the side. The bird staggered under the impact. She stepped lightly on to the flexed upper leg. The next instant, she swung up on its back, straddling the banshee like a rearing pony. One arm went around the front of the neck while the other drew back. The firelight flashed on metal in her hand—*the cooking knife!*—just before she plunged the blade into one of the fleshy plates.

With a cry even more terrible than its hunting wail, the banshee hurled itself up and backward. Its head jammed into the branches at the shelter entrance. Droplets of blood sprayed in all directions. Wrenching free, it threw its head from side to side with such violence that Kyria went flying.

Kyria landed on the remains of their bed, and the dried needles cushioned her fall. She scrambled to her feet and assumed a fighting crouch, but she no longer had a weapon. The knife remained lodged in the banshee's head.

As quickly as he could, Edric mentally grasped the glowing ribbons in the banshee's energy body. When he tried to wrench them apart, they resisted his efforts. Pain raced along his nerves. He took the pain, reversed it, and poured it back into the banshee's channels. The nodes and ribbons brightened. He drove *laran* energy into the banshee's nervous system, as much and as fast as he could muster. It felt as if he were stripping his own nerves raw, shoving psychic energy through himself at a brutal rate. A red hue washed across his visual field. He smelled smoke.

He was burning—no, it was the fire that burned. The bloody haze across his eyes turned him almost as blind as the banshee. Something screamed, but he could not tell if the sound had come from his own throat or the bird's. He couldn't keep this up, and he dared not slack off. It didn't matter if he crippled himself. If this didn't work, he wouldn't survive to regret it.

Dimly, he felt the impact as he toppled to his knees and then his side, but he didn't—*couldn't*—give up. He sensed the banshee's brain flare up like tinder, hot and blinding white.

And then, almost beyond believing, the brilliance faded. At first, its edges curled like pine needles as they burned out. Patches of darkness appeared in the center of the brain, dots that spread and coalesced into irregular shapes.

A racketing cry filled Edric's skull and as quickly died. Something large hit the ground a short distance away. All he could see now was an empty void. But he could feel, arms and legs and hardness underneath him, and warmth on his face.

"Edric!" A woman called out from what seemed like an immense distance. Was he dead then, and was this the Overworld? "Edric, are you all right?"

He managed to crack his lids open. His eyes watered in the glare from the fire. The banshee sprawled on the ground, its head on one edge of the pile of burning wood. Smells arose from it—burning flesh and feathers, and something not entirely physical, the stench of burned-out neurons.

A horse whinnied, and the woman murmured to it. "Easy, easy . . . sweet girl. It's all right. Edric, answer me— say something!"

Edric thought of getting to his feet, but his body refused to obey his wishes. He felt as if he had just fought a tenday-long battle with a horde of berserkers. Every joint twinged and every muscle ached, but otherwise he seemed reasonably sound. Of body, anyway. Aldones knew what he had just done to his mind. If he could think at all, he wasn't dead, which the banshee clearly was.

The fire went bleary in his vision. The air felt colder, but he could not tell whether it was because he was going into shock or because the fire was dying. Or both. Outside the shelter, snow began to fall on the downward-slanting branches, or so he dreamed.

He dreamed, too, of Kyria. Of seeing her laugh in the brightness of a summer day or flushed with the exertion of a dance. The dream of holding her in his arms was so vivid that it lead inevitably to images of other, more intimate embraces. In his mind, she was as passionate in lovemaking as in everything else. The bed beneath them shifted under their combined weight.

"Kyria," he murmured. "Kyria . . ."

Cool fingers trailed along his temples. *Sleep, sleep.*

He slept, this time deep and dreamless.

— ✦ —

Hunger woke him, and cold, and the force of his shivering. His belly cramped, as after a long session of *laran* work. As much as he craved sleep, he knew to heed the signs of his body's depletion. The next moment, as he forced his eyes open, memories of the night before brought him fully awake.

The fire, which should have long since gone out, was burning brightly at the entrance to the shelter. More than that, above the flames hung several skinned ice-rabbits on wooden spits. He almost swooned at the smell of meat roasting, but hunger won out. As he sat up, the cloak in which he'd been wrapped fell away. At the far end of the shelter, the mare looked up and swiveled her ears in his direction.

Kyria slipped through the entrance. At the sight of her, the fight with the banshee came back to him—dodging the monstrous bird around the fire, Kyria climbing on top of it, stabbing it with that little knife, himself seizing the currents of life energy in the banshee's body, in its brain. Burning out its nerves with his own *laran*, with his *storm sense,* his ability to *call the lightning.*

Shuddering gripped him. He fought it and the sickening grayness that lapped the corners of his vision. He was alive. They both were.

"Awake at last," Kyria said. "And hungry, I'll bet."

Silently Edric blessed her practicality. She didn't pelt him with questions he had no strength to answer. Eating the roasted ice-rabbit turned out to be a tricky business because his hands were shaking so badly. Fortunately, the meat was cooked well enough so that once he'd bitten through the crispy skin, he could pull off bits. He was so hungry, he barely tasted it. Kyria offered him a handful of dried moss to wipe his hands and chin. By the time he'd done that, bone-deep weariness enveloped him.

— ✦ —

The next time he woke, he was alone again, but no longer shivering with the aftermath of intense *laran* work. He was only a little hungry—Aldones knew how much rabbit he'd wolfed down—but clearer in his mind. He wasn't dead, or even in imminent risk of dying, and the realization filled him with astonishment.

He went outside to relieve himself, noticing that the carcass of the banshee had been dragged some distance from the shelter. Snow covered the body, several nights' worth, he judged. No wonder he'd been so hungry.

While Edric was inspecting the stiff, snow-buried carcass, Kyria came back. She rode the mare with the ease of long experience. She slid from the mare's back, rushed up to him, and hugged him hard. Then she drew back, blushing.

"I'm sorry, I didn't mean to presume—to be overly familiar. I'm just glad to see you recovering. We can travel tomorrow, can't we? We need to leave this area before another banshee comes hunting. I'm sorry, I know I'm talking too much. I'm just so glad you're all right, I'm nervous. I don't know what to say."

"Please stop apologizing. We wouldn't be here talking if you hadn't jumped on the banshee, a deed worthy of a hundred ballads."

"Let's get in out of the cold, or we will undo all my heroism."

Edric stood back while Kyria led the mare into the shelter. "Is there any more ice-rabbit?"

Laughing, Kyria showed him where she'd hung the rest of the cooked meat. He built up the fire while she rubbed down the mare with what looked like plaited strips of inner bark. She explained that she'd gone in search of fodder for the horse and had found patches of dried grasses that were only lightly covered with snow. "It's not enough to put back the weight she's lost, of course, but better than nothing."

As they ate, Kyria asked about the fight with the banshee, clearly curious to hear Edric's understanding of the story.

"I don't know how to describe what happened," he said. "It's not something I can put into any words you'd understand. I haven't told you before, but I studied for some years at Tramontana Tower."

"You are a *laranzu*, then? And Gifted with *laran*?" Kyria asked, her face filled with awe as if he were a direct descendent of Aldones, Lord of Light.

Edric hated that she looked at him like that. Once, long ago, those with psychic Gifts had been revered, sometimes worshipped. His teachers had no patience with such superstitious nonsense. "*Laran* isn't divinely granted," he said, "nor is it sorcery. It's a talent that some have to varying degrees, and to use it safely requires training and discipline. What I did with the banshee involved *laran*, although I do not believe anyone at Tramontana, or Arilinn or Hali, for that matter, has ever done such a thing."

"I have heard that the *leroni* at those Towers are the most powerful and skilled on all Darkover. Clearly, they don't know everything."

Smiling at this, Edric got up and went outside. While they had been eating and talking, night had come, and swiftly, as if a star-studded cloak of inky velvet were suddenly thrown across the shoulders of the world.

Kyria came to stand beside him, so close he could almost feel her warmth. His *laran* barriers were still in tatters from his battle with the banshee, and it seemed as if they had lost their separate skins, that all he had to do was breathe in her essence and they would be one person.

"*As for my own consent*," she had said just before the banshee attacked, "*you have had my heart since the first moment I saw you.*"

As you, beloved, have mine, he thought.

But how could he hope for such a joy? She was not free to give herself to him, any more than he was free to accept such a gift. He would marry whoever would most benefit Aldaran, an alliance dictated by politics instead of love, even as she had been betrothed to Scathfell.

Too heartsick to find words, he turned away from her and went back inside the shelter.

12

As Edric and Kyria loaded the horse and left their shelter, the swollen red sun had cleared the eastern peaks, although shadows still lay like violet pools across the last night's drifted snow. The trail rose into the barren heights, how far they could not tell. Fortunately, there was only a little wind and the sky was clear. They went on foot in order to spare the horse. Climbing would generate body heat, at least as long as their strength lasted, and if luck were with them, they would descend before the next nightfall.

Kyria kept her eyes on the trail, silent for so long that Edric feared he'd offended her. "Before all this happened, the banshee attack I mean, something troubled you," she said with that disarming frankness of hers. "I asked but you never answered. The time to do so is now."

"It is of no importance."

"I don't believe you. Something lies between us—an ancient feud between our families, I know not what. Everything was easy when we knew nothing of each other's histories. Then it all changed, and I wish we could go back to being simply Edric and Kyria, nobodies out of nowhere."

"Leave well enough alone." He could not meet her eyes, could not even look at her. "I will escort you to a safe destination and be on my way."

"If I had not seen you take on that banshee with your bare hands, I would think you a coward for refusing to answer my question," she said, her temper rising.

"I'm not so brave as all that. *You* were the one who jumped on top of the banshee with only a cooking knife."

She slowed her pace to negotiate a steeper section of trail. Loose stones littered the ground, making the footing treacherous. "Which of us is the more reckless, then? You may have the title if it pleases you. I don't want it. I freely acknowledge the foolhardiness of any man who refuses a woman who takes on banshees with *only a cooking knife*."

Edric laughed, despite himself. What would life be with such a woman by his side? Then the moment passed, and he sobered. She would not give up until she had wrested the answer from him, and he would not lie to her.

"Very well," he said, keeping his eyes on the trail before his feet. "I will tell you, although afterward we may both wish the words unsaid. What happened was *Scathfell*."

"Scathfell? My promised husband?" She halted abruptly and then hurried to catch up with him. "What is he to you, that you speak his name with such feeling? Have you a grudge against him? Has he wronged you or your kin? Or is he guilty of some infamous act, some vile perversion?"

"I know nothing of him personally, either good or bad," Edric temporized. "But the name Scathfell is recognized throughout the Hellers."

"Then you know more than I, for all I know is that he is richer and grander than my own family, and generous as well. None of us expected me to marry so well."

Edric went on in silence. Why would Gwynn-Alar Scathfell send halfway across the Hellers range for a wife who could bring him nothing in the way of political or financial advantage? Why make an offer that an impoverished family could not resist? "You said that you and your promised husband had never met," he said. "Why then did he seek this betrothal?"

"Truthfully, I have no idea. I'm boyish and have a lamentably sharp tongue. Alayna is prettier and sweeter of temper, and would make any man a better wife. You've met her, so you know it's true. No, do not laugh. I have no false modesty when it comes to such things."

"You must allow me to disagree, *damisela carya*," Edric

said, smiling despite himself. "I cannot imagine—" He was about to say, *a more desirable wife and companion.*

"But I am the elder," she went on, "and so it was only proper that I be the one when Lord Scathfell sent a marriage offer for a daughter of my House."

"And what is the name of your House, if it is not forbidden for you to say?"

"'Tis no great and terrible secret, if that's what you mean. We may be poor, but we are honorable and respectable for the most part. Not outlaws like those *reish*, those stable-sweepings of Sain Erach. I am the daughter of Pietro Salvador, Lord Rockraven."

Edric reeled as if he had been physically struck. He felt the blood drain from his face. *Rockraven . . . the lightning-control Gift.*

Kyria put her hands on his shoulders, searching his face. "Please tell me what is wrong. And no more evasions like what you said, or didn't say, about Scathfell. Why does the name of my family offend you?"

"I am surprised, not offended." He took her hands in his and lifted them to his lips until he realized what he was doing. "We are distantly related. Aliciane of Rockraven was my grandmother."

Kyria's face lit with a smile. "Great-Aunt Aliciane? Who could have guessed? She scandalized the entire family by becoming *barragana* to Old Lord Aldaran, you know. Her father disowned her, or so I was told, and her story is still used as a warning to us girls. That's what I meant about my family being *mostly* respectable."

After they had climbed in silence for a time, she said, "Aldaran . . . If you are descended from my kinswoman, you must be a member of that family, then? A distant cousin?"

Here it was, the truth that could not be hidden. "I am actually the lord of that realm, although my mother has acted as regent during my long sojourn away from home."

Kyria's mouth formed an O. "*Vai dom!* I had no idea—"

"I am still the same plain Edric you met in the traveler's shelter. I still put on my socks like any other man, as you know."

"I do, indeed." She blushed, perhaps remembering how she had warmed him that first night in the grove.

"Surely there is no need for formality between two

people who have fought a banshee together. I would rather you judge me for what I have done, not as Lord Aldaran."

"But you *are* Lord Aldaran, just as you are a Tower-trained *laranzu*. I know you do not like me to fuss over those things, so I will do my best to be irreverent."

"Always."

"Yet this explains why you spoke the name Scathfell with such heat. I have heard of the feud between Aldaran and Scathfell, who has not? You are kin, aren't you?"

"Yes," he replied, "and the families were once on good enough terms to consider an alliance by marriage. The betrothal ended with the death of the Scathfell boy, which they blamed—rightly or wrongly—on Old Lord Aldaran, and relations have never recovered. They have reason to hate us, and we in turn cannot forget how they attempted to seize Aldaran by force."

"The war that ended in King Allart's Peace?"

"The very same."

"It's a sad thing when men who ought to be as brothers are at each other's throats," she said. "I hope you and the present Lord Scathfell are on better terms."

"I'm not sure we're on any terms at all," Edric said, focusing on putting one foot in front of another. "I certainly haven't had anything to do with him since I left home to study at Tramontana, and Mother is far too good a diplomat to needlessly incite trouble."

They went on for a short time in silence. "Regardless of the feud between Aldaran and Scathfell, I now understand the reason Scathfell went to such lengths to bind you to him." Edric heard the bleakness in his own voice, but Kyria deserved the truth. "The lineage we share, our Rockraven blood, is why Scathfell wanted you. You're right, it had nothing to do with you, Kyria, or any wealth you might bring him, but because of something far more valuable than gemstones or land: what you carry in your genes."

Kyria frowned. "What? A predisposition for assaulting banshees with cooking knives? A talent for trapping small fur-bearing animals?"

"Storm sense. Which, in its fully realized form, means the ability to not only detect but *control* cloud and rain and lightning. It runs in my family, and yours."

"Why would Scathfell want *me*? I am no battle witch."

"You not only carry the potential but the ability itself. I know this because I have sensed your mind from the time we met in the shelter. You have *laran*. Untrained, to be sure, but present nonetheless."

Kyria looked away, and for a moment he thought she would reject everything he'd said. Then she lifted her head, her expression forthright. "Ever since I was a little girl, I could feel when a storm was coming. My father said I used to have nightmares about lightning even when the sky was yet clear. But my nightmare storms always came. I was never mistaken."

"We are alike, for I have the talent, too," Edric said. "I can not only sense storms, I can send them where I wish. I can, if you will excuse the colloquial phrase, *call down lightning*. I went to Tramontana Tower to learn how to control my Gift so that I would never misuse it, as has been done in the past."

"That's how you killed the banshee. It just crumpled, though you never touched it. And afterward, you slept as if dead, as if you had drained your life force."

Edric nodded. "I hope that will be the end of it, that I will never be forced to either use my *laran* or see someone I—" *love, say it!* "care for perish horribly."

Realization dawned. "Now I see what you meant when you said Lord Scathfell had no interest in me as a person. Any Rockraven daughter would have sufficed, so long as she could give him sons with the lightning Gift."

"A Gift that would offer a means of revenge against the defeat his father suffered at the hands of mine, a generation ago."

Revenge makes monsters of us.

Kyria's cheeks went very pale. "Children should be cherished, not sacrificed to an endless feud."

In this, at least, he could reassure her. "The truce has lasted since before I was born, but it's uneasy at best, a result of Scathfell's inability to wage war and my own disinclination to do so. That hardly constitutes a stable peace, although it is better than open conflict."

"Then you must promise not to assault him, if not for his sake, then yours." She paused, her cheeks flushing. "Forgive my, my lord. I had no right to dictate how you must manage your own affairs."

"You need not apologize, for you spoke the truth: I must take steps to mend the old breach, although I do not yet know what I might do." If he had never provoked Scathfell, neither had he done much to promote better relations. There hadn't been much he could do while at Tramontana, but now he must make overtures of friendship and find a way past this festering stalemate.

"As for myself, I will *never* provide Lord Scathfell with a brood of storm-Gifted warrior sons," she said. "Yet that might not be so simple. When he learns I have escaped from Sain Erach, he will come after me. He'll search everywhere. If what you say is true, I'm too valuable for him to do anything less. Where can I hide? If I go home, he'll hear of it and demand my return. Papa could not give me sanctuary, even if it were lawful for him to do so. The betrothal contract is binding. And Rockraven is no fortress. If Lord Scathfell sent armed men, as his father did against Aldaran, we could not mount anything like an effective defense. If we tried—" Her voice rose with her emotions. "Papa might be hurt—killed. Or my brother, Valdir, and then what would Ellimira do? And the children? Or Rakhal and my other brother, Hjalmar, rushing home to defend them? All for my sake? No, I will not allow that to happen!"

She drew herself up straighter. "There is only one way out for me. The world must believe I am dead. My family will mourn me, but we would have likely never seen one another again, anyway, Scathfell is so far." She stumbled to a halt, her eyes very bright. "It is better for my family this way. They will not risk Lord Scathfell's wrath and yet will enjoy all the benefits of the match. Under the terms of the contract, Papa will not be obliged to return the bridal gifts."

Edric nodded, impressed by her grasp of the situation. Before he could say anything, she went on.

"As for my—for that man, let him find another wife. A fat, rich one with no *laran* at all."

Edric chuckled despite himself. "That would be a fitting match." Then he felt a sudden, icy chill at the realization that *Alayna* carried those same genes and she was now on her way to Scathfell under Ruyven's solicitous care. He saw in Kyria's face, in the dismay that flared up in her eyes, and sensed through their psychic rapport, that she had reached the same conclusion.

"If Lord Scathfell thinks I am dead," she said, "he will marry Alayna in my place. She'll be lost without me, will have nowhere to turn. She'll be in his power. Edric, this is terrible—we can't let that happen! But what can we do? I can't very well march up to his castle gates and demand her release. I do not want be the cause of yet another conflict between your two families, yet it seems that one way or another, Scathfell's dreadful plan may yet succeed."

Edric took her in his arms, a reaching out to her with mind and heart. Her hair smelled of snow. For a long moment, he could not think of anything that would make the situation more bearable. Then he remembered his mother saying that nothing was certain but death and next winter's snows.

"Take heart," he murmured. "Scathfell has not succeeded yet, and many things may happen, things we cannot imagine now. As you yourself said, the betrothal is binding, not only upon your family but upon him. He must make an effort to negotiate your release. He cannot look elsewhere for a bride until your death is confirmed. Who knows how long that may take? And Alayna may refuse him. She's not as outwardly strong as you, but I believe she has hidden wellsprings of determination. She found a way to speak with me privately, to beg me to come after you, and this despite *Dom* Ruyven's chaperonage."

Kyria nodded, sniffling. "She does have a mind of her own under all that sweetness. And if he does not fulfill her notions of a romantic suitor, she may very well refuse—no, she will be his guest, vulnerable to pressure he might bring to bear on her. He can lock her up until she agrees—"

Almost unawares, Edric sent Kyria a pulse of mental calm and felt her panic abate. He held her at arm's length, forcing her to meet his gaze. "None of those things has happened, and may not. Scathfell cannot court your sister while you are presumed alive, and then nothing else can be done during the mourning period. Even if everything transpires as you fear, it might be a happy match for both of them. It is not certain that their children, if they have any, will have the storm *laran*. Meanwhile, I promise you I will do everything in my power to mend relations with Scathfell. If he no longer feels threatened, it will not matter which of us has the storm Gift, except to warn the farmers about rain."

She responded with a brave attempt at a smile. "That plan does not offer much hope, but I cannot think of a better one."

"In time, one may present itself."

"Or, as they say, Durraman's donkey will learn to sing." As the moment of levity passed, Kyria's expression turned sorrowful. "I suppose this means Alayna, too, must believe I am dead. I do not see how we might get a message to her without the risk of it going astray. If Scathfell finds out and thinks she conspired against him or—who knows what he might think? From all accounts, he has grown up in the shadow of that old feud, and that may well make him suspicious of everything and everyone. It's simply too dangerous. But it will be like ripping out my heart to never see her again."

In a quiet voice he said, "I would lift this burden from you if I could."

"Thank you, but there is nothing to be done. I shall grieve for a time but not nearly as long as she will. At least *I* know that *she* is alive and well. But now I must disappear. Edric, will you help me?"

"You will always have a place with me. I wish I could marry you—I would do so in an instant. But I have lived my life with the hard truth that the Lord of Aldaran must make a powerful alliance."

"And I am penniless and now House-less, a true nobody."

He considered asking her to become his *barragana*, but the next moment, his mind churned with what the Tower healers had taught him about genetic lines and lethal recessives and how the old breeding programs concentrated *laran* traits by matching close relatives. If he took Kyria as his mistress, sooner or later they would want children; he certainly would, and from the way she had talked about children being cherished, she would, too. If those children inherited the storm Gift from both parents, what might it do to them? Kill Kyria in childbirth as Dorilys had killed her own mother? Become so unstable as to be a danger to themselves and everyone around them? As a trained *leronis*, his mother might know, but she was not here to consult. He told himself he ought not to inflict such harsh possibilities on a gently reared young woman—the same woman who hurled herself at the banshee, the same woman who'd saved his life.

"I love you," he said. "Even if I can promise you nothing else, I will always love you. Will you accept my protection, since that is all I can in honor offer you?"

Kyria gazed into his face as if she were casting truthspell in order to read his heart. "And I love you," she said in a voice that seemed to arise from the very core of her being. "Before Lord Scathfell's offer, I had never thought to marry at all, having nothing for a dowry, so that is hardly a disappointment. But—" and here her voice trembled in a way that sent shivers through his heart, before she steadied herself, "—I would a thousand times rather be with you, as your companion or friend or anything else you want of me, than to marry the richest lord in Shainsa."

13

They climbed, and climbed, and made it to the highest point of the pass with an hour or two of daylight left. It was a good thing, too, for the winds were already whipping the falling snow so hard it dashed into their eyes and between the folds of their clothing. Star was near done in from the long, hard ascent, but they dared not pause, not even to catch their breaths, before stumbling down the far slope.

Once past the summit, the snow came at them even harder, but the wind at least was not so wild. He saw then that they had come up the easier slope. At times, it felt as if he were falling rather than walking. Grit and loose stones combined with the snow to make the trail slippery. Once Kyria lost her footing entirely and would have gone tumbling headlong down the slope if she had not held on to the mare's stirrup. She twisted sideways, almost going to her knees. Edric caught her up and held her for a moment. Her face had gone ashen with exhaustion and cold.

"We have to keep going," he said. "This snow will be the end of us if we don't find shelter."

Nodding, she gathered herself. "I'm all right. I can go on."

"Not on foot, you can't. Here, I'll boost you onto Star's back."

Kyria set her lips together, and he feared she would

refuse, and they'd end up in a useless debate when they most needed their strength for the trail. But she let him give her a leg up into the saddle. He took the reins and went on as fast as he could trust his footing.

He felt the waning of the day even before the light began to fail. Shadows took on a subtle violet hue. Soon the temperature would drop, and still they had not found a place out of the elements. The snow gave way to mist, reducing visibility even further. It grew thicker, and he feared that between the oncoming night and the mist, he would lose sight of the trail. Then the bulk of a tree, twisted and stunted but unmistakably a mountain pine, loomed out of the mist. A short time later, the mist lifted, and they looked down on a vale. The land looked poor but not barren. Rocks and copses of the same pines dotted the slopes. At the very bottom, shrouded in twilight shadows, lay a cluster of buildings, and pinpoints of yellow light gleamed in their windows.

Kyria gave a wordless cry of relief. Edric's eyes stung, and he bit his lip to keep from sobbing. They were going to live, after all. He had not realized until that moment how frightened he'd been that the mountains would be their death. *Her* death.

Dark had almost fallen by the time they reached the farmstead. They traveled the last stretch by the light of stars and moon, always guided by those beckoning motes of flame. As Edric walked Star past pens of rangy goats, a dog barked. A man came out, lantern in hand, to investigate.

"Hallo, the house!" Edric called.

"Who goes there, in the night?" The man sounded wary but not hostile.

"Myself and my . . ." Edric hesitated, then decided that a small lie was worth giving Kyria the additional protection. " . . . my wife, travelers though these mountains."

Kyria's glance flickered in his direction, but she looked otherwise composed. He imagined her doing her best to resemble a dutiful wife and deciding the best way to accomplish that was to not speak at all.

"Just the two of ye? Come closer, then. Show yer faces."

Edric led the mare into the illumination of the lantern. The man was of middle years, dressed in a long jacket of what looked like goatskin with the hair side worn facing the body. Edric saw no suggestion of deceit in the man's face, only the fierce pride of the mountain folk.

Keen eyes measured Edric in return. "Ye look like decent enough folk, and I'd not turn away nor man nor beast what comes to me for shelter. We hold by the old ways here."

"We have no weapons," Edric said, holding his hands away from his body. Mountain hospitality, once extended and accepted, meant a complete cessation of any previous animosity. Feuds, no matter how bitter, could not pass the threshold.

"Do I have yer oath ye'll harm none here and will ye take mine in return?"

"Gladly I give you my word of honor."

"That's it, then. Come on, get ye inside. Anndra! See to the horse!" The man swung the lantern toward the house as a younger man, almost as tall but with the slender build of a teenager, trotted forward.

A few minutes later, Edric and Kyria found themselves seated before a patchstone hearth. He gave only their first names. In return, their host named himself Rannirl, his wife Nira, his younger son, two daughters, and a babe still in Nira's arms, and the other members of his household, his widowed aunt and her two sons, strong men a little older than Edric, who lived in the second house. With four men to work the land and enough children to mind the goats and barnfowl, they enjoyed a degree of prosperity. Eventually, the men would want wives of their own or go off to work for one of the larger estates or even become soldiers, but for the time, they all seemed content. The women clustered around Kyria, while the men and the younger children held back.

The evening meal was a simple one, rounds of tangy goat cheese, roasted root vegetables, and a dense, surprisingly filling pudding of barley and nuts. Everyone ate in silence, as the children darted shy glances at Edric and Kyria.

"What is this place?" Edric asked.

"Thyra's Meadow," Rannirl answered with a hint of a blush. "She was me mam, none finer, fierce as an eagle. 'Twas once known as Three Goat Meadow."

"It's good to honor your mother," Edric said, his heart

lifting. Three Goat Meadow was one of a series of farms on the borders of Aldaran lands. They were closer to home than he'd dared hope.

"Aye, that it is. Ye're welcome to bide here awhile, for yon fine mare looks near dead in."

A day or two of rest would not cause an undue delay. No one was on the hunt for them, not here. "We thank you for your hospitality. Depending on how the horse recovers, we'll bide here, as you so generously offer."

"'Tis no more than decent folk offer travelers. Nor snow nor hunger care aught for a man's loyalties."

The older of the girls tiptoed to Edric's side and held out a hand for his wooden trencher. He remembered the ways of the mountains, how Rannirl and the other men would not look directly at Kyria, and kept his own gaze averted. The last thing he wanted was to insult his host's daughters. Murmuring among themselves, the women of the household gathered up the dishes and took them to the corner of the main room that served as a kitchen.

"Can you show us the nearest road to Aldaran Castle?" Edric asked. "We lost our way and found you only by fortune."

"The mountains'll play tricks on even the canniest traveler," Rannirl agreed, "hard-ice and avalanches, not to mention banshees and wolves, both the two-footed and the four-footed kind. Ye've the blessings of the gods to have made it safe this far. As for the way to Aldaran, we're but a half-day's easy pace from the Haverford Road, that loses no man. Anndra'll guide ye when ye're ready. Nay, nay, 'tis no pother. 'Twill be a holiday for the boy."

No thanks were necessary for what was demanded by the laws of hospitality. Indeed, as Edric was coming to understand, it would be embarrassing to shower his host with praise for only doing what honor required.

"So ye're bound for the castle?" Rannirl asked. "Do you have folk there?"

"We are . . . we have a place in the household," Edric answered.

"That's it, then, for the old lord ever dealt well with us, his lady regent as well, and I hear the young 'un's a fair copy."

"I have never heard anything to his discredit," Edric said, which was true enough, for no one at home or the Tower had ever criticized him to his face.

Nira and the girls brought out blankets, which they set about turning into a bed on the floor in front of the hearth. Rannirl, looking a bit flummoxed by all the feminine activity, excused himself to go check on the horses, and Edric went with him. They worked in silence, making sure of water and fodder, and Edric examined Star with special care. She had her nose deep into a net of hay and barely twitched as he ran his fingers on either side of her spine, pressing to detect sore muscles. Rannirl, having seen that his own animals were eating contentedly, nodded to Edric and headed back to the house.

When Edric returned, the house lay silent except for the hush of embers falling into ash. The hearth gave off a gentle glow, and by its light he saw that the bed had been made up, piled high with comforters. One bed, he noticed, and Kyria had curled up on the side away from the hearth. He didn't think he could sleep with her so close . . . so warm. It was his own fault, he told himself, for saying they were married. At the time, it had seemed a good idea; he'd heard a fair amount about the prudery of mountain folk. An unmarried man and woman traveling together would either be turned away as immoral or else cease to be unmarried via the informal nuptial customs of the mountain folk, which involved only sharing a meal, a fire, and a bed.

Lord of Light, by the next morning we'll be considered married, even if we lay there like lumps.

The temperature was already falling, except for a narrow area directly in front of the hearth. He pulled off his boots and outer clothing, leaving only his body linens. Moving carefully, so as to not waken Kyria, he slipped between the covers. The coverings of the comforters were coarse enough that their feather stuffing—chicken feathers, no doubt—poked through. After only a few minutes, his skin prickled with them. He stretched out, trying to focus his mind on each and every place he was being stuck by a chicken feather. His ears caught the sound of Kyria's breathing, and the rustle of the comforters with the rise and fall of her ribs . . . her chest . . . her breasts . . .

He was definitely not going to get any sleep at this rate.

But he would get through this night if he had to practice every single exercise taught to entering students at Tramontana, over and over again.

And then the covers lifted on Kyria's side, and he inhaled the faint, familiar smell of her skin. The bedding shifted beneath him. With one hand she touched him, fingertips gliding over the contours of his muscles. At first, her touch was hesitant, as if she had never caressed a man before, but then the contact gained in sureness as she held him close. His heart thundered in his ears. He was melting and burning all at once. Even as he drew breath to protest, her mouth came down on his, her lips like silk, like fire. He'd never taken aphrosone, but this was how he imagined it would feel, his senses reeling drunkenly.

As if in a dream, thinking to make her stop before *he* could not, he pushed her away as gently as he could. "Kyria, stop. We can't do this."

He could hear her breath, fast and light. "Do you not—not want—"

"Gods, yes!" He had no words for how much he *wanted*.

She pressed one hand over his heart. "This is the last chance we'll have. Once we reach Aldaran, you'll go back to being the powerful lord of the castle. We will never be anything to each other but Lord Aldaran and a penniless, unmarriageable woman, given a roof over her head only through your generosity."

The bleakness of her words shocked him. "Not charity. Given gladly."

She placed one finger on his lips. "I'm not finished. You will remember what we were to one another, but only for a time. There will be another woman, a bride, a mother to your children. All the things I can never be."

"Don't say that!"

"I hope that you love her—not only for her sake, but for your own. I would not have you endure a loveless marriage."

Fondness might come with time, good will, and healthy children, but Edric had no illusions about any marriage between two people who were lucky to see one another at all before their wedding day and might have nothing in common beyond submission to their families.

"I understand a great deal more of the world than you

give me credit for, *caryo," she said.* "What I wish for us is this night only. This memory to keep me warm . . . to keep my heart warm."

Her eyes were pools of darkness. He felt himself falling into them. All his reasons, all his fears blew away like so many grains of dust.

"And my heart as well," he whispered as he pulled her to him.

14

As Alayna watched Edric ride away in pursuit of Kyria, she felt as if half her heart went with him. She might be untutored in the ways of the rich and powerful, but she understood that Ruyven had no intention of placing himself at risk on her sister's behalf. Edric, who had no obligation to their party, was willing—eager, even—to rescue her.

Lord of Light, watch over him and grant him success.

"*Damisela.*" *Dom* Ruyven took her by the arm with such firmness that she had no choice but to go with him. "Bless all the gods, you have taken no injury. Yet what a shock to your delicate system—the suddenness of the attack, the shock of being severed from your precious sister. We must not expose you to any further danger."

Alayna suppressed a shudder at his unctuous manner. Until now, he had treated her with distant politeness, when he had bothered to address himself to her at all, thinking first of his own comfort and safety, then of Kyria's. The bandit attack had changed that. All of a sudden, *Dom* Ruyven, who had never spared her more than a passing glance, and never a word as to how she fared, treated her in the most solicitous manner.

She extricated her arm. "Are you sure this is the best way to make contact with the kidnappers? What if they return *here* but we have gone? How will they know where to send their demands?"

"My dear, you must have faith in the reputation of Scathfell as a power not to be trifled with. Your sister will tell them the name of her promised husband and they will not dare to harm her. These men understand what a valuable hostage they have. Everyone knows who Lord Scathfell is and where his castle lies. I assure you, they will make haste thither, which is why we ourselves must also do so." He guided her to her horse, adding, "We must not risk your suffering a similar fate. The faster I conduct you to Scathfell Castle, the safer you will be."

The party divided, with Francisco and his strongest men escorting *Dom* Ruyven and Alayna. The cook, Timas, remained behind with the wounded, to follow as best they could.

By the end of the day, Alayna's energy flagged. Although she had thought herself hardened to travel, portions of her lower anatomy had gone numb. Despite her weariness, she refused to complain or request a stop. Every hour of delay meant another hour Kyria remained in captivity. What was her own discomfort compared to *that*? No, she must not allow herself to think of what Kyria might be suffering.

Surely, she reasoned with herself, *they will not harm her, will not—* She stumbled over the thought. *Lord Scathfell will hunt them down if they injure her in any way. Barbaric they may be, but not incapable of respect for a lady.*

All the arguments she summoned paled in comparison with the increasing need to *hurry, hurry, hurry!*

The thought pulsed through her mind, repeated with every step her horse took. Glancing around, she saw that the entire party had halted. *Dom* Ruyven, who had been riding in front of her, dismounted heavily, and the other men were swinging down from their horses.

No, she tried to protest, although no sound came from her throat beyond a whimper. *We can't stop now—there's still daylight left—we must go on!*

"Put up the tents! Prepare my bed!" *Dom* Ruyven's voice sounded like a crow's.

"*Damisela*, if you please." Francisco stood beside her horse. Grasping the headstall with one hand, he held out the other to help her dismount.

Alayna leaned forward to free her right foot from the stirrup, lost her balance, and ended up sliding over the horse's back. Francisco caught her before she reached the ground. He wrapped one arm around her, steady as a rock. She felt his breath on her face as he set her down. Nevertheless, she protested, "Must we halt so soon? Can we not travel a little longer?"

"Lady, you are nigh exhausted. You must rest or you will not be able to go on. How will that serve your sister?"

She noticed for the first time that his eyes were hazel, almost green. Her heart pounded with more than weariness.

He led her by the hand, urging her to sit down, "Here, on this rock; it's not too rough." Meantime, the men saw to the horses and prepared the camp. He must be just as fatigued as any of them, she thought, and here he was with the responsibility for their comfort—what little there was to be had—and safety for this night. He didn't *have* to speak so gently to her. But he had, and she was too tired to sort out its meaning. Kyria would have something teasing and insightful to say. Tough, level-headed Kyria. But Kyria was in the hands of those awful men.

Blessed Cassilda, watch over her. Bring her back to me.

Alayna laid her forehead on her folded arms. Her face felt hot. *I don't know how to live without her.*

——— ◆ ———

Alayna roused to a touch on her arm. She was lying on her side on a smooth flat rock, although she had no memory of falling asleep. Captain Francisco knelt beside her. The setting sun lit his eyes.

"Come, my lady. Your place is ready." He held out a hand to assist her. He'd set aside his gloves at some point and so had she; their bare fingers touched.

I will be all right. All will be well.

He led her to the best-situated of the tents. "You must tend to your own needs, but you will have a measure of privacy. If there is anything I can do to ease your rest, you have but to ask."

"I have already endured far worse conditions."

"But then you had your sister to care for you—" He broke off, lowering his eyes. "Your pardon, I did not mean to remind you of today's calamity."

"Captain, I am grateful for all you have done. You have been guide, protector and, I hope, friend." She thought of asking him to use her personal name, if only for the pleasure of hearing it on his lips, but decided that would be too bold. Perhaps later . . . it might be a long ride to Scathfell. Yet when she'd said *protector*, his face had tightened. She regretted the effusiveness of her thanks.

"I bid you good night, *damisela*. Now I must see to my men and horses." And with that, he bowed and left her.

Inside the tent, she removed her cloak and sat upright to eat the bowl of meat and nut porridge that one of the men brought. The porridge was as gummy and tasteless as paste, but it warmed her. She managed to finish it all, then placed the bowl outside her tent flap, pulled off her boots, and wrapped herself in her blanket and cloak before falling asleep.

In her dreams, she wandered through a great house, its immense chambers richly furnished, but cold and covered with dust. Cry out as she might, no human voice answered, only the echoing emptiness. Faster and faster she ran, slipping on the bare floors, whirling down one corridor and up the next, searching for she knew not what. Then, in the manner of dreams, she became aware of someone or some *thing* following her, shadowing her footsteps, always out of sight but drawing ever closer until she could feel its breath on the back of her neck . . . *hunting* her.

At home, when she'd had childish nightmares, Kyria would wake her, stroking her hair and speaking to her so gently, so sensibly, that the terror would blow away like autumn leaves. Now she must fend for herself and be the lady Francisco treated her as. She might not have Kyria's outdoor skills, but she was not entirely helpless. One thing always within her power was to hold her tongue and refuse to complain.

The next morning brought the sound of men's voices and horses moving about, the clatter of cooking utensils, and the smell of *jaco*. Light, the brightness of a clear dawn, slanted through the edges of the tent door. Alayna thrust her feet into her boots, shook out her riding skirts, and crept outside. She glanced around for a suitably dense cluster of brush. When she returned, she found a bowl of water outside her tent with a scrap of cloth folded around a chip of soap. The water was still warm.

The men were taking turns eating and making ready to travel; Francisco was off supervising packing up camp.

Dom Ruyven smiled as Alayna accepted a bowl of porridge. "Fair morning to you, *damisela*," he said. "I trust you rested well."

"As well as can be expected, thank you."

"Your sister's fate weighs heavily upon you, as it does upon us all. Fear not, all will come well, I am sure of it."

"I do not mean to doubt your word, *vai dom*, but how can you say that? Kyria is not yet returned to us. For all we know, the bandits will demand a ransom so high that Lord Scathfell cannot pay it."

"My dear," *Dom* Ruyven said, "you have little experience of the great folk of the world. Your sister has made a most advantageous betrothal, and her promised husband is a powerful lord. Once you are safe within the walls of his castle, you will understand the difference."

He meant, of course, that she was an ignorant country girl from a family so poor they had not two copper coins to rub together. And, she admitted with a rueful sigh, he was right.

Her meal finished, Alayna took her place in line with the others and they set off again. In places, the path was stony, with a rocky wall on one side and on the other, a hillside so steep it was practically a cliff. Once, they crossed what must have been the remains of a landslide. The horses slipped on loose stones, sending little avalanches down below them. By the time they stopped at midday, they were well below the tree line.

Dom Ruyven spread his cloak on a stone for Alayna. He brought her midday meal and tended her with such care that she began to suspect he fancied himself a prospect for her hand. She found the idea revolting—he was old enough to be her father. But as his behavior toward her was otherwise perfectly proper, she decided she had nothing to fear. At the moment. As long as Francisco was nearby.

She called to him, and her heart rose as he turned to her. "Are we very far from Scathfell Castle?"

Francisco stayed where he was, examining one of the horses. "Another four or five days at this rate of travel, by my reckoning." At a sharp look from *Dom* Ruyven, he added, "*damisela*."

"So long! But we have come out of the worst part of the Hellers, haven't we?" she asked, pointedly looking around her at the spring-fed foliage.

"Indeed, but we have another pass to traverse. And Scathfell itself is a mountain fortress."

"Indeed it is," *Dom* Ruyven added, wiping the last crumbs of waybread from his lips. "Strong stones breed strong men, it is said, and there are no stronger or braver men than those of Scathfell."

"If the captain is any example, I am in utter agreement," she murmured, keeping her eyes on Francisco, who had turned away, inspecting one of the horse's front hoofs.

"*Damisela*, I have the greatest respect for the captain's competence. I'm eminently sensible that it was by his skill and knowledge that any of us escaped being murdered, or worse, by those bandits, not to mention getting us through that terrible storm." *Dom* Ruyven lowered his voice. "But he's no more than a hireling, unlikely to ever rise higher, and a nobleman's daughter like you ought not to be casting dewy eyes upon him."

"I *haven't*—!"

"No need to protest. You did not realize the impropriety of your conduct or how it might be noticed."

"I have *not* behaved improperly," Alayna cried, glad she was still on formal terms with Captain Francisco. "And nobody has *noticed* because there is nothing to see."

"I assure you, *I* have noticed. I say these words, difficult as they may be to hear, only for your own good."

"Why should *you* trouble yourself for *my own good*? You are not my guardian or my kinsman."

"Nonetheless, I am responsible for your welfare," *Dom* Ruyven answered with a smile she did not for an instant believe, "and your virtue. A hazardous passage, such as the one we have endured, filled with perils of all sorts, can engender certain misplaced feelings of gratitude. Pray, do not grant such sentiments sway over your better judgment. It would be most unfortunate if you later found that certain, shall we say, *opportunities*, were no longer available to you because of a moment's unguarded behavior."

She stared at him, momentarily incapable of speech.

"Yet allowances must be made," he continued. "You are innocent, unaware of the ways of the world and the capriciousness of its favor. Therefore, it is my duty to caution you against errors, to guide you. But you are a sensitive young woman. I see how heavily your sister's fate weighs upon you. Your concern does you credit."

"I—I thank you." *I think.* Half the time she thought *Dom* Ruyven was nothing more than a silly, pampered lordling who thought only of his own comfort. Then he came out with a comment like that, so sympathetic she was left not knowing how to react.

"Do not trouble yourself with matters about which you can do nothing," he went on. "Lord Scathfell is an honorable man and he very much desires this union with your sister. He will see that everything is set right."

15

Scathfell Castle lay at the end of a valley, broad where they approached and tapering as the mountains crowded in on one another. From the shoulder of a mountain jutted an immense rocky promontory, surrounded on three sides by cliffs. A fortress sat atop it, the walls as stark and sheer as the cliffs.

"There it is, *vai damisela,*" exclaimed *Dom* Ruyven. He was riding at Alayna's side, for the road now accommodated two or three abreast.

Something in *his* tone made Alayna feel uneasy. The castle lowering over the valley did not seem an entirely welcoming place. Those walls were made to keep things out. Or to keep them in. She was not sure which prospect disturbed her more.

Meanwhile, there was plenty to see, farm fields and pastures, barns and granaries. A village sprawled around the base of the promontory. Smoke rose from one of the outlying buildings, perhaps a smithy. Metal ore was a rare commodity, so the facilities to refine and forge it indicated that the Lord of Scathfell was well off, indeed.

A short while later, *Dom* Ruyven rode out ahead, doubtless wanting to appear in command. Alayna was amused and then relieved when Francisco, who had been riding in the lead position, dropped back beside her. In answer to her questions, he pointed out the various crops being grown, the pens for sheep and cattle, the mill and forge and other points of industry, furnishing everything that folk might need.

"Lord Scathfell must be a very rich man indeed," she murmured.

"Aye, that he is, for this valley is fertile, but even it cannot support the castle population by itself. Food and other goods, like wool and leather, are collected from vassal farms, which often have little enough to spare. In good years they get by, but when there's been a poor harvest and a harsh winter, even the castle folk go hungry."

"Surely that cannot be." She turned to Francisco in astonishment, and then blushed at her audacity in contradicting him. "I mean, at home in Rockraven we had far, far less. Kyria and I and our sister-in-law, Lady Ellimira, would not have new hair ribbons above once in three years, and come spring, we were all heartily sick of nut-porridge thrice a day, but we always had something to eat." She refrained from adding that this was in no small part due to Kyria's traps, for what would Francisco think of his lord's promised wife doing something so hoydenish?

The skin at outside edges of his eyes crinkled, even if he did not laugh aloud. He *wanted* to, and that sent her heart into little leaps of delight. "'Tis clear you know a thing or two about managing a thrifty household, an admirable thing in a woman. If it were just Lord Scathfell and his household, and even a passel of courtiers like *Dom* Ruyven, there would be more than enough to go around. Even those poor families who scrabble out a living on soil that's little better than gravel would not want. But my lord keeps the castle fortified as if war were upon him, with an army standing ready to muster at his call. Such men don't come cheap, nor would they tolerate your nut-porridge. They must be paid in coin and fed with meat, and so even this fair valley cannot produce enough."

With those words, Francisco's lips pressed together. He looked as if he repented having spoken so frankly. "Your sister will have the best once she is returned to us, and you, as her honored guest, will not lack for anything."

"We had little enough luxury at home," she assured him.

"I suppose it will be pleasant to not worry about the patches in my—" She was about to say, *chemise*, but was it proper to mention undergarments to a man not her kin? "—my skirts."

"My lord's generosity will surely extend to a new gown or two."

"But I must take care to regard such things as special treats and not become accustomed to them."

As they talked, the trail wound through a cleft in the rock. It climbed steeply, narrowing so that the party was forced to go single file as a convoy of empty carts descended past them from the castle. Their way led straight into the mountainside, where a raised portcullis guarded the entrance. Armed men stood watch on either side. Here they all dismounted, for the tunnel was not tall enough to accommodate riders on horseback.

Alayna delayed, hoping that Francisco would help her, would hold out his arms, and she would fall into them. And then, just for a moment, she would feel those strong arms around her. She might even rest her cheek against his chest. It was a silly notion, but harmless. And why should she not wish for such things? He was, after all, a man, and she was a woman. She had no aspirations of a match as grand as her sister's. It would be a very fine thing to be married to a captain in the service of her brother-in-law. He found her beautiful, she was certain of it, and never before had she been so glad of the effect she had on men.

As if her longing had summoned him, Francisco came around to her horse's shoulder. "My lady," he said as he held out his arms. Although she was perfectly capable of getting off a horse by herself, she allowed herself to slip into his arms. But the next moment did not come about as she had imagined. He did not press her to him. Instead, he set her on her feet and took a step back. *Dom* Ruyven had already proceeded into the tunnel, and Francisco went to organize the rest of their party. She had no choice but to go along.

The tunnel floor rose steadily, the walls moist with condensation, and chilly as well. Sounds echoed weirdly in the confined space. Next came another raised gate, its pointed bars like the teeth of an open mouth.

This must be the best-defended castle in the Hellers. She

could not imagine any enemy—not the bandits of Sain Erach, nor even King Allart Hastur, come all the way from Thendara—foolhardy enough to attempt an assault. The mountain would throw them back as if they were straw.

Alayna stepped into the sunlight beyond the tunnel's mouth and peered up at the castle. Its walls loomed over her, straight and sheer. The tops, what she could see of them, were broken by openings—for archers, she supposed. A flight of steps led to massive doors of wood bound with straps of bronze. Armed guards waited to either side, their faces unreadable beneath their helmets.

One of the doors swung open and a man in a garnet-colored robe emerged. His white hair was bound back from his face, and he carried a staff. A ring of keys jingled from his belt. He bowed deeply to *Dom* Ruyven and offered formal words of welcome. The two men then conversed in hushed tones, too low for Alayna to understand more than that *Dom* Ruyven was relating their encounter with the bandits. She wished beyond words that she could go to Francisco and shelter in his strength, but he had taken her horse and led it to the side, and there was no way within the bounds of proper deportment that she could approach him. When a couple of stablemen emerged from around the side of the castle and took the horses in charge, Francisco and the others went with them.

Don't leave me, she wanted to cry out. *When will I see you again?*

Dom Ruyven, apparently satisfied, disappeared through the open door. The robed man swept down the stairs. "*Vai damisela*! On behalf of my master, I welcome you. I am Zefano, *coridom* to Lord Scathfell. You must be exhausted from your long journey, not to mention your many ordeals."

Alayna curtsied and followed him up the stairs and through the opened door. The chamber inside was so spacious, it could have housed half of Rockraven, but was clearly only an entrance hall. A large door opened at the far end, with smaller doors to either side. A boy of eight or ten emerged from one of these, bowed to Zefano, stared wide-eyed at Alayna, and bowed again.

"Fetch *Domna* Dimitra, fast as you can," Zefano commanded. When the boy sprinted back through the smaller door, Zefano turned to Alayna and explained, "She will be

Damisela Kyria's lady-in-waiting and is best equipped to see to your needs."

A short time later, a woman of Ellimira's years bustled through the same door. She was no servant, for she wore a dress of pearly gray wool, edged with lace like frost on glass. Except for the color, which was elegant but boring, it was the most gorgeous dress Alayna had ever seen. Certainly, no one at Rockraven owned anything like it.

"Welcome to Scathfell, *vai damisela*." Without waiting for a response, the woman tucked Alayna's hand into the crook of her elbow and drew her toward the main door. "*Dom* Ruyven said you were snow-bound and then assaulted by brigands. You must have had such a dreadful time! But you are safe with us now."

The main door led into an even grander chamber. Alayna had no time for closer examination, as they were now across the hall and through another door, up one corridor and another door, then up a set of wide carpeted stairs that doubled back on themselves, down another corridor and more stairs—wood, this time, glossy with age and polish—until Alayna lost all sense of direction.

"Here we are!" *Domna* Dimitra paused before a door, one of several leading off a corridor, and flung it open. "This will be your suite, my lady." She stood back for Alayna to enter.

Suite?

Alayna stepped into what must surely be the most charming room in the world. Honey-gold wood paneled the walls, and the tapestries and carpet had been chosen to enhance the color of sunshine. A divan and two chairs had been arranged around the fireplace where a small blaze burned. Some aromatic wood had been added to fill the room with a sweet smell. The bedroom beyond was, if anything, more lovely than the sitting room, with its dressing table and wardrobe, and the four-poster bed with draperies to ward off the night's chill, all in shades of butter and caramel.

"This cannot be for me," Alayna protested. "Surely, such a grand chamber must belong to Lady Scathfell."

"This was to be your sister's room, until her marriage *di catenas* is solemnized," *Domna* Dimitra assured her. "But since you are here and she is not, there is no reason you should not enjoy all the comforts befitting your station. I will send a maid to help you undress and provide a bath." She opened the door to the wardrobe. "And here you will find suitable clothing."

Alayna and Kyria used to borrow one another's clothing. Well, *she* used to steal *Kyria's*, usually whatever was newest and brightest. But they were no longer children, and Kyria, who was to be Lady Scathfell, was in the hands of those brigands. Heart aching at the thought of her sister's situation, Alayna turned away from the open wardrobe. "If these were intended for my sister, I cannot wear them."

"More will be made for her upon her arrival. You will not be depriving her of her due, I assure you." The lady-in-waiting paused, her lips pursed. "I understand your concern about *Damisela* Kyria, but we cannot have you going about the castle looking like you have been on the trail for a month of tendays." She drew out an overdress of jade-hued wool, its front panel and sleeves touched with embroidery. "This should look very well with your coloring. There is a skirt to match, and a shawl to keep off the drafts."

Conscious of how grubby she was, Alayna touched the garments with only the tip of one finger. The tunic and under skirt were as soft as a puppy's ears, and as for the colors, surely not even Queen Cassandra Hastur wore raiment so bright.

Within a surprisingly short time, Alayna found herself attended by a maid who helped her out of her trail-stained clothing while another filled a tub in the adjacent chamber with steaming water that smelled slightly of sulfur. Beside the tub, a rack held towels, a dipper for rinsing, various brushes and bottles, and a basket containing chunks of soap.

The water was almost too hot to get into, but Alayna managed it, bit by bit. The maid took up a cloth, worked the soap into a creamy lather, and began washing Alayna's back. The massaging movements felt surprisingly good. Alayna had dreamt of life in a grand palace, but her imagination had never before extended to being bathed by someone else.

The maid brought in a ewer of hot water that smelled like apple blossoms. After lathering and rinsing Alayna's hair three times, she poured the water over her head as a final rinse and worked the fragrant liquid in. Then she

wrapped Alayna in several layers of towels, sat her on a
stool, and worked through her hair with a long-toothed
comb. To Alayna's surprise, the comb slipped through without tangling.

"'Twouldn't do to rip out half that lovely hair," the maid
said.

"I was dreading combing it out," Alayna admitted.
"What is that stuff?"

"Slippery apple bark, with a little hawthorn," the maid
replied.

"What's your name?"

"Sadhi, *vai damisela. If you would please sit* here by the
fire, I will dry and arrange your hair. We should have just
enough time to get you ready."

"Have I somewhere to go?"

"Indeed. You're to be presented to Lord Scathfell himself."

—— ✦ ——

Alayna examined her reflection in a mirror so large she
could see herself, head to toe. Sadhi had braided and coiled
her hair low on her neck, with a few tendrils framing her
face. The green wool overdress flowed over her curves,
cinched with a belt of green and yellow. She looked for all
the world like the Blessed Cassilda in the springtime.

She smiled, and her image smiled back, and she imagined how she would look to Francisco. He might even attend Lord Scathfell this very evening. She must manage to
speak with him.

Alayna followed the maid Sadhi back down a maze of
corridors and stairs until at last they arrived at the dining
hall. *Dom* Ruyven stood there, so regally attired that for a
moment, she failed to recognize him. She halted the proper
distance from him and dropped a curtsy. The green skirts
swept gracefully around her, swirling as she rose.

Dom Ruyven held out his arm for her, and they went in.
A long table, glossy with polish and bedecked with beeswax
candles, had been set for ten, with one place at the far end.
Lord Scathfell's, she assumed. Servants in livery stood here
and there along the far wall. Men and a few women, dressed
in the same splendor as *Dom* Ruyven, stood talking and
drinking from goblets. Alayna's heart faltered, for Francisco

was not among them, and she had no idea who they were or what was expected of her.

"Is one of them Lord Scathfell?" she whispered to *Dom* Ruyven.

"They are courtiers and dependent kin, nothing more," he replied. "They have donned their finery to meet the future Lady Scathfell. My lord will join us shortly, now that we are all assembled."

He introduced Alayna to the guests. She'd never met so many new people at once and doubted she would be able to remember all their names.

When they finished the circuit of the room, one of the servants brought her a silver goblet on a tray. Its contents steamed lightly and smelled of winter spices. She took it, waited for *Dom* Ruyven's nod of approval, and sipped. It was wine, which she had tasted only on holidays. It burned her throat, but she managed to not sputter. A subtle warmth spread throughout her body. *Any more of this and my head will start spinning.* Alayna had seen what too much hot spiced wine did to her older brothers, and she certainly did not want to behave *that* way in front of a great lord. Then she noticed how the ladies held their goblets but did not drink, so she copied them. *Dom* Ruyven, she noted, did not drink much, either.

The large door at the far end of the hall opened, a pair of armed men took up stations on either side, and a man entered who she knew, instantly, must be Lord Scathfell. He had the same strong waist and broad shoulders as Francisco, undoubtedly from many hours at swordplay, and his attire was rich but not flamboyant. Until that moment, Alayna had not really thought what to expect, only that he was to be her brother-in-law, so of course she must do her best to be cordial to him. And he was rich and powerful, so she must be respectful. Now the courtiers and ladies parted as he approached, clearing a path straight to Alayna.

Dom Ruyven bowed deeply. Alayna looked around for what to do with the goblet, but there seemed to be nowhere to put it, so she curtsied as best she could. By the time she straightened up, *Dom* Ruyven was saying, "*Vai dom,* allow me to present to you *Damisela* Alayna Rockraven, sister to your promised wife. *Damisela,* Gwynn-Alar, Lord Scathfell."

To Alayna's surprise, Lord Scathfell held out his hand. She placed her own in it, and to her even greater surprise, he kissed the back of it. His hair was a rich chestnut color, as was his neatly trimmed beard. The bristles tickled a little.

"You are most welcome to Scathfell Castle," he said. "It gladdens my heart to see how well you survived your ordeal."

"Captain Francisco saw to our safety and comfort," she said, then added, "as did *Dom* Ruyven." *And my sister? What news of her?*

Lord Scathfell's gracious expression did not alter. "Let us save further discussion for the dinner table. You will sit at my right hand, Ruyven, and the lady will take my left."

The left side was traditionally reserved for the woman of the household. *Dom* Ruyven seemed to think nothing amiss, however, and before Alayna knew it, Lord Scathfell himself was escorting her to dinner while the others took their places.

When they were seated, the servants brought in tureens of soup while Lord Scathfell engaged Alayna in conversation. He inquired if she found her quarters comfortable and if she lacked anything to make her easy and at home. He sounded genuinely concerned that she felt welcome and her needs be met. She stumbled through a reply, bewildered by the notion that the sumptuous chambers and even more luxurious bath, not to mention the elegant gown and now this delicious soup, could be in any way inadequate. She had nothing like this at home, and with that thought came a pang of longing for her family—Papa and Valdir and Gwillim, and even Ellimira, but most of all, Kyria. To say she was homesick and desperately worried about her sister seemed ungrateful, so she focused on her soup.

"I see you are not one of these fashionable ladies who pretend to never consume more than a mouthful here and there," Lord Scathfell said, "for fear that they will be thought overly robust."

"I suppose there are such ladies," she murmured, "but being delicate is not always a good thing. I wish I had been stronger, or I would not have fallen so ill when we were caught by a heavy snowfall."

"You seem perfect to me, just as you are."

Blushing, she bent to finish the last bit of soup.

The soup bowls were removed and platters of meat and root vegetables, baskets of bread, and bowls of stewed apples were brought out. Alayna was grateful for the diversion. Keeping her gaze lowered, she concentrated on the next course.

"Ruyven has already rendered his account of the journey," Lord Scathfell went on. "I would like to hear yours, if it is not too distressful."

Alayna set down her eating knife, considering how to answer. Her own discomforts paled by comparison to what had happened to Kyria. "I cannot remember having been so cold in my life, and I grew up in mountains very like yours. But Captain Francisco took good care of us all, as did *Dom* Ruyven, of course." *I'm repeating myself. What must he think of me?* "The captain located a traveler's shelter, where we passed the worst of the storm."

"So Ruyven told me. Also that you encountered a fellow traveler there."

Alayna glanced at *Dom* Ruyven, unsure how to answer. Her host had turned the conversation in this direction for a reason. Edric had been so kind, she did not like to violate his anonymity or divulge information that later might cause him difficulty. For all she knew, he might be a wrongfully accused outlaw with a price on his head.

"Yes, and afterward we went on for a time together," she said cautiously. Surely Ruyven would have told that much.

"What sort of man was he?" Lord Scathfell asked.

"My lord, I hardly know. He was of assistance with the horses, I believe."

"Not overly coarse in speech or appearance," *Dom* Ruyven answered. "His horse had the look of quality, but he traveled alone. I concluded, therefore, that he was no one of consequence. We did not exchange full names or other information under the usual conditions of shelter truce."

"Of course." As if that settled the matter, Lord Scathfell bent to his meal.

Alayna picked at hers. The meat was too heavily seasoned for her taste. Finally she gave up, and forgot her resolution to remain insipidly silent. She didn't care that Lord Scathfell had the power to throw her out. He also had the power to pay those hideous men what they asked, to have Kyria restored to her.

"Please tell me, Lord Scathfell, if there is any news of my sister? Have the bandits sent a ransom demand?"

"We have not yet made contact with her captors," he replied, his tone gentle. "No message has arrived, but do not let that trouble you. Within an hour of your arrival, I dispatched riders to Sain Erach. One way or another, we shall soon hear." He placed one hand on top of hers. "There is every reason to hope, *vai damisela*. We know the identity of the brigands and where they nest. They will not dare to harm a valuable hostage."

"That is what *Dom* Ruyven told me. At the time, I was so distressed by the abduction, I could scarcely hope."

"In this, Ruyven is as knowledgeable as any man, having served not only here but in the court of King Allart Hastur himself." Lord Scathfell bent close to Alayna and dropped his voice to a conspiratorial whisper. "He may not look like a hero, but few can equal him in scheming, plots, and nefarious intrigue."

Dom Ruyven, who had clearly been meant to overhear the remark, made a dismissive gesture, but it seemed to Alayna that he was secretly pleased.

Servants took away the last plates and moved the tables aside. By the time they had finished, a group of performers had set up. Lord Scathfell himself placed Alayna beside his own chair, where she might have the best view.

The musicians were skillful, far better than any she'd heard at Rockraven, and she'd never seen anything like the acrobatics and juggling. How strong and supple the performers were, with their leaps and somersaults, and the way they juggled so many balls at once. Once or twice she thought how much Kyria would have enjoyed this evening.

Now and again Lord Scathfell smiled at Alayna. She was so filled with the excitement of the evening, she smiled back. Before she knew it, the performance ended. Lord Scathfell signaled to the *coridom*, who handed a purse to the troupe leader, and they exited the room.

Alayna settled back in her chair, a little sad that the evening had come to an end. Truthfully, she was tired, but she wouldn't be able to sleep, she was so wrought up. Servants brought more trays with goblets. She took one because she was expected to. The goblet held something akin to *jaco*, only with a heady aroma. By the time she'd finished it, the

musicians had begun playing again. She recognized the
promenada as one she'd danced at home. Of course, it was
impossible for her to join in. She had no kinsman to dance
with. There was *Dom* Ruyven, who had met her parents, but
he was engaged in conversation with one of the courtiers.

"*Damisela* Alayna?" Lord Scathfell rose to his feet and
faced her, one hand extended. "Will you grant me the honor
of the first dance?"

Even if she had not been delighted with the opportunity,
she would not have dared to refuse. To be singled out by the
lord of the castle! Ellimira would have been beside herself.

Alayna placed her hand in his. His fingers closed around
hers, exerting pressure to conduct her to where she was to
stand. She had heard of how a skillful male dancer could
guide even the most inexperienced lady through complicated patterns, but never before had she had moved so effortlessly in time with the music.

All too soon, the musicians played the final cadence. The
lines of dancers paused, men and women facing each other.
Lord Scathfell bowed, but not so low that she could not see
his smile, mirroring her own. She executed a curtsy that
would have done Ellimira proud, then he escorted her back
to her seat.

She did not remain there for long. Soon one of the courtiers approached her for the next dance. He was as old and
as richly dressed as *Dom* Ruyven. The dance was one she
knew, or near enough that no one noticed if she stepped
wrong. Its liveliness made more than a few words conversation impossible. She thought wistfully that if Francisco were
here, she would have no need for words.

She had scarcely two moments' rest when *Dom* Ruyven
came to claim her for the next dance. At this rate, she would
be engaged for every number, and it would be a close contest which would give out sooner, her feet or the musicians.
This one was slower, the dancers interweaving and occasionally exchanging partners.

"Are you enjoying the evening?" *Dom* Ruyven asked.
Although a bit red-faced, he proved to be light on his feet
and, to her surprise, Alayna enjoyed dancing with him.

"I am, thank you for asking." At that moment, Alayna
couldn't help but wonder if it were seemly to be engaged in
revels planned for her sister, when Kyria still languished in

the hands of those horrible men. *But not for long*, she reminded herself.

Despite the exhilaration of the dancing, and the attentions of Lord Scathfell as he claimed a second and then a third dance, Alayna's energy began to flag. She did her best to smother a yawn, lest her current partner think she was rude or, worse yet, bored with his company. She wondered how to politely excuse herself.

Just as the dance ended, Lord Scathfell made his way across the floor to where Alayna stood. "I fear we've overtired you, and for that I beg your forgiveness."

"There is no need, sir." Alayna indicated the hall. "This was a truly splendid welcome."

A smile hovered at the corners of his mouth. "And you were the jewel of the evening. I will not detain you with the flattery you so richly deserve but bid you good evening and good rest."

Alayna, having no idea of how to respond, curtsied and murmured, "*Vai dom.*"

Domna Dimitra conducted Alayna back up stairs and down hallways until they arrived at the suite. A fire had been lit in the bedroom, a branched candlestick illuminated the mantle, and a tray on the bedside table bore a goblet of warm milk sweetened with honey and a plate of tiny scones. *Domna* Dimitra lifted off Alayna's dress and eased her into a high-necked nightgown. Even though she was tired, Alayna downed the scones and the milk. Then, pleasantly warm, she sank into the softness of the bed.

"Good night then, sweetling," Dimitra murmured, reaching for the candlestick, but Alayna was already asleep.

16

The fire was still burning when she woke. Or maybe it was a new fire, tended by a silent servant. Alayna snuggled under the covers, reveling in the sensation of being truly warm. The last time she had slept anywhere but on the ground had been in the traveler's shelter where they'd met Edric, and she and Kyria had shared one of the alcoves. Remembering Kyria had a sobering effect. When Alayna went to the window, she saw that the sun was well overhead.

What a slug-a-bed I've turned into!

She went to work with water and soap, and materials she found on the washstand for cleaning her teeth. Just as she finished, a discreet knock on the door heralded Dimitra, and Sadhi carrying a tray that contained a sumptuous array of breakfast foods, surely enough to feed half the Rockraven family. Alayna was sure she couldn't possibly eat that much, but decided to take a taste first. One bite led to another and another, until she scarcely drew breath.

After the maid removed the tray, Alayna glanced up at Dimitra. "What am I to do now?"

"Lord Scathfell's ridden out today, so you are not obliged to present yourself." Dimitra pulled the covers down for Alayna to slide back under. "Sleep as long as you like. You'll need your strength for tonight."

"Why, what—?" Alayna covered her mouth in what she hoped was a suitably ladylike manner even though she yawned so hard, her jaw popped. "What is happening to-night?"

"Another, much larger ball. The headman of the village and his wife will attend, and the officers of the castle guard and the army, as well. It will be a grand affair, one you'll want to be refreshed for."

"More dancing . . . I wonder." *If Francisco will be there.*

Before she could finish the thought, she melted back into sleep.

——— ✦ ———

Alayna spent most of the rest of the day alternating be-tween dozing and daydreaming in bed, luxuriating in the delicious sensation of being warm and comfortable, without obligations.

Once Kyria had been restored, there would be another round of festivities, even more joyous because they were to celebrate the formal wedding. So she, Alayna, must look her best to honor her sister and her new brother-in-law. She might be only a poor country girl, but she knew what was required to make a good showing of herself. Last night, everyone had made allowances; she'd just arrived, after all, and she'd been through such an ordeal, and besides, every-thing had been made ready to welcome her sister, not her, so no one expected her to be prepared. Tonight, however, everyone would be watching *her*.

Before Alayna could figure out how to summon Sadhi or Dimitra, both appeared. Sadhi carried yet another tray of covered dishes, from which came the most mouth-watering smells. Alayna looked over the hand-sized meat pies and basket overflowing with nut rolls.

If I keep eating like this, I will soon be as big as a plough horse.

"There will not be a banquet tonight," Dimitra informed her. "Lord Scathfell will dine privately, so it is best to fortify yourself while you can. This simple fare should last you through the evening."

Alayna took one of the meat pies. She started to remark that Scathfell must be wealthy indeed, if a meal like this was considered 'simple,' but then she remembered Francisco's comments as they passed through the farmland. Everything came with a price.

Dimitra selected a gown from the wardrobe, a proper lady's dancing attire of thick, cream-colored spidersilk, shockingly low in the neckline. Alayna didn't care, it was so gorgeous. Lace edged the neckline and sleeves. The matching slippers were a bit too narrow, but of leather so soft it molded itself to her feet.

"It fits as if it were made for you." Dimitra touched Alayna's hair. "How to arrange your hair? It's so lovely in its own right, I wonder if we should choose a simple style."

"I am no child, to wear it unbound," Alayna said.

"Yet you are a young, unmarried woman, and you have no need of artifice. I doubt even a jeweled tiara would be as much adornment as your hair itself. But perhaps you are right. The gown is certainly that of a woman grown, so we must not risk you appearing like a child in her mother's best dress."

Alayna flushed, for Dimitra's words had the effect of making her feel exactly like that, only not her mother's dress but her older sister's. What would Kyria think if she saw Alayna now?

Kyria would laugh and tell me not to take myself so seriously. She would say I always cared about finery more than she did.

"What's the matter, sweetling? Are you ill? Or does the gown not please you, after all?"

"No, it is splendid. It's that I miss my sister very much. We have never been apart, not even for a single day."

Dimitra put one arm around Alayna's shoulders and gave a motherly squeeze. "It does you credit to think of your sister, but I am sure she would not want you to fret. Lord Scathfell will see to her rescue. Everything will turn out for the best, you will see." She sounded so certain that Alayna allowed herself to be persuaded.

The musicians were already playing as Alayna followed Dimitra into the Great Hall. She stared at the assembly, her confidence wavering. There were no performers, as on the previous night. Instead, she looked out at a sea of ladies and courtiers, dressed in bright, rich colors, men in uniform, and folk in farmers' rough cloth, standing to the side while more elegant couples formed a doubled line.

Here came Lord Scathfell himself, holding out his hand to her. She remembered herself in time to curtsy, before he led her out onto the floor. She danced the first set with him, and then the next, each as effortless as their dances the night before. After that, courtiers and officers, first one and then another, asked her to dance. The room swirled with color and movement. Although she looked, she did not see Francisco.

"*Vai damisela*, is aught amiss?" Her dancing partner, a courtier dressed in purple and yellow, bent over her with an expression of concern. His name, which he'd taken pains to give her, was *Dom* Nevin Morrisco, and he was a kinsman of Lord Scathfell. "Are you ill? I shall summon a healer at once."

Alayna gathered her wits. She'd missed a figure of the dance and almost collided with the lady of the opposite couple. "Please do not trouble yourself. I'm overheated from dancing, that is all."

"Then allow me to help you to a chair and bring you something to drink."

Clearly, *Dom* Nevin hoped for an intimate conversation as he guided her to a seat near a shadowed alcove and then lingered. She reminded him that she would like something light to drink. While he was gone, she took the opportunity to move to a more prominent location between two older women, to one side the wife of the village headman, to the other an older woman, who Alayna took to be a widowed aunt but was actually the household *leronis*, Jerana.

Dom Nevin returned a few minutes later, bearing a goblet. "Refreshment for my lady."

With the first heady sip, Alayna felt her head spin. He'd brought her hot, spiced, *fortified* wine.

Just then, the headman approached and took his wife away to dance. *Dom* Nevin slipped into the empty seat before Alayna had time to draw breath. "The whole castle is talking about you, you know. Everyone knows you are here as a companion to the future Lady Scathfell. We did not expect someone so enchanting in her own right."

Alayna found it increasingly difficult to breathe. The gown was too tight, the room too hot. She then discovered two things: that she really was very thirsty, and that she would become intoxicated if she drank any more fortified wine. Kyria would know what to do, but Kyria was not here. Alayna's vision went swimmy with tears.

"*Vai damisela*?"

Lord Scathfell stood before her. *Dom* Nevin sprang to his feet and executed a flourished bow. Alayna seized the opportunity to thrust the goblet into his hands. She got to her feet, clenching her teeth against the wave of renewed dizziness, and slipped one hand around Lord Scathfell's arm. He looked pleased rather than offended by her forwardness. To her relief, he did not proceed to the dance floor but to his own chair. At a gesture, servants brought up a second chair and placed it alongside. She sank into it gratefully.

"*Shallan* for the *damisela*," he murmured to one of the servants. "Well watered."

Before Alayna could think of what to say, the servant returned with a folding table, on which he placed a tray bearing a goblet. Beads of condensation covered the outside, and when she took it, she found the contents were chilled and delicious. Kyria would have loved it. How long would it be before Alayna saw her again? The thought dampened the gaiety of the evening.

Presently the servant took away the tray with its empty plate and goblet. "Would you care for more?" Lord Scathfell asked.

"No, thank you, *vai dom*. I am quite refreshed."

"But something still troubles you."

"My lord, last night you said that riders had been dispatched to the bandit stronghold for word of my sister, and for that I thank you. How long must we wait before we hear from them?"

"That I cannot tell you, for there are so many things that might go wrong: the roads, the weather, the process of bargaining with Sain Erach, or something entirely unforeseen. I place the greatest faith in Francisco, however. If anyone can negotiate this ransom, he will."

He leaned toward Alayna and took her hands in his. His fingers felt warm and strong, so strong. "I understand how terrifying the uncertainty must be for you. Like you, I have lost someone dear to me. My brother died when I was too

young to understand what had happened. I prayed every
day for him to come home."

He spoke with such unaffected candor that Alayna felt
as if he had opened his heart to her. "I'm so sorry."

"That is why I can now say to you, do not lose hope.
Nothing can be gained from worry, only from action. I
promise you, I will do everything in my power to ensure
your sister's recovery. In the meantime, I hope you will partake of Scathfell's entertainments, such as they are. There is
nothing wrong in diverting your attention from troubles
you have no power to resolve, only endure."

Before he could say anything more, Dimitra approached
them and curtsied. "Are you here to deprive me of my
charming companion?" he asked.

"Indeed, my lord, I think she has not sufficiently recovered from the ordeals of her journey to be carousing two
late evenings in a row." Dimitra took Alayna's hand and
helped her to rise. "Come now, sweetling. There will be
dancing enough to come, but only if you do not make yourself ill with exhaustion."

"We must on no occasion allow that," said Lord Scathfell.

Alayna dropped a curtsy, perhaps not as deep as was due
his rank, but graceful nonetheless. At the rate she was practicing, she would soon become as proficient as any great
lady.

As they made their way through the maze-work of the
castle, Alayna concentrated on not tripping over the hem of
her beautiful gown. At last, they reached the end of the
stairs and headed down the corridor to Alayna's suite. A
few more times, she thought, and she'd be able to find the
way herself.

"*Dom* Nevin paid you particular attention, I note," Dimitra said. "He is a fine catch. Rich, you know, and well-
connected. He's Lord Scathfell's mother's second cousin.
Or did he mention that?"

"*Dom* Nevin did convey the general sense. He was trying
to make a good impression, I think."

"As well he should." Dimitra opened the door and stood
back for Alayna to enter. "He's in the market for another
wife."

Alayna turned and stared at her. Another *wife*? *How
many does he have?*

"He's a widower twice over and needs an heir. His first wife was Delia-Mhari Reynart, poor thing. She died in childbirth, as did his second wife, but Lady Delia left a living child, a daughter, who must be five or six now. So of course he must want a mother for her, as well as a wife to bear him a son." Dimitra began loosening the laces of Alayna's gown. "Or sons, just to be on the safe side."

"I'm flattered that anyone might think I'm a match for him."

"Lift your arms, sweetling. So you say, but you must look at the facts. There's no other future for you, hanging about until you shrivel up like last year's apples. Or going home where, I understand, the only prospects are chervine herders and woodsmen. A fine life you'd lead." When Alayna did not answer, Dimitra rattled on, "Do you mean to say that it has never crossed your mind to hope for a more advantageous alliance?"

Alayna, now in only her shift, turned to face her. No one here knew of Kyria's intention to provide her with a dowry, and it was wiser to keep it that way. "What I hoped—and still do hope—is to marry for love."

"What does love have to do with marriage? Love comes afterward, from good will and healthy children, if it comes at all. And if not, you simply occupy different quarters and see each other only at festivals."

Alayna was so appalled, she could not think of what to say. Was this to be Kyria's future? But surely Lord Scathfell would see the fine person Kyria was and would fall in love with her. Kyria would be happy in her marriage, and if matters worked out with Francisco, so would Alayna.

"If not *Dom* Nevin, then another," Dimitra said as she brushed out Alayna's hair and braided it for sleep. "With your pretty face and this glorious hair, you won't want for suitors." She tied off the end of Alayna's braid with a ribbon, blue like the ribbons that adorned her nightgown. "Ah, I see you will have sweet dreams tonight, if that lovely smile is any indication. Is it *Dom* Nevin who inspires it, or some other lord?"

Blushing, Alayna replied, "He was not in attendance tonight, nor last night, either. In fact, I have not seen him since my arrival."

"Not seen? Not *Dom* Ruyven Castamir, then, for he was

right there on both nights. Come, tell—oh, no! You cannot mean one of your escort party. They're competent, to be sure, but none of them have any lands or rank. You must not throw yourself away on someone so far beneath you, not when you might have *Dom* Nevin."

"The man I mean *is* an officer—a captain—and as worthy of a lady's favor as any I have ever met." Alayna retorted.

"Captain? Do you mean Francisco Alvarez?" Dimitra's tone turned to one of pity. "Dear child, did you not know? He is married and has a child. He had scarcely enough time to kiss his wife before Lord Scathfell sent him off to arrange the ransom for your sister."

17

Alayna spent the days that followed like a sleepwalker unable to awaken from a nightmare. Despite her attempts to follow Lord Scathfell's advice, she could not stop thinking about Kyria, and then she was reminded of Francisco and his mission, and then she thought about Kyria again. Her feelings for Francisco had been nothing more than a foolish infatuation with an older man who was kind to her when she was alone and desperate. At least she had not thrown herself at him in any manner that might cause embarrassment. As for Edric, she concluded that his rescue must have failed or he would have sent word, or conducted Kyria here himself.

It had been spring when Alayna and Kyria left home, and now autumn was fading. There were no more balls, and those lords and ladies who had come for the wedding celebration returned home, with the exception of a few courtiers like Nevin and Ruyven. For companionship, there were a handful of elderly female relatives, the household *leronis*, the wife and young daughter of the *coridom*, and Dimitra.

In the last fine weather, Alayna sat with several other castle women in the garden courtyard, open to the sun but sheltered from winds by an arbor of rosalys and trilobed ivy. They took turns singing while working at needlepoint.

Producing colorful, wear-resistant pillow covers seemed to be the responsibility of women everywhere.

At one of these gatherings, Alayna heard a clamor coming from the direction of the front gates: men shouting in greeting, horses neighing.

"Someone's come!" Shayla, the *coridom's* young daughter, said. Her needlework tumbled to the ground.

"They cannot be soldiers from Aldaran, or the alarm would have sounded," her mother said. "Pick up your work, child. Being trampled underfoot will not improve your stitches."

It is the party that went after Kyria! Francisco has brought her home! Every fiber in her wanted to go running to the gates. She could not bring herself to speak.

Dimitra clapped her hands for everyone's attention. "I will send a page to find out what's going on. Meanwhile, let us behave like ladies instead of the uncouth spawn of Trailmen."

The other women resumed their work with not a few glances toward the castle gates. Dimitra settled herself on the bench beside Alayna. "My dear, you will not have long to wait. Lord Scathfell understands perfectly well the devotion you feel toward your sister."

"Yes," was all she could say.

As the moments dragged by, Alayna found poise was increasingly difficult to maintain. Sometimes she felt her cheeks heat unbearably, but the next instant she thought she was on the verge of fainting. Had she not known better, she would have thought she'd drunk too much of *Dom* Nevin's strong wine. Her head swam with it, and her pulse raced.

What is taking so long? Why does he not send for me? Surely Lord Scathfell would not be so cruel as to keep them apart after such a long and anxious separation.

Has something happened to Kyria? No, that was not possible. There must be a perfectly innocuous reason for the delay, such as the greeting of two people betrothed to one another, meeting at last. And he would find much to appreciate. Perhaps he had fallen in love with Kyria at first sight and could not tear his eyes away. And Kyria, standing before her promised husband, seeing his eyes filled with adoration, feeling the same passion arising in herself . . .

Alayna allowed herself to luxuriate in the romantic

images. Yes, that was a reason she could not object to. Speaking even a few words to summon Alayna might be more than he could do, so enchanted was he with his bride.

She roused at the sound of the page's running footsteps on the garden stones. She had no idea how much time had elapsed, although the other women looked restless, unhappy with waiting. Well, they would have cause for celebration soon enough.

The page whispered to Dimitra, who turned to Alayna. "You are to attend Lord Scathfell in his presence chamber. I will escort you there."

Dimitra set a brisk pace from the garden, along the pathway and through the castle. Alayna recognized the doors leading to the Great Hall, but then Dimitra headed down a corridor and toward the front of the castle. Yes, there was the foyer and here, a door that was new to her. Beyond lay a chamber that, while modest in size, dwarfed the Great Hall in its formality. A raised dais topped by a massive throne, now empty, dominated the far end. Other than the throne, there were no chairs.

Alayna took in the room in a glance, for her attention was immediately drawn to the cluster of men at the far end. At first she saw only their backs, their travel-stained cloaks and boots. As she reached the space in front of the dais, she saw Lord Scathfell, his face so taut and livid that she scarcely recognized him as the charming host of only a short time ago. He no longer wore the rich attire of the welcoming balls but leathers dyed in the colors of his House, and he looked like a huntsman standing over his captured prey. Kneeling at his feet, head bowed and hair falling across his face, was Francisco.

"Here is *Damisela* Alayna." Lord Scathfell bit off each word. "Tell *her* why you have failed to ransom her sister, as you were commanded to do. What are you waiting for, man? Get up. Face her."

Francisco lifted his head. His face was almost white. It tore at her to see him so humbled.

Alayna would have hurled herself down on the floor beside Francisco, except someone grabbed her shoulders from behind. So strong was the grip that her muscles froze. She could not have turned around to see who it was, even if she had wanted to.

"Don't interfere. It will only make things worse." Low and harsh, *Dom* Ruyven's words took Alayna by surprise. She nodded, just the slightest movement of her head, but he did not release his grip.

Francisco stood up. He moved as if his limbs had turned to chalk. His expression did not change as he faced her.

"Once again, I have failed in a mission entrusted to me by my lord," he said, his voice flat. "The bandits at Sain Erach were unable to negotiate a ransom. They have no hostage to exchange. Your sister is dead."

Far away, a woman let out a piercing wail. Then blackness closed in around her.

"Stand back," Dimitra commanded. "Let her have some air."

Alayna swam back into bleary consciousness. She was lying on the floor in a gloomy chamber, all dark stone. Dimitra knelt beside her, stoppering a vial. A handful of men formed a rough circle around them. Alayna recognized Lord Scathfell and *Dom* Ruyven, but Francisco was not among them.

"As you see, *vai dom*, she has merely fainted," Dimitra said.

I will not faint. Ever. Again.

Lord Scathfell gathered Alayna in his arms and helped her to her feet. He handled her as if she were something precious. "That was unspeakably brutal. Please believe me, I had no idea you would be so affected. I hope you will find it in your heart to forgive me."

Alayna looked up into his face. He was not making fun of her. In fact, he was still clearly furious, although not at her. She received the distinct impression that his anger was on her behalf.

He lifted Alayna's hand to his lips. "Go now and rest. Dimitra, take her back to her chambers and make sure she has every comfort. You and you, go with them. Ruyven, I need you here."

Alayna found herself ushered back through the castle. She held herself as straight as she could, out of fear that if she showed weakness, one of the guards would pick her up and carry her.

Once they'd arrived at the suite, Dimitra sent Sadhi for warming stones for the bed and then undressed Alayna, all the while clucking like a mother hen. "No one blames you for being overcome, sweetling. To lose a sister is bad enough, but in such a wretched manner? The *vai dom* is beside himself. You could see it in his face. He has a temper, we all know that, and especially when someone belonging to him is harmed. Mark my words, those murderers at Sain Erach will regret this day. There, there, you just have a good cry. You poor thing."

Alayna found Dimitra's attention a bit overwhelming. Every few moments, tears would well up, Dimitra would see them, and the process of commiseration would begin again. Alayna was soon so exhausted that she did not protest when Dimitra urged her into the newly warmed bed.

The rest of the day passed in a misery of drowsing and weeping, and trying *not* to weep because Dimitra kept watch in the sitting room and would hear and come in. As the hours went by and the day darkened into night, Alayna ended up with the same conclusion: Kyria must have died during a botched rescue attempt. There was no other reason for it. The bandits certainly would not have killed her when they could be richly paid for exchanging her alive.

Her death was my fault, all mine. If I had not urged Edric to go after her, none of this would have happened. Francisco would have succeeded, Lord Scathfell would be overjoyed, and Kyria would be here.

Everyone would have been happy, if it weren't for her meddling. What had she been thinking? Some romantic nonsense about daring rescues?

They didn't even have Kyria's body for a proper funeral. How would she say good-bye? Oh gods, what was she going to tell her father? How could she bear his grief as well as her own?

It would be far better for her to sneak out of the castle in the middle of the night and perish of cold in the mountains. She had nothing left to live for. Francisco was lost to her, and now Kyria as well, and she couldn't go home ... and she was getting absolutely maudlin, feeling far too sorry for herself.

Outside, night had fallen full. Shadows shrouded the

bedchamber, illuminated only by the fire she could not remember being lit and the candelabra on the mantel. She heard a knock on the outer door, then a man's voice, too indistinct to make out words, and then Dimitra's hushed reply. A tap sounded on the bedroom door and Dimitra entered.

"Ah, you're awake."

"Who was that, at the door?"

"Messages from Lord Scathfell, *Dom* Ruyven, and *Dom* Nevin, all inquiring about your condition. I must say, you've acquired a host of worthy admirers in such a short time."

Of course, Lord Scathfell would ask. He was her host. As for *Dom* Nevin, the less she thought about *him*, the better.

"I told them you're in no condition to receive visitors," Dimitra went on, "Men have no idea how a woman's heart works. They think we're all too delicate to walk from one end of a ballroom to the other without assistance—except when it comes to bearing them one son after another. Once you're married, sweetling, you must take care to keep the upper hand."

Alayna started to protest that she had no thought of marriage, especially since she was in mourning. Still, she could not resist saying, "I hope Lord Scathfell can forgive me for making such a scene. The news about my sister—and then poor Captain Francisco—"

"That one does not deserve your sympathy." Dimitra's mouth twisted in disapproval. "He's in disgrace, as well he should be. It was remarkable for Lord Scathfell to show him leniency. Another lord might have cut off Francisco's right hand or hanged him from the top of the castle walls—"

Alayna stifled a horrified gasp.

"—but as it is, he paid Francisco his wages and exiled him. The punishment must be made public, you understand. It's not so harsh; the captain will find work somewhere else. But Lord Scathfell is still in a sore temper about the loss of his promised bride. If you so much as mention Francisco by name, he might just change his mind and execute the captain."

These last words had the effect of withering any further discussion.

Alayna woke the following morning to rain slanting down from a sullen gray sky. At home, when the weather was *shivery sog*, as Kyria liked to joke, she'd find one excuse or another to stay in bed *just a little longer*. The remembrance brought new tears, and tears brought spasms of sobbing, until she was so exhausted, she fell asleep again.

Sometime later, Dimitra entered, bearing a stack of fine white handkerchiefs, which she set down on the bedside table. She held one out to Alayna. "Come now, sweetling, dry your tears. You haven't touched your breakfast."

"I haven't?" Alayna sat up and ran the handkerchief over her face. Her eyelids felt hot and puffy. She hadn't even noticed the breakfast tray.

"It's well into afternoon now. You must eat something or you'll make yourself ill. Or, worse yet, spoil those pretty looks."

"I'm not hungry." Alayna threw herself back on the bed, her back to Dimitra. "And I don't care what I look like."

"There, there." Dimitra stroked Alayna's hair and back.

"Don't touch me! Don't try to comfort me. There's nothing anyone can do to make me feel better." Even as the words burst from her, she knew she was behaving like a spoiled child.

Dimitra removed her hand. Alayna shrugged the covers back over her and pretended Dimitra had gone.

One morning, a tenday later, Alayna opened her eyes to see sunlight streaming through the windows. Somewhat to her surprise, she realized she was hungry. A tray bearing a covered plate and a pitcher sat on the table before the fire. Alayna could not remember how long it had been there, but she seemed to remember similar trays on the bedside table. This one gave off the smells of fresh *jaco* and yes, sausages.

She was not only hungry, but her hair was tangled and greasy. Sodden handkerchiefs were strewn about the bed and under her pillow. When she tried to get out of bed, her body responded sluggishly. She couldn't remember a time when she'd felt this stiff. Maybe the winter she was eight, when she and Kyria had both come down with a lung fever.

Kyria. The memory tugged at her, but the pain felt blunted, as if she had no more tears to shed.

Kyria would have a fit if she saw me now. I'm such a mess. And such a brat. Here I am, a guest with no rights beyond simple hospitality, and Domna *Dimitra has tried so hard to be nice to me.*

She must find a way to apologize. But first, breakfast. By the time she finished, she felt better enough to examine the pile of notes tucked under the tray. They were from *Dom* Nevin. *All* of them. She read the first one, glanced at the signatures of the others, and threw the lot in the fire.

As if on cue, Sadhi appeared to retrieve the tray. "Will there be anything else?"

"Yes, please. If it's not too much trouble, I should very much like to bathe and wash my hair. And get dressed. And speak with Dimitra, if she has a moment to spare. And send an apology to Lord Scathfell. I'm afraid I've been rather a burden to everyone."

"It's been no trouble, *vai damisela*. Everyone understands what you've been through."

The maid returned a short time later with a parade of servants carrying buckets of steaming water. She soaked up the warmth and the sheer, sensual pleasure of having her back scrubbed and her hair soaped and then rinsed. She was sitting in front of the fire, wearing a clean dressing gown, when Dimitra came in.

"You're looking much better, sweetling. Sadhi tells me you're eating again. I am glad to hear it. Jerana, our *leronis*, said you were in no danger, but I worried, nonetheless."

Alayna sprang to her feet and took Dimitra's hands. "You were so kind to me, and I behaved like a spoiled child. Can you forgive me? As for Lord Scathfell—what must he think?"

"As for Lord Scathfell, the best amends will be to see you smile again," Dimitra replied in a gentle tone.

"I dare not face him. Not yet, anyway. If he spoke to me, I'd probably burst into tears. The poor man has his own sorrows to contend with."

"I assure you, Lord Scathfell will not be undone by a few tears. But perhaps you are wise to take things slowly. What do you say to joining the other ladies at their needlework this afternoon? Will that be within your strength?"

Alayna had never considered needlework strenuous, although it was certainly a suitable occupation for a lady. Not like—no, she would not think of the pranks Kyria had got up to.

Dimitra must have had a word or three with the other women. When she and Alayna entered the solarium, no one asked difficult questions or commented on Alayna's pale cheeks or the way her clothes hung loosely. Jerana, sitting apart from the others and setting tiny stitches in squares of fabric, looked up with bright, measuring eyes. Marianna, the *coridom's* wife, was teaching her daughter how to knit socks. The scene looked so domestic and homelike that Alayna felt a fresh torrent of tears ready to gush forth.

I can't do this, Alayna thought, but really, what else was there to do? If she stayed in bed one more day, weeping and sleeping and weeping some more, she'd go mad. She lifted her chin, determined to *behave* like a lady even if she didn't *feel* like one.

"This is a pleasant gathering," she said, curtsying as one did to equals. "Shayla, would you like me to wind that skein of yarn into a ball?"

"Yes, please." Shayla answered, leaping up and handing her knitting to her mother. "I've dropped another stitch and I can't find it. I give up!"

"Come, let's sit here together," Alayna said, lowering herself to a bench that could accommodate two. "Would you rather hold or wind?"

"Hold, I think. That's something I can't mess up. Unless you—but then—I didn't mean—"

"It's all right." The words came with surprising ease. Tears receded. "I believe I can handle the winding without tangling the yarn too badly. And the good thing about winding, like knitting itself, is that if we make a mess of it, we can always undo the work and begin again."

"Yes, that's true." Shayla slipped the looped skein over her wrists and held it out.

Alayna, having done this work since she was too young to remember, found the end and began winding it into a ball, neither so loosely that the strand would tangle nor so tightly the yarn would stretch and become less resilient. She found the simple rhythm soothing, unlike fancy needlework, where she had to keep her mind on what she was doing. Shayla chattered away about the puppies that had just been born to Lord Scathfell's favorite dog.

Kyria and I used to talk about such doings at home. Sitting here with Shayla was almost like having a little sister.

"Now," Alayna said when the ball was half-done, and Shayla no longer looked so intimidated. "I gather you're having difficulty with double-pointed needles."

"I don't see why we can't make socks with the regular one-pointed ones."

"So did I when I seemed to have five thumbs. It took me forever to learn to turn the heel properly, but the only way to avoid a seam that will give blisters is to knit them in the round. How many needles have you broken?"

Shayla's eyes went round. "*Broken*? Um . . . none. I didn't know you could *do* that."

"Knit enough socks and you'll find out." Alayna dropped her voice to a whisper. "I broke six in one tenday the winter I was twelve. My sister-in-law said I did it on purpose, but I think it's more likely I was growing so fast, I didn't know my own strength. Don't you think?"

Shayla giggled.

— ◆ —

As one tenday progressed into the next, bringing intimations of approaching winter, Alayna began attending the women's musical gatherings as well. Much of the time, the gathering consisted of Alayna, Marianna, and Shayla. Jerana sat in a corner with her eyes closed, but did not sing or play.

Shayla begged Alayna to teach them new songs. At first, Alayna had not the heart to sing, or to sing anything except laments, but after several requests, she made an effort. They sang rounds, and "A Summer's Lass" and several versions of "Fra' Domenic's Pockets," which had them all laughing uproariously. Wiping her eyes, Alayna realized how long it had been since she'd laughed.

"Very good. So charming!" *Dom* Nevin applauded from the opened door. He strode to Alayna, took her hand, and brought it to his lips. "My dear, I had no idea you were such a songbird."

Alayna pulled her hand away in a manner that was, if not outright rude, decidedly unencouraging. "Pardon me for speaking frankly," she said, "but it was not a public performance. We sing for one another here, for our own amusement only. I beg you to leave us so that we may continue."

He made a careless gesture. "It was never my intention to embarrass anyone, if that's what you mean. Although I hardly know why you are so modest about your singing. It was a delight to hear you."

With an effort, Alayna held her tongue.

"Why, your voice would grace any gathering. Whatever man marries you will have no cause to hire a singing-woman when his own wife is far superior."

Alayna's cheeks grew hot, remembering that her own kinswoman, Great-Aunt Aliciane, had gone to Aldaran as singing-woman and later became that lord's *barragana*, even while his wife was alive.

I will hurl myself over the castle walls before I become your singing-woman. Oh, Kyria, why did you abandon me to the attentions of such an odious man?

"Be at ease, ladies, for I did not come here to disturb your revels, charming as they are," *Dom* Nevin was saying. "Having no other means of speaking to *Damisela* Alayna, I took advantage of this opportunity."

Marianna and Shayla rose and edged toward the door, but Dimitra lingered.

Don't leave me alone with him. "You could have sent me a note," Alayna said.

He blinked. "I did."

Alayna suddenly thought of the stack of notes, all from him. She also remembered burning them, unread, except for the first. "They must have gone astray," she murmured.

She got to her feet and pulled herself up to her full height, which wasn't very much compared with his. "Very well, since you clearly have something to say to me, here I am. *Domna* Dimitra, please remain as my chaperone, as is proper."

"I'll be just outside, in case you need me." Dimitra slipped out the door, leaving it ajar.

Dom Nevin waited until Dimitra was out of sight. "Fair *damisela*, you cannot be entirely insensible—surely you must realize how much I admire you. Indeed, you are the most beautiful, the most enticing creature I have ever laid eyes on. Perhaps you think I flatter, but these words spring from my most sincere feelings for you." He paused, clearly awaiting a reply.

"Thank you."

"You may well wonder why I choose to make my affections known at this time." He began pacing, gesturing as he spoke. "I have long felt myself in need of a wife, firstly to secure the happiness of the marital state once more. There may be some men who can live without female companionship, but I am not among them. I feel—I *appreciate* the presence of women in my life. Moreover, I wish to provide motherly guidance for my daughter. I have therefore fixed my desire upon *you*, my most adored lady."

Alayna stared at him, appalled that he would make advances to her while she was still in mourning for her sister.

"Besides your obvious attributes," he said, still pacing but at least not moving any closer, "you possess an impeccable lineage, for did not Lord Scathfell promise himself to your own sister? When I learned of the betrothal and that his promised wife had a sister, I thought I could do no better."

"You cannot be serious," Alayna burst out.

"Once again, your modesty does you credit. I assure you, I am in utter earnest." *Dom* Nevin halted, took a step toward her, and lowered himself to one knee. "I entreat you with all my heart to do me the honor of becoming my wife *di catenas*."

"I cannot possibly marry you."

"Why not? I am cousin to Lord Scathfell, as you know, and I have a good estate of my own. One to which I would otherwise have returned, had your beauty not kept me here."

"Have you forgotten how recently I learned of my sister's death? Even if you came back next year, or in five years, my answer would be the same. Besides, I have no dowry."

"No dowry?" *Dom* Nevin got to his feet, his knees creaking. "But surely—well, it makes no difference. If my kinsman required none of your sister, can I be any less magnanimous? Once we are joined, it will not matter."

Alayna had run out of words. He was in earnest. This was no joke, no bad dream. He had issued his proposal within Dimitra's hearing, which meant the news would be all over the castle by nightfall. If she refused him, she might offend

Lord Scathfell. Nevin was his kinsman, after all. What if he insisted? She'd heard tales of young women forced by their families to marry. When her brothers and their friends thought she wasn't listening, they'd told of such brides being drugged with aphrosone on their wedding nights to make them willing.

"Thank you for the honor," she managed to stammer. "I must—I need time to consider it."

On those words, he left her.

18

After *Dom* Nevin departed—with a bow so highly flourished it put the acrobatic entertainers to shame—Alayna remained rooted to the spot. If she moved, she thought, she might faint again, and she could not risk it. Unless she acted speedily and decisively, she'd end up married to him.

The door remained ajar, as it had been during their interview, and chance granted her a glimpse of *Dom* Nevin handing Dimitra something—a purse of coins, Alayna thought.

She arranged the whole thing, the notes, his barging in on us, and then leaving me virtually alone with him. For all I know, he put her up to it—and now she's got her reward. How much more will he pay her once we're wed?

Now Alayna had no fear of fainting, she was far too angry. She drew herself up and took a deep breath. "Dimitra, are you still there?"

"Yes, sweetling." Dimitra stepped inside and closed the door behind her.

"You overheard?"

"I stayed near, in case you should have need of me."

Alayna forced a smile. "Then you know *Dom* Nevin has proposed marriage to me."

A nod, a dip of the head. "I gathered as much. Let me be the first to wish you happiness."

"I did not give him an answer."

"After he has paid you such attention. What are you thinking? That you will get a better offer elsewhere? I assure you—"

"No, no, I have no intention of teasing him." She swallowed hard, though it took every shred of her self-control to maintain a suitably decorous expression. "I told him I needed time to consider. Marriage is not to be entered lightly, especially *di catenas*, which cannot be dissolved. I must regard this marriage as the only one I will ever undertake. I want to be sure of my feelings."

"If you mean love, then do not be foolish. Love is a fleeting thing, a passion of the moment, and those who marry for it all too often regret their rashness. A good match, one based on mutual understanding and advantage, is much more likely to lead to happiness than infatuation."

Something in the older woman's voice struck Alayna as poignant, even sad. Dimitra had never spoken of her own life, whether she had ever married and if she had been happy. She was called *domna*, so Alayna had assumed she was widowed, but the term might also be used as a title of respect for any older woman.

"How can I love a man I've barely spent an hour with? How can he love me?" Alayna affected an insouciant shrug. "But I suppose you are right, and such things do not matter, or are not the *only* things that I should take into consideration. I've led a sheltered life in the country, you see. We were all terribly surprised when Lord Scathfell made an offer for my sister. I myself did not hope to marry, certainly not a man as distinguished as *Dom* Nevin."

"I see that you are aware of the honor he does you by his proposal." Dimitra sounded smugly satisfied. "Then why do you hesitate? Such opportunities do not come along every day. Why not jump at the chance?"

"You believe I should accept him, then?" Alayna made a play of picking at her skirts, which allowed her to avert her face. She did not entirely trust her ability to mask her revulsion.

"Of course! Isn't it obvious this is the best outcome? But you must not hesitate or he may begin to doubt your sincerity. What will become of you if you allow him to slip away? You may never receive another such offer, one that will guarantee you a life of comfort. Heed my advice, for it is the same as I would give to my own daughter."

Alayna drew back, fearful that Dimitra would not stop before she had wrested a firm promise to accept *Dom* Nevin.

"Come now, sweetling, it's not as difficult as all that." Dimitra put an arm around Alayna's shoulders and guided her toward the door. "Why don't you have a nice lie-down? Once you're rested, I'm sure you'll see things more clearly."

"Yes, I think you are right. Today has been very tiring, and I'm not back to my full strength. I keep thinking of my sister ..." Alayna did not have to feign the catch in her voice. *Kyria, I still miss you so.*

Realistically, Alayna told herself, she could not remain at Scathfell Castle indefinitely. Marrying for love was a dream, nothing more. No handsome lord would seek out her hand or any such romantic nonsense. Lord Scathfell ... but he was as far above her as she was above the pot boy.

There was only one way out for her. She'd have to ask *Dom* Ruyven to marry her.

——— ✦ ———

As soon as Dimitra took her leave and closed the outer door behind her, Alayna began rummaging through her rooms for paper and pen. She pulled out drawers and opened boxes, pushed aside hanging garments and lifted up piles of folded shawls and underthings. She found a couple of books, expensive ones bound in fine leather, but still nothing to write with. Was this a deliberate attempt to prevent communication, or didn't fine ladies write letters? It was all too easy to conclude that Dimitra had removed any writing materials for the purpose of making sure Alayna never communicated with anyone except under supervision.

Alayna considered and discarded the notion of tearing off a strip of sheet and marking it with a charred bit of wood, except she'd need a knife to make a slit in the hem so the fabric could be ripped, and any bits of half-burned wood had been neatly removed, leaving only a bed of fine ash.

Just as Alayna finished tidying up the evidence of her search, Sadhi tapped on the door and entered, once more carrying a tray. "*Domna* Dimitra thought you might care for a bit of midafternoon refreshment. And a fire?"

Alayna glanced at the pitcher—sure to be *jaco* again, for apparently the entire castle lived on the stuff—and a plate of exquisite little nut and honey rolls.

"This looks lovely. Thank you so much, Sadhi. And thank *Domna* Dimitra for her thoughtfulness." Alayna seated herself while Sadhi poured a cup of *jaco*.

"If I may be so bold, *vai damisela*, I—*Domna* Dimitra and I—are most happy for you, although we will of course miss you when you leave us."

"Happy for me? Why?"

"Why, for your upcoming betrothed to *Dom* Nevin."

Alayna fumed inside. "Any such understanding is premature, I assure you, and I will thank you to not repeat it. Come back later for the tray. I will rest until dinner time."

"Very well, miss."

The room fell silent and, without a fire, chilly as well. Alayna shivered, then got herself under control. She might be concluding wrongly that Sadhi was acting as Dimitra's agent, and that the two of them were bent on keeping Alayna prisoner in her own rooms until she accepted *Dom* Nevin's proposal. There was one way to find out.

Alayna cracked open the outer door and peeked outside. As far as she could see in either direction, the corridor was empty. She dipped back inside just long enough to snatch up one of the shawls from the chest at the foot of her bed, and hurried toward the staircase. Here she met a couple of maidservants, their arms full of folded linens. Their chatter ceased when they spotted her.

She reached the ground floor without being challenged. Checking room by room, she made her way along the great central hallway. At the far end lay the entry and foyer, and one of these doors led to the Great Hall. There must be a place men gathered during the day. What *did* they do if they weren't tending cattle or supervising the nut harvest or meeting with the livestock manager, all the things her father and brothers did? Practicing with their swords? Polishing their saddles—no, they'd have stable boys to do that. Being fitted for new dancing shoes? Alayna reflected that she might know a great deal about running a small, impoverished estate, but very little of the lives of fine folk.

Almost by accident, she stumbled into a chamber tucked between a gloomy, echoing, unlit hall and the kitchens. A fire danced in the ample hearth, the soot-darkened stones attesting to its frequent use. Worn carpets cushioned the floor. The air bore a slightly masculine smell, leather and outdoors. Two men were sitting at a table, playing a game of castles.

"Excuse me—" Alayna began.

The men looked up: Zefano the *coridom,* and *Dom* Nevin. *Dom* Nevin got to his feet, looking very pleased, and offered Alayna a half-bow. Zefano did likewise, only his bow was deeper and his expression respectful.

"*Vai damisela,*" Zefano said. "How may I be of service? It isn't customary for ladies to venture unescorted into this part of the castle."

"I'm sorry to intrude. I'll leave you now."

"Of course, you will do no such thing," said *Dom* Nevin. In a few long strides, he crossed the carpet and seized Alayna's hand. "My darling, I'm utterly thrilled that you have sought me out. Zefano, leave us. This is a private matter."

Don't go, Alayna pleaded silently, but the *coridom* bowed to *Dom* Nevin and left the room, all the while avoiding Alayna's eyes. And there she was, her hand clasped in *Dom* Nevin's.

"I see in your eyes that you have come to give me your answer. No, you need not speak it aloud. Your actions speak louder and more eloquently than any words."

"I beg you, sir, to release my hand. You've misunderstood me completely. I have no answer for you. The only reason I'm here is that I got lost—"

"Lost in the wonder of love, I have no doubt. Let us seal our promise with a kiss."

So quickly Alayna could not pull away, he shifted his grip from her hand to her shoulder. He drew her in, holding her hard against his body. At the same time, he circled his free arm around her upper body. She pushed against his chest, but it was like thrusting against a rock wall. His face lowered over her, his lips almost upon hers.

Alayna was filled with revulsion. She might be young and unsophisticated, but she'd grown up on a country estate. She'd heard more than one tale of how a marriage might be secured against the woman's will.

Kyria would know what to do.

The thought brought the memory of Kyria's common sense and forthrightness.

This is what Kyria would have done, she thought, bringing one knee up between *Dom* Nevin's thighs. Her skirts hampered her movement, and she was off her mark, so her knee jammed into his thigh, but it was enough to startle him. His grip loosened. Alayna stepped down hard on his foot. Her slipper didn't make much impact on his thick leather boot, but he was already caught off guard. She seized the opportunity to wrench herself free of his grip and scramble backward.

"You—" Whatever he was going to say was cut short when the door at the far end of the chamber swung open.

Lord Scathfell entered, followed closely by *Dom* Ruyven. Alayna was so glad to see them, she could have wept.

Lord Scathfell's expression turned quizzical. "*Damisela* Alayna. *Dom* Nevin."

"*Vai dom.*" Nevin bowed, but not quickly enough to hide the scarlet rising in his cheeks.

"Are we interrupting?" Lord Scathfell asked, carefully polite.

Gazing directly at Lord Scathfell, Alayna said, "*Dom* Nevin was just taking his leave of me."

"Indeed," said Lord Scathfell.

"My lords." After another deep bow, this time to Ruyven as well as Lord Scathfell, Nevin hurried from the room.

"Now then," Lord Scathfell said in the same kindly tone Alayna remembered from the ball, "what's all this about? You're white as new snow. Has Nevin imposed himself upon your kind graces?"

Alayna fell into the nearest chair and burst into tears.

"Ruyven, you'd best find *Domna* Dimitra. This is a woman's province, not either of ours."

"No," Alayna managed to gasp. "Not her!"

After a murmured discussion, Lord Scathfell pressed a goblet into her hands. "Drink this," he said. "It will doubtless taste vile to you, but it will help, I promise."

Her hands were shaking, and her body still heaved with sobs. He put his hands over hers and held the goblet, tilting it so that the pungent, stinging fluid flooded her mouth. His skin was warm, and his touch gentle. She swallowed, tried hard not to choke on it, and swallowed again. Fire ran down her gullet and filled her belly. Whatever this stuff was, Nevin's fortified wine was tame by comparison.

When Lord Scathfell lifted the goblet to her lips again, she shook her head. "No more, please. I'm better now, as you see."

"I rather doubt you've drunk enough to make a difference, but I will not urge you if you do not wish it. Now tell me, what is the matter? How did you come to this chamber, reserved for the men of my household, and what has Nevin done to distress you so?"

"I came looking for you," she said to *Dom* Ruyven.

"Me? Whatever for?"

Now she felt like even more of a fool for thinking *Dom* Ruyven would have any interest in marrying her. For all the attention he'd paid to her on the trail, they were nothing to one another, that much was now clear.

I'm such a fool. Fresh tears welled up in her eyes.

"You need not answer that, since it so clearly distresses you," Lord Scathfell interjected. "But I would like to know what Nevin has done. You are, after all, in my castle and under my protection. If he has given offense, I would hear of it so that I may deal with him as he deserves."

Alayna wailed, "He asked me to *marry* him."

Lord Scathfell's expression closed up, but not before she caught a moment of surprise and then barely masked rage. She remembered what Dimitra had said about him having a temper, but his voice told her that the anger was not at her but in her defense. "Tell me," he said.

"I put him off," she explained. "I told him I needed time to consider—but now he thinks I mean to accept him and I can't—I won't. I'm sorry, I know he is your kinsman, but he's *horrible* and *Domna* Dimitra thinks I should—and she's been practically *throwing* me at him—and I don't know what to do."

"And you sought Ruyven's advice because he had been as a father to you during your difficult journey?" Lord Scathfell took her hands in his. His touch was so light, she could have broken free as easily as sighing but found she had no wish to.

"Nevin has his place," said Lord Scathfell, "and yes, he is kin, but I know his nature. I would not force any woman, let alone such a tender flower, into an unwilling marriage with him. You, my sweet lady, deserve so much better."

It was all Alayna could do to sit still and not bury her face in his hands, covering them with her tears.

"Ruyven, I believe it is time to give my kinsman useful employment elsewhere."

"I will see to it with pleasure, *vai dom*. I presume you intend a long assignment, very far away?"

One corner of Lord Scathfell's mouth twitched into a half-smile. "An emissary to King Allart's court in Thendara would suffice. If he leaves now and rides with haste, he can just make it before winter sets in."

You're sending him away for my sake? Alayna could scarcely believe her ears.

Ruyven offered an abbreviated bow, one to a superior with whom a person is on affectionate terms, and left the room.

"Now," Lord Scathfell said once they were alone, "that was not so difficult, was it?"

Alayna's moment of relief drained away. "I am grateful to be freed from his advances, which I assure you were neither welcome nor encouraged. But it is now impossible that I remain here indefinitely as your unmarried guest. *Domna* Dimitra knows of the proposal, so it is not secret. I'm sure the servants have all heard by now. I will be thought a flirt and a tease—or worse. I fear my only hope is to marry some man who is—well, *less intolerable* than *Dom* Nevin."

"Sweet *damisela*, there is no reason for you to marry any man who does not please you."

"I beg you, do not make fun of me," she cried. "I understand that I have no place here. I had one only while my sister was promised to you and this castle was to be her home. Now she is gone, and I cannot claim even that."

Lord Scathfell was shaking his head now, with an unreadable half-smile that made her heart sink.

Struggling against tears, she hung her head. "Forgive me. I presumed too much. If you will allow me to trespass through the winter, until the mountain passes are open again, and arrange for an escort suitable for someone like myself, I will go home and face Papa with the news of Kyria's death."

"Go home?" Again, she heard a sharpness in his tone.

I've asked too much. It's outrageous to think he can spare men and horses for such a long journey of no benefit to himself.

He took her hands in that gentle way of his. His fingers caressed hers. "Do you truly wish to leave me?"

She looked up, astonished.

"You braved mountains and bandits, all the long miles between your home and mine, in order to keep your sister company," he went on. "Such steadfast devotion is worth more than all the pearls in Temora. Now your sister is gone, lost to both of us. Will you remain with me in her stead?"

Alayna's brain seemed to have turned to jelly. "I don't understand what you are asking."

"Silly girl, I am asking you to be my wife."

"Your—*wife*."

"This may not the proposal you dreamed of, but as your father is not here, we must arrange matters ourselves. I did not offer myself to your sister out of love, but I intended to be a good husband to her, and the match was advantageous to both her family and myself. It has been a long time since Scathfell was home to a family."

He paused, his vision turning inward for a moment. Then he smiled. "You, on the other hand, I have come to know, although not nearly as well as I should like. I see that you are modest and charming." He stroked the back of Alayna's hand, and a shiver ran up her spine. "And loving."

This was not at all how *Dom* Nevin had made her feel. This was wonderful. "You truly mean it?" she whispered, half afraid she had misunderstood.

"Dearest *damisela*, I swear I would never toy with your affections. I meant to marry a Rockraven daughter, and I still do, although I never thought to find one I could so easily love." Lord Scathfell bent to kiss her hand, this time on the palm. She felt the kiss all through her body.

"Then, yes." More tears spilled down her cheeks as laughter shook her. "Yes, yes, yes!"

His features softened into a smile that made him look younger and even more handsome. "Will you seal your promise to me with a kiss?"

Alayna leaned forward, lifting her face to his, and closed her eyes. He cupped her face. She had not realized how warm a man's hands would feel against her cheeks or the tenderness with which he might place his lips on hers. This was not like the Midwinter Festival Night kisses from her brother's friends, not those wet sloppy things. Lord Scathfell's lips were smooth, and she felt a light prickle from his beard. She wanted to kiss him back and was not sure how. He slipped one hand around the back of her neck, under her hair, cupping the tender skin that only a husband might touch. As he did so, the kiss deepened. Her lips softened and parted, as if she were kissing him with the inside of her mouth. She felt the pressure of his teeth and then his tongue, touching her so delicately and fleetingly that when he withdrew, she wanted to pull him close again. Her entire body was on fire. Her nipples ached and the secret place between her thighs pulsed with the beating of her heart.

Heat flooding her cheeks, Alayna opened her eyes. Lord Scathfell was looking at her with a curious expression. "I do not displease you, then, my promised wife?"

She could not speak, only shake her head. *Displease me? I had no idea such a wonderful man walked the world.*

"And it is your will that we be wed *di catenas* at Midwinter Festival?"

"Lord Scathfell, I—"

"You must call me Gwynn-Alar when we are alone. Or Gwynn, even better."

Alayna pressed one hand flat between her breasts, as if she could still the frantic movement of her heart.

"I take that as assent." Rising, Lord Scathfell—*Gwynn*—bent over to kiss her brow. "We will speak more of this after I deal with Nevin. After all, we will have the rest of our lives together."

A moment later, two of the castle guards entered. "Escort the future Lady Scathfell anywhere she wishes to go," Gwynn said. "But see that *Domna* Dimitra attends me without delay."

Bracketed between the guards, Alayna returned to her suite of rooms. Her heart beat fast and light, like the wings of the little red-capped birds that nested in the hedges in the summer. She felt dizzy, as if she'd drunk too much hot spiced wine. Only a fraction of an hour ago, she'd been desperate to avoid marrying *Dom* Nevin. Now she need not worry about her future again. She thought of Kyria and stumbled. Kyria would have wanted her to be safe and happy. A thought came to her, that this marriage and the security it brought was Kyria's parting gift.

Then I will make the most of it. She would see to it that Gwynn never had a moment's regret. *I won't be like Ellimira, ordering everyone around. I will be kind and gentle, and Gwynn will think himself blessed to have such a loving wife.*

It did not matter if Nevin was sent away, for he had no power over her. As for Dimitra ... *Can I ever trust her again?* But was it right that a single mistake should cost Dimitra her place? Perhaps she had reasons Alayna knew nothing of.

They had gone most of the way to the women's portion of the castle, but Alayna turned and, with a determined stride, headed back the way they had come.

"*Vai damisela!*" The guards had to run a few steps to catch up with her. "Your quarters are this way."

"I wish to speak with my intended husband again," she replied without slackening her pace. "Right now."

Gwynn was still in the men's parlor, sitting in one of the large, comfortable chairs. Ruyven was with him. Both men turned their heads as she burst through the doors.

"My lord, I am sorry to interrupt, but I've had a moment to think about our last conversation, and I would not want you to behave against your own best interests on my account."

"My dear, let us have no false modesty or protestations that you are somehow unworthy of becoming Lady Scathfell," Ruyven said, scowling.

"That is not at all what I meant," she shot back, then turned to Gwynn. "I would not build our life together on the pain of others, no matter how well deserved. You decided to send *Dom* Nevin away to protect me, and for that I am more grateful than I have words to express. I expect that *Domna* Dimitra will be brought here any moment for equal punishment for her part in the matter. You must have had good reasons for including both of them in your household to begin with. I don't know about *Dom* Nevin—you said he has his place, so I assume he was useful to you in some way, if only for the duty one kinsman owes another."

Gwynn and Ruyven exchanged glances. "I think it best that Nevin makes himself useful elsewhere," Gwynn said. "Your honor in this matter does you credit, but he has shown he is not to be trusted. He might treat you with respect for a time, out of fear of my displeasure, but in his mind, he will always see you as a young woman he can impose upon. I will not tolerate that behavior toward my wife."

"But until this episode, *Domna* Dimitra fulfilled her duties admirably. She cared for me and helped me adjust to life in the castle." *She was the closest thing I had to a friend.* "I was angry with her because I saw her acting in her own interest or *Dom* Nevin's, not out of regard for my own happiness. If she repents, I will forgive her. Will you do the same?"

"That depends on the sincerity of her remorse," Gwynn said.

"If I may, *vai dom*," Ruyven spoke. "The *domna* and I have never been on more than polite terms, so you know I harbor no favoritism toward her when I urge you to consider *Damisela* Alayna's request. Dimitra must be taught a lesson in no uncertain terms, but a pardon following censure and the threat of dismissal is not a bad strategy. If she knows you may send her away at the slightest lapse in judgment, she will perform her duties all the more assiduously."

"As usual, my old friend, you counsel me wisely." Gwynn laid his hand on Ruyven's shoulder. "Ah, I see Dimitra has arrived. Let us see what we can accomplish. Alayna, *preciosa*, you need not remain if you do not wish to."

"I will stay," she said, and caught the flash of approval in Gwynn's eyes. As Lady Scathfell, she might be called upon to watch or even to inflict even worse censure. At his gesture, she took a seat behind his right shoulder.

Dimitra curtsied formally to Gwynn. "*Vai dom, vai damisela*, how may I serve you?"

"Thank you for coming so promptly," Gwynn said, his voice easy, as if he had nothing in mind more taxing than a conversation about the weather. "I trust you are well. Your quarters are adequate? Your duties are not onerous?"

The lady-in-waiting glanced from Gwynn to Alayna and back again. "I could not ask for a better situation, as my lord knows."

"Indulge me by telling us what your responsibilities entail."

"Why, I provide the same assistance as I would to any mistress of the castle. I help her to select appropriate garb and take care of her clothes, I dress her hair, fetch her jewels from the locked case, and so forth. I supervise the maidservants, so that her room is always tidy, the fire laid on, meals provided in her chamber when appropriate, and hot water brought when my lady wishes it. In addition, because the young lady is unaccustomed to the ways of Scathfell Castle, I offer guidance . . ." for the first time, Dimitra hesitated.

"Excellent. And does this guidance extend to advice concerning suitable companions? You would encourage her to associate with those worthy of her station and discourage those beneath her?"

"Yes, my lord."

"And what sort of relationships would you feel it your duty to promote? If you learned that a man of this court desired *Damisela* Alayna for his wife, and he was a person of good family with the means to support her in comfort and provide for any offspring they might have, would you try to persuade her to accept him?"

Dimitra paled. "I have done nothing except in my lady's best interests."

"*Indeed*."

An uncomfortable silence filled the room. The wind was suddenly audible, and the room was colder. Dimitra was no fool; there was no point in denying what she had done, yet she made no attempt to justify or defend herself. She merely stood there, with obvious effort at dignity, waiting for what would come next.

"You dared," Gwynn said, "you *dared* to interfere in the life of a young woman in my charge *without consulting me*? You took it upon yourself to try to persuade her into a marriage not of my choosing?"

Dimitra sank to her knees. Tears glistened in her eyes. Her hands twisted the fabric of her skirts. "My lord, if you would permit me to explain—"

"Silence." Gwynn got to his feet. "You had the insolence to usurp my prerogative as Lord of Scathfell in determining the fate of a noble young lady who would have become my kinswoman, if circumstances were otherwise."

In the quiet that followed, nothing was heard but Dimitra's barely suppressed sobs.

"You schemed to deliver her to my kinsman, that vermin Nevin, who has already buried two wives." Gwynn pressed on. "Do not protest it was out of your love for her, meant only to secure her happiness. Such a lie will strangle you, if I do not. No, it was for your own profit. You do not deserve the title of lady-in-waiting, you who are no more than a common procurer."

With this, Dimitra broke down completely. Her body shuddered with wave after wave of sobbing, yet the only sounds that came from her throat were choked gasps.

Alayna grasped the seat of the chair, hard enough to make her knuckles ache, to keep from rushing to Dimitra's side. What the older woman had done was cunning and self-serving, but no lasting harm had been done, especially compared to all the kindness and help Dimitra had shown her. *Without her, I would have been miserable during those first few days, and then when I learned about Francisco.* And even if that were not true, she thought, no one should have to suffer this way without the chance to speak in her own defense.

Dimitra mumbled something, her words unintelligible.

"What's that? You have something to say?" Gwynn's voice offered no hint of solace.

"What I did was unpardonable. I have no hope, but for your mercy. For—forgive me."

Gwynn held up a hand for stillness. No one dared move as the moment stretched on. "Look at me, woman."

Dimitra took a ragged breath, visibly gathering herself, before she lifted her head. Her cheeks were reddened, her eyes swollen.

"I will not forgive you, for such treachery deserves no pardon. But the future Lady Scathfell may, if she chooses." Gwynn turned in his chair, indicating Alayna.

Confusion gave way to astonishment on Dimitra's face. "My—my *Lady Scathfell*?"

"*Damisela* Alayna and I have pledged ourselves to one another, that promise to be consummated *di catenas* at Midwinter Festival," Gwynn said. "Such was my intention, while you were scheming to deliver her into the hands of a lesser man."

"I—I had no idea," Dimitra murmured.

Alayna could not remain still any longer. "*Domna* Dimitra, are you sorry for what you did?"

"*Vai damisela*, I wish I had never thought of such a thing."

"And do you promise to never do it again? To speak and act openly with me and to follow my wishes and those of my intended husband?"

"I wish I had done so! I wish I had never met *Dom* Nevin."

Alayna went to Dimitra and raised her to standing. "Then I forgive you. I cannot forget what you did, but when I remember, I will also remind myself of how kind you were when I first arrived. I wish to always have your wisdom and experience to guide me."

Dimitra kissed Alayna's hands, much to Alayna's embarrassment. "Let us put this whole painful episode behind us," Alayna said.

After Dimitra had withdrawn along with Ruyven and the guards, Gwynn held out his hand to Alayna. "I was harsh with her, I know. I wanted to make sure there was no chance she would revert to her old ways."

"I believe her repentance, but then, I believed her false words before."

He kissed her brow and then held her close, her cheek pressed against his chest. "You are a jewel among women, did you know that? No, how could you, coming from the back end of nowhere and then subject to flattery from the like of Nevin?"

"What if he learns you called him *vermin*? Although I suppose that as lord of a realm, you may call him anything you like."

His laugh rumbled through his chest. "He has been called worse things by me, and to his face. You must stop thinking like a rabbit-horn and more like a lady eagle."

"I—I will try."

"And do not trouble yourself on Nevin's account, for he will thrive at King Allart's court. In fact, I would not be surprised if he himself has been scheming for a way to get sent there."

19

When Alayna arrived back at her chambers, every detail of the sitting room had been made perfect in her absence, from the brightly burning fire to the bouquet of dried straw-flowers in its vase of polished green stone. Dimitra herself stood waiting. She curtsied as a servant to her mistress, more reverently than she had done before.

Alayna began to compliment Dimitra on how pleasant the room was, but then held her tongue. It was Dimitra's responsibility to ensure that these rooms, and clothes and meals and anything else Alayna might fancy, were all seen to.

"It's been an eventful day," Alayna said, deliberately looking past Dimitra, rather than meeting her gaze. "I'll rest for a few hours. Be sure to have suitable attire ready for dinner tonight with Lord Scathfell."

"Very well, my lady. I wonder—"

"If it's about today, you're not to speak of it."

Dimitra froze for an instant, then went on. "I wonder if you would care to bathe beforehand."

"A pitcher of warm water will suffice." Alayna proceeded to the bedroom. Dimitra followed and in silence helped Alayna off with her shoes and clothes. Neither spoke.

How many walls we build, shutting one another out,

Alayna thought as she slipped beneath the comforter. She missed Kyria even more than ever.

— ◆ —

Alayna and Gwynn dined alone, except for a guard at the door and a pair of servants, who brought out platters of food and then stood along the wall. The food was simple — bread and roasted vegetables seasoned with herbs, and bowls of a nut-grain mixture with a splash of sauce — not the overly rich fare of the welcoming feast.

After they had been served, Alayna found herself at a loss for what to say. It was thrilling to be here with Gwynn, and she still felt a little dizzy with the speed with which her life had changed. There was so much she wanted to know about him, besides that he was handsome and charming and firm in her defense. Gwynn immediately put her at ease, entertaining her with stories of growing up in the castle. To her surprise, she found there wasn't much difference between life as a child at Rockraven and here at Scathfell Castle, except that he'd had only one brother, quite a few years older, the one who'd died. Clearly he'd adored his brother. She'd heard the lingering pain in his voice whenever he mentioned his brother or his parents.

"Your own family was much larger, I believe, very different from mine," he said, sopping up the last of the sauce with a bit of bread.

"There was Papa, of course. Mamma died when I was little, so I don't remember her much. In order of birth, we are Valdir, who's married to Ellimira and has two boys with another babe on the way, and then Hjalmar, Fiona, Kyria, Rakhal, and me. Fiona went away when she married, so I haven't seen her in a long time." At the name *Kyria*, Alayna felt a pulse of sadness. *I will never cease to miss her.*

"Speaking of home, I was wondering . . ." she said, setting down her eating utensils.

"Yes, my dear?"

"I would so like my family to know of our happiness. I confess, I was reluctant to even mention sending them a message about Kyria. My father will be so distressed. They all will. But now this news might soften that pain, at least I hope so."

"What a kind heart you have, and of course I will

dispatch a rider, weather permitting. Is there any other wish of yours I can fulfill?"

Heartened, she went on. "I have so many questions about what to expect once we are married." She blushed, thinking he might decide she meant intimate matters. "Things like my household responsibilities as lady of this great castle."

"I expect you will be far too busy raising our sons to trouble yourself with domestic matters."

"May I not do both? At home, my sister-in-law Ellimira kept the household ledgers, supervised the kitchen and housekeeping servants, counted and repaired the linens, taught us girls to sew our own dresses, and so many other things. She was busy from before dawn until everyone else was abed. Please allow me to be of use. I have some skill in managing a household, though a much smaller one."

Gwynn sat back in his chair, looking thoughtful. "I've done without a lady chatelaine for so long, since my mother died, that I haven't thought about it. Zefano sees to what must be done. I suppose his wife helps him and Dimitra does, as well."

Alayna might have forgiven Dimitra but did *not* want her performing the duties of Lady Scathfell for one moment longer.

"Do you not find matters here to your liking?" he asked. "The food? The clothing prepared for your sister, which is now yours?"

"Yes, it's all splendid. But people cannot live on festive meals all year long." She indicated the remains of the meal. "This is more like what we will eat every day, or so I hope."

Now he laughed. "I had no idea that such a beauty would have good sense. You are quite right, of course, for the feasts and the balls upon your arrival were a rare occurrence. Indeed, we have had little cause for celebration since I was a child."

Alayna gathered her courage and reached out to touch his hand where it lay on the table. "You mentioned having a brother who died. There is so much about you, and Scathfell itself, of which I'm hopelessly ignorant. But I'd like to share your burdens."

Gwynn's expression turned stony, although he did not pull away from her touch. "Some might say it is folly to

speak of such things to you, that should you learn what
awaits you here, you will flee back to your own family."

"Why? What can be so dreadful to make you think
that?"

"You have a right to know what you are sealing yourself
to in marrying me," he said, and his bleakness made it sound
as if she had just consigned herself to Zandru's coldest hell.
Her heart went out to him. When she said nothing, he went
on, "For a generation now, as you may know, my family has
waged a feud with the neighboring realm of Aldaran, who
are also our kin. My elder brother, heir to Scathfell, was
betrothed to Dorilys of Aldaran when they were but children. He died, and although it was never proven, my father
suspected the girl herself of some vile sorcery."

Alayna nodded. She'd heard of that ill-fated betrothal,
enough to make her feel ashamed that Dorilys, the Witch-
Child of Aldaran, was the daughter of her own Great-Aunt
Aliciane.

"I was too young to understand, but even I saw how it
changed my father. He never forgot, and he never forgave,"
he said in a tightly controlled, almost expressionless voice.
"Then one thing led to another. War followed, and in the
end, he was forced into a humiliating surrender. He returned home so broken, he barely knew me. He died a short
time afterward. My mother was so consumed by grief, she
did not long survive him. I blame her death on the Aldarans,
as well."

"So you lost both your parents and your brother—your
entire family."

He nodded grimly. "You wonder why I keep so many
soldiers. It is because the Aldarans are not to be trusted, not
a single one of the lot. The feud is not over, my love, not
while I remember what was taken from Scathfell. Not while
there is an Aldaran heir perched in his fortress."

Blessed Cassilda! Alayna forced herself to remain calm.
"So you—we, I mean—are we still at war?"

"At present, we are technically at peace, having been
forced into a humiliating surrender. But this peace cannot
be relied upon. I cannot build Scathfell's future on quick-
sand, apt to dissolve at a moment's notice and plunge us all
into bloodshed. Until now, I could do no more than be vig-
ilant and prepared. So many lives have already been lost to

Aldaran witchery that to go against them by ordinary arms would be suicide. I would not lead my men into senseless slaughter. Long have I searched for an answer to this impasse."

The muscles around his eyes tensed, and his vision seemed to turn inward. "I kept my heart guarded, except for Ruyven, for how could I take a wife and sire sons, knowing that they might face the same hideous death as my brother—blasted by sorcerous lightning?"

By this time, Alayna's head was spinning with sad history, the schemes and counter schemes, and most of all, the grief and fear that gnawed at him.

"Then it came to me," Gwynn went on, "the old proverb about *fighting fire with fire*. The Aldarans had the advantage, the Gift of lightning control, whereas we have had only a little *laran*—only enough to sometimes sense the truth of another's words or to feel another's emotions if they are strong enough." He paused, his face softening in a tender smile. "This is why I know you are so sweet, so . . . good."

Alayna flushed. In the past, others had called her *pretty*, but never *good*, not in the sense he meant it. She understood now that none of her peccadilloes mattered. What Gwynn referred to was an essential aspect of her character, one she had never considered had value. Suitors wanted golden curls and flirtatious smiles, didn't they? Not . . . goodness? Courtship, like life itself, turned out to be nothing like her childish imaginings.

"Then it came to me," he went on. "I may not have power over lightning, but *I can ensure that my sons do*. That Gift came to Aldaran through a Rockraven woman the old lord kept as *barragana*. It was never part of the Aldaran genetic heritage. So I sent to your father with a marriage offer for one of his daughters, to bring that Gift to Scathfell, with all its power to defend my lands and people."

She'd been a fool not to have realized it earlier. Gwynn had said he sought a Rockraven daughter, *any* Rockraven daughter. No one at home had questioned why such a powerful lord would choose a wife from a penniless house, and Father had been too glad of the bride-price to ask too closely.

Gwynn gazed at her, his formerly somber expression

melting into one of tenderness. "Couples often begin their married lives with little knowledge of one another. I thought that was my lot, too. I never expected fate to bring me someone like you, Alayna. When you came to Scathfell, I thought you charming. And the most beautiful woman I'd ever seen. But when you had the courage to refuse Nevin, and then when you pleaded for Dimitra, I knew I had found much more. You are not only sweet and lovely, you have courage and insight. And compassion. Until you agreed to marry me, I had no notion of how much I needed those things—how much I need *you*."

— ◆ —

The wardrobe Dimitra presented for Alayna's consideration comprised the cream spidersilk ball gown and three tunics with underskirts, one of them a horrible shade for Alayna's complexion. Alayna paused in looking over the garments spread out over bed and chest. At home she'd had one holiday gown, one everyday dress, one split riding skirt with jacket, and one nightgown, all of them hand-me-downs. Plus a cloak, assorted shawls, hats, scarves, and mittens, none of which truly belonged to her, the way the rest of the family members snatched them up whenever convenient.

It occurred to her that this array might represent an enormous expenditure on Gwynn's part. She remembered what Francisco had said about the farms not being able to support so many fighting men. This feud with Aldaran must end.

The first matter to tackle was the bridal gown. She could not in conscience have a new one made up for her, but perhaps if she altered the cream spidersilk, it would serve. Her gaze lit on pearls set in the embroidery of the russet tunic.

"This will do," she told Dimitra. "We'll pick out the pearls and stitch them here and here, like this . . ."

Dimitra's expression of reserve, which she'd worn like a mask since her humiliation, softened. "Instead of scattering them, for they're so small they can hardly be seen, we might place them along the neckline and down the center of the bodice."

The woman had a good eye, Alayna admitted, finding the best way to show off not only the pearls but the décolletage. She blushed to think of how grown-up she'd felt at that first ball and how naïve she'd been. On Midwinter, she would become mistress of this castle and wife to a great lord. If Evanda answered her prayers, a year hence she would also be mother to the heir of Scathfell.

Gwynn looked tense when Alayna came down to dinner, but she was in such a good mood that he eventually softened. "And what have you been up to that has so pleased you?"

"For that, you must wait for your wedding day," she teased.

"Lord of Light! Not married yet, and she's bossing me around." At her wide-eyed expression, he added, "My love, I was joking. Since I outgrew my childish breeches, no woman has ever been able to persuade me against my wishes." He spoke lightly, as if the matter were a joke, but Alayna caught the hint of steel beneath his words.

"I will of course defer to you in all things," Alayna said, lowering her eyes.

"I see I've offended you. Forgive me, for I am accustomed to giving orders to men, not my intended bride. Their duty is to obey me, not to debate the wisdom of the courses I have chosen."

"You do not ask others for their opinions?" *And sometimes realize that they are right and you are wrong?* What a mismatch he and Kyria would have been, she who never hesitated to make her own thoughts known and to browbeat her brothers into agreement.

"Certainly, but that does not give them, or anyone, license to defy me, or Dimitra to contradict you."

"That is not a fair comparison," Alayna pointed out. "When I first arrived, I knew little of castle life. I consulted her in many things. Other than the one misstep, Dimitra's counsel has been sound."

"Perhaps your trust was not well placed. Had you commanded her according to your own wishes, she might never have had the audacity to interfere with your private concerns."

Alayna sat back in her chair, taken aback that he should blame her for Dimitra's treachery. He must not understand how overwhelmed she'd felt on learning of Kyria's death, how inattentive and malleable. But when she opened her mouth to explain, she found she could not do it.

Gwynn drained his goblet and smiled at her. "Come, do not take offense. Winter will soon be upon us, and then Midwinter Festival and our nuptials. Let us be easy with one another. Scathfell has enough enemies in the world without our creating strife within these walls."

"I presume you mean Aldaran," Alayna replied, still fuming. "*Why* must Scathfell and Aldaran still be enemies? You've said yourself that the feud happened in your father's time and that the present Lord Aldaran has made no hostile move against you. Then what point is there in maintaining an army—" *and impoverishing the people in your care*, "—when it may never be needed? Has it occurred to you that just *having* such a force makes it all the more likely that it will be *used*? You're like the man who has already drawn his sword—one peep out of Aldaran and you'll use it without even thinking, without even *talking* to them."

"Why do you rush to defend my enemies?" Gwynn shot back, his face tight. "I expect such snake-tongued speech from those disloyal to me, but never from my future wife."

"I am *not* defending them!" Alayna threw up her hands. "I don't know *what* we're talking about, truth be told. The folk at Aldaran mean nothing to me. But I would not see you carry the burden of your father's tragedy."

"That may be true, but it is not an excuse for challenging my authority."

This is my husband-to-be. I must not quarrel with him. "I meant no disrespect," she murmured.

"You want me to *forget* how my brother and father died," he plunged on as if he had not heard her, "and the grief that took my mother's life?"

"Of course not," Alayna said, feeling sick at having provoked him. He was a proud, stubborn man. She must take great care never to repeat her mistake. "But surely there is cause—*now*—for joy? For hope that our children will know peace?"

"Would that it were that simple. You have a sweet and forgiving nature, but the world of men is cruel. I do not *want* to start a war, but if one is forced upon us, I will not see Scathfell defeated, *ruined*, again. You speak of swords, and those I have, as many as I can afford to keep. But against the sword of Aldaran, the lightning Gift, such weapons are a paltry defense. I watch Aldaran carefully, because our only hope will be to strike them hard and fast, before they can bring the battle to us."

He sighed, looking more careworn than she had yet seen him. "If I appear distracted, it is because I fear that Aldaran will seize upon the occasion of our nuptials to launch an attack. I know little of the current lord, only that he is the son of his father, and for that reason alone I dare not trust him."

Gwynn was defending his people in the best way he knew, perhaps the only way possible. How could she do anything but rally to his side?

20

Midwinter Day dawned clear and very cold. Alayna, still in her dressing gown as she looked out the window, decided it was so frigid, snow would warm things up. Below, the main halls were decked with greenery and the fragrance of the boughs seemed to carry even up here. This would be the last night she'd sleep in her chambers. Her belongings would be moved to the suite adjacent to Gwynn's, and tonight she would sleep in his bed.

At home, she would have been prepared for the consummation of the marriage by Ellimira, as her nearest married kinswoman. In her turn, should Alayna be blessed with daughters as well as sons, she would instruct them. But who would instruct her? She could not go to Dimitra. Although they were perfectly polite to one another, it was the courtesy of mistress to servant, nothing more. Yet if she went to Gwynn's bed untutored, she would feel but half a wife.

Tears stung her eyes. She'd felt so emotional these last few tendays, she'd cried at the falling of a snowflake. No matter how many times she told herself this marriage was the best possible future for her, it did no good when *the weepies*, as Kyria used to call them, struck her. Since there was nothing else to be done, she got out not one handkerchief but three, curled back in the chair, and let herself have a good cry.

By the time her sobs had subsided into hiccoughs, she felt considerably better. In fact, an idea had come to her: *you must see* Domna *Jerana.*

Jerana arrived promptly at Alayna's summons. They sat companionably over cups of *jaco*, watching the snow that began to fall, first gently, like bits of goose down, then faster and thicker. "A good night to be abed," Jerana said with a perfectly straight face, and Alayna laughed. As calmly as she could, Alayna explained what she wanted.

When they had established that Alayna was not entirely ignorant of what passed between men and women, Jerana became more serious. "You must bear in mind that every husband and his wife are intimate in their own way. Oh, some things never change—"

"—like kissing."

"Indeed. But there are no books stored at Arilinn that say *this* must be done, or at a specified time or in a prescribed order—or *that* is forbidden. The most important thing is that both lovers desire it. It need not give them each the same degree of pleasure, so long as neither finds it repugnant. Do you understand what I'm saying?"

"That my husband may wish—may ask me to do something not entirely to my liking? That I may permit it anyway in order to please him?"

"Not exactly. When we love someone, of course we want to make him happy. In the marriage bed, however, nothing that truly makes one party unhappy is good for the couple together. When one is less experienced than the other, she—for usually it is the wife—may not yet know what gives her the greatest delight. A certain amount of exploration is necessary. She may accede to her husband's wishes in order to discover whether they are *hers* as well."

"I have never lain with a man, so how can I tell what I like if I do not try different things?"

Jerana nodded. "An open mind is a good thing. Also open communication, so that you need not hesitate to tell your husband when something is distasteful to you. Women sometimes think they must put their husband's desires above their own or that it does not matter whether they themselves find pleasure in love-making." She paused, looking at Alayna over the rim of her mug.

"I have never thought about the matter. I truly enjoyed the kisses we exchanged, but I always supposed that lying together was for the man's pleasure. And for the getting of children, of course."

"Why should only men desire sexual union, when a little education is all that is needed for women to feel equal ardor? Some initial discomfort is common the first few times, but if it worsens or you find yourself dreading your husband's embraces, then you must come to me. I am trained as a monitor and healer. Do not suffer needlessly when I may be able to help."

They chatted for a time longer, until the *jaco* had gone cold, and it was clear that Alayna could summon no further questions. Just then, there was a knock at the door.

In swept Dimitra, who looked very fine in her best gown of gray wool. She was followed by Sadhi, and then Marianna and Shayla. They brought out the cream spidersilk gown, onto which they had stitched the pearls from the russet tunic. As they held it up, Alayna's heart leapt in her throat, for the gown had been transformed from a luxurious garment into a glorious one, not the less for the love so evident in every detail.

"I don't know what to say," Alayna cried. "Thank you all so very much."

"Just wanted to do our lady proud," Marianna said.

"Nothing's too good for the mistress of Scathfell," Sadhi added, remembering herself with a curtsy.

After admiring the trousseau, Jerana took her leave. A moment after she departed, there came a knock at the door. It was Zefano, flanked by not two but four household guards. He carried a brass-bound casket. After placing it on the table in the sitting room, he took a key from the ring at his belt and opened it.

"*Vai damisela*, who after today will be our *vai domna*," he said, "I present the Scathfell jewels."

Arranged on a tray of midnight velvet were several antique gold necklaces set with rubies and emeralds, an assortment of rings and earrings, and a small, luminous moonstone on a silver chain.

"My lord bids you to choose what you will for today's

ceremony. These treasures have been passed from mother to daughter since the founding of Scathfell. They are to be yours, to be held in trust for your eldest son's wife."

"Oh, my lady!" Sadhi breathed.

Dimitra scowled and the girl scurried away. Then Dimitra bent over the casket, her eyes alight. "If you would allow me to make a suggestion, *Damisela* Alayna, I would select—"

As she reached for the casket, Zefano blocked her way. "The choice is for Lady Scathfell to make." By his tone, he thought it sacrilege for a mere lady-in-waiting to lay hands upon the jewels.

Alayna's gaze lit upon the moonstone pendant. It came into her hand as if it welcomed her touch, and warmed almost immediately. "This."

Zefano relocked the casket and took it away, followed by the guards. Dimitra wrapped the pendant and the pair of silver earrings that Alayna had selected in a square of silk and tucked them away. Marianna and Shayla left after offering Alayna many wishes for her happiness, and Sadhi went to prepare Alayna's bath.

— ✦ —

An hour before the appointed time, Alayna stood before the full-length mirror and studied her reflection. After a long, luxuriant bath, Sadhi had massaged her with scented creams that made her skin glow. Dimitra had dressed Alayna's hair into plaits wound with white ribbons and strands of tiny silver-cloth flowers, most of them coiled low on her neck and secured with a butterfly clasp of honey-colored wood— Dimitra's gift. A few tresses were left unbraided to flow over the shoulders. The tendrils had been arranged to display the earrings without overpowering them. The moonstone pendant nestled at the cleft between her breasts, and it seemed to Alayna that it glowed faintly with its own inner light.

"Oh, my lady!" Sadhi exclaimed. "You are as beautiful as the dawn. As beautiful as Blessed Cassilda herself."

"Hush, child, do not speak such nonsense," Dimitra said. "'Tis bad luck to praise a bride so highly." Nonetheless, her eyes shone.

"Marianna and Shayla—you two deserve all the praise," Alayna said. "You did a splendid job with the gown."

Dimitra said in a softer voice, "You wear it well."

It was not yet time to go down, but Alayna was too excited to sit still. She wished again that Kyria might have lived to see this day. Grief tugged on her heart, but the pangs felt distant, less fierce, as if they were happening to someone else. She loved Kyria as much as ever, but the loss of her sister was no longer the defining experience of her life. At this time tomorrow, she would be a married woman, a great lord's wife.

The wait seemed interminable, with Alayna shifting from one foot to the other, and Dimitra making pleasant remarks about the weather, the roads, the guests, and the wedding gifts sent from all around. At last, however, a page tapped on the door and recited in his clear, child's voice that all was in readiness and would the *vai damisela* be pleased to join Lord Scathfell in the Great Hall.

Dimitra went down with Alayna, helping her manage the full skirts on the stairs. At the bottom, she smoothed the fabric and checked the fastening of the butterfly clasp, made sure the silver chain holding the moonstone was secure and that every curl and plait was in place. The castle guards bowed as the two women walked by. Alayna felt their gaze even after she had passed.

And then they were outside the doubled doors of the Great Hall. She heard music within. One of the two guards at the door put a hand on the latch.

Dimitra held up a hand. "Deep breaths now, my lady. Ready?"

So might my own mother have spoken, had she lived and were she here. Alayna, not trusting herself to speech, nodded.

"In we go."

As they entered, a hush fell on the assembly, neighboring nobles and their wives, senior officers, Zefano and his family, other folk she did not know. They parted to make way for her, and there at the far end of the room, Gwynn sat in his throne-like chair. Ruyven stood beside him, bedecked in brocade and lace. Alayna spared him only a glance. Once she saw Gwynn, she could not look away. He drew her like a lodestone, or perhaps she drew him, for he got to his feet, powerful and graceful. And the expression on his face, the astonishment writ clear as sunrise, sent a thrill all through her.

Dimitra had told her that she must go to him, for his was the higher rank. As she did, her heart urged her to rush into his arms, but she kept herself to a stately pace. She halted a few paces in front of him, then began a curtsy. Her knees trembled as she found herself sinking deeper and deeper until her skirts flowed out around her.

"*Vai dom.*" She meant the title as a whisper, but her voice rang out, sweet and clear. Perhaps it was the silence of the chamber that made it seem so.

"*Vai damisela.*" As if her voice had released him from a spell, he crossed the distance between them, bowed, and extended his hand. She slipped hers into it and found herself lifted to her feet as if she weighed no more than a feather. He did not release her hand but bent over and carried it to his lips so that each met the other halfway.

The next moment, people began talking and moving again, although in a more subdued manner than before. First one and then another of the guests approached, bowed, and introduced themselves. Gwynn spoke a word or two, treating some in a more familiar manner than others. She wished them all a joyous festival and thanked them for coming.

Ruyven left his place, approaching her and Gwynn. A page brought up a box, much smaller than the casket of jewels. Ruyven drew out the paired *catenas* bracelets, beautifully shaped copper lined with something else — rose gold, perhaps — to prevent the copper from reacting with the skin.

I will wear this for the rest of my life.

The metal felt surprisingly warm as Ruyven clasped it around her wrist, then Gwynn's around his. The bracelets were locked together, so that for this moment they too were joined.

As if in a dream, she heard Ruyven say, "Parted in flesh, may you never be so in spirit. May you be forever one." Then he unlocked the bracelets. The assembly burst into cheering, which fell away only when the music struck up again.

She was married. She was his. Through the haze of astonished delight, she reminded herself that it was her place to lead him in their first dance as husband and wife. She held out her hand, and he took it. The *catenas* glinted. Her feet knew which way to go, when to advance and to pause, and it was a good thing, for her senses whirled in a most pleasant way. They danced one and then another set, revolving around each other and the other couples in complicated figures.

Gwynn brought her wine, and she drank it all, not caring how strong it was. He was her husband and she wanted no barriers between them. "Let us take a break from dancing," he said.

"Am I flushed?" She felt quite warm.

"You look perfectly lovely, but it is courteous to examine the wedding gifts." Gwynn indicated a table running the length of the hall. It was heaped with ornamented boxes, baskets adorned with ribbons, bolts of fabric, even a saddle, which she thought odd but said nothing as Gwynn praised it highly. Many of the gifts were household items: a rolled-up tapestry, boxes of beeswax candles, and the like.

"What is this?" He stopped before a long box, the sort used to transport fragile goods on horseback. The lid had been pried loose but left in place. "I thought I had seen all the gifts as they arrived."

"It must have just come. May I?" At Gwynn's nod, Alayna lifted the lid and slid her hands into the curling wood shavings. The velvet wrapping was well-tied and many layers thick, but with a little juggling, the two of them were able to free what lay within.

"A *rryl*?" Gwynn looked puzzled.

The instrument had been shipped with the strings loosened to prevent breakage or undue stress on the wooden frame. It was meant to be tuned at its destination. Though unable, at the moment, to assess the quality of its sound, she could see it had been made with care and skill. The wood was a rich red-brown, the lines graceful, and delicate carven flowers twined up the sides. Even better, it was perfectly balanced and exactly the right size for her small hands.

"It's splendid," she cried. "Now I can play and sing for you—oh, so beautifully on this."

"I look forward to hearing you."

"Here's the note," Alayna said. "'*For Lord and Lady Scathfell, that you may find delight in one another.*' It's signed, Edric-Donal, Lord Aldaran. How lovely! And how strange."

"Aldaran?" Gwynn's expression darkened. "He *dared!* Does he mean to insult us both?"

"I think he meant the gift as a goodwill offering. *Caryo*, don't scowl like that, not on our special day. Would it have suited you better if Lord Aldaran ignored us entirely? Or sent some extravagant gift that would impose an obligation in return? This is much better, something small and beautifully made."

"Very well," he said with an effort at composure, "if it pleases you, my wife, then you shall have it. But do not expect me to listen to any tunes you coax out of it."

"Do not expect to get out of hearing me play," Alayna teased. "You have never once attended our singing. You do not know if I am a silvertongue or a crow."

"Does the gift please you?"

"You know that it does."

"Then I suppose I must consider the possibility—only a possibility, mind you—that it was sent in earnest. That somehow the moons have changed places with the sun, and Aldaran genuinely wishes for better relations between us. That should not be difficult, for they could hardly be worse, short of armed conflict."

Alayna, her heart full of love and pride, smiled up at him. "I pray that Lord Aldaran proves worthy of your—I will not say, *trust*, for that must be earned. Your willingness to allow him to demonstrate that he too wishes for peace. Speaking of which," she picked up the note again, "I don't suppose you've ever met this Edric-Donal?"

"Hardly. Why do you ask?"

"On the journey from Rockraven, we spent the night at a traveler's shelter. I believe we spoke of it my first night here. We shared the shelter with a young man who called himself Edric. He had no companion or servant, so he went on with us for a time until after Kyria was taken. He would not give his family name, nor did we, for *Dom* Ruyven said that anonymity is the rule at such shelters. At least, I think it was he who said it, and then none of us inquired. Edric is not an uncommon name, but I wonder . . . could it have been he?"

"What would the Lord of Aldaran be doing, journeying alone through the Hellers? I never heard he was foolhardy or lacking in wits."

"The Edric we traveled with was neither." Edric-of-the-trail had not carried himself like a man of low station. *He tried to rescue Kyria, but he failed.* The *rryl* might very well have come from him, not only as a gesture of friendship but of apology.

"Come, my wife," Gwynn said, holding out his arm for her. "The night is still young, and the musicians have started up again. Let us set an example for the others and lead them in dance."

She placed her fingertips on his arm and allowed him to guide her to the center of the room. They took their positions for the next dance, a lively reel.

"You must not overtire yourself," he murmured, for only her to hear. "Later this evening, a dance of only two people awaits you."

Alayna blushed, but there was no time to formulate a reply. The music swept her up, whirling and skipping, always with glances at her new husband. The figures of the dance brought her to circle *Dom* Ruyven. His face was red and beaded with sweat, but he smiled at her, a courteous, distant smile. Alayna felt a twinge of gratitude that she had not needed to contrive a marriage to him. He probably would have declined, anyway, so what did she care if he looked at Gwynn with adoration? This evening, it was enough that Gwynn had eyes only for her.

— ✦ —

The dancing went on forever and yet was soon ended. The musicians put up their instruments, and full goblets were passed around.

Dom Ruyven proposed the first toast. "To the best lord and master any of us could wish for, may his happiness increase!"

"May his bride increase!" one of the men added after everyone had taken a sip. From the way he slurred his words, he was already drunk.

"With many sons!" one of the women called—Marianna, Alayna thought.

Gwynn held his own cup to Alayna's lips. She had to steady it with her hands, but she managed without spilling any on her gown. Everyone laughed uproariously, although it took her a moment or two to understand the symbolism. He'd given her ... liquid. And she'd accepted.

"Come away with us!" A covey of women—Dimitra and Sadhi, Marianna and Shayla, the *leronis* Jerana, and a few others Alayna did not know well, guests and officers' wives—surrounded her, cooing as they bustled her away from Gwynn.

"You'll never get a baby wearing so many clothes!"

"We'll have to make her presentable for her husband!"

"And *only* for him!"

They rushed her up the stairs before she had a chance to draw breath.

"Who brought the radish?"

"Radish?" Alayna exclaimed, giggling. "I'm not hungry. For vegetables, at any rate."

"Ay, she's a sharp one."

"She'll soon find out what's pointy and what's not."

They arrived at Gwynn's chambers. Alayna had never been inside, but the women hurried her through the door, past the outer sitting room, and into the bedroom. The bed was enormous and ornate, its posters thick as pillars. The top of the comforter-laden mattress was so high, Alayna feared she'd need a ladder to reach it.

"I can't possibly sleep in that."

"Poor thing, she does not know what takes place on a maid's wedding night!"

"Oh, sweetling, you aren't going to *sleep*."

With that, they surrounded her, unlacing her bodice, lifting the gown over her head, releasing the butterfly clasp so that her hair tumbled down her back. She stood there, clad only in her shift, and that too was soon gone. The gauze nightgown went over her head, but it was little better than nothing at all. Alayna, glancing down, could see every curve of her own body.

"Into bed with you," Dimitra said, flipping back one comforter and then another. "It won't do to catch your death of cold."

"No worries on that account," one of the other women responded. "She'll soon be warm enough."

Alayna slipped between the sheets, thinking that if she tried to speak, her teeth would surely chatter. Perhaps that was the point of being half-naked in a chilly room—she'd be so glad of her husband to warm the sheets that she would not care what happened next.

"Do you want aphrosone, my lady?" That was Jerana, speaking low. "It will make tonight more pleasurable, although you will not remember in the morning."

Alayna shook her head. She might be cold, but she was not afraid. If she should conceive—and she prayed to the four gods and any others that might be listening that she did—she wanted to remember this first night together.

When at last they left her, the worst of the shivers had subsided. Her mind drifted, too excited to sleep, but she must have drowsed, for she jerked awake at the sound of men's voices outside the door—raucous, some raised in song. Not the outer door, either, but only the length of the room from her. Gathering the covers around her, she sat bolt upright. The single candle added its light to that of the fire.

"Are we going to stand here all night talking, or have I your leave to go in to my wife?" Gwynn's voice sounded as if he'd had even more to drink than earlier. A few moments later, he came in, closed the door behind him, and leaned against it, eyes closed. His entire body seemed to be saying, *Thank gods, that's over with.*

"There you are," he said as, with a smile, he made his way to the bed. He stood over her, hands on his hips. "Whatever is that they've dolled you up in?"

She fought down a giggle. "I believe it's a bridal nightgown."

He sat down beside her, the mattress giving under his weight. With his back to the fireplace, his features were cast into shadow. "Then we'll have to do away with it."

Alayna slid down under the covers. "I'm cold enough already!"

"In that case, my dear wife, I shall have to warm you up."

Alayna watched as he pulled off his shirt. He caught her glance and grinned, his teeth gleaming in the subdued light. Then a few quick movements, and he lifted the comforters to slide in. Only then did Alayna realize how nervous she was. Would it hurt? Would she enjoy it? Would her own ignorance dismay him? "I don't—"

"Shhh." He placed a finger across her lips, following a moment later with his lips.

He had kissed her before, and she had done her best to kiss him back, not many times but enough to enjoy it. This kiss did not end. It went on and on, getting deeper than deep. Shivers ran through her, hot shivers that yearned for more. Gwynn shifted, resting on one elbow as he continued to kiss her and stroke her with his free hand—shoulder, back, sliding down the side of her waist and up the front of her ribs to brush her nipples through the gossamer fabric of her nightgown, which sent another spasm of shivers through her. Then down over the curve of her hip, her thighs, and up again, with each circuit lingering longer on her breasts and moving closer to her inner thighs, then up ... Everywhere he touched made her ache and burn all at once.

"Shall we remove the nightgown now?" His breath tickled her ear. Now he was kissing her neck, working his way to the cleft between her collarbones.

She sat up, pulled the gown over her head, and threw it halfway across the room.

When she lay down, he lowered himself on top of her, supporting his weight on his arms. He kissed her again and again, then down her neck and—*oh, gods, how could it feel any more arousing?*—her breasts. Why had no one ever told her that a man's mouth on her nipples would make her delirious? She drank it all in, drowning in every kiss, every heartbeat, the pressure of his thighs between hers, the way he reached down to stroke her ...

The last thing she remembered, before all sense left her, was his whispered plea, "Make me a son tonight."

21

Alayna woke to the disconcerting sensation of someone nibbling on her earlobe. She was lying on her side, looking toward the watery light of a winter dawn, slanting through a nearby window. Her bare shoulder was cold, although not the rest of her, buried under mountains of comforters. Her back was especially warm, pressed against a very warm, muscled body. Her first coherent thought was alarm that she seemed to be wearing nothing at all, but almost immediately she remembered that she was in bed with her husband. His lips moved down the curve of her neck and one hand ran in long, sensuous strokes from shoulder to breast to hip, evoking with a blush, sensations she remembered from the night before. Did he mean to—? Blessed Cassilda, by the shape and hardness of his body, he *did*.

She woke again to a brighter room and a fire filling the air with sweetness—cedar, she thought drowsily. Part of her wanted to drift back to sleep, but she was hungry, and it was long past time she should have been stirring. Her inner parts were sore and sticky, and the sheet under her felt damp. Jerana had warned her what to expect.

The door cracked open, and Sadhi peeked inside. "Good morning, my lady, or rather, good afternoon, for it's well past midday. *Domna* Dimitra instructed me that you might care to bathe."

A few moments after that, she led the way through the little door and into a sumptuously appointed bathroom. Alayna sank into the steaming water while Sadhi soaped her shoulders. From the bustle on the other side of the door, maids were at work, changing the sheets and tidying the room.

After a time, Jerana came in. Sadhi curtsied and left them. "How fare you, *vai domna*?" Jerana asked.

"I'm well, thank you. Just a bit tender. I suppose that's to be expected. My husband was most enthusiastic. But I did not find it distasteful."

"You must judge for yourself whether the discomfort is tolerable. I have the means to alleviate it."

Alayna considered for a moment before deciding she rather liked the reminders of her wedding night. They talked for a few minutes more, and then Jerana left.

Sadhi and another maid appeared to dry her, dress her, and lead her past her own bedroom to a parlor that was clearly the private domain of a fine lady. Two chairs and a table with a laden tray had been drawn up near the hearth. Alayna ate all of it, the pile of toast, jam, soft-boiled eggs in their shells, spiced Midwinter buns, and soft cheese. Her stomach felt tight.

After Sadhi, removed the tray, Alayna was left alone in her parlor. The two bedrooms adjoined one another, but the sitting room led into the hallway. Presumably, this was where she would spend her time when she wasn't with her husband or her ladies. What a boring life! Of course, before long she would have babies and then children to look after.

But there beside the divan sat the *rryl*. Alayna cradled it on her lap and began to tune it. She played a ballad or two so that her hands would learn the ways of the instrument, but there was no need. Before long, one song after another flowed from the strings. It sang as she sang. As the last notes of the song fell away, Alayna felt a lightness of heart that she had not known since she'd come to Scathfell. *Since Kyria died.*

A faint sound from the bedroom door broke her reverie. Turning, she saw Gwynn leaning on the doorpost. He looked more at ease than she had ever seen him, and his eyes smiled as well as his lips.

"You are well, my lady wife?"

She did not know what answer to give. Did he mean, had she taken physical hurt from their intimacy? Was she as pleased now with their marriage as she had hoped to be? One thing was certain, she had not anticipated how her heart would open to him along with her body, or the over-whelming, almost delirious sensation of lying in his arms with no barrier between them.

"My lord husband, I am."

"Don't stop, please," he said. "I had no idea you sang like an angel. There has not been such music in Scathfell since I was a child. Not since my mother died. You have already brought such joy to my life."

Perhaps this gift may help to heal the grief, and the old feud as well.

"This was a thoughtful gift," she said, setting the *rryl* aside, "one that surely deserves acknowledgment."

"Perhaps. When the roads are open in the spring, I will consider sending a message. Now, if you have finished at-tempting to persuade me of Aldaran's benign intentions, there is a matter I came here to discuss with you."

Instantly contrite, Alayna sprang to her feet and went to him. "How thoughtless of me. What is it?"

"Oh, nothing dire, my serious little wife," he responded with a chuckle. "It is customary in this part of the Hellers for husbands and wives to exchange gifts at this season. I thought to offer you a horse from my stables so that you may go riding in the spring and summer, with a suitable escort, of course, and assuming Aldaran has not launched an attack. I know that you can ride but not whether you take pleasure in it."

"A horse for my own use—I would like that very much." To escape the confines of stone walls, to ride out in the open air.

"That's settled, then."

"I have no gift for you," she said.

"But you will. Perhaps you already have." Gwynn put one hand on her shoulder, the other cupping her belly. He pressed his lips to the curve of her neck, which sent shivers through her.

Alayna pushed him away before his kisses could get any more urgent. "Gwynn, please . . . I'm still sore from last night . . . and this morning."

"Oh, my dearest, I'm so sorry. I did not mean to hurt you."

He looked so contrite that Alayna hastened to reassure him that she was not injured, just tender, and that she would shortly be well.

Within a few days, the newlyweds had settled into a routine. Gwynn rose early and went about the business of running the castle, tending to his lands, training his soldiers, and whatever else he did, given that it was winter and much of the mountainous area would be snowbound for months. Alayna spent her days at needlework or playing the *rryl*, much to the delight of her women companions. Without telling Gwynn, she set up daily meetings with Zefano, learning the ways of the castle, with the aim of gradually assuming the duties of a lord's wife.

Storms came sweeping down from the mountainous heights. Sometimes Alayna imagined the stone walls trembling in the force of the gales. Drifts piled high, and only the inner courtyard was passable, sometimes needing to be swept clear every hour. She supposed the roads must be tended as well, for Gwynn showed no sign of relinquishing his military readiness.

After two months, however, the worst of winter seemed to be passing. Snow still fell every night, as it did at this season and altitude, but not with the thickness of before. A day here and there turned bright, the courtyard stones gleamed with melting ice, and Zefano began talking about preparations for warmer weather. These mostly involved cleaning accumulated grime from the winter.

One evening, when Alayna had indulged herself with a hot bath, she noticed that her breasts were fuller than usual and mildly sore. She ran her hands over her body. Except for the slight changes, she could detect no other sign that she might be pregnant. Her belly had never been completely flat and seemed no bigger now. When had her last women's cycle come? She could not remember. Before the wedding? She'd never got into the habit of keeping track.

And she had shared Gwynn's bed every night since they were joined.

I must tell him. He will be so pleased. She almost leapt from the bath in excitement.

Then caution took over. She might be in error and did not want to raise his hopes. Jerana might be able to use her *laran* to tell.

If it's a girl, I'll name her Kyria. A boy—Pietro for my father? Or shall I let Gwynn choose? He's so sure it will be a son.

— ✦ —

Alayna woke in the early hours. Beside her, Gwynn snored softly, rhythmically. For a moment, she could not think what had roused her from sleep. Then she became aware of the wetness between her thighs. The fire had died down to a few embers, not enough to see by, and she dared not pull back the covers for fear of waking him. She bunched the skirt of her nightgown between her legs, trying to think what to do. Then indecision gave way to panic, and she bolted for her own bedroom, pausing only for a candle.

Alone in her quarters, Alayna felt another trickle, and then a cramping low in her belly, so sudden and sharp it took her breath away. She bent over with it. The spasm faded a moment later, although not entirely. Not trusting to the steadiness of her hands, she set the candlestick on the stone hearth. A small spot of blood marked the front of her nightgown, but when she twisted the back around, she saw that it was drenched.

A knock at the outer door and Dimitra's voice called, "My lady?"

"Go away," Alayna gasped.

The door slowly eased open. "*Vai domna*, I am sorry to disobey you, but Sadhi heard a noise and reported it to me—Blessed Cassilda."

The next moment, Dimitra grasped Alayna's shoulders as another cramp seized her, worse than before. Then everything happened at once—Dimitra shouted for Sadhi. Hands lifted the sodden nightgown, lowered her to a bed spread thickly with towels, washed her with warm water, tucked layers of padding between her legs, pulled a new gown over her shoulders, eased comforters up to her shoulders.

Racked with yet another wave of pain, Alayna curled into a ball. *I want to die, I want to die. What is happening to me?* But she knew.

She roused at the sound of Jerana's voice, a cool touch on her brow and a few murmured words, too indistinct to understand.

Help me. Help my babe.

Blue light glowed within Jerana's cupped hands. Although Alayna struggled to make out the source, something brighter-than-bright twisted deep within the brilliance. Her stomach clenched. She gagged, trying not to retch.

"Do not look at the starstone," Jerana said. "It is not keyed to your mind and can be dangerous."

"Can—can you save—?" Alayna forced out the words, but could not bring herself to voice her fear.

"I do not know," Jerana replied. "That is what I am trying to find out. No, do not try to sit up. Close your eyes and let me do my work. Breathe slowly, that's it."

Alayna tried her best to comply. The muscles of her pelvic floor kept trying to wring themselves into knots. She could not draw a proper breath, and she could keep her eyes closed, no matter what. She squeezed her brows together until they threatened to go into spasm.

"Heavens, child, I meant to relax, not to tighten every muscle in your face." Jerana smoothed the space between Alayna's brows just as another spasm began.

"It hurts!"

"Yes, *chiya*, I know. Such is the lot of women everywhere. Dimitra, fetch me tincture of golden-flower from the herb room, the same of valerian. And motherwort, if there is any."

"Is that safe?" Dimitra added something Alayna could not make out.

"It is the lesser of the ills she must contend with." Jerana's clothing rustled as she got to her feet. She was giving instructions, something about hot water and plenty of towels, wine warmed to the temperature of blood—

There had been so much blood.

Someone held a cup to her lips. The rim clinked against her teeth. The smell was acrid. She tried to push it away, but her hands were caught and held, and the next moment she needed, *needed* to scream, and warm, bitter wine flooded her mouth. She swallowed convulsively.

"Again," said Jerana.

The fumes stung her nostrils, but the inside of her mouth had gone numb, and she could hardly taste the next swallow, or the one after that. Her body rebelled, or perhaps it was yet another agonizing spasm. This one, however, did not build to a peak as had the ones before. It lifted her so that it seemed some other woman lay on her bed, blood soaking into layer after layer of toweling, heart beating light and fast like that of a snared bird.

It's too late, she thought, but could not summon the energy to care.

———— ◆ ————

"She's coming around." The voice was light, feminine, young. *Shayla?*

"Summon the *leronis*." *Dimitra.* "And send word to Lord Scathfell."

Alayna tried to open her eyes. They felt gummy, as if she had cried herself to sleep. *Have I been ill?* And then she remembered.

"My lady, if you'll permit me." Dimitra ran a damp cloth over Alayna's lids, loosening the crusts. "How do you feel?"

Alayna's body felt heavy, as if she had lain abed with fever for a tenday. "Please," she whispered, "tell me."

Dimitra stood beside the bed. She looked weary, as if she had not slept in days. "You were pregnant, *vai domna*, four or five tendays gone. The *leronis* could not be entirely certain, although she examined the discharge."

Tears stung Alayna's eyes, her body responding to what her mind could not comprehend. "Does my husband know?"

"My lady, you have been abed for three days, with maids in and out. How could he not? He's been pacing the halls, demanding news every hour. Not even *Dom* Ruyven could calm him down. But the *leronis* advised him as soon as you were out of danger."

The door swung open and Jerana entered, sat on the bed, and took Alayna's hand. "*Chiya*, you are awake at last. You slept for a long time, even after the effects of the sedative herbs wore off. After an ordeal like yours, the body craves rest, so I did not want to wake you too soon."

"Is that why I feel so weak?"

"I will answer you, but only a question or two. Then I

need to monitor you. Understood? Then, no, it is not the prolonged sleep that makes you feel weak, but the amount of blood you lost."

"With the baby?"

Jerana's face closed up. "Yes."

"But—"

"Two questions is enough. Lie still now. And you, *Domna* Dimitra, make sure I am not disturbed, not even by Lord Scathfell."

"Very well," came Dimitra's reply from somewhere by the door.

Jerana folded the bedding down. Alayna closed her eyes and tried to breathe evenly. She felt a feather light touch here and there—between her brows, then on her breast-bone, then below her navel. She thought she also felt a slight disturbance in the air as the *leronis* ran her hands up and down, barely skimming Alayna's body. How long this went on, Alayna could not have said. She grew drowsy, then fidgety. Finally Jerana gave a sigh and said, "That's enough. Clearly, you're well enough to find it difficult to lie still."

Alayna sat up. "I can have another babe?"

"That remains to be seen, although I could not find the cause of the miscarriage. It lies beyond my skill, but more often than not, no reason is ever discovered. Take heart, for most women who suffer such losses go on to have perfectly healthy children. But you must not try for another pregnancy until your body has fully restored itself. You lost a great deal of blood."

"But—how will I—I mean, my husband *expects*—"

"He will have to wait, just as he would if you had delivered a live birth," Jerana said with a touch of acerbity. "But do not worry. When your bleeding stops, it will be safe for you to resume relations. I will prepare a tea for you to prevent conception."

Too overcome to speak, Alayna hung her head.

Jerana patted her hand. "It will be easier if you do not share a bed for a time. I will speak to Lord Scathfell to make sure he understands these measures are for your welfare and the health of the children you eventually will bear him. If he has complaints, he must take them up with *me*."

Alayna did not feel like eating until Sadhi brought her a bowl of beef broth with some thinly sliced toast. When she asked for more, Sadhi looked uneasy and said that the *leronis*—she lowered her voice, as if Jerana had sorcerous powers and might be listening from anywhere—had permitted only a little light food. It had, after all, only been three days.

Three days. She had barely suspected she might be pregnant and now she was not.

She slept. The moment her eyes opened again, she drank more broth, then slept again. Each time, the light slanted at a sharper angle through the windows, and with each awakening, the feeling of numbness lessened. She felt sad but not sad enough to weep.

Finally, she opened her eyes to a room lapped in shadows, lit only by the single candle and the light of a fire. Echoes of dreams clung to her, bits of her old life at Rockraven, of Kyria screaming, of the moment when Dimitra told her that Francisco was married. She wandered through a deserted castle—not this one, but some place she had never been—looking for something or someone with an urgency that bordered on terror. Rarely had she been so grateful to leave the world of dreams.

From the other side of the outer door, she heard a man's voice, muffled by the thickness of wall and door. "Hello?" she called.

A moment later, the door swung open. In came Gwynn, carrying a tray, which he placed on the table within easy reach. He sat on the bed beside her and took her hand. His fingers tightened on hers, and she felt a slight tremble. A long moment passed, one in which Alayna realized that he was at a loss for words.

"I'm so sorry," she cried.

He drew a breath like a sob, without sound. Something wordless and overwhelming flooded up inside him. She could see it in his eyes, her strong, strong husband adrift on helplessness and loss and fear. Then his face closed around the raw emotion of the moment.

"I'm so sorry," she repeated, feeling utterly inadequate to address the depth of what she had just seen in him.

"As am I. But Jerana assures me that we can have other children. I must be patient. The most important thing is that *you* will recover. In the meantime, we must think of something to cheer you up, something to look forward to. What if, as soon as that harridan Jerana has released you from your bed, we go down to the stables and pick out a nice, gentle horse for you? When you are able and the weather permits, you may explore the valley with a suitable escort."

"I should like that very much. I cannot tell you how dreary it has been, being cooped up. I suppose I will have to wait months and *months* for the weather to be mild enough."

"Indeed not. Although you would not think so now, to look at the ice and drifted snow, the worst of winter is already past. Before you know it, the passes will begin to open."

Spring—and then summer, with warm afternoons and wildflowers on the slopes, if Scathfell were anything like Rockraven.

"As soon as it is possible to travel, I will send a messenger with a note of thanks to Aldaran for the *rryl* that has given you so much pleasure. Does that make you happy?"

As Alayna lay back with a tender smile, she thought that he must have been very worried to now seek to please her in this way.

— ◆ —

By the time Jerana released Alayna from bed rest and allowed her to venture outdoors, the snow was already beginning to melt in the warmth of midday. The icy crusts froze again every night, but slowly and surely, the snow receded.

Alayna returned to Gwynn's bed and felt strong again, strong enough to bear another babe. Only the tea Jerana brewed for her prevented it.

What does that old woman know about marriage and children, anyway? I feel perfectly well. There's no reason to wait any longer, and Gwynn so wants a son. And so do I.

Without a word to anyone, she began dumping the tea into the chamber pot.

22

After looking over the horses in the stable, Alayna decided to stick with the tall, strong bay that she had ridden all the way from Rockraven. Although originally a soldier's horse, the animal had tolerably easy gaits, far better than those of the stag pony on which she'd learned to ride, and seemed grateful to carry such a light burden.

To begin with, she kept to the stable courtyard under the watchful eye of the head groom. Either the poor man had forgotten she'd ridden all the way from Rockraven or else was terrified of his master's wrath, should she topple to the ground. Alayna allowed herself to be cosseted. At last, even the head groom admitted that she was a good enough rider to venture past the courtyard, and she was allowed to go down to the valley.

Two of the junior officers, neither of whom she knew and neither of whom would make the slightest conversation, accompanied her. Aldones only knew what Gwynn had said to them or what dire fate awaited them if she came to any harm, so she contented herself with making comments to her horse about the weather and the quality of the grass. She would much rather have had Francisco's company, as on that first approach to the castle, but he must be far away, exiled. She would never find out if they could have been friends, now that she was married, too. If he had been only a dream when she had no other prospects, he had been a kind-hearted dream.

One day, as Alayna was returning to the castle, a rider came galloping up the road. He must have ridden hard and fast, for his horse was lathered with sweat. His cloak flapped behind him like enormous wings. She thought he wore livery but could not be sure.

Aldaran? In response to Gwynn's note of thanks?

On her arrival, she handed the bay's reins to the head groom and headed for Gwynn's presence chamber, where the guards outside the door would not let her pass. She thought of several choice things to say to them and then thought better of it. If she wanted to convince the lord of the castle that she was a worthy councilor, one who ought to be included in any news, then she had better behave like one.

"Very well," she told them, "I shall respect my husband's prerogative of privacy. When he emerges, would you be so kind as to inform him of my interest?"

They bowed to her but offered no assurances. Alayna lifted her chin and swept off to her chambers. Dimitra met her there, hands primly clasped at her waist, a slight frown furrowing her brow. There were dark circles around her eyes.

"Any news, my lady?"

"I saw a rider come up the valley, but I didn't get a good look at him. I wonder where he came from."

"From King Allart Hastur himself." Dimitra helped Alayna out of her jacket and then bent to ease off her riding boots. "The whole castle's abuzz with it."

"All the way from Thendara," Alayna exclaimed. "And before the passes are fully open. The errand must be urgent."

"Do you know what it's about, my lady? Not another war, I hope."

"I'm afraid I know no more than you. I will wear the gray tunic, if you please. When Lord Scathfell is at liberty to speak with me, I intend to be ready."

"And the moonstone pendant, *vai domna*?"

"Yes, that will do very well."

When Alayna studied her reflection in the mirror, she

thought, *I might not always feel like it, but I look like a proper Lady Scathfell.*

A knock at the door announced a page with a request to join Lord Scathfell in his presence chamber. With Dimitra a step behind, Alayna headed in that direction with the greatest speed consistent with a lady's decorum. They arrived to find the messenger standing before Gwynn, who sat, very straight and regal-looking, on his throne-like chair. Alayna tried to read his expression, but it was impassive, giving away nothing. Guards, many more than usual, stood at attention, and Ruyven watched from the side.

The messenger was a slight man, small enough not to overburden a horse on a long, hard ride. He did not turn at her entrance but remained facing Gwynn, so that she could not get even a glimpse of him. She offered her husband a formal curtsy, so that no one—in particular, this messenger from the powerful Hastur king—might fault the dignity of Scathfell.

"Thank you for coming so swiftly, my lady wife," Gwynn said. "Messenger, repeat what you just related to me."

The messenger did not so much as glance in Alayna's direction. He had been standing with feet apart, but now a change came over his posture so that his very character appeared to alter, and she realized that his training had included not only memorization of words but of the delivery of the man who had originally spoken them. One of her brothers—Hjalmar, most likely—had spoken of such messengers and called them Voices. They were said to be capable of relaying several hours of speech without altering the phrasing or emphasis. She had thought Hjalmar invented them, but seeing this man before her take on the appearance of quite a different person, she no longer doubted.

"Allart Hastur of Elhalyn, King of the Domains . . ." and a whole host of titles, " . . . sends greetings to Gwynn-Alar, Lord of Scathfell, and requests the pleasure of his presence at his court in Thendara, and that of his wife and any of his household whom he chooses, for this Midsummer Festival season. Accommodations will be provided in Comyn Castle."

If Alayna had not been on her best, most formal behavior, her jaw would have fallen open. King Allart Hastur was inviting—*or commanding?*—Gwynn—*and her!*—to appear before him and his court in Thendara? It was a most extraordinary and unexpected message. She hardly knew what to think of it. An honor or a trap? Or the chance she'd never hoped for to enjoy the delights of a great city, music and dancing and she knew not what else. But she must not let the prospect cloud her judgment. Her gaze sought out her husband, but if Gwynn were annoyed or affronted, he gave no sign. In fact, he appeared to be *amused*.

"What say you to a summer journey to the Lowlands?" Yes, Gwynn was definitely amused.

"Such an undertaking must be carefully considered," she said.

"There you have it," Gwynn addressed the messenger. "I thank you for your trouble. You must have had a hard journey, for snow yet lies heavy on the mountain passes." He beckoned to one of the guards. "This man will show you to a hot meal and a bed. Be as a guest in this house until I have determined what answer to make."

The messenger's expression shifted, and his shoulders sagged. The fatigue of the trail showed clearly in his bearing. Murmuring thanks in a voice quite unlike the one he'd used for King Allart's message, he bowed to Gwynn and then followed the guard from the chamber.

Gwynn waited until the doors had closed behind them. "Ruyven, come with me. You, too, Alayna, for this concerns you." Without looking back, he led the way to the men's parlor. Once seated in the center of the room, with guards posted outside the doors, they could not be easily overheard.

It seemed that nobody, least of all Gwynn, had any forewarning of such an overture. "I've had no dealings with the Hastur lords or anyone else in the Lowlands," he said, frowning.

"But only a generation ago, your father made alliance with the king's late brother, Damon-Rafael," Ruyven pointed out.

"To his sorrow," Gwynn replied.

"I hardly think that association recommends us to Allart," Ruyven went on in an even, reasonable tone. "Damon-Rafael tried to usurp his throne, after all."

"If the Hastur lord has not menaced Scathfell for all these years, why would he do so now?" Alayna asked.

Gwynn's frown deepened. "Feuds are easily begun but difficult to mend. I will not say *impossible*, for nothing is certain except death and next winter's snows. If Allart Hastur now schemes to get me to walk willingly into his clutches, he will be mightily disappointed."

Alayna tried not to think of the balls and concerts she would miss. She was a married woman, the lady of a great castle, not some light-minded flutterby.

Ruyven made a sound like a snort. "It is hardly logical that Allart would avenge the brother who tried to assassinate him and, as I understand the story, marry his widowed queen."

"These people are not like us," Gwynn said. "They're Lowlanders. You never know what to expect."

"Or they may be perfectly reasonable, honorable people, despite their customs," Ruyven said.

"I wonder—" Alayna began. "I wonder if he would have specifically invited a woman if he intended—" *to capture and slay you* "—less than royal hospitality?"

"Unless he means to end the lineage of this family for all time," Gwynn said grimly.

Alayna was so shocked at the idea—luring not only a man but his wife into harm's reach and then doing away with them both—that she sat back in her chair, speechless. Gwynn was so strong and vital, she had never thought of Scathfell as being vulnerable in that way. Then she remembered that *Dom* Nevin was a kinsman. The thought of him inheriting Scathfell, should Gwynn die without a son, was odious beyond words.

"What if the greater risk lies not in accepting this summons but in refusing?" Ruyven said. "Would that be considered an insult? And would a man like Allart Hastur avenge the slight by force of arms?"

"Indeed, that is the question, one I fear we cannot answer by sitting up here in our mountains," Gwynn replied. "Nor can we foretell what benefit might come to us by going, not if we had a Tower of *leroni* at our command."

Alayna thought of something and, haltingly, expressed it: might Gwynn be able to forge an alliance with Allart Hastur to strengthen his position against Aldaran? The Hastur king had once been Aldaran's friend, but might he change sides as a result of this visit? Did the invitation indicate his willingness to do so?

Somewhat to her surprise, Ruyven, who had so far ignored what she had to say, listened attentively. "That would explain the invitation and, if true, would be too great an opportunity to pass up," he said. "I believe Aldaran will be far less likely to attack if he loses the backing of the king."

"That is an excellent point, worthy of serious consideration," Gwynn said. "We will discuss the matter tomorrow, after I have thought about it."

— ◆ —

Over the next few days, while Gwynn conferred with Ruyven and others in his court, Alayna began to suspect that she might be pregnant again. After the miscarriage, she had begun keeping track of her cycles, and one had been very light, only a few spots of blood; now she was late for the second. Her breasts felt a little fuller, as they had before, and the smell of breakfast made her feel queasy. She determined to not say anything until she was certain, especially not to Jerana, who would scold her about stopping the tea. So far, none of the women attending her seemed to have noticed. As for Gwynn, she would wait before she said anything, at least until she was sure the danger had passed. She did not want to get his hopes up.

On the third morning after the messenger arrived, Gwynn informed her that he had decided they would go to Thendara. All things considered, he explained, the possible benefits of an alliance with Allart Hastur, combined with the king's reputation for fair dealings, outweighed the risks. They were sitting in Gwynn's parlor, eating breakfast together, which was unusual enough in itself. Alayna was trying hard not to react to the sausages—fat, spicy ones, browned crisp and sitting in little puddles of their own grease, that ordinarily she would have adored. But Gwynn was so focused on his news, he didn't seem to notice.

"That will please you, won't it?" he asked. "To go to a big city and mingle with the fine folk there? I'm afraid we'll have to leave right away if we're to arrive for Midsummer Festival. The roads will still be under snow in places. But you had a taste of that on your way here."

"As long as I am warmly dressed and with you, *caryo*, then I shall be all right."

Ruyven was already waiting for them in the presence chamber. Then the messenger was brought in, looking considerably less trail-worn than before. He stood, his face expressionless, his body as straight and uncommunicative as a stick.

When Gwynn had finished addressing him, however, a change came over the messenger. His posture shifted into that of a much more confident man. "Then I am bid to tell you in the name of King Allart Hastur that quarters suitable to your rank will be prepared for you in the castle at Thendara, as for other noble guests who travel from afar. King Allart himself will vouch for your safety, and you will not find more comfortable accommodations anywhere in the city." Then the alteration in voice and mien passed, and the thin, slightly awkward messenger stood once more before them.

Gwynn paused for a moment before answering. "On behalf of myself, my wife, and our party, I accept the invitation." Alayna knew his voice well enough to know how pleased he was. There was a little more discussion on such matters as how many guards and servants might be housed, and Gwynn seemed happy with the assurances. The messenger paused, his face blank as he committed the interview to memory, and then bowed and withdrew.

"Well, Ruyven," Gwynn said, still clearly in a good mood, "I'll want lists of who is to come, how many men and baggage animals, and likely accommodations along the route. How soon can you have that for me?"

"Within the hour, my lord. I have been preparing a plan since the messenger first arrived."

"And what if I'd refused? All your labor gone to waste?" Gwynn said in an easy, bantering tone.

Ruyven bowed, and Alayna saw this banter was a long time amusement for the two men. "My labor is in your service, *vai dom*, and as you yourself pointed out, the road to Thendara is long. It is a pity air-cars cannot fly in this part of the Hellers, or King Allart might have sent one for us and we would have a much quicker journey."

"Air-cars!" Alayna had heard of them, flying craft powered and guided by *laran*, but had never imagined she'd see one. The batteries required a working Tower circle to charge, and the pilot must also be a trained *laranzu*. To own such a craft must be hideously expensive.

"Very pretty toys, I am sure, but hardly practical for us mountain folk," Gwynn said. "I have never flown in one, but I believe they hold only a couple of passengers and very little cargo. My lady, I expect you will require three pack horses and five maids. I know the wiles of women, you see. It will be all *balls* and *concerts* and *invitations* and *gossip-gossip-gossip* with every other young noblewoman in the city."

Alayna flushed. "It is true that I look forward with pleasure to those things. I have lived a sheltered life far away from any city, as you well know, my lord. Is it so wrong to enjoy them while you men are at politics?"

"Not at all. Little goose, can't you tell I'm teasing you? Has winter here in Scathfell Castle turned you so very serious? Then I prescribe a season of gaiety."

"As for the pack horses and maids, may I remind you that I traveled all the way from my home with only my sister for female companionship and *one* pack animal between us?" Alayna retorted.

"She has spirit, my wife! Very well, I will not inflict more clothes or attendants on you. Choose your own maid and what gowns you wish. I am sure you can have more made up for you in Thendara—Ruyven, help me here. Is that not how it is done?"

"Indeed, *vai dom*, for how else could the lady partake of the latest fashions? A gown that is all very well for our little court here may be hopelessly unsophisticated by Thendara standards."

Gwynn threw back his head and laughed. "There speaks the man who intends to buy three suits of the finest styles for himself, at great expense, all in service to his vanity."

— ◆ —

The preparations for the journey from Rockraven to Scathfell had been nothing compared to what must be done now. Gwynn had not been entirely joking about the number of baggage animals, for they must carry not only food, warm clothing, and trail tents for the entire party, but attire and ornaments for their first days in Thendara—before the

opportunity to shop—and gifts for the king and queen as
well. Ruyven arranged everything, and there was very little
for Alayna to do except select what clothing and jewels she
wished to bring. The prospect of new, fashionable attire
pleased her more than she was willing to admit. As for a
lady's companion, Dimitra was the logical choice, although
since the miscarriage, she had looked surprisingly haggard
and far older than her years. Alayna feared that the demands of tending to her mistress on a long journey were
beyond her strength. In the end, Alayna chose Sadhi, who
might not be the most sophisticated but was earnest and
hard-working and overjoyed with the prospect.

At last everything was ready and they set out on a warm-
ish morning. The first part of the journey wound along the
valley of Scathfell and through the mountains in the surrounding lands. As the days passed, the mountainsides
changed from snow on bare rock to slopes of dense forest.
Freshets of melt water cascaded down from the heights,
joining streams that filled the air with music. Birds sang in
the brief midday warmth, and the best archer in the company brought down a deer now and again, and they dined
on fresh meat. The nights brought snow and sometimes
freezing sleet and once, the howls of wolves.

Sadhi was as solicitous for Alayna's comfort as it was
possible to be, given the travel conditions. The end of each
day left Alayna more fatigued than normal, but she did not
want to be the reason for prolonging their journey so much
that they arrived after the season had ended.

At last, they looked down on the Lowlands, over hills
that seemed nothing compared to the rugged peaks of the
Hellers. In the distance, lakes glimmered, and forests grew
so densely they appeared almost black. Yet Alayna detected
the scars of war, swathes of charred earth where nothing
grew. She had never seen anything like it. Their road led
through it, and she quailed at the necessity of riding through
such territory.

As they descended, however, she found that the sight of
the blasted land was not so terrible. This damage had been
done a generation ago, before the Peace of Allart Hastur
put an end to hostilities. New green showed here and there
in the blackened fields, and a tilled garden or newly thatched
hut testified to the resilience of life.

If there is hope here, after such destruction, Alayna thought, *then there is also hope that our children will live in peace.* King Allart had brought about the cessation of the brutal conflict with Ridenow; why not the feud between Scathfell and Aldaran?

"Look there!" The guard who had been riding at the front pointed aloft and there, against the brightness of the sky, Alayna spotted a long, sleek shape as it dipped toward them and circled low. "An air-car!"

In the few moments while Alayna watched, the captain dug out the truce-flag and waved it about. The air-car made a final circuit and then sped off in the direction of Thendara.

Three days from the mountain pass, they reached the outskirts of Lake Hali with its glittering sands and strange, cloud-like waters. At one end, Hali Tower rose like a finger of pale, translucent stone, glowing with a faint blue radiance. Beyond it lay Thendara. Comyn Castle, in the heart of the city, had been raised by a circle of *laran* workers, and massive, *laran*-charged generators provided heat and light. At the time, she had not put much faith in the story, but now, as she looked at the glistening white towers, she could believe anything.

As soon as they approached the castle courtyard, servants and horse grooms rushed to greet them. The air-car, it seemed, had brought news of their imminent arrival, and everything had been made ready for them. Now that they had arrived, she was grateful when Gwynn placed her and Sadhi in the care of the friendly, middle-aged attendant, clearly more than a maid yet less than a lady-in-waiting. She bustled them through an entrance hall that was grander than the Great Hall at Scathfell and brilliantly lit with glowing globes attached to wall and ceiling. They went up one passage and through another, until they reached a suite of rooms that surely must be grand enough for the Hastur king himself but were reserved for Gwynn and Alayna. Glow-globes lit these chambers, and there were excellent fires as well.

The servant, whose name was Ylethia, got Alayna settled without making her feel the least bit awkward. In the parlor a hot meal had been laid out.

"Where is my husband?" Alayna asked, thinking that she could not begin without him.

"Oh, probably finding out that King Allart does not

expect him to present himself until tomorrow morning."
Ylethia lifted the cover of the largest serving dish. It was
roasted barnfowl, the skin browned and crackling, surrounded by an array of root vegetables. "Your husband's a
considerate man, I'm sure. Wouldn't want you to faint from
hunger, not when the remedy is at hand." Ylethia picked up
a long knife from the tray, carved off a section of breast
meat, speared a large serving of vegetables, and set the
plate before Alayna. She stepped back, hands on her ample
hips. "Eat up now! Eat up!"

The first bite was so succulent, it almost flowed down
Alayna's throat. She was reaching for her second helping,
along with bread and dried fruit, stewed into melting softness and delicately spiced, when Gwynn came in. His hair,
slightly damp, had been freshly combed, and his face
scrubbed clean. Ylethia curtsied to him and left the two to
enjoy their meal.

"I'm glad to see you settled, and that you did not wait for
me," he said, bending to kiss her. "You must take excellent
care of yourself."

"As you see, I am doing my best. Is all well with the rest
of our party?"

Gwynn sat down and began helping himself to food.
"Everyone's safely housed, the stables are impeccable, and
if these chambers are any indication, we are indeed honored guests."

He wasn't completely convinced, though; she could hear
it in his voice.

"There's to be an audience tomorrow morning," he continued, "not just for us but for the other noble folk who
have traveled far. Then a ball tomorrow night."

Alayna remembered her first ball at Scathfell Castle and
could not keep from smiling. Then the smile drained away
as she realized *Dom* Nevin would undoubtedly be here.

"I expect that the Great Houses will attend," Gwynn
went on, "Alton, Syrtis, Ardais, Aillard, Leynier no doubt.
Maybe the upstart Ridenow, for word is that the king has
made an effort to bring them into proper society."

"Do you know these people?"

He shook his head. "Only by name and reputation. Since
my father's time, we haven't had dealings with any but our
own—and Aldaran."

She sighed inwardly at the obstinacy of men. "You still think them your enemy, even after they sent that beautiful *rryl*?"

Somewhat to her surprise, Gwynn said, "You are right to chide me, *preciosa*, although the habits of a lifetime are not easily set aside. When I am with you, I begin to have hope that our future may be better than our past. I no longer feel alone. The *rryl* was a thoughtful gesture, and while I do not yet trust Aldaran's motives, I cannot find fault with a gift that has brought you so much pleasure."

"As I have said, it might have been made for my hands. And do not pretend *you* have not enjoyed the music."

"I cannot imagine not liking any music you make." His fingers closed around hers, warm and firm, and Alayna felt a rush of pleasure. She wished she had brought the harp with her. Perhaps she might be able to borrow one while she was here. The servant, Ylethia, might know whom to ask. *Tomorrow.*

They talked for a while longer, mostly of inconsequential matters, and retired. Gwynn fell asleep almost immediately, but Alayna lay awake, trying to adjust to the bed that, while comfortable, was nevertheless strange. She remembered how excited she'd been about traveling to Scathfell with Kyria, never dreaming that she might one day sleep in an even bigger, grander castle. Tomorrow or the next day, as soon as Gwynn's responsibilities to their host permitted, she would ask him to take her about the city. She fell asleep, drifting on visions of a dizzying array of shops and street merchants, strolling musicians, dancers and acrobats, non-human *kyrri*, all thronging the streets of shimmering white stone.

23

Alayna stirred from sleep into near darkness. For a few dizzying moments, she could not think where she was. This was not her bedchamber, nor Gwynn's, although he lay beside her, snoring lightly. Not her bed, either. Dreams clung to her like mists, dreams of giving birth. *I'm awake. I'm in the castle in Thendara. I'm awake.*

With that thought, her eyes focused on the glow globe on the nearest wall. It cast a faint, blue-white illumination across the room. The heaviness in her lower belly was no dream, however.

Blessed Cassilda, not again.

Half in dread yet moving stealthily to avoid waking Gwynn, she slipped one hand beneath the lower edge of her nightgown and between her legs. No wetness. She sagged back against the pillows in relief. The ache receded. Most likely it was a response to the long day's travel and to being in a strange place. Whatever it had been, it was over.

Try as she might, sleep eluded her. Their upcoming appearance at court was fraught with danger. What did they know about the king's motives and intentions? What if he meant them ill? Two of Gwynn's best fighting men stood watch outside the door, but they could be overpowered or ensorcelled by the *leroni* of Hali Tower, sworn to Hastur service. If she woke Gwynn, he would frown, even if he didn't scold her for *womanish vapors*. She wished Kyria were here. Kyria would talk sense into her and set her to laughing at her own fears, and the two of them would fall asleep with smiles on their faces.

The sound of women's voices and a muted clatter from the parlor caused Alayna to jerk awake. Sunlight filtered through the closed curtains; she'd managed to fall asleep, after all, and she was alone in the bed. At the sound of a tapping on the door, she called, "Who is it?"

"Sadhi, my lady." The maid came in and proceeded to draw the curtains. She looked as if she'd been too excited to sleep. "There's a hot breakfast, if you've a mind for it."

"What time it is?"

"Late enough that *Mestra* Ylethia says you risk being late for the audience with the king. Lord Scathfell's already gone down."

Alayna raked her fingers through her hair, finding it tangled and disorderly. "I don't think I could eat."

"Then take some *jaco* while I set things in order here."

The *jaco* made Alayna feel homesick for Scathfell, so instead she sipped a little fruit juice and nibbled on toast. Sadhi sat her down on a padded stool and brushed out her hair. The gentle, rhythmic strokes soothed her, and she felt almost cheerful when Sadhi set the brush down. Within a short time, Alayna's gowns were spread out on the bed.

In short order, Alayna was dressed, her hair arranged in a braided coronet low on her neck, standing in front of a full-length mirror. To her eyes, she looked pale, although that was to be expected after so long a journey, but the green tunic made her cheeks look porcelain, not ashen. Sadhi beamed at her. Then Gwynn and two of his guards arrived, along with an assistant *coridom* in Hastur blue and silver. Gwynn looked as handsome as ever, but Alayna knew him well enough to see tension in the way he held himself as they went down to meet the king.

The *coridom* led them down a wide hall, halted before a single, elaborately carved door, opened it, and bowed to let the Scathfell party enter. Alayna, her hand on Gwynn's elbow, blinked in the warmth and comfort of the room. She had expected a vast, formal presence chamber like the one at Scathfell Castle, only grander. But even with the place of honor at the far end, the chamber felt more like a comfortable family parlor. There were seats aplenty, and cushioned ones at that, so that everyone might be at ease, not just the king.

And there he was, Allart Hastur, the most powerful man on Darkover. Queen Cassandra sat beside him. Both looked haggard around the edges, as if the cares of office had worn them down. Neither wore what Alayna thought of as courtly attire; Allart's simple robe was of Hastur-blue wool, although he did wear a pendant of silver set with tiny, glinting white gems. Likewise, Cassandra was simply and comfortably dressed. Her hair, ebony streaked with silver, was bound with a circlet of the same gem-set silver as her husband's pendant. Her hands were folded in her lap, and she projected a sense of serenity. Alayna sensed the abiding affection and understanding between this aging couple. With Evanda's blessing, she and Gwynn might one day know the same.

Someone—a court official of some sort—introduced them, and she and Gwynn came forward. A smile lightened the king's face, and as Alayna glanced up from her deep curtsy, she saw traces of the young man he had been.

"Scathfell, be welcome to my court and to Thendara." The king made a little speech about hopes for an age of peace, friendship between the Domains, and the healing of old injuries.

Either he speaks from the heart or he's the best actor that ever lived, Alayna thought. But she sensed no dissemblance in Allart Hastur. He truly believed what he said.

Gwynn responded with a speech of his own, expressing gratitude for the king's hospitality. The back-and-forth appreciation went on for a time, and Alayna's attention drifted to the queen. Cassandra's gaze flickered between her husband and the new arrivals, but she noticed Alayna's interest, and when their eyes met she gave a small, almost mischievous smile, as if they now shared a secret.

Then the introductions and greetings came to an end, and Allart led his wife from the room. Alayna felt unreasonably disappointed that she would have no chance to speak with the queen.

The next moment, the assembly got to their feet and soon one and then another came up to Gwynn and introduced themselves. Apparently no ceremony was required once the king had exited. Alayna recognized some of the names: Leynier, a Lady Aillard from Valeron, and several Hasturs of Carcosa, who were evidently a different branch from the Elhalyns. She was sure she would never remember which faces went with the names, except for a woman of middle years who introduced herself only as Arielle of Hali Tower and was clearly a high-ranking *leronis*, perhaps even a Keeper.

After a time, servants brought in trays of watered wine and bread twists dusted with crystallized honey. The assembly took on the atmosphere of a party, with lively talk of the dancing that evening. Everyone seemed to be on good terms with one another.

The *leronis* and Lady Aillard sat together, talking quietly. As Alayna joined them, the excitement of having been presented to the king left her drained. She did not think she could conjure something witty to say if her life depended on it. Fortunately, the two women had apparently decided she was shy. They shifted their chairs to include her but asked her no questions. It was just as well, since sitting did nothing to alleviate her fatigue. Her body felt heavy, especially her lower belly and thighs, and she was sure she would be unable to make it back to their chambers unless she were carried like a sack of root vegetables. At least, she could think clearly enough to know how mortifying that would be.

Arielle must have noticed Alayna swaying in her chair, and she summoned a tray-bearer, took a goblet, and offered it to Alayna. Alayna did not really want anything to drink but hoped it would help, so she sipped the wine, which turned out to be sweetened with honey and lightly spiced. Ordinarily, the combination would have been disgusting, but now it tasted delicious. Warmth flowed through her, rising from her stomach to her cheeks, and the feeling of heaviness eased. Alayna found herself remarkably content to sit there with the conversation flowing around her. When, after a time, the assembly began to disperse, Lady Valentina Aillard invited Alayna to join her for lunch.

The meal, held in the Aillard quarters, was a simple affair and not nearly as stuffy as Alayna expected. The other

guests included half a dozen ladies, although not the *leronis*.
From the way they hugged and greeted one another by first
names, they were old friends. Some were close to her own
age, and one, a girl with freckles and flaming red hair, was
somehow related to the Altons. None of the others gave
their family names, and Lady Aillard insisted that Alayna
call her Valentina.

"To tell the truth, I still think of my mother when I hear
Lady Aillard," Valentina said. Turning to include her guests,
she announced, "Everyone—here is Alayna, who comes to
us all the way from Scathfell in the Hellers."

Alayna found herself the center of attention. After a moment or two of feeling overwhelmed, her reserve left her.
Upon hearing that she had seen almost none of the city, the
others pelted her with descriptions of all the places she
must go and things and people she must see.

"Tonight, of course, is a ball," said the red-haired girl,
"and we shall all be there and dance the women's rounds
together."

"Yes, and sigh over the men as they cavort through the
Sword Dance," another giggled, blushing. "How I long to
see them."

"Yes," said another, "that will be the high point of the
evening."

"Oh no, the high point will be what happens *after* the
dancing."

"Will your husband exhibit his skills tonight?" Valentina
inquired. "He's quite handsome, you know, and it will please
all the ladies to see him perform."

"I hardly know," Alayna murmured. Gwynn certainly
could dance, but his mind had been fixed on the political
reasons for the journey.

"Then you must persuade him," said the girl who longed
to see the Sword Dance. "It will be so fine to see a new
face."

"And new—well, what is *below* the face," her friend
added.

*Good heavens, were these young women lusting after the
dancers? And proposing my husband be among them?*
Alayna's cheeks burned.

"Ladies, please!" Valentina said, raising her hands. "Flirt
with the men all you wish tonight, but spare the delicate

sensibilities of our new friend. She is from the mountains, can you not see, with all their modest ways."

Kneeling at Alayna's side, the red-haired girl took her hand. "I'm a rude, vulgar thing for not having realized you're shy. I can't help it. It's the fault of my unfortunate birth, you know. Can you ever forgive me?"

Alayna fought and lost the battle to not giggle, for it was hilariously close to what she might have said to Kyria after a quarrel. All but the part about *unfortunate birth*. Did she mean—? Yes, she meant she was illegitimate, *nedestra*. And yet here she was, included in the gaiety of noblewomen. The ways of Thendara were strange, indeed. There was no help for it, then, but to embrace the girl and swear eternal sister-hood, at which everyone laughed and clapped and declared Alayna one of their own.

The gathering went on for some time after that, with jokes and teasing, and even a song or two, accompanied by Valentina on guitar. Alayna looked longingly at the instrument but was already beginning to feel weary again. When Valentina announced that it was time to rest so that they would be refreshed for an evening of dancing, Alayna re-turned happily to her own chamber and fell, still dressed, across her bed.

— ✦ —

Alayna woke muzzy-headed from having slept too long in the daytime. She heard the sounds of Gwynn in the adja-cent dressing room, and then Ylethia appeared to whisk her away for a bath. When they returned, spread on the neatly made bed was the most beautiful gown Alayna had ever seen—had ever *dreamed* of. The dress itself was pale green, simply cut in a fashion that would flatter most fig-ures. The neckline was modest and the bodice designed to skim the body rather than hug it as it flared into a full skirt. Over it went a net of crocheted threads of the same color, so fine as to be barely detectable, except for the motes of silver-green brilliance at each knot. Alayna reached out a fingertip, half afraid to believe her eyes and half-afraid that the delicate net was all too real and would tear at the slightest touch.

"'Tis not so fragile, for all that it looks like a moonlight dream," Ylethia said. "The overdress was bespelled by the circle at Hali Tower, so it will withstand far more ill treatment than the dress itself."

"Where did it come from?" Alayna asked in amazement.

"'Tis a gift from Queen Cassandra. Shall we try it on?"

Alayna, too stunned to protest, allowed Ylethia to slip the dress and then the net over her head. The spidersilk settled over her body as if it had been made for her, and she hardly felt the weight of the net.

Just then, Gwynn emerged through the doorframe. Once she would have thought he looked splendid, wearing the same attire he'd worn when she first met him. But Thendara had changed her eyes, and she now saw that what once looked grand was in fact old, perhaps his father's, pressed and cleaned carefully, but reeking of impoverished nobility.

He stared at her, his eyes wide. "Where did you get that dress?"

"It's a gift from the queen." As Alayna looked down at the beautiful dress. "If it does not please you, I will send it back to the queen with my thanks."

For a long moment, he said nothing. Ylethia slipped from the room and closed the door behind her. Undoubtedly, the entire castle would be abuzz with the gossip that Lord and Lady Scathfell had quarreled over the queen's gift. Alayna's knees felt so wobbly that only an effort of will kept her on her feet.

Gods, what was wrong with her? She pressed one hand to her belly. *Being pregnant has made me emotional, that's all.*

"I am *not* displeased," he said, his voice husky. "You look like a goddess in that dress. I was momentarily taken aback by the richness of the gift."

She almost heard his thoughts in her mind. *We may not be as poor as the farmers in the valley, but we cannot compare to the Hasturs in wealth.* Her pleasure in his compliment faded.

"You have been greatly honored by the queen," Gwynn went on in a more normal tone of voice, "and I by the king in being asked to perform the Sword Dance tonight. There are to be only four of us, so it is a privilege. Being so distinguished bodes well for us."

With a pang, Alayna wished Gwynn could enjoy the pleasures of the evening without always considering the political ramifications. But the grief and fear and anger of

the past haunted him still. She wondered if he would ever
be free of them.

Music and lively chatter filled the Great Hall, spilling out
into the corridor when Alayna and Gwynn approached the
opened doors, Ruyven following only a pace behind. Alayna's heart sped up at the same time her mouth went dry.
Until that moment, she hadn't realized how many people
would be present. The balls at Scathfell had not included a
fraction so many. Her fingers tightened on Gwynn's arm.
He, too, was on edge, keyed-up. Only Ruyven seemed at
ease.

Relax, Alayna told herself as she forced a deep breath.
*There will be a moment of sheer terror, but once you begin
dancing, you'll be fine.* Oh, but what if she didn't know any
of the fashionable city dances? What if she fell on her face,
disgraced Gwynn in some way? Regardless, it was too late
to withdraw now. At the door, a servant in Hastur livery
bowed to them with a smile.

And then she could not think at all, because entering the
Great Hall was like being plunged into a tempest of brilliant colors, movement, warm lights, laughter, and a lilting—
and familiar, bless the gods!—tune from the musicians.
Jewels sparkled around the necks and in the hair of the ladies; their gowns glowed in the lights, skirts flaring as they
moved through the patterns of the dance. The men were as
gorgeously dressed and sometimes even more ornately,
short capes and jackets of intricate brocade or fur-trimmed
velvet, and many glittering ornaments. Some wore tartans
in their House colors, fastened with brooches of heavy silver and precious stones.

"A festive array, indeed," Ruyven murmured. Alayna
suspected he was taking mental notes for improvements
to his own wardrobe, but she could not summon any ill
will toward him. Instead, she was grateful for his presence,
for Gwynn always seemed steadier with his friend by his
side.

Gwynn paused, alert as a hunter, as he scanned the assembly. "Come, we must pay our respects to our host." He
indicated the king, who stood talking with a group of ele-
gantly dressed men. The queen was not with them, probably

elsewhere in the Great Hall, attended by a collection of ladies.

"Scathfell!" Smiling, Allart Hastur gestured them to approach.

"Your Majesty." Gwynn bowed, and then Allart said, "No titles tonight, my friend. We are all equals here—that is what *Comyn* means, does it not? So be at your ease, for you are among friends." He proceeded to make introductions.

Alayna tried to memorize the names and faces, but they blurred together. One was an Aillard lord, but she had no idea of his relationship to Valentina. The men greeted Gwynn cordially and he replied in kind, although Alayna heard the guarded tone behind his words. He had no reason to trust anyone here, and until the king made a concrete offer of alliance, his purpose in inviting them remained in doubt. Yet between the holiday merrymaking and the wine at the refreshment tables, everyone seemed to be in excellent spirits and ready to enjoy themselves.

As should we. She would much rather be dancing than standing around listening to a bunch of men tread the fine line of diplomatic maneuvering.

"Scathfell? That's halfway across the world, isn't it?" one of the older lords asked, but in a friendly way, as if Gwynn had done something extraordinarily gracious in traveling all this distance.

"Hardly so far as that," Gwynn answered, somewhat stiffly.

"Well, well, it's good to have you in our company. When it comes to Midsummer Festival, the more the merrier," another chimed in. His reddened nose hinted at the source of his joviality.

"And Midwinter! Let's not forget that," said a younger man with shoulder-length, rust-colored hair. An Ardais, Alayna thought.

"Alas," Ruyven put in, "the passes will be completely snowed in then, so we must make the best of this present conviviality." At this, the red-nosed lord and a couple of the others laughed. Gwynn relaxed a little.

"What are we doing, standing around like old grandfathers?" Allart said. "Here is a lovely lady who must surely prefer dancing. Lord Scathfell, Lady Scathfell, I again bid you welcome. Please enjoy yourselves!"

Alayna tried to not look pathetically grateful as she followed Gwynn out on to the dance floor. She glanced back at the king and saw, or imagined, a shadow fall over his face, a dimming of the easy friendliness. His vision turned inward, as if for a moment he saw something quite different from the elegant festivities. Then a cluster of dancers blocked her view, the musicians struck the opening chords of a reel, and it was some time before she was free to do anything but concentrate on the dance steps.

They danced the reel and then a courting dance that was close enough to one she knew from home when she and Kyria were each other's partners. When it was over, Gwynn looked distracted, impatient with dancing, and Alayna regretfully resigned herself to sitting with the other women. Even in such a hospitable gathering as this, it was not proper to dance with a man who was not her husband or kin.

It was not *fair*! She had just arrived and now she was relegated to a corner with the spinsters and grandmothers—and was expected to look as if she didn't mind. How could she *not mind*? But as she struggled to compose her expression into an approximation of agreeableness, Ruyven approached and asked if he might have the honor of squiring her through the next dance.

The dance began, a spirited set with pairs of couples working their way up and down the line. There was one musical passage where she skipped away from Ruyven, only to return, join arms, and whirl away. As she remembered, he was an excellent dancer, light on his feet. He had the knack of guiding her through the changes of direction so that she appeared to be a better dancer than she actually was. At the end, she was breathing hard, and a pulse throbbed in her temples. Sweat beaded her brow. But the other ladies looked just as flushed with the vigor of the exercise and none of them gave any sign they were in the least self-conscious.

With a courtly air, Ruyven asked if she would care for refreshments, providing a way that she could take a break without having to admit to being out of breath. As he escorted her to an area where a group of ladies were sitting, she realized she did, indeed, feel fatigued, and more so than she would have expected from only a few dances.

As they approached, Alayna spied Queen Cassandra in the center of the little group. Cassandra beckoned to her with a friendly smile. "There you are, my dear. How beautiful you look tonight! Sit here by my side and tell me what you think of Thendara. We have not had the chance to get to know one another."

Murmuring thanks, Alayna took the proffered seat. Her heart would not slow down, no matter how she tried to take slow, deep breaths. A cramp began building in her lower belly —

Oh no, not again, not here . . . not again.

"My dear, are you quite well?" Cassandra asked. At her gesture, the other ladies rose, curtsied, and left them. A moment later, one of them returned with a goblet of fruit drink for Alayna.

"It is nothing, *vai domna*." Then, because she must explain or be thought rude, Alayna added, "It is the excitement of being here in Thendara, among so many strange people — and very fine folk at that. I never traveled before I came to Scathfell."

"Perhaps you will join me and my ladies while the menfolk are about their business, during your visit here. We will be your family away from home."

"I would like that very much."

"I was once very much as you are now, young and bewildered. I remember a ball in this very chamber, right after King Stephen Hastur died, quite unexpectedly, I might add, from an attack on the air-car in which he and Allart were traveling. Folk today take for granted the peace we now enjoy, but it was not always so." Cassandra's chest lifted in a barely perceptible sigh. "My family was determined to see me married. Allart and I, you see, had been handfasted at an early age, but we hardly knew one another." She gave a little laugh. "He was so somber in those days, like the monk he had been. I could barely get him to look at me, and I could not decide if he were *emmasca* like Prince Felix, or did not care for women in that way, or was still bound by his oath of celibacy."

Alayna ventured to say, "But you resolved your differences."

"Indeed we did, although it was not easy. Yet the experience has left me with an abiding faith in the ability of two people to find happiness together, no matter what the difficulties. Do not fret because your husband has other things on his mind besides dancing."

Alayna looked down at her hands, clenched in her lap, and wondered that she had been so obvious.

Cassandra signaled to one of the servants and sent him off with a request to the musicians. "Come, let us amuse ourselves. Our husbands may think they are all-important, but we do not need their participation in order to dance."

The orchestra played several chords, at which the central area cleared of men, leaving the women to form two concentric circles, facing one another. Cassandra directed Alayna to stand beside her in the inner circle.

"I don't know this dance," Alayna whispered.

"Don't worry, most of it is slow and easy to follow. The music speeds up toward the end, so that the *damiselas* who wish to attract husbands can display how prettily they whirl about. My days of such antics are long over, so I shall slip away, and you can follow me if you wish."

Cassandra proved to be right, the dance was easy to follow. Several of the older ladies missed a beat here or a step there and no one took any notice.

Step, step, dip, sway, step . . . The dance flowed on, gradually increasing in tempo. A young lady skipped into the center, whirling so that her skirts flared out about her like the petals of an opening blossom. She held a garland of ribbons and brandished them aloft. Alayna, who had never seen any dancing like this, and certainly not from a woman, stared.

"That's our cue," Cassandra said. As if pre-arranged, the outer circle opened to allow her and Alayna passage. They had not gone more than a few steps when *Dom* Nevin emerged from the crowd, directly in Alayna's path. She froze.

"*Vai domna.*" Nevin executed a courtly bow. His mouth twitched in a barely concealed smirk as he held out one hand. "The pleasure of the *secain*?"

Blood drained from Alayna's face. She was so appalled, her throat closed up, and she could not make a sound. The effrontery of the man, to suggest she—his lord's wife—join him in the notoriously licentious dance. It was her responsibility, hers alone, to refuse the invitation.

"Come now," Nevin said in that oily tone of his. He had

clearly noticed her hesitation and said, "It is not improper for you to accept. We have been introduced, you know, and I am your husband's kinsman and therefore yours."

I'll challenge him to a duel myself, rather than say yes.

"You must excuse my young charge." Cassandra put a motherly arm around Alayna's shoulders. "I have given her strict instructions to not overexert herself at her first Thendara ball. You, sir, will simply have to wait for another chance. I suggest you apply to her husband."

Without waiting for a reply, Cassandra hurried Alayna away. Within a few moments, they were seated again. The queen's ladies appeared as if magically summoned, surrounding them with a wall of fluttering fans and bird-like chatter. To Alayna's relief, Cassandra did not press for an explanation. The queen summoned more fruit drink for her, fortunately not fortified with wine, and let Alayna sit quietly.

"Thank you," Alayna said. And although she wasn't sure if she should offer a more detailed explanation, that much she wanted to express.

"Think nothing of it." Although Cassandra's tone was light, almost dismissive, her face hardened as her gaze fixed in the direction where Nevin had disappeared into the crowd. "Court life, as one might expect, attracts certain personalities, much the way a rich larder attracts insect pests. One learns to recognize both."

Alayna stared, then realized she was doing it and lowered her gaze. The queen's expression was perfectly composed, yet . . . was she *laughing*? Comparing Nevin to a cockroach? Gwynn had used the word *vermin*.

"Of course, politeness demands courtesy toward kinsmen, even if they do not return it." Then, as if she were musing aloud, the queen added, "Men think the province of war belongs solely to them. They have no idea of the battles fought, for good or ill, on the dance floor."

She turned to Alayna with a dazzling smile. "But we will have our revenge. *We* get to sit here, at our ease, while they make fools of themselves by cavorting about with their swords. Look, the Castle Guardsmen are bringing the blades out now. Let us hope your, ah, persistent but unwelcome gentleman has the wit to depart before he must perform or be thought a coward."

Alayna tried not to giggle at the notion of Nevin leaping and whirling in the patterns of the Sword Dance. She had heard that different places had their own styles, and now found herself curious what these Thendara performances would be like. At home, as was customary, only her brothers had taken part, as a sort of contest to see how fast they could execute the various steps. Once, in the privacy of her own room, Kyria had arranged a pair of sticks on the floor so she could practice. Alayna remembered the two of them collapsing in giggles and then smothering their merriment for fear of discovery. At the sound of footsteps coming down the corridor, both had dived under the covers, leaving the incriminating sticks on the carpet.

Delightful memories, yet her mind kept returning to Cassandra's comment about powerful men who lacked honor. "*Dom* Nevin wanted to marry me," Alayna said, "but Gwynn came to my rescue, if a most welcome proposal could be considered in that light."

"Then you are fortunate in your husband, as I am in mine."

Whatever more the queen might have said was forestalled as the music resolved into a single drone-pipe, skirling out a challenge. The entire assembly fell quiet, and a space opened up so that Alayna, seated beside the queen, had an unobstructed view of the circular area where the dance was to take place. The glow globes dimmed, and shadows pooled along the walls and over the faces of the onlookers to either side. Torches flared from their sconces along the periphery, adding to the primeval atmosphere.

Four dancers took their positions on the far side of the circle. Two of them were men Alayna did not know, although one might have been one of the aristocrats she'd seen in audience with the king. The third was Gwynn, looking fierce in the wavering light. Fierce, and strong, and proud. Behind her, ladies murmured in appreciation.

A fourth dancer appeared to be the youngest, lean and fit. Alayna could not make out his features in the dimmed light, yet there was something familiar about him. She'd been introduced to so many people since arriving in Thendara, they had doubtless met, though she'd forgotten.

Behind her, one of the ladies said to another, "Ah, Elisa, this will be a rare sight. Do you remember two Midsummers ago, we had only one halfway decent sword dancer, and he was too hung over to pay attention to what his feet were doing? I swear I feared for his life and bodily integrity, but perhaps the sword master had made sure to provide him with suitably blunted blades. Can you imagine the scandal if he'd slit his own throat on the dance floor!"

The other lady giggled, hushing as the queen glanced her way.

Now the drone-pipe music began in earnest, and one of the men—not Gwynn, nor the youngest—moved, rising slightly on his toes and pivoting. Alayna's breath caught in her throat, for she had never seen anything like the gliding steps with which he circled the swords. None of her brothers had stretched their arms over their heads in this manner, elongating the entire body. The next moment, she thought, he might change into an eagle and take flight. He wound through the steps once, and then again in precise repetition.

"Not very original, I'll warrant, but a pretty enough sight," the lady behind said to her companion.

"Even if we have seen it a dozen times before," came the reply.

"What do they mean?" Alayna asked the queen, keeping her voice low.

"Some dancers follow a memorized set of movements," Cassandra replied, "but the finest improvise within the prescribed steps. The true artistry of the dance requires not only physical prowess but imagination. And, I suppose, passion."

Keeping the queen's words in mind, Alayna now saw that although the dancer executed the opening steps very well, he repeated them with no detectable variation. What she was seeing was not an inspired performance but one that had been carefully rehearsed, using a limited number of gestures. The music swelled as he bent, picked up the pair of swords, and lifted them over his head, blades crossed. The audience responded with a burst of applause that seemed to Alayna polite recognition of a modest but well-executed performance.

After bowing to the audience, the first dancer quitted the floor and handed the swords to the Guardsmen, who replaced them in their proper position. The drone-pipe quieted for a few moments and then resumed with the now familiar challenge melody. This time it was Gwynn who stepped forward. Of course, Alayna thought. It would have been rude to ask him to go first; the dance was part ceremony, part competition, and courteous diplomacy for a visiting dignitary must be observed. The opening dancer had clearly been chosen because he was competent but not extraordinary. It would not be difficult for Gwynn to outshine him.

The king is courting my husband.

Instead of repeating the opening moves of the first dancer, Gwynn turned his back on the swords and faced the audience—not just the general assembly, but the exact place where the king stood. Sweeping his arms out, he stepped wide and deep, then spun to face the swords. Again outward, this time in the direction where Cassandra sat, and again that smooth step. He circled the swords and with each stride he bent his knees deeper and deeper. Then, when it seemed he could not go any lower and still move, he leapt into the air and came down into a swordsman's stance. Although Alayna had not seen him reach for the swords, there they were in his hands.

The ladies behind Alayna burst out in cries of appreciation. Alayna gathered that this particular step had not been seen in the Thendara court before.

Blades flashed as Gwynn lunged this way and that, slashing through air so fast that they blurred in her sight. The maneuvers looked more like sword fighting than dancing, but perhaps in the end they were the same.

Shivers brushed her spine at the power—the *dangerousness*—of this man. What did she really know about him? She shared his bed, his home, his name, but this fierce, almost animalistic whirling, this making love to steel, she knew nothing about.

Gwynn's movements embodied barely contained ferocity, a cloud leopard stalking its prey, as he began a series of slow, graceful spirals, using the swords as if they were extensions of his arms. The piper responded to the vigor of the dance, quickening the tempo. The drone-pipe took on a dark, untamed quality. Gwynn landed in a lunge, one sword extended in front and the other straight out behind him. For a moment, he held the pose. Not a muscle quivered, and even the very tips of the swords did not waver.

For a moment, no one moved. No one breathed. Then the audience burst into cheers. Still Gwynn held the final pose. He seemed to be saying that their approval meant nothing to him, that the dance had been its own reward.

The word that sprang to Alayna's mind was *magnificent*. Gwynn was magnificent, and now all of Thendara—all the lands of the Domains—knew it.

24

The third dancer waited while the swords were replaced. Of the performers, he was clearly the oldest, for gray streaked his hair, long enough to be knotted at the base of his skull. He stood looking down at the swords as if pondering a philosophical question as the pipes repeated the overture. His movements, as he bent to pick up the swords, were unremarkable; he might have been a servant picking up after his master and not a dancer at all. For a moment, he held them upright as if testing their weight and balance. Then he shifted his grip, fingers on the hilts, blades in perfect alignment. His footwork looked simple; certainly, he did not leap or pirouette, and his strides were restrained.

Watching him, Alayna had the sense that every stylized movement, every shift of weight, every minute change in the angle of the swords was carefully controlled. Nothing about his performance was showy, but neither was it easy. This understated display could only be executed after decades of dedicated study. His focus never wavered. This dance was not for the audience, but whether it was for the man himself, in honor of his teachers, or as a tribute to the gods, she could not tell.

Behind her, ladies whispered to one another, but not about the dancer. She overheard one ask, somewhat querulously, why they were wasting everyone's time with that old man. She wanted to see *real* dancing. Her friend hissed back that any time Lord DiAsturien wanted to perform, the king would accommodate him, and if she were wise, she would keep her opinions to herself.

The applause was as reserved as the performance itself. Alayna, clapping, caught a glint in the old man's eye. He did not care about those who had not seen the artistry in his dance, only those who had. As he left the floor, the drone-pipe fell silent.

The last performer stepped from the shadows and waited until the piper signaled readiness, standing with his feet slightly apart, balanced on the balls of his feet, hands loose at his sides. When he began, it was with a simplicity of movement that Alayna found strangely affecting. Here was no master of fighting arts but a man who had learned these forms as a boy and executed them now with an elegance arising from coordination and balance, skills clearly learned elsewhere. Even when he picked up the swords, he did not display any prowess in their handling. By comparison to Gwynn's virtuoso brilliance or the precise subtlety of Lord DiAsturien, this dance was modest.

Behind Alayna, ladies fluttered their fans, clearly bored, although they had the good manners not to begin talking until the performance had come to an end. It did so all too soon. Alayna kept waiting for some flash of dazzling skill, but there was none. The ensuing applause was muted, more out of politeness than any real appreciation. The cheering that had greeted Gwynn's finale had been overwhelming. If this had been a contest—and now she realized that in a very significant way, it had—Gwynn would be the clear victor.

The ending of the fourth dance released the audience. As the ladies rose, their gowns rustled like the wings of small birds taking flight. Alayna wanted to rush to Gwynn's side, but she did not know the protocol for taking leave of the queen, who had shown her such particular attention.

Cassandra solved the problem, turning to Alayna as she got to her feet. "Come, my dear. We must thank the performers—all of them, but especially your husband. He has made a stunning debut in court, you know. He's certainly carried away the hearts of my ladies. You shall have to look lively, since they will be making moon eyes at him all evening."

King Allart was talking with the performers, shaking each one's hand in turn. Perhaps by chance, Gwynn was the last.

"Wait." Cassandra reached out a hand, and Alayna halted in mid-stride. "We must not interrupt the diplomatic proceedings."

And yes, the king was introducing Gwynn and the other dancer. Each bowed to the other, and they exchanged a few words just as the lights brightened. Alayna had a clear view of their faces.

Lord of Light! Edric? Whatever is he doing here?

Too stunned to speak, Alayna followed in the queen's wake. She heard Cassandra say, "It seems you have made quite the conquest with your dancing, Lord Scathfell."

"Your pleasure is all the acclaim that I seek, Your Majesty," Gwynn murmured with a courtly bow.

"No false modesty, now. Your lovely wife and I watched your entire virtuoso demonstration. Such skill, fiery but perfectly controlled, is exceptional and deserves all the praise it has inspired. And you, Lord Aldaran, gave a very tidy performance. No hurling the swords into the air and giving us all a fright."

Edric? Alayna repeated numbly to herself. *Edric is Lord Aldaran?* And here he was, standing beside Gwynn. The merrymakers' chatter faded into a blur of sound. Her skin felt like ice. Her lower belly twisted, as if someone had grabbed the muscles there and wrung them hard.

Edric's voice: "Lord Scathfell, look to your wife!"

She was caught as the room slipped sideways. She felt the floor beneath her, although she had no memory of having fallen. Ruyven shouted for aid.

"Give her some air!"

"Send for a healer!"

Blue light flared at the corner of her eyes. The queen's face appeared above her own, turned to speak to someone Alayna could not see. " . . . beyond my skill . . . send for Lady Arielle. . . . Tower monitors . . ."

Edric said something Alayna could not make out, and then she found herself in Gwynn's strong arms, her head cradled against his chest. Someone shouted, "Make way!"

"Hold on," he murmured to her, his voice low and urgent. *I'm sorry, I'm so sorry . . .*

She was being carried somewhere. Walls sped by, gray stone set with translucent blue panels. Her body felt numb, and her eyes refused to focus.

Blue light bathed her, an ocean of radiance. Voices echoed, as if through a snowstorm at a far distance.

"Lay her down here."

She tried to lift her head, but her muscles would not obey her will. What was wrong with her?

"Lie still," a woman said.

Cold, so cold . . .

An eternity later, she found herself under a lowering gray sky, on a vast gray plain that stretched as far as her eyes could see in all directions. From afar, a figure beckoned, but whether male or female, child or adult, she could not tell. Was this the Overworld, where the dead drifted as shades until time wore itself out? Surely that must be Kyria, calling to her.

Alayna began to run, but even as she did so, the figure withdrew. "Wait for me!"

The figure turned, face lit by the diffuse, unchanging gray light. Alayna was even more certain this must be her sister, and she must make the best use of this chance to narrow the distance between them.

But as hard as Alayna tried, she drew no nearer. She pushed herself to go faster, ever faster, with no result. All other thoughts vanished from her mind except the desire to see Kyria again. She forgot where her body lay, forgot the anguish of yet another miscarriage. Gwynn's hand clasped hers, his brow furrowed as the *leronis's* starstone flared into blue-white fire.

Kyria! Oh, Kyria, stay for me!

The featureless gray terrain softened beneath her feet, so that with each step, she sank deeper into it. It took ever greater effort to lift her feet. She glanced down, half expecting to find herself mired in a bog, to find that her entire lower body had turned as gray as the ground. She saw then that the ground was not sucking her down; she was melting, becoming part of it.

Still, she dared not give up the chase. If she had to crawl on her hands and knees, or wriggle on her belly, she must follow where Kyria led. Just then, her feet stuck to the ground so firmly that she fell forward and caught herself on her palms. Instantly, gray tinged her hands, her wrists, her forearms.

Kyria, help me!

For a moment, it seemed the figure was slowing, turning back, but the next instant, it shrank to a dot on the horizon. Alayna tried to pull free from the grayness underfoot. The harder she tried, the deeper it drew her in. She wailed aloud in despair, knowing that she would never see Kyria again. She'd had this one chance, and now it was gone. She was alone, terrifyingly alone, with no way out except to let the grayness take her.

Come back . . . come back to us. A chorus of overlapping pleas resounded in her mind.

Come back? Where was there a *back* to come to? All she knew or had ever known was the dull, unchanging monotone that even now seeped through her core. She no longer felt its chill.

Child, you have wandered into the Overworld, where none but the shades of the dead and those specially trained to withstand its perils may venture. Come back before you are trapped there forever.

This time the voice—a single voice—shook Alayna with its power and clarity. Around her mired body, the grayness solidified. A mazework of cracks broke its surface. When she tried to move, however, it turned into sticky mud. She was well and truly caught, even more so than before. Her efforts had only made things worse.

Don't give up! Follow my voice.

It was too late. She was beyond rescue. Beyond hope. Lower and lower, her head sank. She had neither the strength nor the will to fight the pull of the mud. What did it matter? What did anything matter? All she had to do was let go just a little more, and the weight of her own despair would drag her into the lifeless depths.

The light in front of her brightened, no longer a watery overcast but a shimmering blue. Startled, she lifted her head.

Edric?

Before her stood a man of light, like Edric in form if not

in substance. Her mind could make no sense of his presence here, unless he, too, were dead.

"Edric? What are you doing here?"

"I came after you. The Keeper of Hali Tower herself searched for you, but you did not answer her call. We thought that since you know me, you might be able to see me better." He reached out a hand, limned in blue radiance. "Take my hand, Alayna. We must leave this place with all speed."

She stretched out her fingers. He felt cool to her touch, and for a panicked moment she wondered if he were a creature spun out of the same stuff as the ground and sky. Then his fingers curled around hers. He pulled her to her feet and wrapped her in his arms.

"Where are you taking me?" burst from her. "I can't leave! Kyria—"

"Kyria is not here. And neither should you be."

Alayna pushed against him, although he held her fast. "Look!" she cried, straining to peer over his shoulder. "There she is! I must go to her—quickly, before she vanishes."

Edric shook his head. "Whoever that poor soul is, she is not Kyria."

"But she—she must be! See how she turns to beckon me. Let me go to her!"

"You do not belong here, and it is dangerous to linger. This place is treacherous and will lure you to your death."

"Is this not the realm of the dead? Where else should Kyria be? I thank you for pulling me from the mud, but you must let me go." Despite her attempts to free herself, his grip turned to iron.

"Listen to me, Alayna. This is the Overworld, a place where neither time nor space have any meaning. It has many dangers, but none is greater than the one ensnaring you now. Even if that were Kyria and even if she *wanted* you to come to her, it would be impossible. Do you hear me? You would run and run until you forgot you were ever alive, caught in an endless chase—"

"I cannot give up!"

"—while your body perishes from starvation and thirst. Kyria loves you. She would never wish such a fate for you."

"Kyria would never do that to me," Alayna agreed. She sagged in his hold, resistance draining from her.

"No, she would not," he said, his voice soft. "For her sake, if not for your own, come back to life."

For Kyria's sake. And Gwynn's . . . But how?

"I do not know which way to go," she admitted. "This place is the same in every direction."

Edric turned her to face a tall, narrow tower that glimmered with the same blue light as his own form.

"Where did that come from?" she whispered. "And what is it?"

"That is Hali Tower, or Hali Tower as it appears in the Overworld. I told you that this is a realm of mind, of thought. Those of us who have learned how to safely travel here can shape its substance as we will. Generations of *leroni* from the Tower have envisioned it this way, and have imprinted the stuff of the Overworld with its image. I have merely made use of those memories in summoning it here."

As they took a step nearer, the Tower shifted, moving to meet them. Alayna's courage almost failed her. Buildings, even unnaturally slim and straight as this one, did not change positions. If this gray world was a place of magic, where only those adept in the use of *laran* might travel safely, then how could she trust anything her senses told her? Edric himself might be a figment of her dying mind, or an hallucination born of madness, or a creation of evil sorcery, bent on ensnaring her for its own purposes.

When she halted, Edric turned back to her. "What is it?"

"This place. That thing," with a jerk of her chin toward the Tower. "I don't know what to believe. None of this is real."

"You are right, it isn't real, and for that reason it has an even more powerful hold over the unprepared." He looked thoughtful for a moment. "Do you trust me?"

"If you *are* you!" she shot back, her panic rising. "How do I know? You could be anyone—a spirit of the dead, one of Zandru's demons sent to trap me!"

He dropped her hand and looked down at her, his eyes calm and steady, knowing that if she felt the least compulsion to gaze into them, she would have bolted. But he wasn't trying to use his gaze to bespell her. Instead, as they stood there, he grew more solid. Color seeped into his skin, and his hair took on a reddish tint. She felt the warmth of his breath on her face.

"I *do* know you," she said at last. "You danced at the castle in Thendara. And before that, at the traveler's shelter. Before the bandits came. You went after Kyria."

"So I did."

A dozen memories rose up all at once: the trail, Scathfell Castle, Gwynn's face in the firelight on their wedding night, dancing with Kyria around their bedroom. Homesickness shivered through her, for Rockraven and Scathfell and all the people her heart ached for. Gwynn and Dimitra and Shayla, even Ruyven, for all his fussy ways. Father and Rakhal and Hjalmar, and little Gwillim and even Ellimira, but also Kyria. Always Kyria.

I will never see her again, not in this gray land nor any other, except perhaps in my dreams.

She slipped her fingers through his. "Take me home, Edric."

With that, the Tower came rushing toward them. Just at the moment Alayna thought it would smash into them, the walls enclosed them and she found herself rising up a central stairwell. Her grip on Edric's hand tightened, but he himself showed no sign of alarm. They whooshed to the top level of the Tower, through walls, through doors, until they arrived in a chamber furnished with a couple of padded benches and a cot. A woman lay there, swaddled in blankets, and a man sat on a bench beside her. Blue light flared from the man's hands. The woman looked familiar.

Can that be me, so pale and still? I look as if I'm dead.

And so you were, almost, Edric's voice spoke in her mind.

——— ✦ ———

When Alayna opened her eyes, she was lying on a bed of sorts in an unfamiliar room. Blankets swaddled her against the chill in the air. As her eyes focused, she saw that the walls were curved—a room in a tower—*the* Tower. Edric sat on a stool beside her bed, and one of her hands felt the lingering warmth of his, although he was tucking something into a small packet of cloth. He looked weary, the skin around his mouth pale. A short distance away, an older woman watched. Blue light streamed from her cupped hands.

"Lady Arielle? Where am I?"

"Hali Tower, my dear."

Alayna struggled to sit up, but a wave of weariness pressed her into the cot. Nausea clawed at her throat. *What happened to me?*

"You have been gravely ill, child." Arielle's expression was somber. "You collapsed during the Midsummer Festival ball, but the midwives could do nothing for you. We thought it best to bring you here, where you might receive monitoring and *laran* healing. King Allart and Queen Cassandra, who studied in this very Tower, insisted on it."

Alayna shook her head, sending fresh waves of sickness through her. The babe—but then she remembered the ball and the days leading up to it.

I've lost the babe, haven't I? she dared not speak the words aloud.

"Hush now," Arielle said in a kindly tone. "You've been dosed with herbs to help you sleep. We can do many things here, but speeding up a healing such as yours is not one of them. You are safe, and you will be well in time." She touched Alayna's forehead with one fingertip, and that was the last Alayna knew for some time.

— ✦ —

Days passed, marked by increasing periods of wakefulness and a gradual lessening of fatigue. Often Alayna woke to find a white-robed monitor, and sometimes Lady Arielle herself, by her side. When she was able to eat, a novice brought broth and then soft foods. Gwynn did not visit, and this distressed her until she learned that those not trained in *laran* work were absolutely prohibited from passing beyond the Stranger's Hall on the lowest level. Arielle did not relate Gwynn's response, but Alayna imagined him livid with frustration and worry.

Then Arielle delivered the news to her that she had indeed miscarried a second time. For Alayna, hearing the words spoken aloud added weight and finality to her loss. The monitors of Hali Tower had not only managed the blood loss and other physical dangers but also discovered a malformation of the womb that made it impossible for Alayna to ever carry a pregnancy to term.

"You were fortunate to be within reach of Tower-trained monitors instead of at home or on the road," Arielle said, "or you would not have survived. You very nearly died, which is how your spirit made its way to the Overworld. As it was, it took the combined power of a circle to bring you back. Another pregnancy would certainly kill you. We have modified your body so that you will not run that risk again. In all other respects, you will be a normal, functioning woman, capable of enjoying all of life's pleasures except motherhood."

There would be no son for Gwynn. Not now . . . not ever. *Does Gwynn know? He'll be devastated.* "My husband—?"

"Has been informed. He understands there was no choice but to ensure that you never again conceive, for neither you nor the unborn babe would survive. This way, we preserve one life at least."

"For all the good it does me. I have failed him, failed everyone."

"You are too distraught to know what you are saying. It is a great deal to take in all at once, which is why we waited until now to tell you. In your previous, weakened condition, such a shock might have cost your sanity, if not your life."

"Better that it had." *What will he say? That he should never have married me!* "He must have an heir, and if I cannot give him one, he will surely set me aside."

"You do not mean that—"

"I do! What use am I now to him, to my family, to anybody? My life is worthless."

Arielle's face hardened. "You speak this way because you have been brought up to believe that a woman's only value is her ability to bear children. You have been *trained*, as a horse or a dog is trained, to consider yourself no more than a breeding animal." Her anger and disgust were palpable. "If I could, I would wipe such pernicious nonsense from the mind of every man, woman, and child in the Domains."

Stunned at the vehemence of Arielle's reaction, Alayna lowered her eyes.

"Look at me!" Arielle commanded with such force that Alayna responded instantly. "I have never borne a child, nor wished to. I have no need for a husband. I am a *leronis*, beholden to no man save the king, who is liege lord to everyone in this Tower. I have healed hundreds of folk during my years as a monitor. I have spoken mind-to-mind with my fellow *leroni* across all the settled lands. I have made fire-fighting chemicals and mined rare minerals with the power of my mind. I not only earn my living, I can defend myself. Do you think *my* life is worthless because I will never be a mother?"

"No," Alayna replied in a small voice, once she was able to speak. "You are a great lady, a sorceress." Arielle winced at the superstitious term but said nothing, so Alayna went on. "I know you mean well, but I am not Gifted like you," she managed to say in a calmer voice, "and the lord of a great estate must have an heir. If I cannot give him one, then he will set me aside for a wife who can."

"Dear, foolish child, he will do no such thing. Whatever inheritance arrangement he makes, *that* is not among the possibilities." Arielle touched a fingertip to the bracelet encircling Alayna's wrist. "Marriage *di catenas* may be little more than slavery for many women, but it offers this advantage: it cannot be undone, except by death. Your husband has been sending messages every day, inquiring after your health. Do you think that the behavior of a man who cares nothing for you?"

As Alayna remembered his face in the warm light of their bedroom, she felt sure of his love.

25

When Alayna saw Gwynn waiting outside the gates to Hali Tower, all doubts vanished. His face, which had been white and taut on first sight, relaxed into a grin. He rushed to the threshold and caught her in his arms, despite the presence of the Tower workers who had assisted her to walk. She felt crushed, smothered, and yet so relieved she could have shouted, had she been able to draw breath. Tears sprang into her eyes, and when at last he drew back to gaze into her face, she saw tears in his, too. She tried to speak, but the only sound that emerged was a sob.

Arielle stood by to supervise the leave-taking as they prepared a litter for Alayna's return to Thendara. There was no need to say anything beyond the exchange of instructions regarding the litter and Alayna's subsequent care. "She is to rest at least two hours every morning and afternoon." She gave Gwynn a severe look. "No dancing, no gadding about the streets of Thendara. And *no worrying*."

Any reservations Alayna had harbored about the necessity of the litter vanished after the first hour of travel. If this was a good road, and it was said to be one of the best, then she did not want to think what it would be like traversing rough ground. The jerking movement eased as they entered Thendara, and the dirt road gave way to paved streets, but by that time, Alayna was too exhausted to care. Her knuckles had gone white from gripping the edges of the litter.

Ruyven had assembled a small army of servants who then carried Alayna through the entrance hall, up a wide flight of stairs, along corridors and finally to the suite of rooms she and Gwynn shared. Sadhi had made her bed ready and was waiting with a pair of equally motherly maidservants. In short order, the men—including Gwynn, who looked both reluctant to leave and embarrassed at so much feminine commotion—were shooed out, Alayna was eased out of her clothing, into a nightgown, and then into the bed itself. A warming pan had been placed at the foot of the bed, and a wave of relaxation passed from her toes to her face.

Finally Sadhi admitted Gwynn to the bedroom. "How are you feeling?" he asked, bending over her bed.

"Did they tell you?" *Everything?*

Something in his eyes shifted so that for an instant, they looked like the hooded eyes of a bird of prey. "They told me that *laran* was the only way to save your life and that only the *leroni* of the Tower had the skill. They are a law unto themselves, I think. One of them made a point of telling me that the only reason the queen was allowed—*allowed*—to attend you was that she herself had once studied there."

"Yes," she said, thinking it wiser to not mention that Edric had been there, too. She was so weary, she could not think clearly.

Alayna's eyes closed without her conscious will as Gwynn went on talking about how, despite their airs, the Towers were nonetheless beholden to their liege lord—in this case, Hastur—and a good thing, too, for who knew what they might do if left to answer only to themselves. He was talking to fill up the time, venting his frustration and worry. Perhaps there was more, a nagging fear that the day might come when the king who commanded the most powerful Tower would dominate all the others. And now his own hope of an heir who need never be beholden to a Lowland king was gone.

— ✦ —

Judging by the light, it was early morning when Sadhi came in, helped Alayna to the chamber pot, washed her face and hands, combed and braided her hair, and then changed her into a fresh nightgown. Gwynn did not appear, and his side of the bed showed no sign of having been slept in, not that Alayna would have remembered his being there, she had slept so deeply. He must have slept elsewhere to avoid interrupting her rest. If she'd dreamed, she could not remember.

Sadhi brought in a pitcher of an aromatic tisane, a little toast, and a soft cooked egg. Alayna felt well enough to sit up but only for a few minutes at a time, necessitating several tries to finish the meal. She lay back against the pillows. "Where is my husband?"

"Have you a message for him? I'll take it, although I can't promise to find him right away. Word is, his lordship and the king, and several other lords as well, will be in council much of the day. Midsummer, after the Festival itself, all the lords and those ladies who hold power in their Houses, they gather together at the king's behest."

"And do what?"

"Oh, talk about this and that. Trade, marriages, water rights, the settling of disputes."

Gwynn was gone all day, as was Ruyven. Alayna slept so much of the time, she hardly noticed their absence. She did, however, feel a pang of disappointment when Gwynn sat with her briefly in the early evening and then departed. Her conscience chided her, for the dinner engagement was one of several at which Gwynn hoped to make connections with other powerful Houses. She probably wouldn't be able to stay awake for the banquet, anyway. The affair was expected to last through the early hours of the following day, if not dawn, or so Gwynn said.

Having ordered Sadhi to her own rest, Alayna tried to drowse, but her mind was too restless. She kept imagining all the things that could go wrong between Gwynn and Edric, and then her thoughts returned to how the succession for Scathfell might be assured. A foster son? Or did Gwynn have *nedestro* children? He'd never mentioned any, but perhaps that was out of regard for her dignity. A kinsman to inherit? *Zandru's hells, let it not be Nevin!*

Sighing heavily, Alayna flopped on her side, wishing she'd asked Sadhi to find her a book. Even if she had, the candlelight was adequate for finding the chamber pot but not for reading. She'd been too incoherent to ask Arielle when she might have visitors, not that she knew anyone here. Edric couldn't very well see her—a man who was neither husband nor kinsman must not be admitted to her bedroom. And she wouldn't dare ask for the queen.

She flopped over to the other side, aware that she was working herself into a fit of self-pity. She'd *wanted* to come here, and even if she spent the rest of their time in this room, she ought not to complain. She'd seen something of the city, and she'd been to a royal ball. Sword dancers had performed for her—well, not exactly for *her* but for the audience that *included* her. And the queen herself had taken notice. Surely that must be enough glamour and excitement for one lifetime. She must find a way to be satisfied and properly appreciative. Back at Rockraven, she had dreamed of encounters with elegant lords and ladies, of dances and gowns and jewels and music, and she had already had her share.

Remembering the ball sweetened her temper. At any rate, there was nothing to be done, except follow Arielle's instructions and hope to recover quickly enough to enjoy a little more of the season before she had to go home again.

I have been fortunate in so many ways. If I cannot have everything I have ever wished for, still I must be content.

A tap at the door broke into her musings. Instantly, she felt a bit more cheerful, which was a pitiable thing—to derive pleasure from a maid come to remove the dinner tray.

"Enter! I'm awake."

The door swung open and a figure, cloaked and hooded, stepped inside. Alayna couldn't make out details in the dim light, but this was *not* a maidservant. Nor was it the queen, who had no need to go about in disguise. She sat up, her pulse quickening.

"Who are you and what do you want?" she asked, trying to sound confident and not succeeding very well. "Are you sure you're in the right room?"

The figure sat beside Alayna on the bed and pushed back the hood. The light from the candles fell full upon the intruder's face.

Alayna's jaw dropped open. It was not—it could not be—

Am I dead? Her vision went swimmy and her ears caught

the muffled thump of her body falling back on the pillows.
Then someone was calling her name and shaking her, or
maybe the bed itself was moving, maybe she was still in the
litter on her way from Hali Tower to Thendara, and she had
fallen asleep. She squeezed her eyes shut, convinced herself
that she could not possibly be awake, and then opened
them again.

Kyria was still there. Eyes bright, cheeks rounded with
health and a bit more plumpness than Alayna remembered.
Mouth grinning in that achingly familiar, we-share-a-secret
way.

Alayna reached out to touch Kyria's hand, then drew
back. She half expected Kyria to go gray and misty, the way
she had in the Overworld. Or to disappear entirely. "How
can you be here? There is something wrong with me. I must
be delirious, hallucinating from fever." She blinked hard,
but the face before her did not disappear.

"Dearest, you are not imagining things. I am as real as
you are."

Real. With that thought, Alayna flung herself into Kyria's
arms. Kyria was *alive*, alive and here in this room, hugging
her back, sobbing and laughing until Alayna could not tell
the difference between them. A whirlwind of relief and joy
had caught her up, and it was all she could do to repeat to
herself, *She's alive, she's alive.*

"But you died," Alayna said at last, pulling away. "They
said you *died*—"

"Hush, I'm here now. Everything will be all right."

"All right? How can you say *all right*? You—you
wretched thing! I cried my eyes out for you. How dare you
deceive me in this way?" Alayna lashed out, but the blows
lacked the force to do more than graze the folds of Kyria's
cloak. "I—thought—I'd—lost—you!"

Kyria caught Alayna's hands and held them. "Calm
down, Layna. I know it's a shock, but I'll explain everything,
I promise. Please stop struggling. You've been so ill, becoming distraught cannot be good for you."

Alayna fought back her tears, taking deep, sobbing
breaths.

"Please believe how sorry I am for having caused you so
much pain," Kyria said. "I wish I could have got word to
you, but I didn't dare. It was too risky. Then when I heard

what happened—how you'd lost your babe and very nearly your life—and that you could not have more children—I couldn't stay away. It was hard enough, letting you believe the worst about me, but if I'd lost you without even a farewell, I could never forgive myself. But you are out of danger now," she went on, entwining her fingers in Alayna's, "and the men will be at their meeting and drinking for hours. So I thought it was not too great a risk to come to you. I thought—I *hoped*—that seeing me and knowing I am alive and well—even if this is our only chance to visit—might be the best medicine. I am so sorry for your losses."

"I will learn to live with them," Alayna said, in between hiccoughs. "For this moment, right now, I can't express *how* happy I am. I feel as if I'm dreaming, and I don't ever want to wake up. But it's all so strange. So much has happened since that ambush on the trail. Gwynn—Lord Scathfell, that is—sent a party to bargain for your release. When they returned with the news—" She shied away from the memory of that dreadful scene. "They said you'd died—the Sain Erach bandits."

"I was their captive, true, but only for a little while. Then Edric rescued me. At your behest, my dearest, most loyal sister. Though I think he would have come after me of his own accord, it touches my heart that he did so with your blessing."

Edric from the traveler's shelter. Edric, Lord Aldaran, of the Sword Dance. Edric, Gwynn's enemy. Edric, who sent the rryl... Alayna brushed away the last of her tears with the back of one hand. "I thought you were dead," she repeated, still too overcome with emotion to think clearly. "I was all alone. I didn't know what to do."

"I would not for the world have caused you such pain if I believed I had a choice," Kyria said. "I did what I thought best in order to survive. Sain Erach was a hideous place, not one you'd wish on your worst enemy. When Edric snuck into my cell, *of course* I went with him."

You could have let me know. As soon as the thought came to her, she realized that whatever her sister's reasons for remaining hidden, they must have been compelling. Kyria was alive and out of the hands of the bandits, and surely that was what really mattered.

"Lie down, and I'll tell you the whole story. I would not

want you to relapse on my account." Kyria tucked the comforters around Alayna's shoulders. "There. So you want to hear all about the rescue and flight through the mountains, all liberally sprinkled with romance?"

"Don't tease. You know I do."

"Very well, although I'm afraid it wasn't at all like the tales we used to tell one another. Edric got me out of that horrible place, just as he promised you, even though all kinds of things went wrong."

Kyria launched into the telling: the flight from bandits, the perils of the trail, and how Edric had nearly frozen to death. From the tone of her voice and her smile whenever she said his name, she had fallen in love with him. When she related their desperate battle against the banshee, Alayna's heart beat very fast, as if she herself were facing such a dangerous predator.

"That part is far more entertaining in the telling than it was at the time," Kyria said. "Neither one of us expected to survive, and we very nearly didn't. So—bandits and freezing cold and giant carnivorous birds," she counted on her fingers. "We finally made it to Aldaran Castle. And then here to Thendara, Edric at King Allart's invitation, and me to Hali Tower on business of my own."

The way Kyria phrased the reasons for making the journey struck Alayna as guarded, as if Kyria's presence must be kept secret. "Hali Tower? What business brought you there?"

"Well . . ." Kyria spread her hands over her belly, and now Alayna noticed the roundness.

"You're with child," Alayna exclaimed. "And it's Edric's?"

"Indeed."

Then we each have found love. "I'm so happy for you. For both of us."

Kyria's expression turned pensive. "I wish it were as simple as the stories we used to tell each other, with happy endings for both of us. It seems we have had the misfortune to fall in love with enemies."

"It's not fair that a grudge between men who are now in their graves should keep us apart. It's high time that feud was over."

"I agree with you, and so does Edric, but such is not the

way of men. It's all very well for the two of us to be as close as close can be, but the situation between Aldaran and Scathfell remains precarious. It would take very little to plunge both realms into war. Edric is doing everything he can to build a truce, if not an alliance, but it will take time. We dare not risk how Lord Scathfell might react if he found out I was alive but had allowed him to believe otherwise."

"He was absolutely furious at the news," Alayna said, "but there was no one to blame except Captain Francisco, who was sent to negotiate your ransom, and the bandits themselves."

"I hope Lord Scathfell did not vent his anger on the captain. It was not his fault I could not go through with the betrothal, and the only way out of it was to disappear and let everyone think I was dead."

Alayna sighed. "I'm afraid Gwynn exiled the poor captain, but at least he did not execute him." She remembered wondering about taking her sister's place as Lady Scathfell, but then she remembered the tenderness in Gwynn's eyes and the way he touched her, and any question as to whether he really cared for her vanished. Despite her grief when she believed Kyria dead, she now had a husband she loved and who loved her.

"So you understand why I did not come to you right away," Kyria said, "and why I am here in secret?" When Alayna nodded, she went on. "I have been staying out of the way, mostly at Hali Tower, where I came to consult with the *leroni*."

"I've never heard of such a thing. Isn't it unusual to come all this way? Oh, no—are you—? Please tell me you are not subject to the same ills as I was."

"No, this was to make sure both my sons are healthy and that their birth will not pose an undue ..." Kyria hesitated, searching for the right words. "No undue risk to me."

"Boys—and *twins*? I will be an auntie twice over. But what do you mean *posing an undue risk*? You look as healthy as ever."

Kyria looked away, but not before Alayna caught the shadowed expression in her eyes. "At home, no one talked about the dangers of the Rockraven Gift, beyond the usual troubles of threshold sickness. I'd always assumed that since I—and you, too—survived puberty reasonably well, we were safe. Most of the time, there is no problem, but should an unborn babe inherit the Gift and manifest it during birth, summoning lightning, the consequences might be fatal."

"I don't understand. How could a babe do that from its mother's womb?"

"How indeed? Such a thing should not be possible, but it has happened. Our Great-Aunt Aliciane died in child-birth in just such a fashion."

Alayna felt as if her head were stuffed with feathers. "How do you know—oh, yes. She was the mistress of Old Lord Aldaran, so Edric would have known."

"Her Gift was inherited by her daughter Dorilys, the one we all called the Witch-Child of Aldaran, and by her son Donal, Edric's father. You and I carry those same genes."

So Gwynn believed when he proposed marriage to me.

After a pause, Kyria went on. "Any child of mine might inherit the trait through me or Edric. Or through us both. I sought the counsel of Hali Tower to make sure this preg-nancy is safe."

"And? What did they say?"

"As you may guess from my relieved expression, their news was good. My sons do carry the Gift, but there is no sign it will awaken early, if at all. That is a blessing in more ways than one. I will have my hands full with two boys, even if they are not shooting lightning bolts at one another."

"Well do I remembering the scrapes Gwillim and Este-ban got into at home," Alayna said. "Not to mention the trouble Rakhal got you into with his traps."

"In his defense, those skills saved my life and Edric's, and were as much my doing as Rakhal's, which is why I have a healthy respect for the mischief children can get into."

"Then they will clearly be in need of a doting auntie. Even if I cannot have children, I will love yours as dearly as if they were my own."

"You will make a most excellent auntie, even though it may not be possible for us to visit for some time. If Lord Scathfell were to learn I am bearing Edric's sons, even if they are *nedestro*—well, there is no telling what he might do."

"*Nedestro*? Then you are not married? Father would

have a fit if he knew. Why ever not? Did Edric not wish to marry you, or is he not free to do so?"

"He has no prior obligation, only the desirability of a political alliance with one of the powerful Houses," Kyria admitted. "That was why we hesitated to make any formal pledge at first. And so we might have continued, except that when we arrived at Aldaran Castle, Lady Renata took one look at us and knew how deeply we had come to care about each other. She's not only his mother but a Tower-trained *leronis*. Edric insisted he would not set me aside, although he accepted that we could not marry *di catenas*."

Thinking of her own courtship, Alayna said nothing. At the time, she had not thought to question why Gwynn wanted her without dowry or powerful family connections.

"Lady Renata persuaded him that, having given his heart to me, he was no longer free to make a marriage offer to any other woman," Kyria continued. "She's a most formidable woman. I believe she spoke so passionately because of her personal experience. She and Edric's father, Donal, were not permitted to wed because their families wanted to use their marriages for political alliances. She didn't openly tell Edric to not make her mistake, but that was what she meant." Her lips curved into a fond smile. "She also promised that we need not fear the Rockraven Gift running in both our bloodlines. She was trained as a monitor, so she detected the presence of twins and advised us to consult the healers at Hali Tower to be absolutely certain all was well."

Alayna wondered how her own life might have turned out if she'd had such expert care. Jerana had done her best, but with tragic results. There was nothing to be done now, except to go on. Returning to her sister's story, she said, "With such a prospective mother-in-law, I am astonished you are not yet married. Doesn't she object to her grandsons being illegitimate?"

"Not that I can tell. Tower folk are open-minded about such things, caring more about a person's talents than whether their parents wore wedding bracelets. Edric would have married me then, but I was not sure it was safe. I may be overly cautious, but a man of his stature cannot take a wife and keep it a secret. Gossip spreads fast in the Hellers, where folk are always hungry for news of their neighbors.

No matter what we did, Scathfell would hear, and at that time, we had little prospect of better relations. I did not want to risk our marriage igniting the old feud. Now I hope things will be different."

"Still," Alayna said with a sigh, "it is a poor thing to think of my own sister as a rich lord's *barragana*. Great-Aunt Aliciane was enough scandal for one family."

"It is not important to me whether I wear the *catenas*." Kyria looked so well and happy, Alayna could not criticize her choices. "Yes, I know, Papa would be shocked, and I do not even want to guess what *Ellimira* would say."

"So your Edric would marry you, but you will not agree?" Alayna said. "What a strange turn of events. It's usually the other way around."

"Lady Renata is still determined to see us wed, and now the situation has changed, we may as well marry. If a wedding cannot be kept secret, then neither can twin sons." Kyria spread her hands over her belly. "Now that I know they will be healthy, I can stop being so noble and stubborn. And ridiculous. I have given in, much to Edric's delight and Lady Renata's approval."

"And we can visit and be together—"

"Not yet, dearest. Let us make sure of the friendship between Aldaran and Scathfell first. There have been so many misunderstandings in the past, I do not want to risk another one. Promise me that you will keep the secret until the right time."

Why did the world have to be this way? Why must women choose between their sisters and their husbands? "I do not like it, but if you feel so strongly, I will promise. Just to please you."

"Ah, do not look so downcast," Kyria said. "All may yet be well, if not at this Midsummer Festival season, then at some future one. Let us give the king's diplomacy and Edric's overtures a chance to mend things between our husbands."

"Well, if we have anything to do with it, they will soon be friends. I really am looking forward to being an auntie." Alayna felt a yawn bubble up. "Was it your idea for Edric to send a wedding gift?"

"It seemed a gods-given opening for a friendly gesture. The choice of gift, however, was mine."

"I wondered..." Alayna stifled another yawn. "It seemed made for my hands alone."

As Alayna's lids fluttered closed, she remembered her joy at making music on the beautiful harp. Images formed in her mind, of herself playing in a firelit room, and she and Kyria singing, and their two husbands easy with one another.

The mattress shifted, and she felt the covers drawn around her shoulders and a butterfly kiss on her forehead. "I'm sorry," she murmured. "I'm just ... so sleepy."

"Then dream sweetly, my Layna. Edric and I will be leaving tomorrow, but I hope it will not be too long before we can be together again."

26

No sooner had Arielle given Alayna permission to resume normal activities then Alayna leapt from her bed, dressed without asking for—or, indeed, *needing*—assistance from Sadhi, and found her way into the public spaces of the castle. She had not gone far before she encountered one of the younger ladies from court, Felisanne MacAran, who greeted her with squeals of delight.

"It's just *too* wonderful to see you! We were *all* so dreadfully worried! You did not think of us at all, I am sure, or of all the *dreadful* parties and balls we were forced to endure without you. Even the queen seemed downcast, and as you know she is *never* out of countenance. But not one of us knew exactly what was wrong with you, only that you were not permitted visitors. We all thought you must be at death's door! But you sly thing, here you are, as radiant as ever."

From this speech, Alayna understood that Felisanne wanted juicy details that she would undoubtedly swear would never pass her lips but which would be all over the castle before the day was out. She gazed at the pink cheeks—undoubtedly rouged—the slightly pinched eyes, and the hint of greed in the pouting lips—and wondered what she had been thinking, to take pleasure in the company of such creatures as this. Kyria was worth a hundred such court women — no, a hundred hundreds.

"I recovered somewhat more rapidly than expected," Alayna murmured just as Felisanne drew breath to ask more questions. "And now you say I have missed all the fun?" She gave an exaggerated sigh and slipped her arm through Felisanne's with what she hoped was a suitably confiding air. "Tell me, is there no further amusement to be had? Not even the teensiest party?"

"The season is not entirely over, although many have already departed. The Valeron folk, you know," Felisanne rattled off a string of titles and estates, including Lord Aldaran's party, " — so only the Lowland Comyn are left, since they have not so far to travel before the first snows of autumn." Felisanne went on and on, taking no apparent notice of Alayna's reactions. " — and those who are not married are as tedious as anyone with whom one has been forced to dance a thousand times. But I have just remembered!" Felisanne stopped in her tracks. "There is to be an intimate gathering in the queen's private courtyard. I was just on my way there. Listen, I have the most delicious idea. Why don't you accompany me? This being a garden event, it does not require formal attire. Your sweet little dress will be perfectly adequate, and as you know, the queen does not stand on ceremony when entertaining her closest friends."

As she prattled on, Felisanne smoothed the skirts of her gown. The pale rose fabric had been embroidered with darker pink blossoms and trimmed with lace and ribbons so that it resembled an elaborate gift package rather than a garment one could reasonably do anything useful in.

Alayna pretended she believed every word uttered by Felisanne, although it took an effort to not burst out laughing. "I would be so grateful for an invitation."

"Then it's settled. You shall come as my guest." Felisanne continued down the corridor. She did not so much walk as totter. Alayna could not get a good look at Felisanne's shoes, but suspected they were extremely stylish and even more uncomfortable.

Cassandra sat on a wicker chair underneath an arbor of vines laden with tiny yellow blossoms that gave off a spicy scent. Arielle was not there, but several of the ladies Alayna had met on the night of the ball were. Heads turned as

Felisanne made her entrance, gazes sliding over to Alayna.
Felisanne lifted her chin and strutted forward, clearly certain that the attention was for her. She halted before the
queen and performed an elaborate curtsy, which Cassandra
acknowledged with a nod.

"Come here, dear child," Cassandra said, gesturing to
Alayna. She indicated that the lady seated at her right was
to vacate her bench and that Alayna should sit there. "We
are so pleased you are well enough to enjoy this fine
weather. The *leronis* Arielle brought us news that you were
out of danger, but we had not expected so swift a recovery."

Everyone seems to want to know why, Alayna reflected.
She couldn't very well say it was gladness that her sister was
alive. "I'm happy to be here, Your Majesty."

"And are you well enough to play a tune for us, do you
think? We've had no entertainment but gossip this afternoon, and since everyone in Thendara already knows everyone else's business, I fear we are a dreary lot."

"I will be most happy to oblige, if someone will lend me
a *rryl*. I left mine at home, rather than expose it to the hazards of the trail. It was a wedding gift."

"Very wise. Perdita, go fetch one from my music room."
With a neat curtsy, the young lady hurried off. "What
amusement shall we have, while waiting for the instrument?
Felisanne, will you sing for us?"

Felisanne executed another of her elaborate curtsies,
murmuring, "If my poor voice can give pleasure, I am at
Your Majesty's command."

With a mild expression, Cassandra said, "We are all
friends here, at least I assume we are. No one expects a
professional performance, only the desire to do one's best."

Felisanne took a deep breath, shoulders lifting almost to
her ears, and sang in a warbling voice,

> *Come all ye maidens young and fair*
> *Who are blooming in your prime*
> *Beware and keep your garden fair . . .*

When she was done, everyone applauded politely. The
queen indicated that Felisanne might take the seat nearest
where she stood, which meant that for a moment at least,
there was a little circle of quiet around the queen.

"You are looking pensive," Cassandra said to Alayna. "Has the entertainment overtaxed you? Will you feel up to playing for us? If you are at all fatigued, you need not exert yourself."

"I am well enough, Your Majesty. It just feels strange to be outdoors. So much must have happened during my illness. I had scarcely arrived and had not seen anything of the city or the delights of the season, except for the ball and the sword dancers, of course, and now *Damisela* Felisanne tells me many of the nobles and their retinues have already departed. The season is almost over, and I missed my only chance to enjoy it."

"Ah! Here is Perdita with the *rryl*. Now we will have the pleasure of hearing you play."

Alayna settled the harp on her lap. As she expected of any instrument owned by the queen, it was well made, its frame skillfully carved in the form of a dancer. The strings were in good repair but tuned oddly, so that Alayna had to adjust several of them.

"I see you have found out my secret," Cassandra said, leaning closer to Alayna and extending one of her hands.

"Oh!" Alayna tried not to stare at the queen's fingers, long and slender as they were, and also six in number.

"We are all different, some in large ways and some in small," Cassandra said. "When I was very young I used to fear what others thought of me because I was not exactly like them. Yes, my hands are not the same as theirs, but it does not follow that they are deformed. As you can see, having an extra finger can be an advantage when it comes to playing the *rryl*."

"I see that you have tuned it to play chords that I, with only five fingers, cannot achieve." Yet something in the queen's manner suggested that she meant more than just the ability to pluck a greater number of strings.

Alayna glanced up from tuning the *rryl*, studied the queen's features, and saw not only a woman of influence who had been kind to her, but someone who had looked deeply into her own character. Someone who knew what it was like to be lonely and frightened. Someone who, had circumstances allowed, might have become a friend.

I could have told her about Kyria. She would have kept my secret, and more than that, she would have understood. But I made a promise and I intend to keep it.

Cassandra gazed back with a serene, almost motherly expression. "I regret that time does not allow for a deeper conversation. I suspect that we share a love of more than music. Alas, the change of the seasons is upon us, and you have a long journey through the mountains to reach your home. But do not be downcast, child. If our husbands have managed their affairs as they ought, we may celebrate another Midsummer Festival together 'ere long."

Next summer, they might sit in this very garden. Kyria, too.

"I hope so, Your Majesty," Alayna replied.

She bent over the retuned harp, set her fingers to the strings in the ordinary manner, and plucked a chord. The tone was so sweet and clear, the instrument seemed to be singing—which was just as well, for she could not have uttered a note. At that moment, thinking of the harp Kyria had arranged for her, Alayna's heart was too full to sing. She began playing a simple air, a lullaby from the hill people around Rockraven that their nurse had sung to her and Kyria. Perdita hummed along with the chorus. By the time it ended, Alayna had settled into the music. She no longer gave a thought to Felisanne, listening with a sulky expression, or to her impending farewells with Cassandra and Arielle and Ylethia and everyone else who had been gracious to her during this time. A reel danced its way out of her fingers on to the strings, setting several of the ladies clapping in rhythm. Even the queen looked as if she would like to get up and dance. Another lively tune followed, and then a courting dance, and then one of Kyria's favorites, "River of Stars."

"Sailing, sailing across the sky . . ." went the refrain, echoed as Alayna repeated the closing cadence, slower and slower, until the music died away into a hush.

For a long moment, no one spoke. The silence soaked into Alayna, washing away the pain of separation from her sister, her anxieties about the simmering feud with Aldaran. And then she felt a lessening of her grief at the loss of her babes, and the loss she was only slowly beginning to comprehend—the loss of the dream of ever holding a child in her arms. She felt no sense of forgetting but rather of acceptance without flinching, without remorse.

Every time I play Kyria's harp, I will feel how we are

connected and always will be. Our line will continue through her sons, and Ellimira's children, blood of my blood, as they say. Bone of my bone.

When they each returned to their suite near the end of the afternoon, Gwynn inquired how she fared but would not touch her except for the fleeting brush of his lips on the back of her hand. Alayna accepted his withdrawal as a reflection of his own disappointment and not as a repudiation. Kyria's visit had given Alayna such hope that she could look with compassion on her husband's grief, firm in the belief that he would make his own peace with it.

"I spent the afternoon with the queen and her ladies," she said, settling in one of the chairs before the fire.

"Good. Then you have not entirely wanted for amusement. Do you think you will be fit to travel in three days' time? Or should I inquire of the Tower healers—?"

She remembered the days of packing and preparation before they left Scathfell. "Is this not sudden?"

He began pacing in front of the fireplace. "My business here is finished, the first snow is already falling in the Hellers, and I have been absent from Scathfell for long enough. If you had not—if circumstances were different, we would be already on the road."

"Then I apologize for having delayed you," she replied, stung. "It was not my intention to inconvenience anyone." Then she took a breath and went on in the gentlest tone she could manage, "This has been a difficult time, with Scathfell's future at stake. Here I am, prattling about a garden party when you have been negotiating with the king."

"It's this place, and never a moment alone. Every word spoken in this city has three meanings." Gwynn threw himself in the second chair. Alayna, greatly daring, took one of his hands in her own. He did not pull away. "Nest of snakes, the lot of them! All but the king, and he means to broker a peace."

"Are we to have peace with Aldaran?" Alayna asked, her heart beating very fast.

"We are not to have war, at least not for now. Edric Aldaran appears to be a more reasonable man than his father, but it remains to be seen whether treachery runs in this generation, too."

"He did send a wedding gift . . ." At his sharp look, she abandoned that train of thought. Friendship purchased with a *rryl*, no matter how splendid, would not withstand the slightest test. She shifted her tone. "If the Sword Dance meant anything, you have nothing to fear from him."

That elicited a hint of a smile, the quirk in one corner of his mouth that she had come to love. "Forgive me, my love. All my life, I have thought of Aldaran as an implacable enemy. When I am with you, however, I begin to hope that things can be different. That you and I, and our heirs, need not live in the shadows of past tragedy. I wonder if this would be a better world if men resolved their differences in contests of dance instead of by drenching each other's lands in blood."

They talked for a time longer. Gwynn was perfectly serious about departing, and most of the preparations had already been made. "I'm sorry there won't be time to order those new gowns, as I'd promised," he said.

"Then Sadhi will have less to pack for me. Besides, what occasion would I have to wear such things at home? My own clothes will serve me as well as ever. I have seen little of the city and the royal court, but I will be sorry for the loss of female companionship. At home, I have no friends of my own age and station. I suppose it is too late to ask if any of the other young noblewomen might visit with us at Scathfell . . . ?"

"Of course, you may invite what guests you choose, if they will make you happy. Shall I speak to the king about a companion for you?"

"Rather, it is the queen who should be asked, and I will do that myself. I would rather have someone who wants to come, and not some poor soul being sent away for the expedience of her family or some such nonsense."

The next morning Gwynn spent with his captain and a professional travel organizer, making sure they had sufficient food and other supplies, and that the horses and mules were fit for travel. Alayna waited until a suitably polite hour, and then sent a message to the queen, asking if she might be granted a visit. The response came back much more quickly than Alayna had expected; the queen would be delighted to see her in the solarium.

When Alayna arrived at the appointed hour, she found the queen attended by only a single elderly lady-in-waiting and Arielle. She breathed a sigh of relief as she curtsied, grateful that she would not have to make her request before Felisanne and the others still at court who would turn it into the worst sort of gossip. *Poor thing, she has no friends, all alone in that awful castle at the back of nowhere. Did you see her gowns — no fashion to them at all. Or should I say gown, for I never saw her in more than one.*

"*Chiya*, come sit beside me," Cassandra said, indicating the cushioned chair in a warm, sunny spot. "I'm happy to have the chance to see you again. Yesterday did not fatigue you overly?"

"Only in the best way, Your Majesty, for I am shortly to endure far worse rigors on the trail than in those few hours in your garden. My husband informs me that snow is already falling in the Hellers. I may not be comfortable riding all day and night, but far better that than being caught dawdling in a blizzard."

Cassandra laughed, and Arielle smiled. The elderly lady appeared to be hard of hearing, for she only nodded her head and returned to her knitting.

"I see that your sense of humor has fully recovered," the *leronis* observed.

"Ah, she speaks her mind, this one," Cassandra said lightly. "Arielle, you have outdone yourself in restoring not only her body but her wits. This is not the little mouse who arrived at court."

"'Tis naught but mountain plain-speaking," Alayna murmured, lowering her gaze. Yet the queen had the right of it. She was not the same girl who had left Rockraven as her sister's companion, eager for romance and adventure. Nor was she the young bride, filled with gratitude at not having to marry that odious Nevin, nor the woman who had stared at the towers of Thendara and been overwhelmed by the gorgeousness of the Midsummer Festival ball.

"But what is the reason for this visit, other than to amuse us?" the queen said.

"With your permission, I would very much like to invite

one of the young ladies of your court to return with us as my companion, and my husband has given the proposal his blessing. Scathfell is remote, it is true, and it may not be possible to find a suitable person in such a short time, but I cannot leave without asking."

Cassandra and Arielle exchanged glances. "Deny it as you will, old friend, you are indeed clairvoyant," the queen said, then turned to Alayna. "Normally, you would be quite correct. Families must be consulted, wardrobes created and packed, and so forth. Not every gently bred young lady is as enthusiastic about a long journey through the mountains as you are, my dear—in any season. But Arielle has just been telling me of a student who, for various reasons that are her secret and not mine, will never be able to work in a matrix circle. She does not wish to return home to an unwanted marriage, but neither can she take the place of someone who *does* have the talent. And then there is Perdita, our own sweet Perdita, who I fear will never get over her broken heart when she is daily reminded of the fickleness of man's affections."

"And of the woman he transferred them to," Arielle added.

Felisanne? Please tell me it wasn't her. Oh, poor Perdita! Alayna kept her mouth shut and in that moment, it occurred to her that being responsible for a heartbroken young woman—one for whom she already had a measure of sympathy—would be a welcome diversion from her own sorrows. She could do nothing about Gwynn's moods, but she might be able to do a great deal for Perdita.

"I cannot release my student without the leave of her family," Arielle said with a little shake of her head. "It would be one thing to give her over to your charge, Cassandra, and quite another to send her so far away."

"Be easy on this matter," Cassandra replied, brushing her fingertips across the back of Arielle's wrist. It was an odd gesture, at once remote and intimate. "I doubt even *her* family will refuse the hospitality of the queen, and I know all too well how difficult it can be to leave a Tower for ordinary life. She will be well with me."

Arielle inclined her head.

"And Perdita?" Alayna asked, now feeling anxious as only one who has been presented with unexpected hope and then seen it taken away can be. "Does she face similar obstacles?"

"I can answer for her," Cassandra said, "for I know of no impediment. She has no immediate family, being an orphan. I suspect that her remaining relatives will be relieved to have her placed even more distantly than she is now. She has always been a biddable child, and will go where I ask her, even if she is presently so miserable that she cannot see it is for her own benefit."

"I will care for her as if she were my own little sister," Alayna said.

"My dear, I cannot doubt the greatness of your heart, and I hope the two of you will come to love one another."

The arrangements for Perdita's travel were quickly made. Ylethia handled obtaining warm, comfortable clothing for Perdita and packing it all up, and Perdita was provided one of Cassandra's own horses, a shaggy little chestnut gelding who looked as if he were part mountain pony.

When Alayna came down to the stable yard on the morning of their departure, she found the men readying the horses. Sadhi was already there, and Perdita as well, her face pale and expression so sad, so bereft, that Alayna wanted to weep.

Perdita curtsied at Alayna's approach as she would have for Cassandra herself. "Please, we have no need of such ceremony on the trail," Alayna said. "If we are to be friends— and I hope we shall—then we need not be so formal with one another. Well, not until we arrive at Scathfell. Then you will address me as Lady Scathfell when others are present, and I will call you *Damisela* Perdita, and we shall have a good laugh when we are alone."

Grooms from the castle stables brought up Perdita's chestnut and Alayna's bay. One helped Alayna to mount— *goodness, had the horse always been so tall?* Gwynn and Ruyven approached, along with the king and queen, who were according them the singular honor of seeing them off.

"Are you ready for the long journey home?" Gwynn said, patting the shoulder of Alayna's horse.

"I am indeed," she replied lightly. "The snow holds no terrors for me."

He turned to Perdita. "I have not had the chance to

welcome you to our party and to Scathfell. I hope you will
be happy with us."

"I am sure I will be, my lord," Perdita murmured. "Thank
you for your kindness in offering me a home."

"May we meet again next Midsummer Festival!" Allart
called, and then they were on their way, clattering out of the
stable yard, through the opened gates, and along the cob-
bled city streets.

Once past the outer walls of Thendara, Alayna looked
ahead to the road as it rose into the Venza Hills. Beyond
them lay more hills, and tendays of travel, and steadily rising mountains . . . and home.

27

The first few days of travel homeward felt like a holiday outing. Summer still held sway on the Lowlands, rendering the days warm and the nights only cool enough to lend a certain delight to snuggling under the blankets. They found an inn at the end of each day's travel, where they all had soft beds, good dinners, and hot water. The horses were fresh after their long rest in Thendara, and the roads wide enough that Alayna and Perdita could ride side by side, chatting about the sights, telling stories, and occasionally singing songs. At night, she slept in her husband's arms, although he did not initiate love-making and appeared not to notice her tentative overtures. Perhaps he feared resumption of intimacy so soon after her ordeal, although Arielle had assured her that was all right.

Most of the time Gwynn rode ahead with his captain, leaving the women alone except for an occasional inquiry.

"He must think us very silly," Perdita said after one such time.

Alayna thought it more likely that he regarded their conversations as if they had taken place in a solarium or sewing room. Such spaces were not strictly forbidden to men, but it was understood that women required privacy and the company of their own sex. *Dom* Nevin's intrusion into the music room had been a breach of manners, to say the least.

The day was wearing toward dusk, and they had been climbing, slowly but steadily, toward the crest of a line of hills. Beyond, Alayna glimpsed the outlines of distant, mist-shrouded peaks. "What weighty subjects shall we discuss, then?" she asked playfully. "The latest fashion in philosophy? Or the intrigues of the court? We must not descend into gossip, of course, so that leaves out who has slighted whom, and all the vexations of—" She started to say *courtship* but held her tongue at the last moment, for that would be cruel, considering Perdita's recent disappointment. "—well, whatever people are currently vexed about. I'm sure there is a long list of things."

Perdita's gaze remained on the pommel of her saddle. "I know not how I have offended you, unless it be my comment about silliness. I crave your pardon."

"You have not offended me," Alayna replied, shamed by the other woman's meekness. "If offense has been taken, it is from my own inexperience. I was not brought up in a grand style, you should know. My family were of good lineage but not well off."

Perdita turned to gaze at Alayna with wide, astonished eyes.

"It's true," Alayna said. "And my older sister was betrothed to Lord Scathfell. I accompanied her so that she would not be alone and friendless in a strange place. But she—" *Remember your promise!* "—she died, and then I became Lady Scathfell. I never realized how lonely that would be. I have women servants, to be sure, and ladies of the castle with whom I play music or sew, but not—not a friend."

"I did not know. The queen said only that you sought a companion. I did not think it my place to inquire why. I supposed you wanted someone to fetch and carry and perhaps to sing to you when you are weary in spirit."

"And so you thought, when I asked you to sing yesterday, that I was judging whether your voice was sufficiently fine? And if it did not please me, it's a bit late to send you back, don't you think? Oh, Perdita, you are not a horse whose paces I must approve."

They had come to the crest of the hills and paused here to give the horses a rest. Alayna looked ahead, over the woodlands that gave rise to even higher hills and to the mountains she had glimpsed earlier, but Perdita twisted in her saddle to look back along the long slope, the pastures and farms.

"Lady Scathfell," Perdita said in a quiet voice, at last turning away from the Lowlands, "I am poor, like you, but unlike you, I have no prospect of a marriage to secure a home for myself. I must earn my bread in whatever honorable way I may. I am grateful for this position, but please, let us not pretend I am anything but your servant."

Was it cruel to take her from her home? I will make sure she never regrets having come with me. Alayna resolved that she would persist, trying one amusement after another until Perdita's spirits were lightened. She did not press the issue now, not with Perdita looking so pensive and gazing back toward Thendara, which now lay far behind even the sight of an eagle. *We shall laugh. And make music. Come next Midwinter Festival, we shall dance as well.*

As they passed beyond the settled lands, there were no more inns or even farmhouses. Now well into the outskirts of the Hellers, they camped in tents. The air was thinner here, dusk came swiftly, and snow fell at night. On the second night, they heard howling, but far off. Alayna lay awake, back to back with Gwynn. From the nearby tent, she caught the sound of Perdita whimpering.

"Gwynn, are you awake?"

"I am now." Then came another peal of howling and a muffled shriek. "Are you troubled, *preciosa*? The wolves are far off. They sounded nearer than they are because of the shape of the hills."

"Not I, as long as I am with you. But this must be terrifying for Perdita. I think I must go to comfort her."

"I suppose city life has not prepared her for the hazards of these mountains. You must set an example for her. By all means, reassure her."

Feeling heartened by Gwynn's confidence in her, Alayna wrapped herself in her cloak and crawled into the tent Perdita shared with Sadhi. Sadhi was fast asleep, but Perdita had curled herself into a ball, hands over her mouth to keep from crying out.

"Hush now." Alayna wrapped her arms around the shivering girl. "There is nothing to fear. It's only wolves."

"W-wolves, my lady? Truly?"

"Just wolves, not banshees, not this far below the tree line." Alayna kept her voice down to not awaken Sadhi. She did not add that the worst danger she had faced in the mountains, aside from the threat of freezing, was from a different sort of wolves, the human kind from Sain Erach. Perdita did not need to hear that. "They won't come into camp, not with so many men and a fire burning. We're quite safe."

"If you're sure . . ."

"I am. My husband would never place us at risk . If this journey were truly dangerous, he would have remained in Thendara until next spring."

"Don't think me silly for being afraid, but I have never been outside the city before, except for a summer's outing with friends, and then no further than Lake Hali. I have spent the better part of my days indoors, most of it in Comyn Castle, and so I am woefully ignorant about life in the mountains."

"As I am about life in the city. Surely you must have seen how awkward I was, and how many mistakes I made."

Perdita rolled over to face Alayna, who then drew the blankets over both of them. "You were ill for so long, you had no opportunity to form alliances among other women. Everyone is on the lookout for her own advantage—what desirable, unmarried lord she can entice, how close to the queen she is seated, what influential people owe her favors, what rich gifts she receives from her suitors."

"How . . ." Alayna searched for the right words. ". . . sad to think only of what advantage one might derive from another, and not the simple joys of friendship. But *you* never seemed that way to me." She could not think how to describe Perdita's quiet modesty in a way that would not seem like the false praises of the court. "Yet the queen seemed to favor you."

"I have been fortunate indeed in her patronage."

From that time onward, an understanding grew between the two young women. They talked whenever the trail permitted them to ride side by side. Alayna indulged her own inclination to cosset her friend, making sure that Perdita was the first to receive a hot drink when they made camp, and had the best of the beds at each travelers' shelter where they passed a night.

At last Alayna knew for certain that she had passed this way before. They were nearing the valley of Scathfell, which led to the castle itself. She remembered riding at Francisco's side and how he had talked about the farmers and herders living there. He was long gone, as was his family, the wife she would never meet. All she could do was hope he had found a master who deserved his loyalty.

Alayna had scarcely time to exchange two words with Gwynn upon their arrival at Scathfell Castle. One of the guards had ridden ahead to announce their return, and the main courtyard churned with grooms to look after the animals, servants to unload them, Zefano the *coridom* watching over it all, and Dimitra and Marianne and a small host of maidservants to attend to the women. Dimitra looked thinner than Alayna remembered, and sallow-skinned.

Perdita tried to be of help in unpacking Alayna's clothing, but she was clearly exhausted.

"Sadhi, take her away before she faints," Dimitra said, and then to Perdita, "You're of no use to anyone like this, girl. Eat something, wash off the trail grime, and get some sleep. Her ladyship and I can do very well without you for a single evening."

Alayna was perfectly happy to let Dimitra sort out the details. All she herself had to do was to sink into the deliciously warm bath that had been prepared for her, eat the expertly cooked meal that waited for her, allow Dimitra to comb her hair and dress her in her favorite nightgown, and slip between the smooth *linex* sheets of her own bed. She was yawning by the time her head touched the pillow.

When she awoke to the brilliance of a shaft of morning sun through a gap in the curtains, she was alone. She reached out to the other side of the bed, but the sheets were cold, the covers undisturbed. The dregs of sleep vanished as she sat up.

Perhaps Gwynn had left her to her own bed so that she might enjoy an uninterrupted rest after the long journey. Perhaps at dinner, when the day's work was done . . .

Alayna gave Perdita a tour of her favorite rooms in the castle, ending with the solarium. Her usual women companions had gathered there for music and needlework. Her *rryl—Kyria's gift*—had been brought out. Alayna introduced them all to Perdita, as she would any noble guest. After they had all chatted for a time, Alayna took up her *rryl* and played a simple air for Perdita to sing. Perdita had a far better voice than any of the others. They passed a pleasant morning together in the sunlit chamber. Then, seeing that Perdita was ashen with fatigue, Alayna announced her own intention to rest from her long journey. She had intended to spend a quiet few hours after sending Perdita to her own room, but she ended up lying down and then falling asleep.

Dimitra appeared an hour before dinner time. While she dressed Alayna's hair with her usual skill, Alayna felt a twinge of pity for her; she had after all been left behind.

"How have you all been during my absence?" Alayna asked.

"Thank you for asking, *vai domna*. There were a few cases of summer fever, but all the patients except one recovered."

"Summer fever? I do not know that illness."

"It's also called spotted flux for the rash that comes with it. 'Tis likely one of the newly conscripted soldiers contracted it elsewhere and brought it here. It strikes the old harder than the young, so poor little Shayla was abed for a tenday, itching miserably. Many of us had it as children and cannot get it again. Those of us who were immune, myself included, took turns nursing the sick."

That explains why she looks so weary. "How dreadful," Alayna said. "But you said someone did not recover."

"Yes. Old Jerana took a bad case, and it went to her lungs."

The old *leronis*! "I'm sorry to hear it. She was so kind to me when I—the first time—" Alayna stumbled. "She will be missed."

"Yes, it is a great loss for us. Do you know if Lord Scathfell will send to a Tower for another *laran*-trained healer?"

Alayna had no idea what Gwynn's wishes were, or even how usual it was for a place like Scathfell to have a household *leronis*, and she had the sinking feeling that a lady of her station ought to know. "I'll be sure to let you know what he decides."

Dinner turned out to be somewhat more formal than Alayna had expected. The table usually reserved for feasts had been set for only four. A fire brightened the hearth, softening the chill that clung to the stone walls. Outside, snow began to fall almost as soon as the red sun dipped behind the western peaks. When she and Perdita entered through the main door, Gwynn and Ruyven were waiting for them.

Servants brought in a tureen of soup while Gwynn asked Perdita about her impressions of Scathfell. "It is nothing to the palaces in Thendara, but I hope you will be comfortable here."

"I am sure I shall." Perdita kept her gaze on her spoon as she dipped it into her bowl. "Lady Scathfell is a most generous mistress."

"Then everything is as it should be," Ruyven said.

Alayna laid down her spoon. Everything was *not* as it should be. "Dimitra told me that while we were gone there was an outbreak of summer fever. Spotted flux, she called it. She also said there was a death among us."

Gwynn's brows drew together, and his lips narrowed. Perdita's spoon clattered against her plate. Ruyven said, "My lady—" but Gwynn cut him off.

"*My wife*, this is not the time or the place to discuss such matters, especially in front of our guest, a tender young woman who has just endured an exhausting journey." He turned to Perdita. "I apologize for the outburst and hope it has not dampened your pleasure in the evening."

Perdita stared at the dregs of her soup. "It is I who should beg your pardon, my lord, for my unseemly reaction. My parents died of the spotted flux when I was a small child." She blinked away tears. "I should not be so emotional, I know. It's just that sometimes I wonder what my life would have been, had they lived. Your lordship is undoubtedly correct, and that my feelings are somewhat—volatile—from fatigue and being so far from home. I am sad for your loss, of course, but happy that the outbreak was not worse."

Seeing Perdita still downcast, Alayna searched for a way to cheer her friend. "How would it be if we presented an evening of music? Perdita has a lovely singing voice and now I have my *rryl* again. You will enjoy that, will you not, my love?" When Gwynn did not answer immediately, Alayna pressed on. "We have been enjoying ourselves in Thendara, while our people here—Zefano and Marianna and Dimitra and all the others—have been hard at work. Let us open the concert to them as well. It will be our thanks to them for their faithfulness in safeguarding our home."

"Put like that, I can hardly refuse," Gwynn said. "You have convinced me."

"Excellent." Ruyven turned to Alayna. "May I be of assistance, *vai domna*?"

"Not with the concert itself, although I thank you for your offer. But if you would undertake preparing a place for us to perform—what do you think, Gwynn? The Great Hall is so large, our voices will be lost. Will the solarium do for a larger group? Or perhaps the men's parlor?"

"I know nothing of such matters. You and Ruyven must choose whatever seems best." Without waiting for a response, Gwynn clapped his hands, and servants took away the soup course and brought a haunch of venison. The next little while was occupied with carving and serving.

"If I may—?" Perdita said shyly, after they had all eaten a little. "I often assisted Queen Cassandra in private concerts, both indoors and in her garden. One must consider the acoustics of the venue as well as the strength of the singers' voices and the size of the audience."

"You see, my dear," Gwynn said to Alayna. "We have an expert in our midst."

"This is most excellent venison," Ruyven said, breaking the pause that followed.

"The cook seems to have outdone himself," Gwynn replied. "Come to think of it, I don't recall dining on venison the entire time we were in Thendara. Do you?"

"Not offhand, my lord," Ruyven said. "But there were so many elaborate dishes with such fancy names, I could not swear to it."

"And you, *damisela*? Can you enlighten us about the consumption of game in Thendara?"

"Her Majesty did not care for venison, so I cannot say," Perdita murmured.

"I suppose you might find venison now and again in one

of the city markets," Ruyven said. "Perhaps one of the nearer estates includes a woodland park for the keeping of deer. We did eat rabbit-horn, if you recall, *vai dom*."

"We did? When?"

"The feast hosted by Lord Syrtis."

Gwynn's brow furrowed. "Aldaran was there."

"And very courteously he greeted your lordship, too," Ruyven said smoothly.

"You are right, my friend. He did make friendly overtures—not just on that occasion but on many. I must take care not to see the hand of Old Lord Aldaran in every syllable the young one utters."

"Lord Edric Aldaran sent us a wedding gift," Alayna said to Perdita. "My beautiful *rryl*, just the right size for my hands."

"Yes, it was a handsome gift," Ruyven said. "Should Lord Aldaran ever take a wife, we must be sure to reciprocate appropriately."

"Well, he is not wed or even betrothed, not that my spies can discover." Gwynn bent over his meat, cutting it into thin, precise slices.

"Spies?" Alayna stared at him. He *spied* on Aldaran? On Kyria's new family? Even after all the overtures of good will?

"Don't look so shocked. I'm sure *he* has spies here. I could rout them out if I wanted to put everyone in the castle, not to mention the whole valley, under truthspell. He could do the same. But then I'd be forced to execute the traitors."

Executions? Traitors? Blessed Cassilda.

Alayna rose. "I beg your pardon, my lords. I am—" How could she say what she felt: *appalled, outraged?* "—overly fatigued. Please do not trouble yourselves on my account. Enjoy the rest of your dinners." She took a step backward and found herself less steady than she expected. An instant later, Perdita was beside her.

"*Vai domna*, you cannot go wandering about the castle without proper attendants," Perdita said in a low but determined voice. Before Alayna could protest, Perdita bustled her out of the dining hall, down the hallway, up the stairs, and into her own quarters.

"I had no idea you were so capable," Alayna murmured

as Perdita eased her on her bed and piled pillows under her head and beneath her knees.

"It seemed more dignified than to call for servants to carry you. I'm shy, as you know, but I'm not helpless. Queen Cassandra understood that about me. I hope that you will come to trust me as she did."

"Do you miss the queen? And your home in Thendara?" Alayna said once she found her voice.

"Lady Scathfell, you have a kind and open heart, which is worth more than all the sophistication of ten royal courts," Perdita said. "Come, I shall rub your hands as I used to do for the queen when she had one of her headaches, and tomorrow we will plan such a concert that the entire castle will talk about nothing else all winter!"

28

The first serious snowstorm of the winter descended on Scathfell Castle on the very day of the concert. By midday, the clouds were so thick and gray, and the fall so heavy, that even the solarium felt gloomy.

After conferring with Ruyven, Alayna assigned the concert venue to the men's parlor. A good blaze in the fireplace and banks of candles combined with the comfort of the chamber to create a sense of intimacy. As they filed in behind the guests of higher rank and took their places along the walls, she watched the servants, the way their eyes gleamed, the whispers, the smiles.

We are a family. It was the closest she'd yet come to understanding Gwynn's devotion to Scathfell and his fierce defense of it.

Gwynn strode into the chamber. As he passed, the nearest bowed or curtsied. One or two, Dimitra among them, murmured their thanks. Dimitra held herself stiffly; in the warm candle light, she looked more drawn and tired than Alayna had ever seen her. Gwynn settled himself in the largest and grandest of the chairs, placed in the front center row, with Ruyven on his right side and Zefano on his left.

Alayna stepped forward and recited the greeting she had prepared. "Thank you all for joining us this evening and especially for welcoming *Damisela* Perdita Vyandal into our midst," she said, pitching her voice so everyone might hear. "As the nights lengthen and the days grow colder, we hold in our hearts faith that the sun will return. Spring will come again. Meanwhile, let us take delight in one another through the dark of winter."

When she finished, there was a scattering of applause and murmurs of agreement. Gwynn met her gaze and she thought she saw a glint of emotion, although she could not discern what it was. When the words "take delight in one another" came to her mind, she had been thinking of him.

Alayna joined the others as they took up their instruments. Besides herself and Perdita, Marianna and Shayla were to perform together. Shayla was too lacking in confidence to attempt a solo in front of such an audience, but she played the hand drum and sang harmony very nicely. As they began a country reel, the *rryl* came alive in Alayna's hands. Marianna played the bowed viol and Perdita a simple wooden flute. Perdita had learned the instrument as a girl, "as every child in Thendara did," and said her playing was not good enough for an audience, but Alayna had persuaded her to join in.

The chamber filled with the lively tune, reprised over and over, as it would be for a dance, but each instrument in turn played a solo variation. Most of the listeners knew the melody and clapped out the rhythm. Alayna suspected that if the floor were cleared of chairs, many would have formed into lines and let the music carry them away.

They followed the reel with a call-and-response courting song, with Alayna's harp and Marianna's viol taking the two parts while Shayla tapped out the rhythm. After several more tunes, all of them traditional and fast-paced, it was time for something slower. As Alayna had anticipated, her fingers needed a rest, and Marianna looked grateful to set down her viol. Perdita came forward.

"I would like to sing for you a lament taught to me by Lady Scathfell. She in turn learned it from the folk of her homeland. It seems to me to belong here, in these beautiful mountains."

They had already decided that the song should be performed without accompaniment so that nothing detracted from the purity of Perdita's voice. After composing herself, she lifted her head and began,

> *Farewell to the place*
> *Where I was raised,*
> *Land of high mountains*
> *Where the mist maidens dwell,*
> *Where the sun rises early*
> *In a sky bright as roses*
> *To sweep away the shades of night.*

Verse after verse poured from her, the yearning of the song-maker transformed into notes so vibrant that Alayna thought her heart might break. In her mind, she wandered on slopes dotted with wildflowers. She smelled snow on the air, and the freshness of a spring breeze. She had no idea what *mist maidens* were, perhaps the daughters of herdsmen or trappers living on the heights, or another name for the nonhuman, supernally graceful *chieri*. When the song ended and she came back to herself, she saw brightness in the eyes of the audience and even a quickly wiped tear.

So the evening went, with solos and ensemble pieces, quick-paced dances and mournful ballads. Perdita sang a few of the new, fashionable tone songs from the court, to polite, restrained applause. Then everyone, performer and listener alike, joined in for a Midwinter Festival children's song. During the finale, the servants standing along the back wall slipped quietly out, as Alayna had instructed. They returned carrying tables and laden with an assortment of holiday treats just as the performers were taking their bows. Soon everyone was milling about, chatting with the musicians and helping themselves.

Alayna caught sight of Dimitra, who stood beside a refreshment table, holding on to it as if she felt faint. The next moment, Alayna was at her side, catching her other arm. "Dimitra, you look unwell. What is the matter? Has something happened?"

Dimitra pulled away, but not before Alayna became aware of how withered her arm felt. Until that moment, she had not realized how much Dimitra had diminished from the round-bodied woman who had welcomed her to Scathfell Castle.

"Just a momentary—" Dimitra said, her voice rough. "'Tis the closeness of the chamber, nothing more. I pray you, my lady, take no notice."

"I will indeed take notice."

"Just let me sit awhile." Dimitra collapsed onto the nearest chair and broke into a fit of coughing.

If Jerana were here, she would know what to do. But she is not. I must do the best I can. "We must get you to your bed, or at the very least a place where you can lie down. Can you stand?"

Dimitra pushed with both hands against the seat of the chair, but it was no use.

Alayna gestured to a servant girl who was headed, empty plate in hand, back toward the refreshment table for a second helping. "You there. Tell Lord Scathfell I must speak with him immediately."

A moment later, the girl returned with Gwynn. He looked and sounded annoyed. "What's this?"

"Dimitra nearly fainted and cannot get to her feet. Someone will have to carry her to her chamber."

"*Vai dom*, I'm sorry to cause such a fuss," Dimitra protested. "I told her ladyship that a brief rest would restore me."

Gwynn beckoned across the crowd to two guards. "The lady is unwell and requires assistance to her chamber."

"*Z'par servu, vai dom*," the older of them said.

How the two of them managed it, Alayna was not sure, but without any fuss or awkwardness, they lifted Dimitra to her feet, one of them on either side as if she were a fine lady and they her two swains. With their assistance, she was able to walk enough to make a stately, if slow, exit.

"That was kindly done," Alayna said to Gwynn. She would have gone on, but at that moment, Ruyven and Zefano approached them. Gwynn explained the situation in a few words.

"It's a pity that Lady Jerana is no longer with us," Ruyven said.

"Yes, that was my thought, too." Alayna glanced at Zefano. "Is there some other woman with healing skills in the castle?"

"I know of none who can do more than bind up a kitchen cut or tend a sour stomach, although a man or two among the soldiers has experience with treating battle injuries," Zefano answered.

"What about the village?" Alayna asked. "Surely they must have a midwife or some grandmother experienced in treating women."

Zefano bowed to her. "I will inquire."

After the *coridom* hurried away, Alayna said, "This is no ordinary fatigue. Seeing her now, after an absence . . . I had no idea she was ill, but she most certainly is."

"Go with her and do what you can to make her comfortable."

Summoning Perdita, Alayna hastened to the staircase and then along the corridor leading to the quarters of the upper servants, like Zefano and his family.

"Did your experience in court include nursing the sick, by any chance?" Alayna asked Perdita as they approached Dimitra's door.

"Alas, nothing formal. The queen was rarely indisposed, and when she needed care, she was always tended by Lady Arielle or one of the other *leroni* from Hali Tower."

Alayna knew that the skills of the Tower healers were far beyond those of ordinary herbal healers. Scathfell no longer included a household *leronis*, so she must make do with her own eyes and ears and common sense, whatever small measure she possessed, at least until more skillful help could be found.

As she lifted the latch, she realized that she had never been in Dimitra's rooms before. She was pleasantly surprised to find herself in a snug parlor, adequate for someone who did not spend many hours there. A fire had been laid but not lit. Candles illuminated the worn, ruby-hued carpet, the little table, and the divan on which Dimitra lay. The guards were still there and had just set her down. They turned to Alayna and bowed, awaiting further orders.

"This won't do. She needs to be in bed." Alayna knelt at Dimitra's side and took her hand. "Lady? Can you hear me? Are you able to walk a short distance?"

Dimitra's bloodless lips moved. "Let me . . . just rest . . ."

If I do that, I may never get her back on her feet.

Alayna gestured to the guards. "If you would, please carry her the rest of the way. Then you may return to your duties, but send a page in case I require anything further. Perdita and I will care for her."

Once the men had moved Dimitra and left, Alayna and Perdita worked together to fold back the comforter and remove Dimitra's shoes and stockings. Dimitra roused enough to sit up and allowed herself to be undressed down to her shift. Alayna managed to not gasp aloud when she saw the condition of Dimitra's body, the emaciation of her arms and chest in stark contrast to the swelling of her abdomen.

After covering her, they withdrew to the sitting room and closed the bedroom door behind them. Alayna dispatched the page for hot water and towels, then sat down on the divan next to Perdita. "I've never seen anything like that," Alayna said. "Her belly looks as if she were carrying a child, but I do not think that is possible at her age."

"There was a lady at court, one younger than *Domna* Dimitra, who looked something like this," Perdita said. "I believe that for a time, there was a rumor she had dallied with one of the courtiers, although that would have been out of her usual character. She left the court and later I heard that she had died."

"Evanda grant that Dimitra recovers."

— ◆ —

Sometime later came the sound of someone rapping on the outer door. Perdita jumped to her feet to open it. Zefano stood outside, and with him was an elderly peasant woman. Her shape could not be discerned under layers of patched-together tunics, scarves, and shawls. She was short, wrinkled, and the hairs that had escaped from her knitted cap were snowy white. Despite her cane, she moved briskly into the room.

"M'lady, forgive me if I don't bow proper. Me old bones have opinions of their own."

"Think nothing of it, *Mestra*—?"

"Tarva," Zefano answered, "the headman's grandmother."

"Well, *Mestra* Tarva, you are welcome—"

"Eh, never mind the pretty titles! Yon lummock rousted me from me bed, and I'd like to get back to it as soon as may be. He says there's a woman needing a healin' granny?"

"Yes, this way." Certain that anyone who talked like that

must know what she was about, Alayna led the way to the bedroom. "Thank you, Zefano. Get some rest yourself."

Tarva lifted Dimitra's arm and ran her fingers over it, pausing to test the pulses at the wrist. Then she folded back the comforter and began feeling Dimitra's abdomen through her shift, pressing here and there. Dimitra moaned and turned her head from side to side. Sweat gleamed on her brow.

Tarva went on like that for some time, unheeding Dimitra's increasing signs of distress. Finally, Tarva made a clucking sound and pulled the covers back up. "There, there, me dove. I know it hurts, but I couldna tell the matter without a bit of poking. Rest now. I'll leave ye be."

Tarva prescribed a mixture of herbs to be taken with wine, and Alayna sent the page off with the orders, after listening to the lad recite them back twice to make sure he'd memorized them correctly. He returned in a surprisingly short time, and Tarva coaxed Dimitra to swallow the potion. "Poor dove, she'll sleep better now. Lady, we must talk."

Back in the sitting room, Tarva lowered herself to the divan and faced the two younger women. "Is she kin, this lady?"

"No," Alayna answered, "but she is of my household, and as chatelaine of this castle, I am responsible for her."

"Well, she's in a bad way, I'm sorrowed to tell ye, and not likely to get any less so."

"You'd best tell me the truth." Alayna decided it was better to receive bad news on her feet. Perdita stood against the wall by the door, hands clasped together in front of her.

"'Tis a growth, not a babe, that swells her belly so. Mayhap it arises from her womb or nearby parts. There's no telling sure. I've buried four husbands and as many sons, and birthed more babes than I can count, and in all my years I've seen but two cases like this."

"A growth? You mean a tumor?" Alayna said. "And it's bad?"

"M'lady asked for the truth straight out, and here it is. 'Tis more than *bad*. 'Tis her death."

For a long moment, the words hung in the air. There was no other sound, except for the faint rattle of Dimitra's snoring from the other side of the bedroom door.

Dimitra isn't dead yet. It's only this woman's word. None of us can know the will of the gods.

"There must be something you can do for her," Alayna said, her voice turning stern. "You're the midwife of the village, aren't you? You know how to treat women's ills."

Tarva shook her head, and her words carried genuine regret. "There's nawt that any medicine I know can do, save to ease her pain."

Alayna crossed her arms and began to pace. "Any *ordinary* medicine, you mean . . ." Her words trailed off as she remembered how her own life had been saved, not by medicine but by the mental powers of the Tower healers. "What about *laran*?"

The old midwife's expression was suddenly guarded. "I know nawt of such things, nor should ye. 'Tis not for the likes of us, that vile sorcery."

Alayna paused, momentarily taken aback. "Why do you call it *vile*?"

"Ye are young, and new-come to these lands. I remember well how it was when the old lord marched on Aldaran. Lightning rained from the sky, not from any natural storm but from spells and brewings. The land itself broke open and swallowed men up, and those that returned had better died."

"Surely you can't blame every *leronis* in the Domains for that."

"If you say so, m'lady." Tarva heaved herself to her feet, using her cane for support. "Ye asked, and I have answered. Now, if ye have no more idle chatter, I'll be on me way to the kitchen to brew up more of the numbing draught. That one," with a jerk of her chin toward the bedroom, "will be needin' a quantity of it 'ere long."

"Please do," Alayna replied with stiff dignity. "And thank you for coming."

Alayna sent Perdita along, in case Tarva should need anything or slip on the stairs, she didn't know what. Wrestling her emotions under control, she forced herself to stand still before the hearth, where the warmth of the fire washed over her. She could not send to Thendara for Lady Arielle or any of the other matrix workers at Hali Tower, not at this season. Scathfell had no *leronis*, but Aldaran, their nearest neighbor, might. Kyria had said that Lady Renata, Edric's mother, had trained at a Tower. And there was Edric himself, Edric who had reached her in the Overworld when her disembodied spirit wandered there. Edric who had brought her back to the world of the living. *I do not know if he or any man—or woman, for that matter—has the power to heal Dimitra, but if I do not ask, she will surely die.*

The problem was going to be the asking. Even if she could get a message to him, would Gwynn permit him to come to Scathfell? And if Gwynn invited him, would Edric place himself in the power of his old enemy for the sake of a woman he did not know?

— ✦ —

Alayna found the men's parlor deserted, except for the servants sweeping the floor and returning the furniture to its usual arrangement. Not a trace remained of the food and drink. Within the hour, everything would be as if the evening's concert had never happened. And if Dimitra died, she wondered, would life at Scathfell go on just as if *she* had never existed?

Alayna made her way to Gwynn's quarters. The hour was now so late that he must have retired to his private sitting room. As she approached his door from the hallway, she heard his voice, muted, and then Ruyven's. *Ruyven. Of course. Ever the faithful friend in times of distress.*

Gwynn and Ruyven looked up from where they sat, chairs facing one another on either side of the fireplace. A goblet sat before Ruyven on the little table, undoubtedly wine left over from the evening's gathering, but Gwynn cradled his in one hand. Ruyven got to his feet and bowed to Alayna, the salute of a high ranking counselor to his lord's wife. Gwynn remained as he was.

"My lady," Ruyven said, "what news? How fares *Domna* Dimitra?"

The enormity of what she was about to attempt dampened Alayna's courage. "She's not at all well, I'm afraid."

"I'm sorry to hear that," Gwynn said.

Taking a seat, Alayna related how Tarva had come from the village at Zefano's behest. Gwynn's expression turned grave when Alayna came to the diagnosis. "Tarva has only a midwife's skill, but she has seen cases like this before. Although she ordered a sleeping draught and can prepare others to ease Dimitra's pain, she offers nothing in the way of hope."

For a long moment, no one spoke. Then Gwynn said, "Dimitra hid her illness so well, and she was so skillful at carrying out her duties, we must not blame ourselves for not having suspected."

"Yes, and we were away in Thendara for a long time," Alayna said. "I never asked if she wanted to come with us. I blame myself for not noticing how ill she was."

"You had your own troubles to contend with, my lady," Ruyven said. "If this disorder, this *cancer*, is as Tarva describes, then it is entirely possible that no treatment would avail Dimitra."

"No ordinary treatment, perhaps," Alayna said, looking not at Ruyven but at Gwynn. "But there are other methods. If she had come with us to Thendara, she would have had access to the same *laran* healing that I did. Perhaps Tarva is right, and Dimitra's cancer is too far advanced to do anything except keep her comfortable as she dies. But I will not admit that there is no hope at all, not when I see in my own mirror the living proof."

Gwynn's eyes darkened, as if a shadow passed over them. "The healers of Hali Tower are powerful," he said slowly, "but they are there and we are here. Dimitra could not make the journey in her present condition, not even in high summer. If Jerana were still with us, the situation might be different. We will do what we can for Dimitra in her final days, and next spring, when the passes open again, we will send to a Tower for a replacement for Jerana. Will that satisfy you, my wife?"

Alayna sat up straighter in her chair. "We have no *leronis*, it is true. And it is also true that we cannot send to even the closest Tower in time to help Dimitra. But we have a neighbor whose household might well include someone with Tower healing skills."

"Near—? You mean *Aldaran*? I cannot believe he would send aid to us."

"When has he offered you anything but friendship?" Alayna asked. "Our wedding gift, his good wishes—his overtures at King Allart's court? Gods, if his past behavior is an indication, he will outdo himself at the chance to be of service to Scathfell."

Gwynn stared at her as if she had sprouted wings. In a quieter voice, she went on, "You have been told the healers at Hali Tower saved my life. That I would have died without their help."

"Yes . . ."

"That is not the whole truth. They tried, but they could not reach me. I had strayed into the Overworld. It was Lord Aldaran who found me there and brought my spirit back to the land of the living."

For a long moment, no one said anything.

"Think of it as a test, my husband," Alayna urged. "I know you do not trust Lord Aldaran, even with all he has done for us, but we have nothing to lose by asking. If he refuses, then Dimitra will die, just as if we had not asked. Lord Aldaran will have revealed the falsity of his words. But if he acts out of friendship, he may not only save our loyal servant but take an enormous step beyond the old feud. Is that not worth a simple request?"

"Is this what you truly believe?"

"It is," she admitted.

"And you, Ruyven? What is your counsel in this matter?"

Ruyven considered for a moment. "Lady Scathfell makes an excellent point. Even so, there are practical matters to consider. Someone would have to go to Aldaran Castle to present the request, and we have no trained Voice. An ordinary messenger cannot be entrusted with so diplomatic a mission. Even more importantly, a journey over such a distance and in weather such as this will take time. Whoever Aldaran sends, assuming he accedes to our request, may need time to prepare and, if it is a *leronis*, she may not be able to travel at speed. We must consider whether *Domna* Dimitra will survive long enough for help to arrive." Here he looked directly at Alayna.

"I—I cannot say, not being trained in healing." She glanced at Gwynn, pleading silently with him. *If it were me, you would take even a small chance . . . or you would have once.* Reading no answer in his eyes, she struggled on. "The midwife said nothing about Dimitra's passing being imminent. Instead, she mentioned the future need for a pain-numbing draught. Tonight Dimitra sleeps soundly. Let us see if tomorrow brings any improvement. I believe that if there is a chance, we must try. As you said, my husband,

Dimitra has been a member of this household for a long time. She may not have always behaved as we might have hoped, but I do not believe she has ever wished me—us— ill. And despite her single lapse," Alayna concluded, lifting her head high, "she does not deserve a death sentence, not when there is anything we can do to help her."

Gwynn set aside his goblet and held out his hands to Alayna. "You are no longer the timid girl who enchanted me at that first ball. You have grown into a lady of honor, a lady who returns service with loyalty and is unafraid to speak her mind."

Alayna slipped her hands into his and felt his fingers tighten. *If only I could tell you everything.* For the present, however, she must content herself with small victories: help for Dimitra and an opening to better relations with her sister's new family.

Gwynn gave her hands another squeeze. "Tomorrow we will see, and if the lady is not worse, I shall send to Aldaran."

"I will go, *vai dom*, if you will it," Ruyven said. He clearly wasn't happy about travel in the winter—Alayna remembered how he had complained during the journey from Rockraven—but there was no one better suited to such a diplomatic mission, and they all knew it.

"My old friend!" Gwynn exclaimed. "You never fail me."

"I am ever at your service, my lord. And now, I will take my leave and go to my own rest. I may need all my strength for tomorrow." With a bow, Ruyven left them.

Alayna felt suddenly so shy, she could not bring herself to look directly at her husband. As long as she did not, she could still hope. She heard the rustle of his garments and felt his warmth on her face, then the brush of his lips on her cheek.

"Go to bed, my love," he said in a husky voice. "I'll join you shortly."

29

Alayna rose slowly from sleep, then more rapidly as she realized she was not in her own bed. Dawn glimmered through draperies but from the wrong direction. The mattress beneath her shifted and a muscular arm clad in winter-weight linex wrapped around her, pulling her close to an equally muscular body. Half afraid that she was dreaming and would awaken alone, she rolled over. Her own nightgown had somehow become rucked up around her waist.

"Aren't you glad you stayed?" Gwynn whispered, shifting to nibble on the side of her neck.

She sighed, for a moment too caught up in the delicious sensation of his lips on her skin to speak. "I thought you joined me in my own bed."

"Mmm. I did, as you may recall, but it was too small. You agreed with me at the time."

"Ouch! I'm sore from last night."

"Sorry. Got a bit carried away." He sounded happy, if still a bit sleepy.

Like a newlywed. And I'm no better, I suppose.

Both of them had responsibilities, and hers would not wait. Much depended on how Dimitra fared this morning.

"Time for both of us to stir," Alayna said. "I've a patient to check on, and you have an estate to run. And a travel

party to get together, assuming the best. Up with you!
Ruyven will not appreciate a late start due to his lord suddenly turning into an indolent sleepy-head."

"Here's a fine thing, you schooling me on a lord's responsibility."

Alayna kissed him on the nose to prove she had not become entirely stuffy, then flipped the comforter back. She
paused at the door leading to her own bedroom. He was
already sitting up and reaching for the trousers he'd left on
the floor.

"Will you break your fast with me?" she asked.

"I'll join you for *jaco* in an hour, nothing more."

Alayna attended to her morning needs, then pulled on
her old green tunic and underskirt, and soft indoor boots.
Just as she emerged into her sitting room, Sadhi entered
through the outer door, carrying a tray with the usual
pitcher and basket of freshly baked nut rolls.

"Just *jaco* for now," Alayna said, pouring a mug and
sweetening it to her taste. "I'll want more, and a couple of
meat pastries and some soft-cooked eggs as well, in a couple of hours. This will hold me for the time being."

"*Vai domna?*"

"Yes, Sadhi?"

"We're all praying to Evanda for *Domna* Dimitra's recovery."

It had not occurred to Alayna that the servants might be
worried, especially those under Dimitra's supervision.
"That's very good of you. When she is better, I will convey
your well wishes to her."

Alayna made her way to Dimitra's chamber without a
single wrong turn. Scathfell Castle, with its twists and turns
and ancient architecture, had imprinted itself on her bones.
Dimitra was still sleeping, although a fire had been lit, and
a platter of cheese and sliced apples sat on her bedside table, proof that one of the maids had been here. Someone
had put a cap trimmed with a narrow band of lace on her
head and tucked the comforters around her body, snug under her chin.

Alayna tiptoed closer and inspected the pitcher: water,
not *jaco*, but with a pleasantly medicinal, herbal aroma.
Dimitra's breathing seemed easier than it had the night before, and regular. Her color looked better, too. Alayna

watched for a time before placing one hand gently on the older woman's shoulder.

"Dimitra, I'm sorry to wake you, but I need to speak with you."

Eyelids fluttered open. For a moment, Dimitra looked confused, her gaze unfocused. Then her eyes steadied on Alayna. "*Vai domna!*" Hands pulled at bedding. "Your pardon for this unseemly sloth. You should not have to—I should have been about my duties—"

"No, you must not get up, not yet." Alayna gently pushed Dimitra back against the pillows. "You were taken ill last night—do you remember?"

"Please, it is not my lady's responsibility to care for—"

"Nonsense. It is *exactly* my responsibility to personally ensure the well-being of the women in this household," Alayna interrupted. "Especially one who has cared for me, one who faithfully continued her duties even when her own health failed."

Dimitra flushed. "So you know."

"After you fainted last night? Did you think I would let such a thing happen and not learn the reason? We sent for the midwife from the village. Dimitra, do you understand what is wrong with you?" Alayna captured the older woman's gaze and would not look away.

"I have suspected for a time. What could I do? I know perfectly well there are no herbs for something like this, and I have never been one to put my faith in superstitions. All that was left to me was to continue my life as I have lived it, executing the tasks given to me for as long as I could, and once my strength failed and the pain took hold, to pray for a speedy end."

Feeling suddenly both helpless and angry, Alayna said, "I wish you had said something earlier. Before we went to Thendara."

"Why, would you have taken me with you? A last holiday for the dying woman? A chance to see the city, the delights of the court? To say goodbye? Of course I kept it from you. I did not—I *do not ever*—want your pity."

"No, I did not mean that, not at all. Dimitra. When I was in Thendara, I had another miscarriage, even worse than the one you and Jerana nursed me through. *Much* worse. The *leroni* of Hali Tower saved me, and I thought— They can sense sickness we cannot detect by ordinary means, and they have methods of healing far beyond the skill of a village midwife."

Dimitra closed her eyes. The lines of suffering in her face deepened. "It is too late."

"You do not know that."

"I know the distance to Thendara and the impossibility of such a journey at this season. I understand you mean well, *vai domna*, but please keep your good intentions, as well as your pity, to yourself. Let me live out the time left to me in peace."

"I will do that, but only after you have heard me out. I know perfectly well that even if you were in good health, you could not travel to Thendara over passes that are snow-blocked for the winter. Nor is there time to send some hardy messenger there and back before next year's spring thaw. But there is a place much closer—within our reach—where a Tower-trained healer might reside, one who might be willing to come here to you."

"What do you mean? What *leronis*?"

"I mean Aldaran. We have lost our *leronis*, but they may still have one among them."

Dimitra shook her head. "Lord Scathfell would never permit such a thing."

"On the contrary, Lord Scathfell has promised me that if you are well enough, and if you are willing, he will send to Aldaran, imploring their aid." Gwynn had said nothing about *imploring*, but it sounded better this way.

"He would do this for me, after everything?"

"I honestly do not know if he has agreed to do this for you or for me, Dimitra. Either way, I am not ready to give up, not when there is still hope, and *I* am willing to do this for you."

Ruyven departed for Aldaran within the hour.

The snow had stopped falling overnight, and the morning air was unseasonably mild, as if the urgency of the mission had tempered winter itself. Wrapped in her fur-lined cloak, Alayna, along with Gwynn and Perdita, and Zefano, and, it seemed, half the castle staff, stood on the steps above the courtyard to bid Ruyven and his escort farewell. Although no formal announcement regarding Ruyven's mission had been made, everyone seemed to know. Alayna found the crowd unexpectedly touching. Dimitra might not have been universally liked, but she had been an essential part of the castle household for a long time.

"How long will it take for an answer?" Alayna slipped one gloved hand into the crook of Gwynn's elbow. "I know you said a tenday, but is there no hope Ruyven might return more quickly?"

He pulled her hand closer. "If this weather holds, and if there are no mishaps on the trail, and if Aldaran welcomes him instead of clapping him into the darkest dungeon ... and if the answer is speedy, one way or another—"

"A simple answer was all I asked for," she exclaimed, laughing, "not a litany of everything that could go wrong. Please, I have enough to contend with without stuffing my head with fearful imaginings."

"I would not have you worry without cause."

"Oh, only *with* cause?"

"Then it is not *worry*, my love. It is *prudent concern*. But all the concern in the world cannot hurry travel through the mountains. I doubt we will see Ruyven before a tenday or so."

The lightness of their banter and the glint in his eyes suggested that the time might be passed very pleasantly.

—— ✦ ——

Just past midday on the fourteenth day, Alayna was sitting with Dimitra when she heard the sound of running feet and the clamor of voices in the corridor outside. She set down the book she had been reading aloud and went to the door. Shayla was there. She paused in midstride and managed a curtsy.

"'Tis *Dom* Ruyven—he's returned, *vai domna*! Word's just come from one of the valley sentries."

"Has Lord Scathfell been informed?"

"Aye, my lady. The whole castle's abuzz with it."

Alayna found Gwynn in the front hall, talking with Zefano and a man in riding leathers and soldier's cloak. "Is it true? Ruyven has returned? Is he—did Aldaran send anyone?"

"Get yourself to the kitchen for a hot meal," Gwynn handed the rider a small purse. "You have my thanks."

"My lord." With a bow, the man departed, ushered away by Zefano.

Gwynn turned to Alayna. "Be easy, my wife. Not only has our friend Ruyven yet again fulfilled his duties admirably, but the party returning with him rides under the Aldaran banner."

Relief swept through her. Edric had not refused them.

Gwynn assured Alayna that it would be the better part of a day before they could expect Ruyven and the Aldaran party to arrive. Minutes dragged on, mounting into hours with infuriating reluctance. Alayna did her best to not inflict her own impatience on anyone else. She played her *rryl* while Perdita sang, attempted to concentrate on needle-work, and delivered the news to Dimitra.

The arrivals passed through the gates just as the eastern horizon turned inky. Light still shone in the west, but in the shadows ice had begun to form. Alayna waited at Gwynn's side on top of the castle steps, Perdita standing behind her shoulder. Together they watched the riders file past, their horses blowing and lathered with a last effort to reach their destination before full night. The torches placed around the courtyard flickered in the gusting wind. First came Ruyven and his guards, two of Scathfell's finest, then a man in a cloak of Aldaran colors.

Gwynn stiffened. For a moment, Alayna was unable to believe what her eyes told her: Edric had not sent someone from his household. He had come himself.

Even before Ruyven had clambered down from his horse, Edric dismounted and bounded up the steps. He moved with surprising agility for someone who had just completed an arduous ride in freezing weather. His riding cloak flared out behind him like the wings of a gigantic bird. Reaching the topmost step, Edric inclined his head a salute proper from one lord to his equal. *"Vai dom."*

"My Lord Aldaran," Gwynn sounded overly formal, not yet quite recovered from his surprise. "If you come in friendship, you are welcome here."

"Vai dom, I do. Lady Scathfell," with a bow, then to Perdita, *"Vai damisela."*

"Thank you for coming," Alayna said. "I only hope it is not too late to help my lady-in-waiting."

Ruyven, having taken a moment to smooth his hair and straighten his cloak, approached. "Lord Scathfell, I bring a Tower-trained healer, as requested." He sounded weary.

"You have fulfilled your mission admirably, my friend." Gwynn clapped Ruyven on the shoulder. "Go to your well-earned rest. We'll talk later."

Gesturing for Edric and Alayna to accompany him, Gwynn passed through the massive double doors. "I must confess, I expected you to send your household *leronis*."

"Both my mother and I trained in a Tower," Edric replied. "Since she feels the cold more strongly with the passing of her years, the hardship of the journey ought rightly to be borne by me."

"I have not heard of the heir of any great estate studying sorcery. My own father harbored deep suspicions about the practice."

"Given our history, he had good reason. But *laran* is not sorcery, although the common folk call it so. It involves not only innate talent but discipline of mind. For those of us who possess that Gift, to neglect its mastery is to place not only ourselves but everyone around us at risk."

Alayna caught a flash of emotion on Gwynn's face and knew he was thinking of how much he had lost because of *laran*. His brother, his parents, what should have been a safe and happy childhood. Many of Scathfell's families also had cause to grieve their fathers and sons. And those were not the only ones. Dorilys—*my kinswoman, Edric's kinswoman*—had perished, as well Aldaran's own soldiers. How easily could loss turn to fear and fear to anger. But now the two families had real hope of building trust instead.

They paused in the entry hall for servants to take away their cloaks. Gwynn turned to Edric. "You must have had a hard ride to arrive so soon. Have you need of rest or refreshment?"

"Thank you for your kindness," Edric replied, "but I had better examine the patient to determine the seriousness of her condition. I understood from *Dom* Ruyven that she was deteriorating rapidly. I would have been here sooner, except one of the horses went lame."

Alayna imagined a horse and rider making their way along the side of a steep hillside covered with pockets of

snow, then going down suddenly—the horse heaving itself
to its feet, standing on three legs, the rider dusting snow
from his jacket. *How badly—? s*he started to ask before
realizing that she did not want to know if a horse, who took
no sides in any feud, had lost its life in the effort to save
Dimitra's.

"We were able to pack the leg with snow to control the
swelling, and let the horse rest for the night," Edric said, as
if he had sensed her question. "The next day, it was recovered enough to go slowly, without additional weight."

"I'm glad no greater harm was done," Gwynn said.

"Yes, we were fortunate. Cold was our ally instead of our
enemy."

"If you will follow me, Lord Aldaran," Alayna said, "I
will conduct you to my lady-in-waiting."

Edric bowed again to Gwynn, then he and Alayna hurried up the stairs, Perdita close behind. Alayna said nothing
though she longed for news of Kyria and her unborn
children—*or had they come into the world already?* But she
dared not ask while they might be overheard. Yet when she
paused at the outer door to Dimitra's quarters and glanced
up at Edric, it felt as if all her longing had risen to her eyes
and threatened to spill out.

"Perdita," she said in as clear a voice as she could imagine, "would you be so kind as to bring a basin of warm water, in case it is required?"

"At once, my lady." Perdita dropped a graceful curtsy
and hurried away.

Bending close, Edric said in a voice that was barely a
whisper, "She's well, as are our sons."

Relief and delight washed over Alayna, with an image of
Kyria lying in bed on sheets so white they glowed, her face
suffused with joy, cradling a swaddled baby on either side.
"And are you married?"

Edric gave her a look of undisguised joy. "Let's go in," he
said.

She lifted the latch. Dimitra was seated in her little sitting room, on the chair before the fire. She was fully, properly dressed, but pain had incised new lines in her face. As
Alayna and Edric entered, she made as if to rise. Her face
contorted with effort. Alayna could hear the rasping of her
breath from across the room.

"Please remain as you are, *domna*. I am Edric Aldaran, once of Tramontana Tower, and I have come to offer you my aid. That is, if you give your consent."

"*Vai dom*. I did not expect—I did not—" Dimitra tried to swallow, her throat working.

"We may not have expected Lord Aldaran to come himself, but he is here, and he is certainly qualified." Alayna poured out some watered wine and held it out to her. "No more nonsense. Edric, what do you need to begin?" If Dimitra had noticed the use of his personal name, she gave no sign.

Edric explained that it would be better if Dimitra lay down, for purposes of monitoring her and determining the exact nature and extent of her illness. Together they helped Dimitra to her feet and into the bedroom. There was no need for her to disrobe, and Alayna placed an extra pillow under her knees and tucked the comforters around her.

"Where should I stand?" she asked Edric as he brought in a straight-backed wooden chair from the sitting room.

"It would actually be better if you left us. I need all my concentration for this work. If you could—" He broke off as a tap on the outer door heralded the arrival of Sadhi. Between them, they sorted out that Sadhi would remain in the sitting room with the door closed.

"My lady," Edric began, "if you would arrange to have food sent up, that would be a valuable service. Like all *laran* work, monitoring requires a great deal of energy that must be replaced, especially if I am to attempt healing work afterward. Sweetened pastries or dried fruit and nuts, if you would, but no meat or cheese. And *jaco*, not wine."

Alayna liked the straightforward way he communicated his needs. He must have learned it at the Tower, for there was none of the arrogance, the entitlement of a great lord in the way he spoke.

Kyria, a wife and mother—two beautiful babes—

"I'm sure the kitchen can manage," Alayna said. "You'll find the *jaco* here surprisingly good. I'll go down to the kitchen," she offered, since Perdita had not yet returned.

At the bottom of the stairs, Gwynn stepped out from around a corner. She smiled at him. "It's quite wonderful, more than I—than we—hoped for," she said. "He's with

Dimitra now, with Sadhi as watchdog against castle gossip. We should have news soon."

She made as if to continue on, but Gwynn blocked her path. "You seem to be on friendly terms with Lord Aldaran. I had not realized you two spent any amount of time together in Thendara."

"Good heavens, Gwynn, don't tell me you're *jealous*! You're entirely mistaken. I never thought of him that way. Never could, given that I am a married woman. Don't you remember that he traveled with us—me and Kyria, and Ruyven as well—on our way here? We didn't know who he was at the time, of course. He said travelers keep their families and alliances to themselves, that the conditions of the trail are the real enemies, not one another. Besides, it was all perfectly proper, with Ruyven looking after us. I'm sure I told you."

"I suppose you did. Or Ruyven did. I was taken somewhat aback when Aldaran himself turned up." This was as close to an apology as Gwynn would offer, and Alayna knew not to press him. "I wouldn't have believed him that trusting, to place himself in my power," he said, adding, "or foolhardy, as the case may be. Where are you off to now, all in a hurry?"

"To the kitchen, to make sure he has something to eat when he finishes his work."

"This is why you have a companion and servants, not to go scurrying about the castle on menial errands yourself."

"In my judgment, this should not wait. Perdita's already fetching warm water, if you must know." Alayna took advantage of Gwynn's hesitation to circle around him and continue on her way. She was not surprised when he came with her. "Apparently," she said, "such work can drain the healer, and if he is able to actually treat Dimitra, we want him to be fit, don't we? Are you *expecting* something to go wrong?"

"He certainly has earned *your* friendship."

"And not yours?" Alayna stopped at the door that led to the kitchen area and whirled to face him. "He's here as your *guest*, Gwynn-Alar, and at your behest. You may have no care for the honor of Scathfell, but I most certainly do!"

To her surprise, he threw back his head and laughed. "My spitfire wife, or should I say, my conscience?"

When he leaned forward to kiss her, she did not pull away.

"I won't detain you from your duties as lady of the castle," he said. "You to the kitchen to provide what our *guest* requires, and I to Ruyven for his report. We will leave Lord Aldaran to his work."

— ✦ —

Alayna lay awake, wondering if Edric had begun, and if he had, what was going on. Time passed, although whether quickly or slowly, she could not tell. Her only measures of time were Gwynn's rhythmic breathing and the beating of her own heart. She turned from side to side, careful to not wake him. Once or twice, when her thoughts went to Edric, images of him came to mind, and she saw that his features were almost inhumanly composed. Blue light flickered across his face. Of the room beyond, and in particular Dimitra, she saw nothing.

She must have drifted back to sleep because the next thing she knew, the drapes had been drawn back to admit the brilliant morning sun. She was alone, although warmth still clung to the other side of the bed. When she got up, she found Perdita had brought hot water for washing, and had laid out the gray tunic and underdress.

"I wasn't sure you'd want breakfast, but there's fresh *jaco* in the sitting room, my lady."

"Thank you," Alayna said, slipping into the clothes. "I'd like to see if there's news about Dimitra first."

A short time later, she found Edric and Ruyven in conference with Gwynn in the men's parlor. The remains of a simple breakfast lay on the table between them. Shadows ringed Edric's eyes, and gray tinged the skin around his mouth. He wore the same clothing as yesterday, only more rumpled.

"*Vai domna.*" Edric inclined his head.

You look as if you haven't slept all night. "What news?"

"Your lady-in-waiting is indeed seriously ill, but with the blessings of the gods, not beyond hope. The tumors have spread to other areas of her body, most notably her lungs. One of these had almost blocked a major airway, which accounts in part for her lack of energy. I feared that if left unchecked, it might cause the lung to collapse. In her weakened condition, it might precipitate a crisis. Rather than risk it, I dissolved the tumor immediately."

Edric looked weary, as might any man who had undertaken a mountain journey in winter and then worked through the night.

Gwynn was saying, ". . . our gratitude for your efforts on behalf of one of our own."

Alayna felt a rush of relief so intense, it almost brought her to tears. With great effort, she maintained control. At the same time she petitioned any god who might be listening that this opening between Scathfell and Aldaran, this softening of Gwynn's anger, might be the turning point in the generation-long feud.

Over the next tenday, Alayna dared to hope that her prayers had been answered. True, Edric spent almost all his time either working at healing Dimitra or sleeping. Or eating—according to the cook, he consumed enough for several ordinary men. Gwynn seemed content to let Edric go about his work.

Work filled Alayna's days, too, especially delegating and then overseeing those tasks that were previously Dimitra's. The work distracted her from all the things she might otherwise worry about, and it also gave her a sense of satisfaction. She'd gone from visitor to bride to a chatelaine who fulfilled her responsibilities to the castle household.

She and Gwynn were finishing breakfast in his sitting room when Zefano entered with a bow. Close behind him came Edric, his features haggard with fatigue but his eyes alight, and then, moving haltingly and leaning on a cane, Dimitra.

Alayna scrambled to her feet, almost knocking over her chair. "You're well!"

"*Vai dom, vai domna.*" Dimitra's face was pale, except for two faint spots of color over her cheekbones, but she had a vitality quite unlike the wasted sallowness of before.

"It gladdens our hearts to see you recovering," Gwynn said. "Lord Aldaran, we are much in your debt."

"Lord Scathfell," Edric replied with the same formality, "it is I who owe you for the opportunity of being of service. After all, this is how friends behave."

"Indeed, it is."

"Now I must beg your leave, for my patient's strength

must not be overtaxed so early in her recovery. I am not at my best, either." He met Alayna's questioning gaze, and she understood that he had pushed on through the night to finish the healing.

Dimitra returned to her chamber, aided by a pair of maids, and when she presented herself to Alayna the next morning, she looked even more rested. Edric stayed in his quarters, undoubtedly sleeping. On the third day, Alayna allowed herself to be persuaded that Dimitra might resume light duties, and Edric bade his farewells. Politely but firmly, he refused the gifts that Gwynn wanted to give him. He was adamant that the only reward he desired was friendship between them, but he said it with such humility that Gwynn took no offense. Then he departed, trotting out of the castle courtyard into a morning of shivering clarity.

30

As Midwinter Night approached, Alayna took charge of preparing the feast and evening celebrations. Between hanging the great hall with evergreen wreaths and ribbons, ordering the meal, and arranging a proper space for dancing, Alayna realized she had no holiday gift for her husband. Nor Perdita, Ruyven, or Dimitra, although she was not strictly obliged to give them anything. Gifts for her friends were relatively easy to think of. Her clothes chest contained a spidersilk scarf perfect for Perdita. Ruyven would undoubtedly be happy with a chair cushion covered with her own needlepoint; she had a supply of those that wanted only hemming and stuffing. A small token would do for Dimitra, perhaps one of the wooden hair combs purchased in Thendara.

But Gwynn? What could she give him that would be fine enough? She didn't have time to embroider a fancy shirt, not with arranging everything for Festival Night. In truth, she owned almost nothing in the way of physical possessions that had not come from him.

The one thing Gwynn wanted she could not give him. Not this Midwinter Night nor any other. What she wanted— to be reunited with Kyria, to see Kyria's babes grow up— she could never ask for.

Thinking of Aldaran—of Edric, of Kyria—brought the image of the *rryl* that had been their wedding gift. She could play better than most, she admitted without false modesty. Although her voice was not as good as Perdita's, she could sing passably well. An idea formed: she would take a familiar melody, one within her vocal range, and set new words to it. A song composed especially for Gwynn would be something no one else could give him. As soon as she made the decision, a dance tune came to mind, the dance "Lilies and Laces." She began humming the melody and trying out one phrase or another. Soon she had devised lyrics to a verse and chorus. So pleased was she, that she went about smiling and occasionally dancing a step or two.

"My dear, something has amused you," Gwynn said as they sat over *jaco* and nut-topped custards after dinner.

"Indeed, it is something wonderful," Alayna responded, "or I hope you will find it so. But you mustn't press me for details."

"A secret, is it?" he said, his tone playful.

"I suspect that, given the season, it will be revealed in the proper time, my lord."

"Oh, ho! It's a *Midwinter* secret, is it? My spies inform me you are hard at work making everything ready."

"Then you have most effective spies," she replied. "Our Festival Night may not be as elaborate as they will celebrate in Thendara, but I hope it will be an event to remember."

Gwynn's joke reminded Alayna of his previous mention of having placed spies in Aldaran. She remembered being appalled at the time, then other things had demanded her attention and she'd thought no more about it. Now, in the warmth of her own home, with her husband in a jolly mood, her thoughts went once again to her desire for closer relation between the two Houses.

"Midwinter is a time of new beginnings," she said, carefully setting down her custard spoon. "The earth lies fallow under its blanket of snow, but every day the nights grow shorter. No matter how cold and lifeless the world seems, it is already moving toward spring."

"A pretty speech," Gwynn said, "fit for elegant ladies and courtly poets, not men of action. Take pity on me, my love, and tell me what it means."

"Only that we, too, are moving into a season of new

beginnings. We light candles in the darkness, don't we? We set aside old grievances in the spirit of fellowship."

"You have already made known your opinion on our relations with Aldaran." Gwynn's tone had lost some of its earlier gaiety, but he did not seem seriously displeased.

Even though Alayna was determined not to provoke him, and certainly not to repeat their old arguments, she could not allow the issue to pass without attempting to move reconciliation forward. "Yes, I have expressed myself, and so have you, my husband. The decision is yours, of course. But in this season of renewal, would it be so terribly wrong to send a message—nothing more, just a wish for a joyful Midwinter Festival?"

Such wishes were customary between neighbors and kinfolk. It would cost no more than a rider and horse for the journey, it would not compromise Gwynn's honor or commit him to any action. A rancorous, deceitful man might hold the messenger hostage or slay him outright, but surely even Gwynn at his most suspicious could not think that, not after Edric himself had come to nurse Dimitra. Alayna looked at Gwynn and could tell that he was weighing the possibilities and risks, just as she had done.

"Well," Gwynn said before the silence had dragged on to the point of awkwardness, "this is an excellent suggestion. As a favor to you, my dear—shall we say, your Midwinter gift?—I will dispatch a rider with that very message. If you would care to include a letter describing Dimitra's recovery, he can deliver it as well. You see, I am not such an unreasonable tyrant as all that."

"I never thought you so, I assure you." In an exuberance of relief, Alayna sprang up and took his hand. Gwynn looked pleased.

And expressed that pleasure in their bed that night.

— ✦ —

Alayna awoke on the morning of Midwinter Eve, as excited as a little girl. She put on an ordinary dress, not her holiday finery, for there was still work to be done downstairs. True to his habit of early rising, Gwynn was already about his morning. Perdita entered the sitting room, balancing a tray with its usual serving of *jaco*.

"Bless you," Alayna exclaimed, reaching for the pitcher. She took a sip and closed her eyes in delight.

If she performed half so well in Thendara, I wonder that the queen was willing to let her go. This is her home now, Alayna thought, *for as long as she wishes to remain.* Since Perdita appeared to be content in every respect, Alayna resolved to speak with her about taking on the formal responsibilities of a lady-in-waiting—not now, with the height of the holiday fervor upon the household, but soon. Dimitra would live, but would likely never recover her former vigor. Another mistress might cast her off or assign her to menial work, but Alayna was moved by Dimitra's plight and resolved to persuade her to accept a comfortable retirement.

"My lady?" Perdita interrupted Alayna's musings.

Alayna plunked the mug on the tray. "Leave that here for Sadhi. I'm off to the kitchens. I hope the cook remembered to hold off icing the spiral buns until they're ready to be served."

The cook had indeed remembered, and a bowl of icing, redolent with holiday spices, sat beside the rack of cooling buns. The baker and his assistants, some of them brought up from the village for the occasion, had been at work since well before dawn, and the kitchens teemed with activity. There was ordinary bread in sufficient quantity that everyone might eat his fill several times over. There were pies stuffed with apple or mincemeat or honeyed nuts and a great cake studded with chopped dried cherries into which had been baked a silver coin. When Marianna had described the anticipation as each child and then each adult was given a piece, everyone waiting to see who would find the coin, Alayna had raised her eyebrows. Rockraven had no such game.

Alayna had visited the kitchens on many previous occasions, but never had the place been so busy or so hot. Between the steaming cauldrons and the fireplaces, it was like a furnace. Onions simmered in savory broth. The meats were already cooking, and the aromas wafted in through the partly opened windows from the spits set up in the courtyard. The chief cook shifted from one foot to another. His eyes darted here and there, clearly trying to keep watch but still pay attention to his mistress. Alayna didn't recognize half the people there, everyone rushing about with arms filled with cooking utensils or baskets of provisions. She jumped when a girl pushed past her with only a "Coming through!" and then recognized Shayla.

Alayna set about preparing a platter of spiral buns and spreading the icing with Perdita's help. She reflected that it must have taken a good deal of persuasion to extract a pitcher of *jaco* from this madhouse, and she hoped Gwynn had already had his. At this rate, he wasn't likely to get any more.

Waving thanks to the cook and his staff, Alayna took herself, Perdita, and the tray of finished buns back upstairs. After setting the table in her own sitting room, she dismissed Perdita to enjoy her own morning. A short time later, Gwynn arrived. Alayna didn't know which she enjoyed more, the memories of her childhood or the domesticity of enjoying a holiday breakfast with her husband.

Gwynn looked up and smiled, dusting the crumbs of his second spiral bun off his fingers. "You are looking immensely pleased with yourself this morning, my love. If this delightful confection was your holiday gift for me, you have succeeded admirably."

"Thank you, but you must wait for your gift. This was shameless self-indulgence. I can't remember a Midwinter Festival at Rockraven without spiral buns. As children, we used to sneak out of bed before Father was awake and beg for our share, hot out of the oven. Of course, Cook would make a big palaver over how they must cool before they are iced. She'd make us wait, but not too long, and the buns would still be hot, so the icing would run down over our fingers. Then we'd be all over sticky and our nurse would scold us. When she stopped laughing." Some day, she hoped not too far in the future, Scathfell children would enjoy those same messy treats.

Gwynn must have an heir. Scathfell cannot go to that scorpion-ant, Nevin. And if it cannot be our own son, he must name another child, a foster son from some other, more distant kin. This was not the first time Alayna had thought of fostering or adoption, but the right time to press Gwynn on the issue had not yet presented itself. Perhaps after the holiday, when life was more normal.

Gwynn placed a small pouch of bright blue spidersilk on the table and pushed it toward her. His mouth curved in a half-smile, as if he were trying to contain his merriment and not quite succeeding.

"What's this?"

"It's a pink rabbit-horn, what do you think it is?"

"I thought *that sending the messenger to Aldaran was my gift.*" *What a dear, sweet husband I have.* "Shall I open it now?"

"Just as it is your custom at Rockraven to indulge in sweet breakfast pastries, it is ours here to exchange gifts in private."

Alayna opened the pouch to find a hair clasp of beautiful soft brown wood inlaid with bits of mother of pearl and a tracery of copper wire. The wood had a warm hue that would set off the color of her hair. He must have gotten it in Thendara back at Midsummer.

"I hardly know what to say."

"Saying you like it would be a beginning."

"I do! I like it so very much. You are too good—you will spoil me."

"No more than you deserve to be spoiled." He grasped one of her hands and lifted it to his lips.

Alayna allowed herself to linger in the moment. It reminded her of how he had been when she'd first arrived: so courteous, so romantic. Now she realized she'd been in love with him from the moment they'd met.

"Wait here." She sprang to her feet and rushed into her bedroom to fetch the *rryl*. It was still in tune, as she had rehearsed the song yesterday afternoon. As she placed her fingers on the strings, she sent a silent prayer to Evanda to sweeten her voice, so that her heart might flow through her music.

Her hands were stiff with tension, and the opening chords came out a little strained. Then the awkwardness melted.

> *Now come winter snows, the season of ice.*
> *The winds blow fierce, and low lies the sun,*
> *Cold has trapped the wings of birds,*
> *But not my heart.*

My heart lies in your keeping,
My hope and my love.

We will walk again in the wood,
scattering the dew, covered in blossoms.
We will see the rainbird in her nest.

Winter's sorrow will never come to us
In love's sweet forest.

A few times, she fumbled a chord change, and once she forgot the words of her final version and went back to the original, less graceful phrases. But it didn't matter. The lyrics danced through the soaring melody.

The song came to an end. A hush settled over the chamber. The harp strings lay still under her fingers. She glanced up at him, and his eyes were gleaming.

"That was—" His voice was thick. He cleared his throat. "No one's ever written a song for me before."

Alayna got up to set the *rryl* aside. "I've never had anyone I wanted to write a song for." She came around the table and held out her hands to him.

He took them, pulling her closer, pressing his face between her breasts. She could not have imagined such a moment. "I wish—" she whispered, "I wish I had more to give you. The world. Happiness. A son."

There. She'd said it.

He shifted her to sit on his lap and looked deep into her eyes. "Do not grieve, my love. It wasn't easy, but I have come to accept that we will not have children together. A man in my position might take a fertile *barragana* and then legitimize any *nedestro* offspring, but I would not insult you in that way. In any event, she could not bear me a Rockraven son."

"Then let us consider fostering a child that you might name your heir, but one we would raise to love and honor Scathfell as much as any natural son."

"We will consider it." He tipped her head to kiss her brow. "In due time, I promise."

Many kisses later, Gwynn went about his own business for the holiday. Alayna wrapped the last two buns in a napkin and placed them on the plate, then wrapped the wooden hair comb she'd gotten in Thendara in a pretty, embroidered kerchief, and took them to Dimitra's chamber. The older woman was sitting before a fire, a blanket across her knees and fingerless gloves on her hands. Her feet rested on a footstool and she cradled a steaming mug. By the aroma, it was not *jaco* but something with mint and honey. Alayna felt a rush of gratitude to whoever had been so considerate.

"Please don't trouble yourself," Alayna said when Dimitra started to set the blanket aside. "Anyone who comes barging in unannounced should not expect elaborate hospitality. I came to see how you fared and to wish you a joyful Midwinter."

"Thank you, my lady." Dimitra's voice was steady.

Alayna handed Dimitra her gift, waving away protests that she had nothing to give in return. She brought the other chair close, sat, and leaned forward. "Think of it as a gesture of appreciation for the good-heartedness you showed me when I first arrived. I must have looked like a puppy caught in a snowstorm, cold and wet and bedraggled, not to mention ignorant of the ways of great folk. But you treated me like a welcome guest."

And whatever happened after is not important, only your kindness.

Dimitra looked as if she were about to protest again but thought better of it.

"In any event, it was my pleasure to bring you something from Thendara," Alayna said, "since you were not able to come there yourself. Here, try a spiral bun. They were my favorite holiday treat when I was a girl, and I understand they're new to Scathfell."

On the first nibble, Dimitra's eyes brightened. "This reminds me of the little buns we had in my own home."

"Do you feel well enough to come down this evening? The great hall looks most festive, and I know Lord Scathfell would be glad of your attendance."

"Then I will come, of course."

"We are all immensely glad that you have recovered."

"I am in debt to you and Lord Scathfell for allowing Lord Aldaran to tend to me," Dimitra murmured, "given the animosity between their two realms."

"Yes, and it was gracious of Lord Aldaran to respond so generously to our request. Perhaps this will signal the beginning of a new era of friendship. Scathfell and Aldaran are, after all, kin."

Dimitra gave her a sharp look. Then, with a sigh: "Midwinter is indeed a time of fellowship. And changes."

"Yes." Alayna realized she was moving her hands in a nervous manner, practically wringing them. She clasped her fingers and forced herself to stillness. "There is something I wanted to discuss with you, speaking of changes." There was no reason to seek Dimitra's consent; as Lady Scathfell, she had the power to dismiss her or any of the women servants on a whim. But it mattered that Dimitra understand this was for her benefit, not a punishment.

"You have been ill for some time now. The last thing I intend is for you to exhaust yourself into another crisis. We must face the situation, which is that you cannot work as before and are not likely to."

Dimitra nodded. The resignation on her face aroused Alayna's pity.

"We are not savages," Alayna said, "to cast aside those who have dedicated themselves to our service when, through no fault of their own, they can no longer perform their duties. In your illness, others have taken up the necessary tasks. I have determined that they should continue to do so and that you will continue to enjoy the comfort of this, your home, for many years."

"I understand that I am being replaced as lady-in-waiting. I expected no less," Dimitra said with a tone of bitterness. "But what work am I do to, then?"

"Why, none at all! You are at leisure now."

"Like an old cart horse or a dog too stiff and blind to hunt."

"If a warm basket by the fireplace or a pasture by the apple trees is what you mean, then yes. I meant it when I said this was your home. Evanda knows this place is big enough so that you can remain here, in your familiar quarters, without the least inconvenience to anyone. When you feel well enough, you can join the women in sewing or music. I may consult with you from time to time." There was only one more thing to add: "Please do not consider this an act of charity. You have *earned* your place here. I will hear no more discussion."

To prove her point, she stood up. Her gaze slipped across Dimitra's astonished features. She headed for the door. "I'll see myself out, as I saw myself in. Be easy, Dimitra. Everyone here wishes you well."

31

The remainder of the day flew by in a flurry of last minute details. Alayna put on the gown Cassandra had given her. Perdita fastened Gwynn's moonstone necklace around her throat, and afterward dressed Alayna's hair, coiling it low on her neck and fastening it with the new butterfly clasp. Alayna sent Perdita to dress in her own holiday attire and waited in her sitting room, although she could not bring herself to actually sit down for fear of wrinkling the lovely gown.

She had not long to wait before Gwynn tapped on the door. He took her hands in his and gazed at her silently for a long moment. The light from the candles filled his eyes so that they seemed to glow with their own inner light.

Their heart-light, Alayna thought. *As mine must surely, also.*

This moment, standing here with the husband she loved—who loved her—was the best Midwinter present she could imagine.

"Shall we go down?" he asked. "We must not keep everyone waiting for their holiday feast."

As they entered the Great Hall together, the place fell silent. Everyone who was not already standing got to their feet and, as one, bowed to Lord and Lady Scathfell. Gwynn escorted Alayna to her place beside him at the head table. When she had taken her seat, he gestured for the others to do so. Ruyven sat at his right hand, and Perdita to Alayna's left. At the adjacent table were Zefano and Marianna, a handful of senior officers, Dimitra and Sadhi, and some of the more highly ranked female servants.

Gwynn lifted his goblet and, around the room, everyone did the same. In a loud voice, he welcomed them all to observe the turning of the year. "On this darkest of all nights, we look ahead to the return of the sun. To lengthening days and brightening hopes. To fellowship and fidelity."

"And fertility!" a man called from the other side of the hall, to uproarious laughter.

"Aye, to that as well," Gwynn said with clear good humor. "May our crops and herds increase, and may these strong walls and the strong arms of our men continue to protect us all."

"To Lord Scathfell and his Lady!" another man cried.

"Lord and Lady Scathfell!" filled the hall.

"Do I need to say anything?" Alayna asked, keeping her voice low.

He sat down, smiling at her. "Did you wish to?"

"No!"

"Then you may permit them to adore you just as you are."

At Gwynn's signal, the musicians struck up a fanfare and servants filed in, carrying platter after platter of festive foods. The first came to the head table, where Alayna was given her choice of meats and pastries, and nut and grain mixtures molded in fanciful shapes, root vegetables carved like flowers, and sauces savory or sweetened with preserved summer fruits.

The musicians, having finished their own meal, began playing simple holiday tunes. Here and there, folk lifted their voices and joined in, even Dimitra. Alayna knew some of the songs, but others were new to her. What the singing lacked in skill or even being on key, it made up for with enthusiasm.

Dessert—flaming, fruit-studded puddings and pies with elaborately decorated upper crusts—came and went, and still people sang. Alayna suspected that the favorite songs were repeated two or three times. Her heart warmed to see these people—*her people*—enjoying themselves. Then, as if by prearranged signal, folk all over the hall stood up to clear the tables and move them to one side.

Gwynn took Alayna's hand as a cadence announced a *promenada.* They moved through the stately paces of the dance, eyes always on each other. For a moment, Alayna lost herself in the dance, as if he and she were the only people in the entire world tonight. As if this music and these measured steps united their own prelude to lovemaking with the movement of the stars and the deep, slow movement of the earth. As if the gods danced with them and through them.

Alayna lost count of the dances, first with Gwynn and then Ruyven, who seemed in excellent spirits, and then a women's dance between Perdita and Shayla, and then—somewhat to her surprise—a reel with Zefano, and then Gwynn again for a courting dance. Perdita was dancing with one of the stable grooms, whose gray hairs suggested he was old enough to be her father, although that did not stop him from flirting outrageously with her or her from laughing just as merrily.

Gwynn escorted Alayna back to her seat. The exertion had made her thirsty, and she took a gulp from her goblet, hoping the wine was well watered. Just then, she noticed a commotion by the doors. Gwynn motioned to one of the guards standing behind the table to check what was going on. Ruyven threw himself into his seat, fanning his reddened face.

The guard bent to Gwynn's ear. Alayna could not make out his words over the laughter and the music and the clomping of heavy shoes on the floor, but she saw the change in her husband's expression. Ruyven must have seen it, too, for all traces of merriment vanished from his face.

"With me," Gwynn said to Ruyven, and strode off toward the doors.

Alayna found Gwynn, Ruyven, and the guard a little ways up the corridor, talking to a man in a rider's heavy woolen cloak and boots. Snow frosted his shoulders, and his cheeks looked painfully red. He swayed on his feet.

Poor man, to have endured cold and wind on such a night!

"—with my own eyes, *vai dom*," the rider said. "By my life, it is true."

"What is it?" Alayna cried. "What dreadful thing has happened?"

Ruyven looked as if he might be felled with a feather.

"My dear, you should not be here," Gwynn said.

"But surely," she stammered, "if this man brings word of some matter so urgent and so dire—does that not concern me as well, as lady of this castle?"

"Go back inside. Pretend nothing has happened." Gwynn grabbed Alayna's arm, his fingers digging into her flesh. She was so shocked that she allowed herself to be propelled back toward the doors.

Crossing the floor with its dancers and merry-makers, she managed to keep her head high and her smile gracious. Every few steps, someone would stop dancing long enough to sweep her a bow or curtsy, or call out, "Evanda bless you, my lady!"

She returned to the head table with her nerves in shreds and her face stiff from smiling. As she eased into her seat, Perdita, who was taking a break from dancing, leaned over. The table was empty except for the two of them.

"My lady Alayna, what distresses you?"

Whatever had happened, Gwynn was not only upset but wanted it kept secret, at least for the time being. She must not reveal what little she knew merely for her own comfort. "'Tis the excitement of the evening, nothing more," she said in as careless a tone as she could summon. She smiled at a couple—one of the cook's assistants and her young man, she thought—as they danced past. Perdita gave her a sharp, unbelieving look but said nothing more.

The next minutes stretched on into agony. Alayna smiled and waved, in between trying not to drink too much wine for fear it would lead her to drink even more in hopes of easing her feelings of apprehension. When Perdita accepted a request for another *promenada* from Zefano, Alayna was glad to be left alone. She dreaded being asked where Gwynn was.

The dancers began to thin out as the older people retired. Alayna remembered Gwynn saying that the noble family typically did the same, so the younger servants might enjoy themselves with abandon. Alayna grew more uneasy with each moment in which Gwynn remained absent.

Finally he slid into place beside her. Alayna lifted her hand to touch his arm, but his posture—so rigid, as if he were clenching his entire body like a fist—rebuffed her. When he smiled, the muscles in his jaw stood out in sharp relief. She could not recall an expression as terrifying as that smile, not since Francisco had brought news of Kyria's death.

The dance ended and still Gwynn did not even glance in her direction. Perdita returned to the table and begged leave to retire for the night. Ruyven came back in but did not take his place at Gwynn's right hand. He bent over and murmured, "My lord, everything has been done as you commanded."

Gwynn turned to Alayna and held out his hand to help her to rise. She slipped her fingers into his, feeling the tension in his muscles and a chill on his skin. Some of dancers paused to call out, "A good Festival Night to you, my lord!" and "Blessed Night!" while others continued on in their round.

Gwynn led Alayna from the great hall, Ruyven following close behind. "Since *Damisela* Perdita has already retired for the night, and you cannot go wandering about the castle unescorted on Midwinter Eve, I will take you to your chambers. Then Ruyven and I have more investigations—more business to conduct."

"Business? Investigations? Tonight?" Alayna dug her feet in and spun around to face him. "Gwynn-Alar, stop right there and tell me what is the matter! You have been in a—a *mood*—ever since that rider arrived. I cannot imagine what news has upset you so. Is the valley under invasion by rabbit-horns? Or has King Allart dispatched an army to occupy the castle?"

His expression, which had lightened with her teasing, darkened. Open-mouthed, she let her arms fall.

Sweet Cassilda, have I stumbled on some terrible truth?

"*Vai dom*," Ruyven said, glancing from Alayna's face to Gwynn's, "your lady has done nothing to cause this situation and therefore bears no responsibility for it. Painful as it must be, she has the right to know. You know I speak from love for you both."

"Whatever it is, my husband, we will face it together," Alayna said.

Gwynn nodded. "There speaks a loyal wife. But this is a

difficult and complicated matter, one best not discussed while standing in a corridor. Let's take this conversation to my sitting room. Ruyven, have wine sent up, and *jaco* if any is to be had at this hour, and then join us."

Shortly thereafter, Alayna sat in her accustomed place beside Gwynn's hearth. He himself stood gazing into the banked fire, his back rigid.

"My messenger returned from Aldaran," he said, "the same one I sent with wishes for Midwinter Festival. He duly delivered the greeting, was given the same to bring back to us, and enjoyed the hospitality of that household. While there, he made contact with the man I had secretly placed some years ago, and he had the opportunity to observe certain things with his own eyes."

Gwynn fixed his gaze upon Alayna. "My dear, you must prepare yourself for a startling revelation. Your sister is alive."

Alayna had such mixed feelings, she hardly knew how to respond. She felt a rush of relief at no longer needing to hide the truth from him. At the same time, his tone and the furrows between his brows made her feel uneasy.

"She not only lives, she is married *di catenas* to Lord Edric Aldaran." Gwynn's voice was so tight, the words came out as growl. "And she has borne him healthy sons. Not one, but two. Twins."

Now he was staring at her, waiting for her response. She must say something, anything. "I am so glad the report from the Sain Erach bandits was a lie. And now she has a comfortable home and a fine husband who loves her and children—what a happy ending to that adventure. I cannot imagine a better."

"Can you not?"

"Now that you have made peace with Edric," Alayna rushed on, her heart sinking in the growing realization that nothing she could say would change his mind, "we can invite Kyria here as soon as her babes are old enough to travel—or we can visit her there. That will bind the two families together even more strongly. Surely we have cause for celebration?"

"You don't see it, do you? My poor, sweet Alayna. Kyria was the Rockraven daughter I bargained for. If she had been my wife, those would now be *my* sons."

"You have a wife now—*me*. And Kyria is married to someone else. So what if it wasn't what you planned? The bond my sister and I share can be the basis for a new closeness between Aldaran and Scathfell."

"How can I be—" his mouth twisted, "—*friends* with Edric Aldaran now?"

"It will take time, but you and Edric will come to trust each other as Kyria and I do."

Blood rushed to Gwynn's features. The tendons of his neck stood out. "You *knew*," he snarled. "You conspired with my enemies to keep this from me. And all the while, your sister was in Aldaran's clutches."

"I did," Alayna admitted, with each moment even more dismayed at the change in him. "Kyria came to me in Thendara when I was so very ill. She asked me to keep her confidence. I regret having to keep anything from you, but I had given my word to my sister. I was the one who begged Edric to rescue her from Sain Erach, and so he has done. And he married her, which cannot be undone. I can assure you, she was happy with the match. If they chose not to inform you, it was with good reason, given your present reaction."

The moment she spoke the last sentence, she regretted it. How could she be so thoughtless as to chide him for being upset when his long-nurtured plans for Scathfell's security had been thwarted, and then to find out she had deceived him?

I cannot give him the sons he so badly wanted, but I thought we had made our peace with that. Now she wondered if he might regret marrying her.

Gwynn took a step toward her, jaw clenched, hands in tight fists. He no longer looked like the man she had come to love, but the ruthless tyrant. In her memory she saw Francisco on his knees, face pale, stumbling through the news of Kyria's death—Dimitra in hopeless tears—

Just then, Ruyven entered, bearing several bottles of wine and three goblets, which he set down on the side table. Gwynn turned his back on Alayna, his gaze fixed on the fire, while Ruyven filled a goblet and placed it in his hand. Alayna refused, but Ruyven poured a small portion for himself.

Gwynn tipped his head back, downed the wine, and held

the goblet out for more. Ruyven complied, his expression unreadable.

He feels cheated. Betrayed. Ruyven will help calm him down, but in the meantime, I must not provoke him further.

With as much poise as she could muster, Alayna got to her feet. "It's very late, far too late to consider a matter of such importance," *and emotionality.* "Shall we continue our discussion on the morrow—or, given the holiday—when we have had a chance to give proper thought to it?"

Still not looking at her, Gwynn picked up the opened bottle. "Do what you damned well please!"

Alayna stiffened as if he had struck her. She sent a wordless appeal to Ruyven, who had barely touched his own half-goblet of wine. He met her gaze with an expression that said, *I'll look after him.*

32

There was no point in waiting up for Gwynn, since he would likely be up until the small hours of the morning, drinking with Ruyven. In the stories her brothers told, that was what men did—drink and carouse.

Alayna could not lie still. She threw off her covers, then found herself shivering and pulled them back on, over and over until the linens were in a hopeless tangle. Finally, she got up and, wrapping the outer comforter around herself, began to pace her chambers.

Let the wretched man drink himself sick, for all I care. He'll come out of it eventually, and then he'll see reason.

At last, chilled and so tired she kept bumping into furniture, she tumbled back into bed. She tried to fix her thoughts on the reunion with Kyria, but they kept slipping away . . .

And then she opened her eyes, and it was morning. The maids must have come in, for a fire emanated gentle warmth, a handful of sweetly aromatic incense had been added to the logs, and its aroma blended with the smell of *jaco*. The water in the ewer on the washstand was still warm. Alayna washed her face and hands, dabbing at her eyes. Despite the evidence that she had indeed slept, her lids burned as if she'd lain awake, weeping, all night. Perhaps the best strategy would be to avoid Gwynn until she looked more composed. She pulled off her nightgown and scrambled into her chemise and woolen stockings, then the old gray tunic and underskirt, and her low fur-lined boots.

Perdita came in a few minutes later, sleepy-eyed. "My lady," she said sympathetically after taking one look at Alayna's face. "I have been neglecting my duties shockingly." She fetched combs and brushes, and set to work.

"I didn't want to disturb your holiday rest for something so unimportant," Alayna said, then cried, "Ouch!"

"You see how *unimportant* this is?" Perdita teased, but she used the comb more gently. "It will take half the morning to set this to rights."

Alayna blinked back tears, hoping that Perdita would assume they were from having her hair yanked. "There is no hurry. The work of cleaning up from last night will still be there. Tell me, was all the fuss worth it? Did you enjoy yourself?"

"I did indeed, more than I did in years past at court. Here at Scathfell I can dance to my heart's content and not worry about hateful, small-minded gossip regarding who favored me and who did not."

Alayna closed her eyes. *Gwynn will be all right. It was a difficult night for him. He would never act on a rash, drunken impulse.*

"Lady Alayna?"

She came back to herself. Perdita had stopped brushing and was peering into her face. "I'm sorry, I think I drifted off to sleep. Sitting up, no less. Did you ask me something?"

Perdita smiled in that sweet, gentle way of hers. "Nothing of any significance. Now, will you break your fast?"

At the thought of food, Alayna's stomach clenched. "I must have eaten enough last night to last a grown man for a tenday. Just *jaco*, I think, while it's still warm."

Perdita brought her a mug, sweetened as Alayna preferred. She drank it without really tasting beyond the first few sips. Then they went downstairs together to assess the condition of the Great Hall. Zefano was busily coordinating the clearing away of furniture and the cleaning of floors, and a number of other activities Alayna could not discern in the bustle.

A man, so rough-faced and burly that surely he must have come up from the village for the event, hefted the boards of a trestle table single-handedly. The ends wavered, swinging perilously close to Perdita's head. Alayna grabbed her friend and pulled her out of harm's way. "Watch out—" she cried.

"Out of the way!" he boomed as he strode away.

A slender figure, clad in black, placed herself in front of him. "You numbskull!" she cried in a tone that would have pierced stone. "You almost knocked Lady Scathfell's head off."

Dimitra?

The man let the boards slip from his grasp. They fell with a clatter. Dimitra had already turned away, summoning two other men. "Here, help this blockhead to carry things properly. And you—" with a stern look at the poor man himself, "next time use what passes for your brains instead of just your muscle."

Alayna watched as the three men picked up the boards, with one on each end for control, and just as carefully carried them away.

When Dimitra turned back to Alayna, she was smiling. "My lady, it's safer for you to not stand in the exact center of the room."

Alayna allowed herself to be escorted to a quieter corner, Perdita close behind. Only then did Alayna notice that Dimitra was not using her cane. The older woman still looked fragile, but less pale.

"What are you doing here?" Alayna asked.

"This?" Dimitra gestured at the bustle with a trace of her old energy. "This is *entertainment*. You don't think I'd pass up a chance to order everyone around? Besides, there's a way of doing this, and Zefano knows only half of it. Never fear, I'll stop before I've worn myself to a thread. But what brings you down here, *vai domna*? Is there anything you need?"

"Only to be of use," Alayna said, although clearly there was nothing she could do, short of snatching up a washing bucket and brush.

"It is not customary," Dimitra said, "at least not here at Scathfell, for the lady of the castle to concern herself with putting things to rights after such a night. 'Twas more than enough that you helped with decorations and special treats."

"I want to know everything about running this household," Alayna said with a lift of her chin.

"And so you shall, if that is your wish." Dimitra's tone softened. "I am not trying to thwart your interest, *vai domna*. I will explain everything I know, all the procedures that were passed down or put into place during my time here. Next year, we can work together, should Avarra spare me that long."

Alayna could see what a difficult time Zefano would have had without Dimitra's help. "That will do nicely," she said.

Dimitra inclined her head in a graceful salute.

— ◆ —

Once Alayna and Perdita returned to her quarters, there seemed to be little else to do except burden the kitchen with a request for more *jaco*, but Alayna didn't want more *jaco*. She wanted what she could not have—for a loving and penitent Gwynn to sweep through the door, beg her pardon for last night's scene, and cover her with kisses.

"How shall we amuse ourselves this afternoon?" Perdita asked after they had sat in silence for a time. "Shall I read to you while you sew? Or shall I bring your *rryl*?"

Kyria's harp. Alayna's heart gave a curious jerk. "I will sit by the fire and rest my eyes, if you will sing to me."

Perdita settled Alayna in her favorite chair, feet on a padded stool, lap robe tucked around her knees. Then she began to sing an old lullaby about a woman who loved the sea and the fisherman who loved the woman. Perdita sang it simply, with only a trill here and there to accent the melody's minor key.

Tears trickled down Alayna's cheeks. She became aware that Perdita had stopped singing. After a moment, Perdita said, "Something troubles you."

"It's nothing, really. I'm still wrought up from last night, that's all."

"Something happened, more than the usual holiday ruckus. You may say it is none of my concern, and that is your right. I must respect your privacy, but I am well aware that Lord Scathfell stormed out of the Great Hall and you went after him. Nor were matters perfectly serene between you when you returned."

Gwynn must be the one to reveal Kyria's existence, but Perdita already suspected something was amiss between them, and that much, Alayna felt she could confide. "My husband . . . got very drunk last night."

"Midwinter is a time of excess, a night of intoxication and oblivion. How else could we—or our servants—bear the rest of the year if we did not have this one night to forget? Midsummer Festival is even worse, especially when all four moons are in the sky. 'Tis said that nothing said or done then should be remembered. Nevertheless, nine months later, there is a flood of babes, many of whom bear no resemblance to their mothers' husbands."

"We heard stories of such things when I was growing up. By comparison, our family celebrations were restrained."

"I told you we Thendara folk are degenerate," Perdita replied with a dimpled smile. "So, you see, your husband's indulgence only indicates his attempts to copy our elevated style."

"It was his—the way he was when he—he frightened me."

"His drunkenness?"

Alayna nodded. "I suppose you are right, and I really am terribly naïve."

"Or fortunate, to have so little experience with the effect wine can exert over a man's mind, not to mention his morals." Perdita's tone gave Alayna the feeling that she spoke from experience. "But men do indulge themselves at holiday time, and what they say and do can be . . . extreme."

"Terrifying."

"Yes, that. He did not . . . did he strike you?"

"No." Alayna was horrified. Why would Perdita think such a thing? *Had—oh gods—had it happened to her?* "No," she repeated, more calmly, "he only shouted. And glowered at me. And was stubborn."

"Of course he was. That is how men behave when they have consumed more wine than is good for them. But do not take it to heart. Your husband is no better or worse than any other man. You certainly did nothing to cause his excess."

At this, Alayna burst into tears. Perdita, alarmed, would have rushed to her, but Alayna waved her off, stammering in between sobs, "I'm all right—just—let me—"

The spasm of weeping passed as rapidly as it had come.

Alayna accepted the handkerchief Perdita held out to her. "Well, that's over with," Alayna said with a sigh. "You must have had lots of experience with this—" With a wave of her hand that could mean anything from Midwinter Festival to drunken husbands to tearful wives.

"I have had the benefit of the wisdom of those who have gone before me," Perdita replied, taking back the sodden handkerchief. "Queen Cassandra always says—"

"Blessed Cassilda. Don't tell me that King Allart—?" Alayna could not bring herself to imagine that dignified monarch in the same state of inebriation as her husband.

"Him? Goodness, no! He was once a *cristoforo* monk, you know."

Alayna stared, dumbfounded.

"Ah, I see you have not heard the tale," Perdita said. "Here, let me arrange for something to eat, and then I will tell it, at least as much as I know and have leave to say. There are a hundred stories about him in Thendara, you know, more than enough to fill the hours until the drink wears off and Lord Scathfell is himself again."

It was as good a way to divert her thoughts as any, Alayna thought, and soon found herself engrossed in the tale.

Toward the end of the afternoon, Dimitra came in. "*Vai domna*, the eating and cooking utensils have been cleaned and polished, and await only your counting before being put away."

Alayna had never heard of such a thing. Clearly, this was one of the responsibilities of the lady of the castle.

"Should I change?" she asked, having no idea how formal an occasion this might be. Her old gray outfit, decent but shabby, might be taken as an insult.

"My lady may of course do as she pleases, but the Counting is a traditional ritual."

"Counting?" Alayna asked as Perdita helped her into the russet tunic and underskirt. Dimitra seemed quite content to let Perdita assume the duties of a lady-in-waiting. Sadhi had not yet made an appearance, presumably because she was still at work, cleaning up from last night. "More than just the spoons?"

"Indeed, yes. The good porcelain, and the serving dishes, and the knives."

"Why—?" Alayna answered her own question. *Because the entire household, plus Aldones knows how many villagers, were in and out. How easy it would be to tuck a precious metal implement into a tunic or the top of a boot.* Loyalty bought only so much honesty, and the villagers and farmers had been bearing the cost of Gwynn's army for far too long.

Damn the army. She should have said something before this. There had been enough opportunities. But Gwynn was now so incensed by the news from Aldaran, any mention of the subject, anything that might be interpreted as a criticism, would only provoke him needlessly. *I must be patient and hope for a way through this mess.*

Dimitra nodded approval of Alayna's appearance, including the butterfly clasp from Gwynn that anchored Alayna's coiled hair at the base of her neck.

The three women proceeded downstairs, and Alayna laid a hand on Dimitra's arm as they approached the kitchen. "Tell me what I am to expect."

"The dishes, implements, and also a collection of ornaments that are used only for Midwinter will be laid out on tables for your inspection," Dimitra explained. "As the Great Hall is cleared, all these things are carried into the kitchen, where they are washed and polished, as may be required, and any damaged items set aside. Guards are posted to ensure that nothing leaves until it is counted. *Mestre* Zefano will meet us there, and he will record your approval and see to it that everything is placed in appropriately safeguarded storage."

"Am I required to actually count the forks and knives?"

"It is customary. And a good practice, I think, not to rely entirely upon servants, however trusted."

Alayna inclined her head and led the way to the kitchen.

The guard outside the door looked as if he'd been on duty since the beginning of Midwinter Eve. Alayna decided against asking him when he'd last had anything to eat. This was his post, an honorable one. She merely nodded to him as she walked past.

The kitchen had been scrubbed spotless. Tables, perhaps the very trestle boards that had almost given her a whack on the head, had been set up in the middle and covered with snowy cloths. Servants—the cook and kitchen staff, maids like Sadhi, and others Alayna didn't know—stood around the periphery of the room. Zefano, record book and marking sticks in hand, waited at the head of the longest table. And there they were, row after row of gleaming implements, stacks of plates, and knives of every possible shape and form suitable for cooking. Short ones, pointed ones, forked ones, curved ones, blunt-tipped ones. Alayna suspected that if a fighting knife or two had been added, she wouldn't recognize it.

"*Vai domna.*" With a bow, Zefano indicated where she was to begin.

The process really wasn't difficult, she thought as she worked her way down the first row. She wasn't expected to name anything, just count it. The items had been arranged in order, so that all Zefano had to do was check off the number. The first time she picked up an eating utensil that was utterly baffling, a sort of corkscrew-shaped fork, he smiled and made a mark in his ledger.

The Counting took well into the evening, and when it was done, Alayna felt as if she knew the front, back, top, and bottom of every plate, eating implement, and cooking utensil in the castle. Although she was weary from standing so long, focusing on first one and then another article, she was glad she'd done it. These things were hers, just as these people were hers.

— ✦ —

Not even the cheerful sitting room fire could entirely dispel the sense of encroaching night. A platter of cheese, cold meat, and yesterday's bread waited for Alayna. Because the kitchen staff hadn't had any rest between the preparations and then washing up and getting everything ready for the Counting, she was content with a simple meal. She hoped they weren't too exhausted to make their own dinners.

The best, perhaps the only way, to enjoy such a meal was to share it. A picnic—on Gwynn's floor or hers, before the fire, yes. She went into her bedroom to the door that led to his and tapped. There was no answer. He might be out and about in the castle, although what that might be, she couldn't guess.

I'll just make sure he has something to eat when he returns.

The latch lifted easily. She could make out rumpled

bedcovers, but no Gwynn. He'd slept, then. An odor clung
to the air: stale sweat and wine from last night's drinking.

Alayna moved toward the sitting room, stepping carefully and silently, although she did not know why. They had
gone back and forth between each other's bedchambers
many times. Yet when she placed her hand on the latch of
the connecting door, her nerve almost failed her. She could
not escape the feeling that she was doing something forbidden. That was nonsense, of course. She had every right to
see how Gwynn fared after last night.

Alayna closed her fingers around the latch. It lifted with
a jerk. "Gwynn? Gwynn darling, are you there?"

The sitting room held the same faintly sickly odor as the
bedchamber, and was as empty. The hearth held nothing but
ashes, and the only light came from three candle stubs, gut-
tering as their wicks drowned in pools of wax. One chair lay
on its side beside a heap of empty wine bottles, at least it
looked like a heap. More than a couple, of that she was
certain.

—— ✦ ——

With each passing day, Alayna longed for and dreaded the
moment when she would encounter her husband again. She
refused to demean herself by hovering around his quarters
like a lovesick, abandoned bride, yet she found herself lingering where he might pass. Her pride led her to disguise
her intentions as she prowled the corridors. She did not
want his absence—or their estrangement—made public.

I've got to stop obsessing about where my husband is,
Alayna thought as she made her way back to her chambers. *There is a perfectly rational explanation for why I haven't seen him—why he's been avoiding me—and I'll find
out in time. But meanwhile, this is ridiculous—infuriating—
childish—*

She came to a halt just as the outer door to Gwynn's
quarters opened and Ruyven stepped through.

"Good heavens," she said.

"My lady," he responded.

Alayna recovered herself. "Ruyven, it's good to see you
again. I hope you've been well."

He didn't look well, for all that he was dressed with his

usual elegance, every ornament in place. His eyes were red and a spiderwork of blood vessels ran along his nose.

"I'm tolerably well, thank you," he said. His voice held a slight hoarseness. "How can I serve you, *val domna*?"

"You can tell me where my husband is."

For an instant, his gaze flickered toward the door. She made as if to move past him toward it. He stepped neatly to block her path.

Alayna reined her temper under control. "Is he in there?"

"He is indisposed and does not wish to be disturbed."

"Did he tell you that, himself? Or are you playing watch-dog for some purpose of your own?"

That set him back on his heels. "My lady, I would never—" She took advantage of his moment of confusion to reach for the latch. "Please do not."

"*Why not?* What is going on that you are so deter-mined—or should I say, so desperate—to keep from me?" Without waiting for his answer, she jerked the latch open and strode into Gwynn's sitting room.

Darkness shrouded the room, except for the glow of a dying fire. The light gleamed faintly on the rounded edges of wine bottles, strewn here and there. The stench hit her like a nauseating wave, rank and sickly. Her stomach roiled and she clasped her hands over her mouth, struggling to keep from retching. She'd smelled it before, only now the reek of many-days-old sweat added to the rest.

She would have rushed from the chamber right then, ex-cept that Ruyven had followed her. He touched one shoul-der, and she spun around. His expression, what she could make out in the uncertain light, was not unkind. He held up both hands, clearly meaning to reassure her that he meant no harm.

"My lady, you should not be here."

I have the right to know where my husband is and what he has been doing. But she knew what he had been doing. She wondered if he'd sobered up in between.

With an effort, she took her hands away from her mouth. "Where is he?"

"He is not here."

"Yes, I can see that."

Ruyven regarded her with a flat, level gaze. She controlled the impulse to shake the answer out of him. He wasn't going to tell her. Of course not. His fiercest loyalty had always been to Gwynn.

There was no point in asking if Gwynn was all right. If he'd been drinking himself into a stupor, he wasn't. But Ruyven would not let him come to any harm. She must content herself with that, and preserve what fragile alliance had grown up between her husband's man and herself.

33

Perdita joined Alayna for breakfast, as had become their custom, and afterward the two of them embarked on a tour of the castle, searching for a space Alayna might claim as an office. If she were to fulfill her duties as chatelaine of the castle, she needed someplace other than her own sitting room. Dimitra suggested a long-disused chamber that still had a working fireplace and was not too distant from Zefano's own workplace. Under dust-laden drapings, Alayna discovered a desk, old fashioned but usable once the wood was oiled, with drawers and compartments for scrolls and writing implements, as well as several book cases that still bore ledgers. The pages were brittle and discolored with age, and the writing had faded to illegibility.

Over the next tenday, Alayna cleaned her new office and set it in order. She could have had the servants dust and polish, but this place was to be hers. Back at Rockraven she knew her way around a bucket of soapy water and a scrub brush as well as any of them. She borrowed an old gown from one of the kitchen maids, tied a headkerchief over her hair, and set to work. Perdita joined her, similarly clad. It quickly became apparent that, despite her attempts at secrecy, half the castle — the female half — knew what she was up to. One or another of them would peek in, sometimes with the excuse of a trivial question or in response to some errand she could not remember sending them on, and would just happen to have a jar of furniture polish or a pile of clean rags. Somehow, in the process of explaining the forgotten errand or setting down the rags, the maid or scullery maid would pitch in.

Dimitra arrived with two kitchen maids, bearing pitchers of *jaco* and platters of cheese and toasted nut-bread as an afternoon repast. Alayna set aside her polishing rags and rinsed her hands in the bucket of soapy water. The maids set down their trays on the desk, which was still covered by an old sheet.

"Whose chamber was this?" Alayna asked, in between bites of toast and sips of *jaco*. "And what was it used for?"

"I believe this was once Lady Scathfell's study," Dimitra said, waiting politely for Alayna to help herself to toast. "The mother of old *Dom* Rakhal, who was *Dom* Gwynn's father."

"His grandmother, then?" Alayna broke off at the sound of men's voices. One voice was very loud and very angry, and clearly Gwynn's.

The next moment he burst into the room, Ruyven a pace behind. His face was flushed, and his hair every which way. He halted, directing a wintry glare at first one and then another of the women. "What in Zandru's seven frozen h*ells* is going on here?"

"Housekeeping," Alayna replied without moving from her seat. "And a snack. Would you care for some *jaco*?"

"Who gave you leave to yoosh—use—this chamber? 'Sss—it's my *grandmother's*!"

Alayna could not see Dimitra's face, but Perdita's, in profile, turned very pale. She wanted to smack Gwynn for terrifying the poor child. "I was not aware I needed your permission to tidy a room that clearly had not been looked after. It's not as if it were already in use. However, I see that my actions have upset you. I—"

"Sh—stolen everything that'sh mine." Gwynn reeled.

Ruyven moved to his lord's side. "*Vai dom*, these women are not your enemies. See, here is your loyal wife and her friend, and *Domna* Dimitra, who has served this house long and faithfully."

"Loyal? *Loyal?*" Gwynn made as if to strike his friend,

but Ruyven avoided the blow handily and took Gwynn firmly by the elbow. "Thrice-damned *traitors*—" Alayna was too shocked to follow exactly what was said, but somehow Ruyven got Gwynn under sufficient control to guide him from the room.

Dimitra rushed to the door and locked it. The key itself, when she pressed it into Alayna's hand, felt cold.

"What does it mean?" Perdita asked in a small voice. She had clearly not yet recovered from her fright in the presence of a very angry, very drunken man, one who had not only tremendous personal physical strength but the power to hang any of them from the battlements. "Why does Lord Scathfell speak of traitors?"

Alayna glanced down at her hands, somewhat surprised they were not trembling. "He didn't know what he was saying." But he had known and had meant it.

"If our efforts here have become a subject of discord," Alayna said, "then we must set them aside for the time being."

Dimitra gave her a curious look and said, "If that is your wish, *vai domna*."

— ◆ —

Alayna judged that it would not be wise to approach Gwynn until he'd had time to sober up and hopefully have a decent meal. Over the next days, she kept an eye out for him. She did not want to appear to be searching for him or, gods forbid, spying. *Sneaking and skulking*—she could imagine his accusations and how his anger would ignite like pitch-pine in fire season. She wasn't sure how to appear *not-sneaking* and *not-skulking* and settled for walking slowly but not too slowly, head high, her smile gracious when there was any occasion that warranted it. In her mind, she practiced what she would say to Gwynn if she encountered him in this corridor, going up those stairs, or in that chamber.

My dear, how lovely to see you again. I've missed you.

He'd never believe that, not even if Aldones Lord of Light descended from the heavens and told him so.

Gwynn! Hello, it's been a while.

And then he'd hear, even if she did not say it, *Where have you been? I demand to know!*

Likely, she'd just stand there, maybe summon a curtsy if

she could manage one without tripping over her own feet,
and wait for him to speak. *My wife,* he might say.

My husband.

You're looking well.

Yes.

The weather has been very fine for this season.

Yes.

Shall we go down to dinner?

If it pleases you, my lord.

Sometimes the imagined conversations would break
down into frantic kisses and avowals of undying love, but
even Alayna at her most romantic understood how impossible that would be. The best she could hope for was an
exchange of perfectly polite, perfectly insipid phrases.

Fine weather.

Yes.

As best she could, Alayna went about her business. On
sunny mornings, she sat with her ladies in the solarium, sewing and making music. She spoke with the cook about the
day's menu, and she consulted with Zefano about the various stores of food; she and Marianna counted linens and
inventoried the various herbal tinctures used for healing.
Zefano found her a bound blank book in which to keep a
journal; it had probably been intended as a lady's diary
from a generation or so ago, when such things were fashionable, or so Perdita told her during one of their after-dinner
meetings.

On one of these occasions, the two friends had exhausted
the day's supply of castle gossip—Shayla had caught the
eye of one of the guards, and he, hers—and fell silent.
Alayna could not stop wondering how long this separation
from her husband would last. Men did return to their real
selves, didn't they?

But which was the real Gwynn—the captivating host and
passionate lover she had given her heart to? Or this brood-
ing stranger in whom vengeance festered like an unhealed
wound? The man who had spent his entire life in readiness
for war?

"Perhaps you will have your meeting tomorrow, my
lady," came Perdita's gentle voice, "and then all will be well,
or at least on the path to being mended."

In a flash, it came to Alayna that their marriage could

not be mended—*Gwynn* could not be mended—until he gave up this insane feud. She wondered how he could ever stop hating Aldaran for the deaths of his parents and brother, and then feeling cheated by the loss of Kyria and the sons he'd hoped for.

"I hope that may be so," Alayna said, struggling to mask her thoughts, "but if not, we will all continue as best we can. At least, winter's worst is behind us. Zefano said that the weather will soon be fine enough to permit a day's outing."

Perdita's expression brightened. "We arrived so late last year, I've had little opportunity to explore the lands hereabout. I am not a great rider, as you know, but even so, I would like to see more of the valley and its folk."

"Then we shall visit them together," Alayna promised. It was high time she took an interest in the farmers and herding folk, as well as the villagers. The fields where the army camped, she could cheerfully avoid.

The notion was so appealing, so lifting to Alayna's spirits, that she had no difficulty in falling asleep at the proper time. On this night, as on many others, she heard voices, Gwynn's and Ruyven's, coming from his sitting room. She no longer tried to make out what they were saying. With the latch on her side of the interconnecting bedroom door firmly jammed, she left them to their own.

She jerked awake at the sound of tapping. Darkness still shrouded the room and the air was chill; as near as she could judge, given the sleep-befuddled state of her mind, it lacked several hours until dawn. Holding her breath, she listened. The sound came again, from the door leading to her own parlor. Grabbing her dressing robe, she made her way across the room.

Dimitra stood there, holding a branched candelabrum. "I'm sorry to disturb you at this hour, *vai domna*."

Alayna made a dismissive gesture. Whatever had gotten Dimitra out of bed could not be trivial. "What's wrong?"

"*Dom* Ruyven has been injured. His servant came to me, frightened half out of his wits."

"Avarra's mercy!"

"Indeed. Will you come, my lady? According to *Dom* Ruyven's servant, he has refused to seek aid, but I think he will not deny *yours*."

"Of course, I will come." Alayna hurried back to her

bedchamber to make herself presentable, for the lady of the castle could not go rushing about in her nightgown, no matter how grave the cause.

Dimitra followed close behind. "Sometimes a calming presence is all that's needed to sort matters out. The servant may have panicked at the sight of a few bruises."

The two women hurried up a flight of stairs to the rooms occupied by unmarried men of good standing. Ruyven's quarters consisted of a sitting room, with a door leading to a small bedchamber. Alayna had only the most hurried impression of the furnishings: several elaborately carved wardrobes and an equal number of chests, a standing full-length mirror. The bed curtains had been pulled aside, not in an orderly way but rumpled. Alayna caught the sweet-tart aroma of Gwynn's best red wine.

The light of Dimitra's candles fell full on Ruyven's unconscious form. His eyes were closed, his hair was disheveled, and dark smears covered one side of his face, running down the side of his neck and chest. The front of his jacket was unfastened. Dimitra lifted one side of it and lifted the candle higher. Glistening wetness drenched one side of his neck, seeping down the front of his shirt. Alayna smelled it now, rising above the reek of the wine: that distinctive, coppery tang.

"Sweet heavens, is he—"

Ruyven himself answered her with an explosive sound that was as much a snuffling grunt. Alayna's gaze met Dimitra's; they were thinking the same thing. Dimitra shook her head, meaning that even if he were as drunk as a Comyn lord on Midsummer, the blood was real. Together they straightened him out, brought water—grown cold at this hour—and towels, and lit as many additional candles as they could find. By rolling him from side to side, they managed to extricate his arms from the jacket and slide it out from under him. It was stained along the opening, but that could not be helped. *And serve him right*, Alayna thought.

Dimitra drew out a little pair of scissors, along with a needle, thread, and an extra candle stub. She held the needle in a candle flame, threaded it, and then set it carefully on the stub.

Beginning along Ruyven's neck and proceeding downward, Alayna washed him. At any moment, she expected to discover a deep slash, perhaps still oozing blood. Ruyven shifted, occasionally muttering phrases Alayna could not make out, interspersed with ones she wished she hadn't. Carefully she cut away the shirt, peeling back the sodden strips, but still there was no discernible wound.

"I don't understand," she said at last, surveying his bare torso, lightly smeared with blood. "Where did all the blood come from? Maybe—oh, Dimitra, maybe it isn't his? Could it be Gwynn's?"

"No, I think it's his. Here, look at this." Dimitra angled the light to shine on the far side of Ruyven's head. Alayna had already washed his temple and cheek, and had not thought to look more closely. "There, under his hair."

Alayna bent over, turning his head for a better view. Indeed, there it was, an open gash in his scalp, a couple of inches above the hairline. Blood flowed sluggishly from it, soaking the pillow. "*This* was the source of all the blood? It doesn't seem possible."

"Scalp wounds bleed profusely," Dimitra observed. "This one will need to be sutured, and best to do it now, when he can't feel it. But I'm afraid my eyesight is none too good in this light."

"That's all right, I'll do it." Ruyven would be far less likely to complain if she, Lady Scathfell, had mended his cut with her own hands.

After wiping the area around the gash, Alayna took up the threaded needle. The skin was more like leather than fabric, and it took more effort than she expected to force the needle through, especially when the oozing blood made the needle slippery.

"I wonder how he cut his head," she said, trying to distract herself. "Likely falling and smacking it against something unforgiving."

"Ask rather why he was falling down, or who he was falling down with. You don't think he became *inebriated* all on his own?"

"Ow!" said Ruyven, as Alayna jabbed the needle back through the lip of the gash.

"Not *inebriated* enough, apparently. Lie still, you wretched man. You deserve every—single—puncture—"

His eyes flew open and he struggled to lift his head.

Dimitra pressed a firm hand against his chest. "*Dom*

Ruyven, with utmost respect, you do not want to do that. Not when Lady Scathfell has a very sharp needle, is about to poke it into your scalp, and has every reason to be angry with the man who encourages her husband in getting drunk."

"Not my fault. Keeping him company—make him too drunk to think—"

"I wouldn't," Dimitra said, every syllable precise. "I really wouldn't."

34

Alayna stationed watchers outside both Ruyven's door and Gwynn's, with strict instructions to alert her the moment either of them stirred. It was not until well past noon that the man assigned to Ruyven found her in the solarium with Perdita. After ordering breakfast to be brought to Ruyven's chambers, Alayna went there, moving at a leisurely pace to give him ample time to tidy himself. Her knocking elicited a groan, which was all the greeting that could be expected from a man who'd been excessively drunk the night before. She found him sitting on the chest at the foot of his bed, wearing the same trousers and boots as last night. His shirt, while clean, looked rumpled. He was poking gingerly at the injured side of his head, and each touch produced a wince. His eyes were visibly bloodshot, and he hadn't shaved.

"*Vai domna*," he said, managing to get to his feet and bow. "You find me somewhat—improperly attired."

"You looked even worse last night. Now sit down and let me take a look."

He sat, although his motion was closer to falling. Alayna crossed to the wash stand, poured out a little water, dipped a corner of the smallest towel, and rubbed it over the ball of fine lemon-scented soap. These she carried to where he sat.

"No, don't touch!" she said, slapping his hand away. "You'll get it dirty, and that's if you don't pull out the stitches."

He winced as she parted his hair and dabbed at the crusted blood. To her relief, the wound looked clean. The stitches had all held, which was something of a miracle, given last night's conditions.

"I take it that you are responsible for doctoring my scalp," he said, "for which service, my thanks." He sounded too miserable to be very grateful.

"I did," she said, setting aside the cloth and basin, "although I was hoping you could tell me how it happened."

He didn't answer, he wouldn't look at her.

"You owe me the truth, Ruyven. Your shirt was so drenched with blood, I thought surely someone had stuck a knife into you."

Before he could respond, the breakfast tray arrived, and she pretended he was little Gwillim, back at home, and she was Ellimira. It wasn't hard. He sat where she put him and sipped the mug of steaming *jaco* she pressed into his hands. She let him drink and nibble on dry toast, which was all he was able to get down. He looked a little better for it, which wasn't saying much. If this is what a hangover looked like, she was glad she'd never been tempted to drink enough to have one.

"Now," she said, keeping her expression Ellimira-like, "you are going to tell me what you meant last night when you said you had been *keeping Lord Scathfell company*—which, I assume, means *getting drunk with him*. Most especially, I'd like to know what you meant by *having got him 'too drunk to think.'* To think what, exactly?"

He gave her a bleary-eyed half-smile. She refused to be charmed.

"Now."

"Lady Scathfell, those matters are private—"

"Something's happened to my husband, and I insist you tell me what it is. You are his closest friend as well as his adviser. I know perfectly well you've been trying to moderate his excesses. That's very admirable, and if that were all there were to it, I would say *thank you very much* and leave the matter. But you were badly hurt last night, and I don't think it was because you fell down on your own. You were with Gwynn—did you two fight?"

When Ruyven remained sullenly mute, Alayna began pacing. "This goes well beyond *let's go drinking together, it's all in fun.* What if it had been Gwynn instead of you, and what if he'd been seriously injured—maybe killed?"

Ruyven appeared to be struggling with himself. Finally he said, "After the news arrived on Midwinter Festival Night, Lord Scathfell spent the better part of the next tenday intoxicated."

"Yes, I gathered that. I observed his condition for myself, as well as a chamber littered with empty wine bottles. I understand that the news upset him, and that men sometimes deal with distressing situations by numbing themselves with drink." Or so her brothers had said. A horrifying thought struck her. "Surely you do not mean that he has remained *intoxicated* since then?"

"Not continually, although the bouts have continued, on and off," Ruyven admitted. "I thought there was no harm in them. Alas, the drink had somewhat the opposite effect than I had hoped. Always in the past, my lord has turned merry and generous, quick to laugh and even quicker to forgive. This time, it stirred up every vengeful, resentful thought and morsel of guilt."

"Guilt? What has he done that he should feel guilty?"

"I cannot speak for the truth of it, only what he himself said, that if only he had investigated properly when word came from the Sain Erach bandits, if only he had not taken the word of lawless men that your sister had perished, then she would now be his wife, and he the father of sons."

"But he couldn't have known. None of us could."

"We were all deceived," Ruyven replied, "or else the bandits themselves made up the story because they had no hostage to exchange. It makes more sense to blame me for pressing on home instead of searching for *Damisela* Kyria at the time.

"I believed that with the passage of time, reason might prevail," Ruyven went on. "His temper would cool, and he would be better able to accept the way things are. Events might not have unfolded as he had wished, but nothing is certain save death and next winter's snows. Soon it became apparent that when he was clear-headed, he cleaved even more strongly to the belief that he had been wronged. He grew even more agitated than when he was drunk. I sometimes joined him in the wine, hoping to restore our old camaraderie or at least prevent him from acting rashly." Gingerly he touched his scalp where Alayna had stitched up the gash. "That might not have been the wisest course."

"I must speak with him," Alayna said, "although he might not listen to me, any more than he has listened to you—and I do believe you tried your utmost, as a true friend. Perhaps if he sees that both of us are motivated by love for him and for Scathfell, we can overcome his objections. But even if he does not listen, I must try."

"Lady, it is unwise to come between a man and his obsession."

"What, will he strike me, beat me, lock me into a tower?"

"I cannot promise he will do none of those things, nor be responsible for your safety. He did not mean to strike me, and yet he did. Would you suffer a similar injury?"

Ordinarily, she could not imagine his assaulting her, but now images rose up, and she remembered the wild light in his eyes when they'd quarreled. Steadying her voice as best she could, she repeated, "I must try. Will you help me?"

After a measured silence, he nodded. "Lord Scathfell will be drilling his troops at this hour. Give me time to complete my ablutions, and I will escort you there."

— ◆ —

The day was unseasonably fair, the sky almost white and the breezes fresh. Alayna's bay trotted along beside Ruyven's horse, both of them with tails bannered and ears pricked. Alayna imagined that the wind made them want to run. As for herself, she felt as if she had been suddenly freed into a world that was much larger and more vivid than the one she had become accustomed to. She drank in the sights, the shape of the mountains, the villagers pausing in their work to stare at her, the animals in their pens; then the well-trodden trail, broad enough to be called a road, that led to the training fields. It climbed a bit, enough for the horses to breathe hard, wound through a gap between the steep-shouldered hills, and then brought her to a view of the army encampment.

Until that moment, she had not thought what to expect. Gwynn maintained a standing army, but she supposed most of the men had gone back to their families for the winter, leaving only a token force behind. But what greeted her was no skeleton corps. To one side stood buildings of wood and stone, row after row of them, barracks she supposed. And stables, and armories, and storehouses. But the greater part of the valley was taken up by men—men practicing, fighting singly or in ranks or even in large groups, one against another. Infantrymen busy with training drills she did not understand, and men on horseback doing the same. Sunlight glinted on swords and the points of spears, with flashes like wind-whipped blades of grass. Their voices and the whinnying of the horses blended into a muted roar.

So many of them.

What a fool she'd been, what a blind, trusting fool, when all the evidence had been before her. She'd *known* that Gwynn had been raised on stories of how Aldaran trounced his father's army, how Gwynn blamed Aldaran for the deaths of his father and brother, and how driven he was by revenge and fear of a repetition of that disastrous, humiliating defeat. She had *seen* what the news of Kyria's marriage to Edric and the sons she'd born him had done to Gwynn. How could she have believed that an exchange of gifts and holiday greetings, and a favor that might have been the cover for espionage, could undo a feud so deeply ingrained?

I saw only what I wanted to see.

This then was where Gwynn went when he was not drinking himself into a fury, nurturing old grudges as if they were treasured heirlooms.

A breeze gusted across Alayna's face. She noted its warmth and the smell of new growth. The ground was not entirely free of snow, but the drifts that remained were mainly in the shadows. If the passes to Aldaran were not already open, they would be soon. And then— *I can't let that happen.*

"Where is he?" she asked.

Ruyven pointed to a road that divided the various training areas. A group of riders were observing a body of men drilling in sword exercises on foot. One wore a familiar cloak. Her cheeks flamed. Before, all Gwynn's talk about needing to defend Scathfell had been abstract. This—this was *real*. The sights and sounds of the men preparing to fight—*to kill*—turned her mouth dry and her palms sweaty.

She could not—*must not*—turn away. If she did, she would
lose her nerve.

"I must speak with him."

As Alayna nudged her horse forward, Ruyven intervened. "Let me take you to the camp offices, the head-
quarters that is, and then fetch Lord Scathfell. He would not
be pleased to see you in the midst of his army, but he may
be persuaded to a private audience."

"Very well," she told Ruyven. "But if he will not come,
I'll not creep back to the castle like a mouse. I *will* speak
with him, one way or the other."

He took her to one of the smaller buildings, set between
those that were obviously barracks and one she took for an
armory. It looked newer than the others. A man wearing a
tunic with Scathfell's insignia over light armor sat on a
bench beside the door. He surged to his feet at their approach, his hand resting conspicuously on the hilt of his
sword.

"*Dom* Ruyven," he said, bowing without taking his hand
off his sword or his eyes off either of them. "My lady."

Alayna recognized him but vaguely, as one of the castle
guards. There were so many she had not been able to keep
track of all their names; now she realized they must have
been rotating between the castle and the encampment.

Within a few minutes, everything was sorted out. Ruyven
went off in search of Gwynn, and Alayna was escorted inside, to a single large room lined with cabinets and open
shelving. A large table dominated the center of the room,
and on it sat a couple of candlesticks, their wax stubs only
an inch or so long, and a broken dagger held down the curling edges of a map. A clay-walled stove sat in the center of
a brick pad but evidently had not been lit, as the room was
no warmer than the outside.

The guard closed the door behind him, leaving Alayna
alone. As she stood there, heart pounding, a chill settled
over her. She expected to see her breath as white mist, but
the air was clear. All the layers of jacket and cloak could not
warm her. She wasn't cold, she was terrified.

So many soldiers, their weapons and horses, all that
preparation. The investment of material, the funneling of
Scathfell's wealth . . . how could all this be undone?

I came here in reconciliation, to begin repairing our

marriage. But this imminent war is so much more important than my private sorrows. I have to find a way to stop it. Yet I can't help thinking I've come on a fool's errand. Gwynn will not disband his army at the mere request of his wife, I don't have that much influence over him. I doubt anyone does.

And yet she must find a way, mount arguments so persuasive that he would see the folly of what he'd done. No, not done, just planned. Prepared for. It wasn't too late; there was still time to undo all this. The army hadn't attacked Aldaran yet. The men could be dispersed, released, sent back to their homes.

She must take great care now. Gwynn had long mistrusted Aldaran. This army might be larger and better equipped than previously, but it was not new. For all she knew, it had begun in his father's time. He would not readily surrender it—he might even regard disbanding his forces as a cowardly act, backing away from battle out of fear of defeat. Then he would dig in his heels and all hope would be lost.

One deep breath after another, Alayna fought to calm herself. If only she had Kyria's courage—but she did not and must do the best with what she had. She'd always been told she was sweet and gentle and biddable, although recently she'd been standing up for herself, standing up to *Gwynn.*

No confrontation. No provoking a quarrel. Speak from love. For Scathfell. For Gwynn himself. For the people who live under our rule.

She remembered pleading for Dimitra, not only after the *Dom* Nevin incident but when Dimitra's life was at stake, and how her words had softened Gwynn's anger. The crucial difference was that he had trusted her then. For all she knew, he hated her now. Yet love might be her only weapon.

She startled when she heard the sounds of men's voices and the clatter of boot heels on the wooden step outside. The door flung open. Gwynn strode in, wind whipping the hem of his cloak. Ruyven followed, a pace behind.

"What in Zandru's seven frozen hells are you doing here?"

Gwynn's words and the impatience, the anger, behind them shattered Alayna's fragile calm. She flinched as if he'd physically struck her. The man standing before her, eyes bloodshot and wild, garbed for combat, sword at his hip, was a stranger. She searched his face but found no traces of the generous lord or the ardent lover. The man she'd fallen in love with.

"My husband," she began, her throat so tight she could barely force out the words, "I haven't had a chance to speak with you—" *since Midwinter Festival—no, don't remind him.*

"Here I am. Say what you've come for and be on your way."

Alayna tried to answer, but her lungs locked up around her breath. Tears stung her eyes, but she didn't care. She could not let that stop her before she'd even begun. "I have been increasingly worried by your absence, so I convinced Ruyven to bring me to you. He did so out of devotion to you, to us both." She sounded stiff and formal, but that couldn't be helped. She prayed he'd hear the sincerity behind her words. "If my presence here displeases you, do not blame him. The fault, if a deep concern for my husband can be deemed a fault, is mine alone."

"I'm well enough, as you can see." Gwynn's tone was icy enough to freeze her as she stood. "But I'm not such a simpleton to believe you came up here to reassure yourself about my health. That was only an excuse to spy on what I've been doing."

He gestured toward the training fields. "There it is, my army! The largest, best trained fighting force these mountains have ever seen. My own father's troops were nothing compared to what I can command. Are you satisfied?"

Alayna feared she'd lost her chance, he sounded so fierce, but she refused to give up. "Please listen to reason. There is no need for such an army. Scathfell is under no threat, certainly not from Aldaran. I know you and I haven't gotten along since Midwinter Festival, but I am your wife, now and for always. I do not want to lose you, especially to such an idiotic, pointless mistake." As soon as she'd blurted out the words, she knew she'd misspoken terribly.

"A *mistake*?" he snarled. "You call defending Scathfell a *mistake*?"

"A war such as you intend can only lead to death—many deaths—many *unnecessary deaths*. Those very men, and who knows how many more at Aldaran? And maybe you yourself!" She was losing control, the words tumbling from her lips. Her heart was so full of anguish, it threatened to choke her. "Now that I've seen—why could you not trust me?—everything we've done to make peace with Aldaran—they are doubly kin to us—"

"Are you quite finished?" Gwynn said when she drew breath.

Alayna could not answer. She could only stand there, trying not to tremble.

"If I have kept my plans from you, it was with good reason, as you have just demonstrated. You think a few years without open hostilities mean we have achieved peace?" He snorted. "Or that a few trinkets and an attempt to infiltrate the castle constitute *good will*? Aldaran hasn't changed since the days of the Witch-Child. They are still a nest of deceitful, murderous *stable sweepings*. The one thing—*the only thing*—that has kept Scathfell standing these long years has been Aldaran's inability to continue their aggression. The Witch-Child burned her brains out, or so it is said, and the old lord had not the stomach to pursue the war. As for Edric, he's such a weakling, he's been locked away in a Tower for most of his life."

"Then what are you afraid of?" Her words came out in a sob.

"That our security depends solely upon the temporary indisposition of our enemies and not our ability to defend ourselves. I dare not rely on anyone else to act in Scathfell's best interest. I—*I alone*—am responsible! So I used the lull in hostilities to devise a plan, one you know."

Dry-mouthed, Alayna nodded.

"When that came to nothing, I blessed the caution that had kept me from dispersing my small fighting force. Then came the news on Midwinter Festival. All you cared about was that your precious sister was alive. You failed to grasp the importance of the news. Aldaran now has the means to breed heirs with that Gift. For all I know, his sons both have it, and if not, the next child may. In a decade or so, Scathfell will face not one Witch-Child but two—or three—or more. Do you honestly believe that anyone who has that much power will hesitate to use it?"

She had no answer, none that he would believe. Anything she said would only push him further into the certainty he was not only right, but fully justified. His fears were terrible: even this army would be useless against a brood of Witch-Children.

There has to be another way.

In the pause that followed, the stillness was so absolute that Alayna was sure her heart had stopped. Gwynn no longer looked human, but like a creature of ash and ice.

"Long have I searched for a way to survive such an assault, and I have found none. Aldaran would destroy us, down to the last stone of the last castle wall. We will be obliterated, as if everything and everyone we hold dear had never existed. Our only hope—*only hope*—is to act now, before the witch-brood has grown into power. To strike pre-emptively and decisively. To put an end to this heap of scorpion-ant eggs before they can hatch."

"Gwynn, please—think what you are doing!" Alayna knew how desperate she sounded. She flailed around for something—*anything*—that would reach him. "This is my sister—your sister-in-law—and your nephews—and the man who would be your friend. The man who saved me when I almost died and who came all the way here to help our Dimitra. If he were truly your enemy, he would have let us both perish. You cannot mean to make war on them."

"*Cannot mean?* Have you lost your wits, woman? That is *exactly* what I mean to do."

"Do not rush into it. Take your time—think things through—"

"I have *thought* long enough. Do you believe I want this war? That I would pursue it if there were any other alternative? If Edric Aldaran had done the honorable thing and turned your sister over to me, then none of this would have happened. If the war is anyone's doing, it's his."

Alayna was too appalled to summon a response.

"At Midwinter, when I learned how I had been betrayed and realized how dire the threat was, the weather forced me to delay taking any action," Gwynn said. "I had to build up my strength and then wait until the weather changed, but my army used that time to good advantage, I assure you. Even now, a single file of riders can get through the snow drifts, but in a tenday, when the passes are fully open, we will be ready to march. Aldaran still believes we mean him well. He will never suspect the havoc that is about to descend upon him."

And on Kyria—and her babes.

Acid raked the back of her throat. Her stomach heaved. She pressed both hands to her mouth, praying she would not vomit.

"My lady?" Ruyven bent toward her. "*Vai dom*, we must get her out of here, lest she become ill."

"Take her away. The fate of realms are the concern of men." Gwynn paused, one hand on the door latch. "It is always a mistake to involve the women."

35

With as much dignity as Alayna could muster, she allowed herself to be conducted back to the castle. Ruyven stayed behind with Gwynn. Her escort clearly meant to ensure that she reached her private rooms safely and without the opportunity to speak to anyone on the way.

Once the door to her chambers had closed behind her, she could not stand still. Her mind seethed, thoughts churning like grains of wheat in a boiling pot. This looming calamity was her fault. She should have seen it coming. All the signs had been there. If only she'd spoken earlier, before Gwynn's preparations became so extensive, his aim so fixed, his resolve so implacable. Her own hopes—not to mention her inexperience with drunken husbands and long-festering resentments—had blinded her to the real danger.

A man does not keep his sword sharpened only to let it gather dust on the wall.

If only the old lords—Aldaran and Scathfell both—had resolved their differences as kinsmen should, peacefully and with honor. If only Great-Aunt Aliciane had never come to Aldaran, or that Gwynn had never thought of marrying a Rockraven daughter. If only those thrice-damned brigands had left Kyria alone. *If only.*

No, this would not do. If she kept on like this, blaming

herself, blaming him, blaming the idiocy of the previous generation, feeding the panic even now rising in her, she would work herself into an hysterical fit. Lowering herself into her favorite chair, she forced herself to breathe slowly and deeply.

Gwynn meant what he said. He would march as soon as the passes opened, within a tenday, and it was useless to try again to reason with him. That would only deepen the rift between them, if he did not place her under guard and key to keep her silent.

She had no idea of Aldaran's military strength. From what she knew of Edric, it probably wasn't much. He'd spent all that time in a Tower, leaving his mother to administer lands and castle, and Alayna had never heard Lady Renata described as hawkish. Edric would have no warning, no chance to prepare a defense, and when Aldaran fell, what would happen to Kyria and her sons? Would Gwynn— and here, Alayna's imagination refused to function. Men, even ordinarily decent men, did terrible things in war. She'd heard enough of her brothers' stories, especially those she wasn't supposed to hear. In the end, however, Gwynn meant to smash Aldaran, to make sure it never again posed a threat to Scathfell.

Over and over, like echoes, thoughts filled her mind:

Gwynn means to destroy them all. He will not listen to me.

I have to do something. I have to save Kyria—and her babes—and Edric.

Gwynn will destroy them.

I have to stop him. I have to save Kyria.

— ✦ —

After a time, Perdita entered, her expression somber. Alayna jumped to her feet and, blinking back tears, took her hands. "I cannot tell you how glad I am to see you, my friend."

"Please tell me what has happened." Perdita led Alayna back to her chair and took the other, facing her.

Alayna related how she tended Ruyven's wound and then convinced him to take her to the army fields and what she found there. Somewhat to her surprise, reciting the events drained them of their nightmarish quality. *I did this* and *I saw this* was so much more manageable than *if only*.

"Lord Scathfell intends to attack Aldaran?" Perdita asked. "I know of the old feud, who does not? But I thought when Lord Aldaran himself came to tend to *Domna* Dimitra, that all would be well. Was I mistaken?"

"If you were, then so was I. But then my husband discovered that my sister is alive and married to Lord Aldaran."

"The one who was supposed to have married Lord Scathfell but was then presumed dead?"

"Word came the night of Midwinter Festival. Do you remember?"

"I remember how happy you and Lord Scathfell seemed, and then he left the room and when he came back, his manner was greatly altered. The two of you barely spoke a word to one another. He must have been dreadfully offended to learn how he had been deceived, if indeed there was any intention to do so. And I suppose that Lord Aldaran must have had a good reason for keeping his marriage a secret."

A terrifying thought crossed Alayna's mind, that Gwynn might seek her own death and then Edric's, to clear the way for his marriage to Kyria. Fertile Kyria. She could not believe it—not Gwynn! He might be—how had Dimitra put it, *paranoid*?—but he was not a wife-murderer. Hadn't he said he would not take a mistress out of respect for her? They had shared a bed, the hopes for a child; she had seen love in his eyes, felt the tenderness of his caresses, and seen how deeply moved he was when she'd sung the ballad for him. Had she been so mistaken about him?

Alayna wrenched herself back to the present, to her sweet friend and confidante. "My husband fears, rightly or mistakenly, that Aldaran means to revive the old conflict. How little he knows of Edric Aldaran. But his mind has been poisoned by having grown up with tales of devastation, murder, and unforgivable humiliation. He lost so much—a brother he adored, his father, and then his mother. I thought he was leaving those tragedies behind, but now the secrecy surrounding my sister's rescue and marriage has confirmed his fears. Now he is determined to go to war as soon as the army can move. That will be very soon now, which is why I must get to Aldaran first."

"Aldaran? Isn't that the worst place to be on the eve of an attack, in the stronghold of the enemy?" Perdita twined her fingers in Alayna's as if to physically restrain her. "No, no, you must not risk yourself—and for what purpose?"

"Why, to warn them. If this attack is a misguided disaster, then how much worse will it be if it succeeds?"

"You wish Scathfell to fail?"

"I *wish* there to be no war at all," Alayna replied, pulling her hands away. "But as I cannot achieve that, the next best thing is for our army to find the gates barred to them, the walls secured. For that to happen, Lord Aldaran must have time to prepare a defense. Then it will not be within my husband's power to harm him or anyone. Gwynn will not be happy about that at all. Dear gods, he will not! Eventually, I hope he will accept the futility of his campaign. He must, though he be reduced to eating stones for bread. He and his men will come home, and that will be the end of it."

"Home, where *you* will not be," Perdita pointed out, "unless you can sneak past a siege and outpace the returning Scathfell army. Think what you are proposing to do, my lady. Can you not send someone else?"

Alayna shook her head. "I cannot be certain anyone else would be believed, and if Gwynn ever found out . . . it would be better if I were not here."

"Is this scheme worth the loss of your home?" Perdita said. "Will Lord Scathfell ever forgive your betrayal?"

"I don't know, but that must not stop me from acting in the best interest of us all. As to how I will return to Scathfell, I have no idea. It would grieve me to be parted from my husband, but even more so to see what he will surely become, should he succeed in this dreadful scheme. That is, if he is still alive when it is over."

Perdita gazed at her for a long moment, so long that Alayna began to fear that she had made a mistake in trusting her. She had to admit to having sounded quite demented. But at last, Perdita nodded. "I see that you are determined, and I will help you in any way I can. With your permission, I propose to enlist the advice of *Domna* Dimitra. She may have knowledge of people and ways, not to mention travel preparations, that goes beyond my own."

Alayna agreed, thinking that surely three heads were better than one.

Perdita returned a short time later, accompanied by

Dimitra. "*Damisela* Perdita has told me of the impending military action and your scheme to counter it," Dimitra said as the three of them settled themselves. "My lady, if anyone else had concocted such a plan, I would presume them mad."

"Not mad, only desperate," Alayna said. "If you can think of any other way, I would gladly hear it."

Dimitra shook her head. "I fear there is none. I have seen and heard more of Lord Scathfell's behavior than you. Servants talk, and I listen. Alas, I do not think you exaggerate the danger. But Perdita asked me to help you, and I intend to do just that. Have you thought how will you reach Aldaran? The snow is not so thick this past tenday, but the passes will be difficult to negotiate, especially for a fine lady."

"I know you will be astonished to hear me admit this, but I am not a *fine lady*," Alayna said, catching Perdita's grin out of the corner of her vision. "I grew up in a mountainous area, not unlike this one, and I have traveled through worse weather than this. It is spring, after all, and a single rider, or a small party, can venture where an army cannot."

Perdita's fair brows drew together. "Surely you were not alone then? When you endured such hardship on the road?"

"No, that was when Kyria and I left our home to come here," Alayna replied. "*Dom* Ruyven escorted us, and there were guards, of course, to protect us and set up camp. Tend to the animals, cook meals. Guide us to a travel shelter during the snowstorm." She tried not to remember how very cold and miserable she had been, and most likely would be again, only this time she would have neither Francisco nor Edric nor even Ruyven to comfort her.

"Guide . . ." Dimitra repeated. "Of course, you had a guide who knew how to arrange winter travel and was familiar with these mountains. And so you need one now."

Alayna shook her head. "I do not know any of the men in the castle well enough to trust. I dare not risk Lord Scathfell discovering my plan."

"Then you must look elsewhere," Perdita said. "The village, perhaps?"

"The village indeed," Dimitra said. "But you must not approach anyone you do not know, especially not a man who may have much to gain by betraying you to Lord Scathfell."

"I don't know anyone in the village."

"But you do, *vai domna*. Tarva, the midwife. Did you not say she tended me before Lord Aldaran arrived? I was very ill at the time, so I do not remember much, and I have been told that my malady was beyond her skill. Nevertheless, once I was able, I sent a gift of grain and cloth to her. If I am not mistaken, she is the headman's grandmother and is therefore the real power in the village."

Alayna felt a little ashamed at having forgotten the old woman. So much had happened since then, she might justify the lapse, but the lady of the castle ought to know the inhabitants of the surrounding lands. "Can I trust her?"

"Such women are accustomed to keeping their own counsel, so yes, I believe you can, or there is no faithfulness anywhere."

Listening to Dimitra's confident words, Alayna was filled with gratitude. She had not thought *how* she might bring warning to Aldaran, only that she must. Now at least she had a first step. With any luck, Tarva would pass her on to others who could help her. For a moment, she reconsidered whether she might ask someone in the village to carry the message for her.

It has to be me, although Gwynn may never take me back. But then at least I will be with Kyria.

"Finding a guide will be only the beginning," Perdita said. "You will need warm clothing—fur, if possible, or good, thick wool—and boots with two pairs of socks, and a sturdy horse accustomed to cold weather."

She ticked off items on her fingers with such assuredness that Alayna wondered how many escapades she had been party to.

"Food, of course," Dimitra added. "A little money. And we will need to keep your absence hidden for as long as possible."

"Goodness, you two have thought of everything. At least, far more than I have," Alayna exclaimed. "Perdita, I had no idea that someone so accustomed to court life in a city, would know about such things."

"Last winter's musical entertainments were all about desperate elopements," Perdita explained.

Alayna laughed outright and Dimitra hid a smile.

"Five different versions, if you can believe," Perdita went

on, "all but one of them ending with the lovers dying tragically, frozen in each other's arms. Singing at the top of their lungs, of course."

"Well, that isn't going to happen to me," Alayna said. "The singing. Or the freezing."

"No, indeed," Perdita said. "But in one of these entertainments, in the one I liked best, the lady's *breda* dons her clothing and takes her place, so the elopement is not discovered until it is too late."

"An excellent idea," Dimitra said.

Alayna studied her friend. They were close enough in size, although Perdita's hair was darker, though it could be hidden underneath a scarf or cowl.

"Perdita, you must also say that Lady Scathfell is unwell and not to be disturbed," Dimitra said, "and I will mention now and again that I have seen you, but you are keeping to your bed. We must hope that Lord Scathfell would not impose on an indisposed wife."

"He will surely be too preoccupied with his army to sit down for a chat with me," Alayna said with a trace of sorrow. "In any case, he's avoided me thus far, and there's no reason to think he wouldn't continue to do so."

The three women spent the better part of an hour, working out more details of their plan. Dimitra was practical, while Perdita made the whole affair sound both exciting and romantic. Alayna herself had a much better idea what was in store for her. If she was very lucky, the skies would continue to be clear and the winds quiet, but she must prepare herself for worse.

— ✦ —

On the appointed day, when everything had been made ready, Alayna rose well before dawn. Perdita helped her to dress in the warmest clothing they could find: wool trousers tucked into fur-lined boots under a divided skirt, topped by a snug-fitting jacket. Plus thick-knitted cap, scarf, and gloves. The outfit was too warm to wear comfortably while still inside, but because it might mean the difference between freezing and survival, she had to bear it. Dimitra had prepared a satchel stuffed with travel food, several changes of socks and undergarments, necessities such as a small sewing kit, and a purse of small denomination coins.

After kissing her friends goodbye, Alayna slipped passed the guards and down to the gates. At that hour, with the faint intimation of dawn lightening the eastern sky, the grooms would already be about their work, feeding their charges and mucking out the stalls. She wished she could have taken her own horse, but the bay would be missed immediately.

As she expected, she was stopped at the gates. She pulled the hood of her cloak forward over her face—not that the guard there would recognize Lady Scathfell on sight—and tried to sound like Sadhi as she explained that she'd come from the village to fill in working in the kitchen and was on her way home. He let her pass without demanding her name.

Hardly daring to believe her stroke of good luck, Alayna proceeded along the road. At first she had to go slowly because of the near darkness, but by the time the village was in sight, she could see quite clearly. Lights shone from every house, and women as well as men and boys were visibly at work. Some of them led or herded livestock: a cow or two, chervines, some sort of round-bodied clucking birds, and a mule. Their voices blended with the sounds of the animals, reminding her of winter mornings at Rockraven.

She settled the satchel over her shoulder and headed for what looked like the center of the village. The first person she encountered was a half-grown boy, who was trying to lead a half dozen chervines away from the livestock pens. His clothes were ragged and covered with patches, and his cheeks looked pinched, his eyes too large in his skull. Bony wrists stuck out from too-short sleeves. When she asked him where Tarva the healer woman lived, he looked at her with an expression of consternation. She watched him hurry away, unable to decide if her accent, her appearance, or the simple fact of her being a stranger was what rendered him speechless.

The next person she saw was a woman, swathed in layers of shawls, a cowl covering her head and shoulders. Her skirts swayed as she balanced two buckets in a yoke over her shoulders. She was not as thin as the boy, but her skin was roughened and dark circles marked her eyes.

"Fair day to you," Alayna said, in the way common folk at Rockraven greeted one another.

"Aye, that it is," the woman replied, slowing to take a closer look at Alayna.

"I'm new here," Alayna hastened to say. "I'm looking for the healer. Tarva."

"Ah, the headman's grandmam," the woman replied with genuine warmth. "That house there, the one at the end of the lane. She's a good 'un, for all she keeps to herself. Birthed many a babe here, and many a babe and mam are still alive for her skill. An' she can stitch up a cut or soothe a fever as well as any I've heard."

This was high praise. These plain folk had no *leronis* to heal them or to see the women safely through childbirth, but they managed nonetheless. "You are very fortunate to have her, then."

"Aye, that we are." With a nod, the woman went on her way, buckets swinging.

Alayna reached the house the woman had indicated. Smoke curled from the fieldstone chimney and the oiled cloth of the windows glowed from the light within. She tapped on the door and heard voices inside, a woman's, a bit quavery, and then a man's. The door swung open and a tall, well-built man stood silhouetted against the brightness of the room.

"Good—" he began, then broke off. "Zandru's hells!"

His voice gave him away, the one voice Alayna had thought to never hear again. For an instant, she stood there, dumbfounded.

"*Francisco*? What are you doing here?"

The last time she'd seen Francisco, Gwynn had railed and roared and sent him into exile. She felt as if the world had turned inside out. "Are you going to invite me in?"

Francisco stood back for Alayna to enter. She noticed the lines in his face, although he looked more careworn than old. He was thinner than she remembered, but not as much as the goat boy, and more warmly dressed than the villagers she'd seen. His garb looked as if it had seen hard usage, shiny at the seams and patched in places. Wherever he'd gone after Gwynn had banished him from Scathfell, he had survived but not prospered.

Alayna stepped over the threshold into a single large room, partitioned with hanging drapes. The hearth filled one wall of the central room, furnished with a table, several

crude chairs, and a spinning wheel. Shelves held baskets
and pottery jars. Bundles of dried herbs and roots hung in
one corner.

Tarva, stirring a cauldron by the fire, was bundled like
the other village women in a shawl that criss-crossed her
body.

Alayna started to curtsy, for she was an uninvited guest
in this woman's home, but caught herself. "I bid you good
morning, *Mestra* Tarva."

"*S'dia shaya,* my lady! I member ye from when I went up
to the castle to tend that poor woman. May all the gods
have mercy upon her, for there was nawt I could do. I pray
her passing was easy."

"Have you not heard, then? Lord Edric Aldaran, who
trained in a Tower, tended her himself. I saw her not two
hours ago, and she was quite well."

"Ah!" Tarva exclaimed, settling her shawl around her
shoulders. "'Twas kindly done, that." She said it as if she
approved of his actions, one healer to another.

"You did not come all the way, and on foot," Francisco
said, "just to tell us of the gracious condescension of Lord
Aldaran."

"And *you* have not explained what you're doing here.
Have you lost your wits? If my husband finds you're here—
but he will not hear that from me," she said. "I beg your
pardon for my hasty words. You were the last person I expected to encounter here."

"Who exactly were you expecting, then?"

"Manners, young pup!" Tarva interrupted. "'Tis a time
for explanations and a time for hospitality. Were yer brains
not so addled by living in strange lands, ye'd know which
comes first."

Francisco glanced away, his posture softening. "It is I
who should beg your pardon, Lady Scathfell. Grams."

Grams? "You are *Mestra* Tarva's grandson? I thought
the headman was."

"Surely a person can have more than one grandchild?"
Francisco answered with a hint of humor. "Arryl, who is
headman here, is my cousin and a fair bit older than I. He
recommended me for training in Lord Scathfell's guards,
and so I left this place. I return from time to time," with a
glance at his grandmother that revealed his affection for

her, "although not recently. But this winter has been hard and food scarce, and then I heard she was ill."

"Hale enough to manage, winter or no, and yet if a trace of the cough will fetch ye here, laddie, I'll not begrudge it." Tarva turned to Alayna. "Lady, I have no *jaco* to offer, but there's still some mint tisane."

"I thank you, but no. It isn't safe for me to linger." She glanced at Francisco. "My husband doesn't know I've gone, but when he does, it's likely he will search the village. He must not find Fran—Captain Francisco. I'm sorry, I don't know what to call you now."

"Francisco will do. Nobody but Grams calls me Cisco." A scowl darkened his face. "So you've run away, without any thought to who you would put in danger."

"I am not so feckless as that, and I have no intention of putting anyone in danger," she retorted. "And I will be happy to leave as soon as I've found someone to act as my guide. That's why I've come, for if anyone knows a likely person, one who has the skill to guide me through the mountains and the discretion to keep our departure secret, it is you. I've left the castle, yes, but I'm not running *away*. I'm running *toward*."

Francisco's tone remained guarded. "Toward what?"

"Aldaran. I've got to warn them that Scathfell is about to attack them with an army."

This statement resulted in so many exclamations and questions that Alayna, despite her repeated insistence that she must hurry, ended up sitting down to a cup of mint tisane and telling the whole story. Tarva's face tightened, and by the time Alayna had finished, she looked a decade older. Alayna supposed she was thinking of how little the village had to spare, and counting the wounded and dead.

"Francisco," Alayna began. "You know these mountains. You served Scathfell for many years . . . you grew up here. I hardly dare ask—I have no right—but there is no one I would trust more. You got us all through the journey from Rockraven, even when it was snowing so badly. And you are a man of honor."

"Some might say that you are mad to think you can accomplish this."

"I may be mad, but I must try my utmost, and that includes finding the help I need."

"You do not know what you are asking," he said.

"You and your family," *there, she had said it,* "may be able to flee beyond the reach of this war. Most definitely, your grandmother and cousin and all the people in the village, and in the valley and the farms and pastures—they will not be able. *They* will bear the cost of this war. In taxes, in food, in conscripts. In lives. If you will not do this for our old friendship, will you not do it for their sakes?"

Francisco's expression hardened but not, Alayna thought, with refusal. She remembered how they had ridden through the valley when she first came to Scathfell, when she still fancied herself in love with him, and he had spoken about how the richness of the valley was continually drained by Lord Scathfell's standing army. How much worse was the plight of those people now.

In a voice resonant with emotion, he said, "My family no longer exists."

Alayna's heart went out to him. "I am sorry to hear it. Forgive me, I had no wish to bring up a painful subject."

"You meant no offense, my lady. They have been gone this past year from a lung fever," he said. "It was a bad winter."

"It seems that all winters are bad now," Alayna said, "and likely to become more so if this war comes about. I am very sorry for your loss, Francisco, but surely you would not want anyone else to suffer as you do, when it might be prevented."

"Seems ye have a choice, laddie," the old woman said. "Go back to the safety ye've made for yerself. Stay out of this, do not risk yerself, for Avarra knows ye've suffered enough. Ye'll be of no use to me if ye're dead. Or ye can serve this lady, for 'tis clear she herself hopes to serve us all." She went to Francisco and reached up to pat his cheek. At her touch, a change rippled through his body, although he did not move. He seemed to be not breathing. "I'll love ye no less for it," Tarva said, "whatever ye choose. But choose ye must, and ye linger on peril of yer life."

He spoke softly, the village accent roughening his voice. "Grams, ye cannot survive another such winter."

"That's for the Dark Lady Avarra to say, not any mortal man nor woman."

He slipped his arms around her, bending to hold her close despite the difference in their heights and the curvature of her spine. For what seemed like many long moments, Francisco held her. Then with a lift and fall of his shoulders, he stepped back. Her eyes were bright as stars. He turned to Alayna. "*Vai domna*, I am yours to command."

Once those words would have filled her with elation, but now they brought only the sickening feeling of destiny closing in around her.

36

Gazing down at his wife and sons, Edric thought there could be no greater happiness. Kyria had fallen asleep while nursing them, a babe cradled in each arm, her skin a pearly glow in the morning light. Her head had fallen to one side, facing little Donal, whose mouth was still attached to her breast. He was almost asleep, but now and again his lips would move. Edric could not decide if the babe were actually suckling or only dreaming of it. Baby Pietro snuggled up to Kyria's other side. He must have finished nursing while she was still awake, for she had covered her breast and tucked her blanket neatly around both of them. It amazed Edric that she could nourish both of them and that they could now sit up by themselves. Although born early, they had thrived.

Seeing the three of them in the abandon of sleep stole his breath away. He had not guessed that such tenderness as he felt now existed.

Even as she slept, he sensed Kyria's mind with his own. Once the barriers between them had been lowered, they were always in light rapport. As if the words of the marriage ceremony had been literally true and they had become one person, one flesh. One spirit. Then he caught himself about to reach out and caress her cheek, but she needed sleep. For the hundredth time, he blessed the gods for bringing Kyria into his life and for giving him the sense to listen to his mother and make her his wife *di catenas*.

Although the boys were twins, born within the space of an hour, Edric had learned to tell them apart. He knew the curve of their cheeks, the sweetness of their scent. What he did not know, and what both Kyria and his mother, who had assisted at their birth, refused to tell him, was which was the elder. Kyria informed him, with that disarming frankness of hers, that if it ever became necessary to the fate of Darkover, she would reveal the order of their birth. But until that time, she would not have her sons subjected to this *eldest and heir* nonsense.

"Would you have them rule Aldaran together?" he had joked.

She'd favored him with a lift of one eyebrow. "That would be an excellent idea."

The quiet lifting of the door latch heralded his mother's arrival. Lady Renata still held herself with the poise of a *leronis* who had trained at Hali Tower and worked there for many years. Now a light frosting of silver highlighted her copper-bright hair. The freckles of her youth had faded, leaving her most pronounced facial feature her large gray eyes. On this winter morning, she wore a loose, fur-lined overdress on top of a high-necked gown. A cowl of dainty knitted lace in the same soft blue draped her from head to shoulders. In no small measure due to Kyria's cosseting, her health had recovered from the lung fever that had summoned him home. But she still took extra care against the cold.

"I thought I'd find you here," she said, her gaze going to the sleeping mother and babes. Edric had never thought of his mother as the doting type. Loving, certainly, and endlessly patient, but practical and level-headed. It was evident, however, that she would very likely spoil her grandsons to a legendary degree.

"You came looking for me?" he said, trying to remember if they had an appointment.

"'Tis a good candlemark past when we were supposed to meet," she replied, keeping her voice low. Her sigh conveyed how much she would like to linger. "Come now, for if the business of the world waited on the slumber of babes, then nothing would ever get done."

Edric followed his mother from the bedchamber and nodded in passing to the nurse who sat knitting before the parlor fireplace, ready when Kyria needed her. "I can think of many things that would be far less desirable than watching such angels sleep."

"It would indeed be a blessing if quarrels waited upon such simple joys," Renata replied as they proceeded down the hallway. "Can you imagine an army forced to stand about while an infant finishes nursing?"

"Yes, that would be the proper ordering of the world."

She opened the door leading to the sunny chamber they used during the winter for estate business. Tapestries shielded the air from the cold stone of the walls. A carpet of Ardcarran weaving, old but still colorful, cushioned their feet. Renata had taken over the room when she assumed administration of the castle during Edric's minority and then in his absence at Tramontana.

Ledgers and loose sheets of paper covered the surface of the table, except for a tray with a pitcher of *jaco*, a pot of honey, and a platter of Renata's favorite nut-studded pastries. She was wont to treat business discussions as if they were as taxing as matrix circle work, and therefore requiring the same sustenance.

Kermiac, the castle *coridom*, rose. "*Vai dom.*"

"Be at your ease, for it is I who am remiss in my duty." Edric took his seat. "What's to do this morning?"

Renata sat back in her chair, watching over the rim of her cup as Kermiac went through his summary of the castle accounts. Edric listened with as much of his thoughts as he could tear away from Kyria and the boys. Kermiac was a good steward, meticulous if dull.

Edric felt a rush of appreciation for the tactful way Renata made it seem he was making decisions, all the while managing the various items of business herself. For example, the tally of food supplies—both for the household itself and for those dependents who required assistance during the winter months until the earliest crops were ready for harvest—fell under the purview of the chatelaine. Kyria would assume these duties as she was able, but for the time being, both she and Edric were just as happy to have Renata continue her capable administration. Aldaran had flourished in Renata's hands during the years Edric was at Tramontana, and it would be a pity to lose her guidance now.

I must start paying more attention to the administration of the smaller estates, Edric thought. One way around the difficulty of succession would be to ensure that whichever son did not rule had lands enough to provide a good living. *It is a terrible thing when brother is set against brother.* It would never happen, he swore to whichever god might be listening.

"Edric?" Renata was staring at him, not unkindly, while Kermiac waited, his hands full of account books.

"Thank you for your service," Edric murmured.

"*Vai dom.*" Kermiac bowed and left them.

Renata favored Edric with an oblique smile. "It was a lucky thing that all he'd asked was if there was anything else you needed."

"Seemed reasonable."

A light tap sounded, and the door swung open. Edric's heart beat faster at the sight of his wife. In the short time since he'd seen her asleep in bed, she'd dressed, tidied her hair, and looked alert and composed.

Her eyes flickered from Edric to Renata. "I'm sorry, have I interrupted you? I saw Kermiac heading down the corridor and assumed you had finished."

"And so we have, my dear," Renata hastened to reassure her. "Would you care for some *jaco*? I think it's still warm, or I can ring for a fresh pitcher."

Kyria declined with thanks, for as she'd confided in Edric she thought *jaco* made the babes fussy. "I will have one of these, however," Kyria said, reaching for one of the pastries.

"We used to eat them by the platterful after a night's work in the matrix circle," Edric said. "I'm afraid I can't stomach the sweetness under other circumstances."

"I, on the other hand," said Renata, "never tire of them. It's a wonder I'm not the size of a cart horse."

"I couldn't imagine that," Kyria murmured in between nibbles.

"I'm lucky. It is said that the same genes that give rise to our Gifts also prevent our bodies from storing extra fat.

This is a good thing. It means I can continue to wear the same gowns as when I first came here."

Glancing down at her own figure, still rounded with breastfeeding, Kyria sighed. Edric, meeting her eyes, spread his hands in surrender.

"Well," Renata said, "perhaps we should spare my son's tender ears from further discussion on this topic."

"My tender ears—" Edric began, but halted at another sound at the door, not Kyria's light tap but a more forceful knock. "Come," he called.

Roderic, the captain of the castle guards, entered. Aldaran had no army and little enough need for guarding, but such need as there was, he and his cadre of men filled. They carried swords but wore no armor, only tunics emblazoned with the Aldaran double eagle, warm and serviceable.

Roderic bowed first to Edric and then to each of the ladies. "My lord, there's a matter requiring your presence. If you would come, please."

Normally Roderic was so placid of temper as to be imperturbable. It was one of the qualities, besides his skill with a sword and his patience in instilling that same skill in others, that made him a good captain. Although Edric could find no fault with the man's tone or bearing, he sensed that something had rattled his captain. He got to his feet, bade the women a good morning, and followed Roderic down to the entrance hall.

"Two people—a man and a woman—just arrived," Roderic explained as they hurried along. "They rode in out of the snow, their mounts half dead and them not much better."

"They must have been desperate to travel at this season. A woman, you say?" At least the weather had been relatively clear. Edric had sensed a storm—a blizzard—gathering on the heights, but if it had not dissipated, it had come no closer.

"My lord, they say they are here to warn you of an impending attack."

"Attack? As in military attack?" Edric could not believe he'd heard correctly. "As in war?"

Roderic paused, meeting Edric's eyes. "That's what they say." It was a measure of how shaken he was that he did not add *my lord*.

"I'd better have a word with them." It was too cold to use the formal presence chamber, and the family parlor, which was where he preferred to meet with guests, was out of the question. One did not discuss war—actual or threatened or even imaginary—in such an intimate environment.

"My lord, if I may," Roderic said with a touch of diffidence. "I took the liberty of placing the strangers in the ward room." This was the snug where the castle guards took their meals and sat at ease. It was warm, being adjacent to the kitchen, and on those occasions Edric met with members of the cadre and the weather was too harsh for the training yard, he preferred to use the ward room. Edric followed Roderic there.

One of Roderic's men opened the door, and as Edric passed the threshold, a woman in a gray wool cloak sprang to her feet and threw herself into his arms.

"Sir—" Roderic protested, even as his two men moved too late to intercept her.

"Edric! It's so good to see you," she cried. Her face was pressed against his shoulder. Droplets of melted snow sprinkled the top of her cloak. She was shaking.

"It's all right, I know her." Edric gently disentangled himself from Alayna's embrace, holding her at arm's length to get a better look at her. She was as pretty as ever, although her cheeks were wind-roughened and her yellow hair had come loose from its braid. A pallor around her chapped lips suggested the edge of exhaustion.

"Why did you not say who you were at once?" he asked. "Had I known, I would never have kept you waiting."

"*Vai dom*, the fault is entirely mine," the other arrival said.

"Captain Francisco. Well met, man. I did not think to see you again."

"Nor I you, sir."

"This is all very well and nice," Alayna broke in. "We can sort out the pleasantries later. Francisco isn't here of his own volition. I practically coerced him into bringing me. And this isn't a social call, Edric. Any moment now, the entire Scathfell army—and it's a very considerable one—is going to descend on you. They were to set out within the tenday when I left, so they can't be far behind. Gwynn is out for blood. He's convinced himself that your babes are going to grow up to be storm wizards or lightning sorcerers or something, and burn Scathfell to the ground. He won't stop until everyone here is dead or run off." She paused, breathing hard. "I don't know how much time you'll have, but even a little defense preparation will be better than being caught completely unawares. So here I am, warning you."

Edric wondered for an instant if the privations of mountain travel had unhinged her mind, but he sensed no unbalance in her. After their sojourn in the Overworld, he knew her mind; there could be no deceit between them, especially about a matter as grave as this. "You came to warn me? That my kinsman, your husband, is about to attack Aldaran?"

"Did I not say so?" She looked as if she wanted to shake him. "He's so eaten up with bitterness, not to mention an immoderate amount of wine, that he's not entirely sane. If there were any other way, if I could have made him listen to me—but Kyria is here and you and my nephews, and I couldn't let him—not without trying." Stammering to a halt, she sank onto the nearest bench and burst into tears.

Edric sent one of the men off to fetch his mother and Kyria as soon as possible.

"I know nothing of this for myself," Francisco said, "but I have no reason to doubt Lady Alayna. I should not have been in the village at all, except that my grandmother had been ailing, and so I risked seeing her, for fear that this might be her last winter."

"I hope she will live to see many a season yet."

Edric did not know Alayna well, not the way he knew Kyria, but it was plain she believed what she said about her husband mounting a military assault on Aldaran. She was overwrought, certainly, but that did not in itself mean she was mistaken. As for Francisco, he was neither inexperienced nor a fool. He was a man of sound judgment, as evidenced by his competence on the trail, and he truly believed Lord Scathfell capable of such a mad venture.

Edric knew all too well the flimsiness of Aldaran's defenses. With the defeat of Old Lord Scathfell a generation ago, there had been no need for any substantial body of fighting men. Even then, it had not been force of ordinary arms, but the unbridled power of the storm *laran* wielded by Dorilys that had turned the battle. Now Aldaran had but a few men, high stone walls, a difficult approach, and years of tranquility.

"It seems," Alayna said, sniffing and wiping away her tears with grubby hands, "that I—"

Whatever she was about to say drowned in the flood of exclamations and wordless cries of delight as Kyria and then Renata swept into the room. Alayna leaped up and the two sisters rushed together, their skirts flying, their arms wound tightly around one another. Edric, in light rapport with his wife, reeled under a surge of unbounded joy. Renata laughed and clapped her hands together like a child. Roderic, who like many of the folk of the castle had a trace of empathic *laran*, looked as if he would like to join in.

Because of the delight of the sisters—hugging and kissing one another, then drawing apart, then embracing again—and the effect on their audience, it took some little while for the uproar to die down. Renata took matters in hand and, with her usual tact, got the two sisters, Francisco, Roderic, and Edric himself upstairs to the office. Edric asked Bennio, who acted as his secretary and librarian, to bring whatever maps could be found of the territory between Scathfell and Aldaran.

Bread, last summer's brambleberry jam, and a pot of calming herbal tea appeared just as they were all getting comfortable. Kyria and Alayna sat as close together as the furniture would allow, and every few moments one or the other would reach out to clasp hands.

Edric made Alayna go over her story again, the message at Midwinter Festival, and Lord Scathfell's reaction, and finally her discovery of the military encampment. Francisco added helpful details to Alayna's descriptions. Scathfell had never entirely dispersed its army after its defeat a generation ago, despite the cost of maintaining men, horses, and equipment. With his ties to the village and his knowledge of the lands surrounding the castle, Francisco had a thorough understanding of the logistics involved. With Alayna's description of the size of the encampment and the former captain's knowledge, they were able to make rough calculations of the size of the army.

The resulting estimate could easily set siege to the castle. With luck and the element of surprise, they stood a good chance of overwhelming Aldaran's defenses. Despite the

elimination of Scathfell's surprise, the castle was not prepared for a blockade. An enemy could batter them with
catapults and assail their walls with scaling ladders. The
springs that supplied water to the castle were well hidden,
but should they be discovered and poisoned, it might mean
a swift and painful end to the conflict.

At least, Edric thought, they did not have a cadre of *leroni*, such as had served Damon-Rafael Hastur, Old Lord
Scathfell's ally. Their spells had crushed the minds of the
defenders even more brutally than the ordinary soldiers
had stormed the physical defenses; illusions of blood and
terror, and unbearable grief, had immobilized the castle
folk. *But Dorilys had broken the siege.* And somewhere beyond the heights, a new storm waited.

The maps, unrolled on the desk, drew Edric's attention
back to the present. Bennio noted distances, Francisco cal-
culated the speed of the army, and they each made a guess
regarding when Scathfell had departed, taking into account
the time Alayna herself had needed to reach Aldaran.

Now that her first flush of happiness at her reunion
faded, Alayna swayed in her chair. The rigors of her journey
had clearly drained her; she'd held herself together just long
enough to deliver her message. With a quick glance at Edric, one that told him they were very much in accord, Kyria
put an arm around her sister. "Come away, dearest. You
have yet to greet your nephews, and we have much to say to
one another. You have done an amazing feat in bringing us
this news, but surely you can take a little time for yourself
now."

Alayna nodded and got to her feet, leaning heavily on
Kyria. Renata rose also, saying, "I must see about a bedchamber for you."

Meanwhile, there was much to be done. Edric had never
mounted a defense against invaders, but here before him
was a man with military experience. "Francisco, you owe me
no allegiance. If anything, I am in your debt for having pro-
tected *Domna* Alayna on her journey here. You are welcome to remain at Aldaran or go your way with whatever
reward you desire. Yet if you would stay, I would value your
counsel. I know you to be a capable commander. You know
how to fight and how to lead men. Aldaran's prospects
would be strengthened by your expertise."

"*Vai dom*, I have no love for Scathfell. He was a fair-handed master, except for impoverishing his own people—my kin—to support his army. I cannot ease their plight, no matter which way this war goes. But I will do what I may to ensure your folk do not share in that suffering. I failed Lady Kyria once. I will do my utmost to not do so again."

The discussion went on, with Edric asking questions, Francisco offering suggestions, and Roderic supplying knowledge about the castle's physical and human resources. Bennio continued in his usual quietly competent way to write down everything of importance. After a time, it became clear that the next step was for Francisco to inspect the defenses. Edric dismissed his secretary and he, along with Roderic and Francisco, began a tour of the castle walls, approach, and towers.

Edric listened to Francisco's shrewd assessments and Roderic's equally astute opinions, wishing he could contribute more. The defense of this castle and the protection of its people were *his* responsibility. But what could he offer, really, having spent the better part of his adulthood cloistered away in a Tower, mastering not spears and swords but his own *laran*? Finally he left them, saying he would expect a full report by the end of the day.

His feet took him tower-ward, as if they knew what he needed. The tower room was not shielded, but it was remote enough to blunt the incessant psychic chatter of ordinary minds. Light sifted in through the slit windows, casting the interior into muted shadows. The air smelled dusty, which was only to be expected. He had not felt the need for isolation since Kyria had come into his life and his heart. Even here, he could lower his psychic barriers and feel her loving presence.

Lower the barriers . . . As he thought it, they thinned and fell away. Closing his eyes, he opened his mind further. He stood not in a tower but on a pinnacle that pierced the clouds. Around him, air currents surged, growing ever more turbulent. Electrical tension shimmered as it built. Clouds, dark-bellied with rain, piled and shredded and piled even higher.

The storm he'd felt earlier had gained strength. It was *aware* of him, of the place in his mind that was like a mirror to its untrammeled strength.

Here, I am here, we are one, it whispered. *Use me. Release me.*

Edric struggled to hold fast, to feel the stone beneath his feet, inert and dense. The storm was still far off and not yet ready to break. It had no power over him. But the winds were rising on the far-off heights and in his mind. He would not yield to the seduction of the storm, but the wind he could use to advantage.

37

The glider soared on the wind, wood and leather flexing under the force of the currents. The parapet from which Edric had launched dwindled below him. Ever since he had taken his first flight as a boy, there had been nothing to compare with the exhilaration of being airborne. He had loved it from the time he was old enough to master his starstone, and it still evoked an era of limitless possibilities. Of a time before his storm Gift woke in full, a time when Aldaran with its fortress walls and vast holdings seemed the safest place in the world.

He knew the dangers of flight, for Renata had drilled him mercilessly in all the ways he could lose control and be smashed on some rocky slope or crag, or be incinerated by lightning, or perish in a dozen other ways.

Today was no pleasure jaunt, gliding through the air currents; he would need to keep his wits about him. And it was cold and would be even colder as he gained in altitude.

A rising current caught one wing tip. Edric felt the subtle change even before the glider tilted. He tightened his grip on the hand holds and righted himself, using the strength of his torso muscles and a touch of *laran* amplified through his starstone. The glider was responsive, the sky an intricate web of fields and streams. He could feel the storm: the hint of ozone, the thickness of the rain-heavy air, the massing clouds. It was still a distance off, up there beyond the heights. Waiting, gathering itself.

Edric turned his back on the storm and let the winds lift him. Below, Aldaran Castle perched on the heights like a gigantic bird of prey. The road leading from the fortress narrowed to a path, growing ever more steep. Approached from this direction, the castle looked formidable indeed. In the days of his ancestors, ordinary men and means had defended it. Since then, however, steps had been carved into the rock on the far side, leaving it vulnerable to attack. Defending the castle on two fronts would stretch their limited resources.

The environs of the castle fell away behind him. There lay Dead Man's Peak, still showing the scars of fire from years ago. And there, wooded slopes, some of them very steep and cut by ravines. Rows of trees marked nut farms. Here and there, pastures had been cleared, and herds browsed on the spring grass. As he flew on, wild, broken hillsides were more prevalent. A raptor, too large to be a hawk, hovered in the distance. An eagle, then: a good omen.

There they were, a mass of men and horses and wagons, marked by bright flashes of sun on spear points. Until that moment, he had hoped against hope that Alayna had exaggerated, that Francisco, who had not seen this force for himself, had been misled. The oncoming army did not march in formation, it surged along the floor of the valley. Despite his height, he could not see the end of it, a vast, many-legged creature that crept slowly, inexorably, toward his home. Such a force could encircle the castle and storm it from several directions at once.

In the few moments he'd gazed down at the invaders, the air currents had carried him closer. Faces, pale ovals, lifted toward him, and the next instant, arrows raced in his direction. He wheeled away, though it cost him height. The arrows spent their momentum and dropped away, falling short, like bits of straw.

He dipped one wing, swinging wide to catch a rising current. A sudden downdraft seized the glider, sending it plummeting. Earth and sky rushed past. Without the constant pressure of wind, the leather wings fluttered. Edric fought down panic. If he lost too much altitude, the next flight of arrows might well find its mark.

Focus, a woman's voice echoed in his mind, sweet and sure, but whether it was his mother's or that of one of his teachers back at Tramontana—or Kyria's—he could not tell.

The contact brought him back to the disciplined calm of his Tower training. His starstone shimmered in his mind, cool unyielding blue. Time took on the same curiously elongated quality as when working in a matrix circle. Time, he had time.

Look there.

Edric searched ahead for the patterns of heat and cold, the movement of the air. Feeling the faintest pressure, he fed energy into it with his *laran*. It quickly strengthened into an updraft. The wings caught it, leather and wood creaking under the lift. He wavered, momentarily unbalanced, before habit took over. His hand shifted on the controls and his muscles flexed, bringing his body into perfect balance with the glider. Like the eagle he had seen earlier, he soared on the wind.

Land fell away, the slopes, the rocky heights. The army disappeared behind a jagged crestline. Edric spiraled down, searching for a landing place that was high enough to permit an easy take off. He wasn't ready to return to the castle, not yet. Not until he'd had time to think through what he'd just seen. He spotted a promontory, steep as a cliff on one side, with a wide flat ledge bounded on the far side by a jagged outcropping of rock to serve as a wind break. He set down there.

Aldaran wasn't ready to fend off an army of that size, no matter how thick its walls. *Time. We need time.* Time to arm, time to gather together materials to rain down on the besiegers. Even a few days might give his people an advantage. *If there were a way to delay Scathfell's forces . . .*

The storm rumbled promises through the marrow of his bones. Closing his eyes, he gripped the front of his jacket where it overlay his starstone.

A shift in the wind—

In his mind, he saw the directions the gathering storm could go and which were the most likely. It did not surprise him that the easiest led toward the oncoming army, for the storm seemed to have a will of its own. It *wanted* to be directed toward his enemies, even as the lightning had *wanted* to be hurled at the Sain Erach pursuers. Another thought came to him: that each time he used his storm Gift, it acquired a measure of control over him in return. That was nonsense, of course, born of his fears about this form of *laran*.

Even as he thought it, the mass of clouds moved into his field of vision. Winds propelled them, piling them gray and thick, heavy with moisture. Gusts laden with rain and electrical tension battered his face.

No, no lightning. Not this time.

Thunder muttered in the distance, or perhaps it was only in his mind. The storm was moving even more rapidly now, gaining in speed. He positioned the glider, slipped his fingers around the hand holds, crossed the width of the rocky ledge, and hurled himself into the air. A current sent him spiraling upward as he caught the faster-moving winds. He seemed to be racing the wind, rising higher than he'd intended. A sense of danger flashed through him, a sudden realization that he was not riding the air currents, *they* had seized control of his glider and were taking him where *they* willed.

Edric tried to tilt one wing downward and turn away, seeking to escape the grip of the air currents. The glider fought his control, threatening to buck like an unbroken horse. The flying apparatus jerked this way and that. One of the handholds almost wrenched free. Air slammed into him, expelling his breath in a rush.

It's only a storm, he told himself. *Wind and water, nothing more.*

What if it *were* more? What if *these* winds and *these* clouds—Aldaran winds, Aldaran clouds—*remembered*? Remembered the young girl who had summoned lightning, bolt after great blue-white bolt? Remembered smashing into the human forces besieging Aldaran?

There, below—

He blinked, for a terrifying moment unsure if what he saw were real or some image from a generation ago. *Masses of men, moving slowly but inexorably forward, crowding together as the passage through the valley narrowed.*

This was *now*, and he was really seeing the Scathfell army. He hung in the air between the black-bellied clouds and the land. The army below showed no sign of slowing. If anything, the gathering storm hastened their pace.

Thunder crackled, all but deafening him. Ice-edged wind rushed around him. He tipped the glider and this time it answered him, allowing him to drop slightly. Lightning hovered at the edges of his senses. Metallic saliva filled his mouth. He could almost taste burned flesh. Power gathered around him. It filled him with longing.

All it would take was a breath, a thought.

With an effort, he pulled his mind free of the lightning's seductive lure. It felt like tearing out part of himself, part of his Gift. His body shuddered, and he almost lost control of the glider.

Winds swirled, catching him, tossing him upward, toward the heart of the storm. Whiteness blotted out sky and land, and icy wetness drenched his skin. The metal clips at the tips of the glider's wings gleamed as if, against all reason, they had been ignited. Electrical tension bathed him. One wrong movement, one momentary lapse in concentration would send the immense power of lightning through his own body. He saw it now, saw that the only way to survive was to discharge the potential. There, into the heart of the army. The storm had built to such a peak of tension that it was inevitable. Through him or around him, lightning poised to strike.

Edric reached for the power within him, the Gift he knew as intimately as the darkness behind his eyes. For long years in a Tower he had trained in its use. In its mastery. Now he reached for that hard-won discipline. His thoughts lifted free of the tumult around him. He steadied himself and focused through his starstone. As the matrix gem amplified his natural talent, the inside of his skull filled with blue luminescence, too bright for his human eyes to bear. He gathered it up, shaped it into a net of mental energy, and cast it outward.

The net looped neatly around the center of the storm, which was not a physical place but a nexus of power. He thought he heard a girl's voice in the tumult—laughing, singing, he could not tell. Then it was gone, and only the rush and roar of the natural winds remained.

The lightning yearned for the land, as the land yearned for the sky. The land *reached up*, but Edric was ready, and a fractional instant later, he clamped his psychic grip on the potential force in the clouds—and *twisted*—

What happened next was akin to trying to cup water with his fingers spread. The storm could not be contained, only deflected. The *laran* net held just long enough for him to hurl the incandescent center of the lightning obliquely away from its course.

Brightness, caustic and blinding, flared around him, yet did not touch him. It slid past him, draining away toward the slope on the far side of the army.

This particular lightning strike might be diverted, but the momentum of the oncoming storm could not be so easily thrust aside. It contained not one but a multitude of such bolts. They were like a cresting wave about to break.

Winds sped past Edric with such force, they sent the glider tipping erratically. Thunder, felt as much as heard, rattled through his body. With another flash and a sound like the cracking of a whip, almost at the same time, the clouds released their burden of water. It came as a deluge, without any preliminary sprinkles. Torrents of near-freezing water turning the air a wall of gray.

Lashing, half-frozen rain and violent downdrafts slammed into the glider. The wings tilted ominously, first this way and then that. It was all Edric could do not to spin out of control. He was still high enough that under other conditions, he might recover, but these winds were too strong.

His breath rasped in his lungs. Bone-deep chill combined with the exertion of his *laran*. Hail pelted him as the cloud sucked colder air from above. He could not tell if he was shivering or if the glider quivered under the impact of the winds. His hands went numb in their gloves. In a matter of seconds, the leather wings and his clothing were drenched.

The storm was moving very fast. There was no time to think or plan, and he was almost above the vanguard of the army. If he could not find a way out of this current, he would be forced to land. He could see the soldiers under their cloaks as they rushed ahead in an attempt to outrun the worst of the storm. Here and there, a face turned up toward him, close enough to recognize mouths open in alarm, and

then hands gesturing. A mounted officer spurred his horse
forward. Even through the rain, Edric glimpsed the muted
gleam of wet steel.

Lord of Light, let me not fall! For if he did, this army
would overcome Aldaran's defenses and swarm over the
walls, killing or taking prisoner everyone it encountered.

As if in answer to his prayer, a rising current lifted the
glider. The craft teetered, shedding water, and the soaked
wood groaned. Edric used his matrix stone to strengthen
the struts. The storm fought him, reluctant to release him
from its grasp.

Before his eyes, brightness flashed, jagged branching
trees that reduced flesh to ashes, fractured stone, and laid
waste the earth. But it was only an illusion, the fate he had
long feared. He had learned, hard and painfully, to give such
things no place in his mind.

The lightning disappeared as quickly as it had come.

——— ◆ ———

By the time Edric reached Aldaran, he had passed beyond
exhaustion. He could no longer feel his hands or feet. It was
all he could do to maintain his tattered concentration on his
matrix and trust instinct to guide him home. Winds, frigid
with altitude and the lingering hold of winter, sliced through
his sodden clothing and deep into his marrow. Ice turned
the leather wings slick and brittle.

Sweating and shivering, Edric brought the glider down
on the slope leading to the main gates of the castle. Trailing
the glider behind him, he flexed his knees to absorb the
impact, as he had been taught. His knees gave way under
him. He lost his balance, but somehow he managed to free
himself from the glider before tumbling gracelessly to the
ground. Two guardsmen raced toward him, concern in their
faces. He tried to wave them off and clamber to his feet, but
his muscles were as responsive as frozen clay. When he tried
to talk, to tell them that he must speak with Roderic, all that
came out of his mouth were incoherent moans. The guardsmen carried him into the sheltered courtyard and then into
the castle.

He floated in and out of strange dream-like states; once
or twice, his eyes tried to focus on the interior of a room. It
was not his, but that was as far as his thinking mind would

take him. Then he drifted through a sea of blue light and was tossed in a storm, its clouds, rain, and waves of coruscating brightness, as if lightning played across the interior of his skull. Finally the world became solid enough for him to comprehend that he was lying on a padded bench in the familiar tower room. His mother must have had him brought to her so she could perform *laran* healing undisturbed. Three or four feather comforters swathed him from the chin down. In the distance, thunder muttered.

"You're awake," Lady Renata said, although whether she was sitting beside him or in Temora by the sea, he could not be sure.

Edric licked his lips and found them dry, but encountered a familiar taste that often lingered after he'd received a *laran* healing. He had no memory of how he'd got up here, but he did remember the storm. And being so cold that he stopped feeling the chill.

"I nearly killed myself, didn't I?" It was a good thing she didn't know about the lightning. "But I made it, and I have news about Scathfell—"

Renata waved him to silence. "I'm not your Keeper. If I were, I'd have a thing or two to say to you about flying off into a thunderstorm—"

"It came up suddenly," he protested, but weakly.

"—but since I'm your mother, I have a different thing or two to say to you—"

"—about flying off into a thunderstorm."

"Your life is not your own, you know. You came dangerously close to overloading your energon channels. Not to mention exhausting yourself from exposure."

He wiggled the fingers that had gone numb. They felt fine, as did his toes and the tip of his nose. "I suppose I have you to thank for not losing a few appendages to frostbite."

"I did what I could. You'll need to rest, or your body will give you no choice."

Closing his eyes and snuggling deeper into the cocoon of bedding sounded like a wonderful idea. *For just a while.* "Kyria, she knows I'm all right?"

"She knows you made it back, and she would not have left your side if I had not insisted." Renata paused, focus turning inward for a moment. "I've nowhere near the strength I once had, but even then, I could not have worked a *laran* healing with someone so distraught and so closely bound to you in the same room."

Kyria would have been furious at being ejected. Best to get the essential business over with so he could reassure her before he passed into a stupor. With aching joints and strained muscles, Edric groaned and managed to sit up. The effort left him breathing hard. "I must speak with Roderic as soon as possible."

"Yes, I expected as much. You kept mumbling about telling him what you'd found. I've set up the office as your war room. If you can make it that far on your own, I'll arrange to have everything you need made ready. If not, I can have you carried down." She made no mention of allowing Roderic to invade her tower working space.

Quickly, Edric assessed the remnants of his energy and judged that he had enough to clamber down the stairs as far as the office. He managed, slowly and with many pauses to catch his breath, to pull on woolen leggings, then loose trousers and a winter weight linex shirt, soft with wear. Just as he was fumbling with the laces of a quilted vest, the door burst open and Kyria rushed into the room. Her face was red and she was out of breath. Plainly, she'd run all the way up the tower stairs. Knowing her, she'd probably taken them two at a time.

She paused, chest heaving. "You impossible man—what did you think you were doing?"

Laughter bubbled up in him, for this was so exactly like Kyria. "You have every right to chastise me," he admitted. "The sky didn't look so bad when I left, or I might not—no, I won't lie to you. I would have gone anyway. We are on the brink of war, my love, and that means ordinary precautions must give way to the necessities of survival."

But if you had been killed . . . Kyria bit her lip and looked away. She rubbed her arms, hugging them to her body, as if she too had taken a chill. *It was a risk you had to take.*

What had he done to deserve such a wife?

Her poise collapsed, and she threw herself down beside him and wrapped him in her arms. He felt how hard she was trying to not cry.

"It was worth the risk," he said.

"It was?" She drew back and gazed into his face. Her cheeks had gone blotchy.

"Indeed, for now I know where Scathfell's forces are, and I was able to delay them, if only for a little."

"I suppose those are good things."

"Those are *necessary* things."

"I saw you when Andres and Tirone carried you in. You were practically *encased* in ice! And babbling away, making no sense. I'm afraid I made rather a scene, but Lady Renata took everyone in hand. Poor Alayna turned white when she saw you. I suppose she was remembering how chilled she got on the journey from Rockraven, or maybe she blames herself or— Oh, dear! Now I'm the one who's babbling, aren't I?"

Edric did not trust himself to stay upright if he tried to kiss her, so he lifted one of her hands to his lips. "You have every cause, so I forgive you. But only if you help me with these gods-forsaken laces. I must meet with Roderic and Francisco while I still have the strength."

"Whoever designed this garment clearly had no idea its wearers would be half-frozen. Or maybe thought they would all have body-servants—or wives—to help them." With a few deft motions, Kyria adjusted the laces. "There! That's better."

By the time Edric had finished dressing, the process made speedier by Kyria's assistance, he felt steadier. This clarity of mind was temporary, however. He had a little time, riding on the healing and the hot food he hoped would be waiting for him, before his energy gave out. His body needed to restore itself, one way or another. If he did not rest—meaning deep, unbroken sleep, not merely sitting quietly—his body would take what it needed. He would rather be in his own bed when he collapsed.

— ✦ —

A short time later, Edric sat in his place before a fire in the new war room, where maps had been unrolled on the desk. On the side table, Renata had set out an array of restorative foods, typical of those consumed after a night's matrix work in a Tower, and hot drinks, none of them alcoholic. Roderic sat across the table, flanked by a couple of officers. Francisco stood a pace or two behind Roderic, looking grim.

Edric sipped the near-scalding *jaco* and went over his tale again. The rain would slow the army, but not deter them. "I might have bought us a few days with the storm," he concluded, "but before this tenday is out, he will be upon us."

Roderic knew the country well and asked questions about the exact location of the army.

"I remember the place where the road narrowed," Francisco said, pointing to the map. "When Lady Alayna and I passed it, I considered the potential of an ambush."

Ambush. Edric remembered how he had directed the lightning to the rock face above the stream, cutting off pursuit by the Sain Erach bandits. He tried to envision the hillsides around the road on which Scathfell's forces were advancing. Was it possible to shear off enough rock to block their passage? Or delay them even more?

Distant lightning hummed along his nerves, and in his mind, a high wild voice shrilled.

If only I had . . .

"I do not think we can send sufficient men to be effective," Roderic was saying, "even if we could spare them from the castle defense."

"Especially if we must face them from more than one direction," Francisco commented.

"I concur," Edric said. His eyesight turned bleary and he was having difficulty keeping track of the conversation.

"*Vai dom*, I fear we have overtaxed you," Roderic said, straightening up from where he had bent over the map. "We still have time before Lord Scathfell arrives, and with Captain Francisco's counsel, we will put it to good use. Rest now, and let us do our work."

Meaning, Edric supposed, that he should not add to their burden with an exhausted, babbly lord. He gathered his legs under him. Somewhat to his surprise, he was able to stand. With a word or two of parting encouragement, he made it to his own bedchamber, where Kyria waited to tuck him under the comforters.

— ✦ —

He dreamed of flying, suspended between the heavens and the earth. It seemed the most natural thing in the world to stretch out his arms and catch the rising air currents. The winds were bracingly fresh but not uncomfortable, no matter how high he went. Gradually he became aware of wispy clouds that thickened as they piled into gleaming heaps. Without conscious thought, he headed toward them.

Mists engulfed him, at first warm and soothing, then turning cool and colder. The air pressed against him like tides of ice. Each new wave sapped the heat from his body until he went numb and no longer cared.

A voice reached him, not the one singing behind the clouds but one he should know. "He's burning up."

Cool fingers touched his face. "I feared as much."

All he wanted was to rest in the gently rolling clouds. But he was cold, so cold.

"—if we cannot reach him—"

Flashes of light illuminated the mist in which he floated. At first they were faint, as if diffused through many layers. They could have arisen from the reflectivity of the clouds. But they came again—a flash and then a pause, then another flash, brighter this time and drawing ever closer. The storm was searching for him.

Why not let it come to him? The pattern of ever more rapid flashes was hypnotic, soothing. Something in him called out to the lights . . . *needed* them.

Then, in the mysterious way of dreams, the cloud layer beneath him thinned into perfect clearness. He saw, spread out on the landscape beneath him, a multitude of shambling forms. Even from this height, he could make out individual creatures, misshapen and menacing. Not men and horses but monsters bent on abominable deeds. Crawling, slithering, slithering ever close to his home. His family. His mother, his wife, his sons whom he loved more than his own life.

Fear chilled him, even more than the mists had, quickly giving way to outrage. How dare they threaten him and his? *Evil, vile, loathsome—he would stop them.*

Lightning answered his flash of anger.

He would smash them.

A girl's voice, laughing and shrieking, near hysteria—

He would blast them.

—past hysteria, into a realm of raw energy—

The firmament exploded into cascades of searing light.

Above him, the storm rumbled. Another flash illuminated the scene below, to be answered an instant later with a deafening whipcrack. Power gathered, more than enough to rout the enemy. *Kill and maim and burn them.*

Use me . . . whispered through his mind. He shivered and burned and *reached*—

And sent the next bolt into the thickest part of the army. It branched and then branched again, until a hundred incandescent tendrils rained down on men and beasts. Great sizzling streams of force shot down, striking again and again. Each one left earth blackened and churned, and shriveled husks that were once living men.

Fire showered the narrow valley. Thunder crackled and boomed overhead. More lightning, and yet more, each bolt filling him, mind and body, with brightness too intense to bear. He could no longer see—he *felt* the devastation going on below him. Despite the deluge, the Scathfell army wagons were burning, as were men here and there, torches in the gathering darkness. Distantly he heard wailing and howling and wordless shrieks of agony. Men rushed about, a few stopping to lift their fallen comrades.

A thought stirred, faint and distant, in his mind, that this was not what he wanted. That these were men like himself, helpless against the immensity of the storm.

He tried to draw back, to withhold the next surge of lightning, but the storm had him in its grip. He no longer directed it with his will. Elemental power poured forth from him.

Thunder crashed, peal after deafening peal. Electrical bolts split the sky and lanced down toward the surviving soldiers. A single man stood firm, trying to rally the troops, bidding them to hold fast. A few men clambered to their feet. The earth around them had turned into a pool of mud. A flash flood was forming as a torrent of rain sluiced down the hillsides.

Raw power surged through Edric, hurling toward the group of men and their leader. Even as it leapt from the clouds, from his mind, he tried to hold it back. He had nothing to grasp it with. As it shot earthward, he managed to redirect it. Only a fraction of a degree, but enough that it struck beside the group of men, not in their midst. The next instant, they scrambled back the way they had come, some on their feet, others dragged along.

Then, as if the great red sun had at last had burned itself out, darkness suffused the firmament. At first, he felt only a diminishing of the incandescent flashes inside him. Then came pauses like the swift falling of night, and ever weaker bolts. No longer thick trunks of light, the strikes appeared as delicate threads that fanned out and fell away.

He heard a distant voice—a woman's voice—but what she was saying and what meaning it held for him, he did not know. Then even that fell into oblivion.

38

Kyria sat on a cushioned footstool, hugging her knees to her chest and trying not to cry. A short distance away, Alayna played with the twins. The nursery was warm and bright, and the familiar baby-smell tugged at Kyria's heart. Her body wanted to give in to the intense, overwhelming feeling of well-being, but her mind would not let go. Her *laran* linked her to Edric, and through her storm sense, she had followed his frenzied psychic flight. She had felt the lightning rampage through him, emanate from him and, worst of all, *remain within him*. The exact details of where he had aimed the storm were hidden from her. In his delirium, he might well have attacked Scathfell's forces, but there was no way to be certain. If that were the case, he had inflicted horrific damage, as bad or worse than the scarred areas around Aldaran Castle. Or perhaps what she had experienced was primarily hallucination, an effect of his fever.

Roderic had sent a party on a reconnaissance mission to the likely location of the Scathfell forces, and Francisco had gone with them. They might be gone perhaps a tenday, depending on what they found and how quickly the wounded, if any, could be brought to Aldaran. Kyria could not bring herself to worry about Gwynn-Alar Scathfell. It must have been dreadful for him, finding out she was alive, married, and a mother, but that did not excuse bringing his army to conquer Aldaran. In a sense, he deserved what happened to him, although she would not say so aloud for fear of distressing her sister.

What had happened to Edric was another matter. If his brain had been permanently damaged by the energies that had been channeled through him, if he was now like his kinswoman, the Witch-Child of Aldaran, then it was not safe to allow him to wake.

If only Dorilys had been born without laran. *Then there would never have been a war with Scathfell and everyone would be happy today.*

No, that was not true. The fight had been complicated by royal politics. If Dorilys had not defeated the besieging armies of Old Lord Scathfell and King Allart's brother, then who knows what might have happened? Aldaran might have fallen. Edric might never have been born—nor their amazing, wonderful sons, surely the most perfect babes ever created. And if she kept thinking this way, she would surely break into tears.

Edric is strong. He learned discipline at Tramontana Tower. He is a grown man, not a child, she chanted silently to herself.

She could not stop remembering how dreadfully ill he'd looked. He had cried out in his sleep, and she'd rushed into their bedchamber. The comforters she had tucked around him so carefully had been thrown off. He writhed, as if trying to free himself from the tangled sheets. His skin glistened with sweat, and his eyes jerked this way and that behind half-closed lids. When she'd called his name, he had not responded. And when she'd touched him—dear gods, his skin had been as hot as if he'd just raced through a forest fire. Nothing she'd said or done, even straining to reach him through their *laran* rapport, had made the slightest difference in his frantic tossing and turning, or in the barely human moans that forced their way through his clenched teeth.

He hadn't known her. Out of desperation and not trusting any of the servants with the message, Kyria herself had gone to fetch Lady Renata. If anyone could help Edric, it would be someone trained in a Tower and skilled in healing; someone who loved him. Renata, sensing Edric's distress, had already been on her way. She had taken one look at her son, and her entire manner had changed. Firmly but not unkindly, she had shoved Kyria out the door.

Now Kyria could not feel Edric with her mind. She was sure she would know if he had died—*no, she must not even think that*—but where he had once been a constant, living presence in the very core of her being, she sensed only a blankness. A wall of flannel and chalk. Kyria felt a rush of despair, not for the first time nor the fifteenth since she had left her husband to Renata's care. Thoughts boiled up, images of Edric soaring into a violent thunderstorm, of grasping the lightning and absorbing it into himself, of flinging bolt after bolt at the approaching army. *Just as Dorilys had done.*

He would not suffer the same fate, burned out from elemental energies no human mind could contain. Nor would he be contained within a *laran* field, neither alive nor dead.

Alayna looked up from where she sat on the carpet. Her delight in the twins filled the room like her music. She seemed serene, except for a faint tension between her brows.

Donal, ever the more adventuresome, rocked forward on his hands and knees, grasping for the wooden ball in Alayna's hands. Instead of giving it to him, she placed it just beyond his reach. Cooing, he lunged for it, then shrieked with delight when his chubby fingers touched it, then howled with dismay as it rolled away. Kyria could not help smiling. Both boys, but Donal especially, made their feelings known without reservation.

"He'll be crawling soon," Alayna said, catching the ball and handing it to Donal.

"You're wonderful with them." Kyria thought it was a shame that Alayna could not have a dozen babes of her own. Perhaps if she had, Lord Scathfell would have better things to do than make war on his neighbors. From the instant Alayna had laid eyes on the twins, she'd doted on them. They, in their turn, responded to her as if they had always known her, especially Pietro.

"Are you worrying about your husband?" Alayna asked. "You have the most peculiar expression on your face."

"*Both* our husbands, although for different reasons. Here we are, two sisters married to men who cannot find their way to even being polite to one another. If Donal and Pietro behave so"—the ball escaped Donal's grasp and rolled toward his brother, who grabbed it with a gurgle of pleasure—"it is because they are too young to know better."

"*We* did not always agree," Alayna pointed out. "I distinctly remember at least one occasion of pulled hair and stolen dolls."

"Let's not forget the rather inventive name-calling that went with it. But we were children. Even though we squabbled, we always made up."

Now Donal wanted the ball back, but Pietro merely clutched it tighter. Kyria snatched up a stuffed cloth horse and offered it to Donal, who settled happily to chewing on the horse's yarn mane.

Alayna sighed. "Somehow, I doubt it will be this simple to get grown men to see reason."

"As much as I hate to admit it, I believe you are right. The world, and the affairs of men, go as they will, not as you and I would have them."

"We must wait for word of my husband." Alayna sounded strained and careworn. "The principle thing now is what has happened to yours."

Meaning, Kyria thought, *whether he has gone the way of our kinswoman. Whether there is any hope for him at all.*

As if summoned by Kyria's renewed anxiety, Renata entered the room. Lines bracketed her mouth, and the skin around her eyes looked bruised. She paused inside the door, and Kyria saw the twins had the same effect on her as they did on everyone who saw them. The tension in Renata's features softened, so that she looked weary rather than desolate.

Kyria struggled to her feet. "How fares my husband? Is he out of danger?"

"I have done what I can for him." Renata lowered herself into the rocking chair where Kyria often sat to sing lullabies. "I can detect no trace of the storm's electrical energy in the *laran* centers of his brain, and his channels are clear. We cannot know for sure whether there is any damage until he wakes. I fear—I *believe* he may be unconscious for some time."

"Oh, no."

Renata shook her head. "Don't say that, for this is a good

thing. Body and mind need to rest deeply to replenish themselves. As difficult as it is for us to wait, this is truly for the best."

"How—how long?"

"A few days. Perhaps longer." Renata did not add what would happen if Edric's period of unconsciousness stretched beyond that.

"I know it is a very foolish thing to go flying in a thunderstorm," Alayna said, almost shyly. "But Edric seemed to be all right when he returned. What happened to him? Was it the same thing that happened to Great-Aunt Dorilys?"

Renata flinched, and Kyria remembered that she had known Dorilys personally, having come to Aldaran for the purpose of teaching her to control her *laran*.

"Exposure to the elements at a time when Edric was already expending vast amounts of *laran* energy caused him to become ill." Now Renata sounded dispassionate, as if discussing a clinical case and not her own son. "It was the resulting fever that allowed the storm Gift to escape his control."

"But that is terrible," Alayna cried, then recovered herself. "Please forgive me, Lady Renata. I did not mean that to be as insensitive as it sounded. I truly wish no harm to my brother-in-law. *He* was not the originator of this calamity."

"Child, we are all of us grieved by what has come to pass. But we have reason to hope. My son's training as a *laranzu* served him well, for the electrical energy was confined to the areas of his brain associated with his storm Gift. And those are areas he has used in a disciplined manner over the years; even racked with fever, such training shielded him from the worst." Renata closed her eyes, resting her head against the high back of the chair.

Kyria had come to love her mother-in-law, and Edric would never forgive her if she allowed Renata to become ill, too. "Lady Renata, I fear you have overtired yourself. Do you need assistance to your own chamber? Shall I call for your ladies? And food! You always have food prepared after *laran* work!"

Renata opened her eyes, a faint smile brightening her face. "I suppose I deserve to be lectured about the proper safeguards. I will take myself to my quarters, and if you will be so kind to have a platter of whatever is sweet and easily eaten sent up—dried fruit, honey pastries, the like. And some *jaco*. I don't care if it's fresh so long as it's heavily sweetened." Sighing, she stood. "But you must promise to let me know the minute Edric stirs, in case he requires additional healing."

Kyria promised. Immediately after Renata left, she ordered food and drink to be sent to her chambers.

"It is all my fault, you know." Alayna lifted tear-bright eyes to Kyria. "If only I'd helped Gwynn more, been more sympathetic to what he was suffering, then he might have been able to leave the dead in their graves and see that your Edric meant him nothing but good. There would have been no cause to go to war. But it was too much for him."

"I fear that all our gestures of friendship could not overcome a lifetime of suspicion," Kyria said with a sigh. "Scathfell suffered terribly in the last conflict, and that was not your doing."

Alayna drew in a shuddering breath, and Kyria feared she would burst into tears, but she calmed herself.

"Perhaps Lord Scathfell survived," Kyria said. "The scouts will report soon, and then we will render what aid we can. We will not leave a single man or beast to perish from cold or their wounds."

"You are very forgiving."

"Why, would you not do the same for Aldaran, if our positions were reversed?"

"How can you ask such a thing? You know that I would."

Kyria could not help smiling. "What a pity it is that the affairs of our two realms must be left to the men, for I am sure that if *we* had anything to say, Aldaran and Scathfell would soon be as brothers."

"Mmm," Alayna replied, looking pensive.

"Now I should go to my husband," Kyria said, pausing on her way to the door. "I must see for myself how he fares, and of course be there when he wakes. Shall I call for the nurse to take care of the children?"

"If you wish, but really it is no trouble at all to look after these two angels," Alayna replied. As if on cue, Pietro reached up to her. She lifted him into her lap, where he leaned against her, sucking his thumb. Alayna laid her cheek against the top of his head.

Kyria was not at all sure what she would find when she entered the chamber where Edric had been moved. It was not their shared bedroom, for Renata had felt the bustle and noise from the adjacent nursery would not be helpful. If it had been up to Renata, Kyria suspected, she would have chosen the tower room as the best place for *laran* work, but Kyria had insisted he be closer at hand. They had compromised on the bedchamber that once belonged to Old Lord Aldaran. It had not been used since his death, but had the virtue of being sufficiently apart from the rest of the living quarters.

And a gloomy old place it is, Kyria thought as she sped along the corridor. Still, it could not be helped. If Edric was asleep, he would not care, and once he woke, he would be free of that dark room.

A guardsman stood on duty outside the massive carved door. He bowed as Kyria passed. Inside, Edric's body-servant, Correy, sat in a chair beside the enormous bed, ready should his master need anything. The room was indeed gloomy; with the draperies drawn, the only light came from the fire in the wide hearth and a few candles in either wall sconces or holders placed here and there. Kyria sniffed, detecting a hint of dust, but thankfully no mildew. At least the fire chased off the worst of the chill, and a handful of aromatic wood chips perfumed the air.

Edric's skin looked waxen in the light from the candles. He was breathing slowly but regularly. When Kyria bent to kiss his forehead, he felt slightly cool but not worrisomely so. At least he no longer burned with fever.

"Beloved," she murmured, stroking his hair back from his face. Closing her eyes, she tried to imagine him gazing at her with the tender expression that never failed to move her.

He did not respond, not in the slightest, and that told her he must be very deeply asleep. In all the time they had been together, no matter how weary he was, he always roused at the sound of her voice. Perhaps it would be better to not put that to too great a test. Renata had insisted he needed rest. Yet Kyria imagined the distinct traces of his personality, quiescent but resilient.

"It looks like I'll be here awhile," she murmured, mostly to herself. In short order, she hauled the draperies open, admitting a flood of late afternoon light. And, unfortunately, revealing the dust that a cursory cleaning of the room had missed.

Correy assisted her in moving the least uncomfortable-looking of the chairs. Settling in it at Edric's side, she wished she were as musical as Alayna. Playing the *rryl* would have soothed her nerves and been a lovely thing to waken to. She considered and discarded the idea of a wooden flute and the needlework that every lady was supposed to have at hand for moments like this. Mending a harness would have suited her mood, but that wasn't practical for other reasons. In the end, she settled for sending Correy to fetch a book — any book — from the castle library. He returned a short time later with a treatise on the care and breeding of chervines, which was as good a subject as any. Kyria fell asleep during the second chapter.

She startled awake at the sound of the door closing softly. Her first thought was that night had fallen. The windows looked out into darkness, although the fire burned even more brightly than before. Her second thought brought her to her feet, gazing down at Edric, who had rolled onto his side facing her. Surely that was a good thing, that he'd moved?

And the third, which had woken her, turned out to be Alayna carrying a tray with several covered dishes and a pot of *jaco*, recognizable from the distinctive aroma.

"You didn't need to—" Kyria cut herself off, rather than say *fetch and carry like a servant*. At home, neither of them would have thought anything of taking a meal to the other.

"Nonsense," was Alayna's response. "I've had so many trays like this brought to me that I couldn't compensate if I spent the next year doing nothing else."

"I don't think either of us will adjust to being a fine lady," Kyria murmured around bites of bean and root vegetable stew.

"It takes time," Alayna said. "You don't want to imitate the ladies in those awful romances we used to playact, but there are things you can learn."

"What, how to not be a bubble-head?"

"You can rest assured, I am in no danger of forgetting

that," Alayna replied with a grin. "I meant that things and people change, and how I see them changes, too. When I first came to Scathfell, I felt like such an ignorant goose."

Sipping her *jaco*, Kyria eyed her sister more closely. Alayna might sound just as feather-brained as ever on occasion, but there was a new solidness, a strength about her. She might have been impressionable and easy to manipulate once, but now it would take more than a lazy servant or a scheming courtier to sway her.

Blessed Cassilda, may her husband be found alive.

— ✦ —

The next few days crept by, with Kyria, Renata, and Alayna taking turns sitting with Edric, although Kyria insisted on taking the longest shifts. Edric was able to swallow liquids, lukewarm meat broth or tea laced with honey. Renata pronounced it an excellent sign.

When she was not sleeping or playing with the twins, Alayna kept Kyria company. The two found much to talk about as they caught up with each other. At times, they laughed so uproariously that Kyria thought they must surely waken Edric, and once or twice she could have sworn she saw him smile, though he slept on.

Alayna's *rryl* had been left behind at Scathfell Castle, but there was a fairly good instrument in the Aldaran collection, one that had once belonged to their kinswoman, Aliciane. Alayna re-strung it and regaled Kyria with old favorites, as well as songs she had learned from Perdita.

Late one afternoon, there came a rapping on the door to Kyria's sitting room. The guardsman outside was one Kyria knew, Andres, and standing in front of him, ill at ease, was a page; one of the boys who ran messages within the castle and its grounds.

"If you please, my lady, the scouts have returned from the battle."

Kyria hesitated, but only for a moment. She could leave the matter to Renata, who had acted as Edric's regent during the years of his minority and while he was at Tramontana. But *she* was Lady Aldaran. It fell to her to act on her husband's behalf. Until that moment, she had assumed he would be awake when Francisco and the others returned. She had never thought to act in his stead.

"Captain Francisco says to tell you," the page rushed on, "they were delayed by the wounded."

"How many wounded?"

The boy's eyes were huge with alarm, pupils so dilated his eyes looked black. "Many."

Alayna came up beside her, brows taut with concern. "I will come, too, in case there is news of Gwynn."

"Correy," Kyria called over her shoulder to Edric's body-servant, "let me know the instant there is any change. Andres, come with me." She and Alayna hurried out of the room, pausing only to dispatch the page to inform Lady Renata of the situation.

Outside the castle's massive double doors, the sheltered courtyard teemed with men and horses, and a pair of heavily laden wagons, everyone milling around and making so much noise that at first Kyria could not tell what was going on. Then she began to make sense of the scene: her own men, *there* and *there* and more issuing from the castle and outbuildings. Men sitting or lying on the carts. Limping, bandaged soldiers even now being supported by Aldaran people. A few men on horseback—Francisco, *there*—and a tall, chestnut-haired man in armor and Scathfell colors, one side of his face crusted with dried blood.

"Gwynn!" Alayna cried, clutching Kyria's hand.

Kyria's memories surged up, of one brutally cold winter when she was a child and her father and every man able to wield a spear or shoot an arrow had gone out to defend the lands around the manor house from an invasion of wolves— both the starving beasts and the equally rapacious human kind. Ellimira, heavy with her first child, had taken charge of preparations at home. No one could have known how many would return, if any, and in what condition. Everyone had pitched in, even little Alayna. Now these people before her—castle folk and former enemies, strangers and kin— were her charge.

She quickly designated where the wounded men were to go first, and which areas were to be given over to treatment. She directed that herbs and other preparations used in treating the injured were to be made available, along with bandages and hot water and anything else that was needed. The livestock were to be taken to the stables and cared for, and hot meals served to everyone.

"*Vai domna!*" Francisco reined his horse to a restive halt before Kyria. Sweat darkened the animal's hide, flecked with lather. He glanced this way and that, and she realized he was searching for Edric.

"Are these all the survivors?" she asked.

"No, only the ones in the worst shape. Some escaped the storm and have disappeared or are making their way back to Scathfell."

"Get everyone inside and out of this cold, starting with the most badly injured. The castle, not the guardsmen's barracks." Looking around, Kyria spotted Kermiac, Aldaran's *coridom*, with a handful of his senior staff at his heels. She rattled off a string of orders, everything she could remember Ellimira doing. When she drew breath, Kermiac nodded gravely and said, "I will see to it all, my lady."

Just then Renata emerged from the castle, leading a handful of women. Kyria recognized some of them as the most experienced with herbs and treating daily minor ailments.

"I've set up an infirmary in the Great Hall, as you ordered," Renata said. "It's about time it was put to good use."

"Captain Francisco," Kyria said, "take the men who are worst off inside, those in the wagons first. Lady Renata will show you where." She turned to Andres, who had halted a pace behind her, as was proper. "You're to assist him. Take whatever other men you need."

The courtyard began to clear at an astonishing rate. A pair of stable boys led the wagon mules right up to the steps so that Kyria and Alayna were forced to move aside as one man after another was carried inside. Some moaned in pain, their bodies so badly burned Kyria did not see how they could survive. Others were able to sit up but not walk, their crudely splinted legs sticking out at angles. One had been strapped to a pair of branches at shoulders and hips. He did not move as two Aldaran guardsmen lifted the stretcher. The smell of charred flesh and the barely stifled cries of agony sent a pang through Kyria's chest. Alayna had taken hold of her hand—Kyria had no memory of when—and held it tightly.

Edric, *her Edric*, had done this.

Francisco, still on horseback, watched it all from near the base of the steps, occasionally shouting out orders. Lord

Scathfell approached and dismounted, or rather half-fell, half-slid to the ground. His face was white and set, except for the swathe of dried blood across one temple and cheekbone. He seemed to be staying upright by sheer pride and strength of will. Squaring his shoulders, he addressed himself to Francisco.

"I can ask no more than what is being done for my men. Now all that remains—"

With a cry, Alayna released Kyria's hand and rushed down the stairs. Lord Scathfell stared at her, his expression unreadable. Alayna, too, felt the awkwardness of the moment. She halted a pace away from him. Kyria thought that if either of them moved, they would both shatter.

A dozen thoughts went through Kyria's mind, the most terrifying of which was that Lord Scathfell realized Alayna had warned Aldaran of the attack.

If he threatens her, I will flay him alive!

Lord Scathfell lifted his face again to Francisco and said, his voice bleak and expressionless, "All that now remains is for me to make my surrender to Lord Aldaran."

"You may do so, in the proper time and place," Kyria said, a trace more severely than she intended, because she was still angry on her sister's behalf.

"My lady, I am at somewhat of a loss, for I do not believe we have met."

"I am Kyria Rockraven-Aldaran, your sister-in-law. At one time we were betrothed."

Lord Scathfell's chapped lips moved, but no words came out. Kyria could not tell what he might be thinking, beyond the obvious fact that he and his wife were now in the hands of those he had sought to destroy. She didn't know him except by his recent aggressive actions and her sister's reports, and those were so contradictory, and the man beside her so plainly in need of care, that she had no time to sort things out.

"Will it please you to come inside, as guest and kinsman to this house?" Kyria said.

"*Vai domna*, I do not intend insult, but honor demands that I make my address to Lord Aldaran first."

"I am *Lady* Aldaran."

Lord Scathfell hesitated, a flush reddening his features. *Perhaps*, Kyria thought, *he realizes how rude that was.*

Blessed Cassilda, the man has an absolute gift for rebuffing those who would be his friends. But he was Alayna's husband, no matter what had passed between them, so Kyria renewed her determination to treat him with the same generosity that she would want Edric to receive, had their positions been reversed. She was going to have an uphill time of it, if the stubborn expression now settling on Lord Scathfell's face was any indication.

Before either could say more, Alayna spoke up. Her voice rang, clear and confident, above the sounds of the courtyard. "My husband, there has been enough suffering because of men long in their graves. Edric Aldaran is not his father, any more than you are yours. Let this be an end to the madness."

He bowed to her, perhaps a shade more formally than etiquette demanded. She responded with a curtsy that would have done honor to the grandest lady in Queen Cassandra's court.

"I think you must have hit your head on something exceptionally hard," Alayna went on, "that you stand out here, half-freezing. Or you would know an offer of hospitality truce when you hear one." She swung her arms wide, encompassing the entire castle, courtyard and all. "Did anyone here ask for your surrender? In fact, has a single person besides you even *mentioned* the subject?"

Kyria could not see Alayna's expression, for her sister's back was to her, but Kyria and Francisco exchanged glances. She recalled how her sweet, timid sister had managed to enlist this man's help on a mission that most would have considered insane.

"I'll tell you what is going to happen." Alayna stopped short of wagging her finger at her husband's nose, but she sounded as if she would like to. "You are going to get yourself inside, and warm, and tended to."

Scathfell did not look convinced, but if they all stood out here much longer, they would soon join the ranks of the incapacitated.

"*Vai dom*," Kyria said, "since it is your desire to surrender, and since a good host considers the comfort of her guests, I hereby accept. Now it is my command to you as my prisoner to go with your wife and obey her every whim. Rest assured, all good care is being rendered to your men, and when you have been fed and rested, you have my leave to ascertain their condition for yourself. Are these terms acceptable to you?"

"These are not what I have any reason to expect, but I do not see that I have any choice other than to accept your generosity." He withdrew his sword from the scabbard tied to his saddle and offered it to her, hilt-first. As he did so, he attempted to kneel, but his balance was not secure. He would have fallen, had not Alayna slipped her shoulder under his arm.

"Put that thing away," Kyria said. "I have no use whatsoever for it, and neither do you, not here." When he did not respond, she said, "Oh very well, give it to Francisco. He will stow it where it can't hurt anyone." When this was accomplished, she managed to convince Lord Scathfell to come inside.

Renata appeared again as Alayna and her husband were passing through the opened doors. By this time, the most badly wounded men had already been carried inside and the horses led away by the stablemen.

"Lady Renata, Lord Scathfell," Kyria said, preceding the couple into the castle. "Lord Scathfell, the dowager Lady Aldaran."

"*Z'par servu, vai angela*," he murmured.

"He hit his head," Alayna explained.

"All who come in peace are welcome here," Renata replied, a trifle distracted. "You will excuse my lack of manners, but I come on a matter that cannot wait. Kyria, you must accompany me at once. Edric is awake."

39

Lord Scathfell had indeed suffered a blow to the head, but the injury was not nearly as severe as Alayna feared. He had a gash in his scalp, just above the hairline, and she remembered from her experience with Ruyven how badly such cuts bled. He was not concussed—so Renata thought when she examined him—just exhausted from a rapid march, the horror of the lightning attack, and then the desperate journey to Aldaran, all the while trying to keep as many of his men alive as possible. He had been willing to bargain his own freedom, his very life, for theirs, and it had taken him some while to comprehend that he was an honored guest, not a prisoner of war.

Gwynn underwent medical ministrations first from Renata and then Correy, Edric's body-servant, the latter apparently dispatched on Edric's own orders. While they were caring for his wounds, night overtook the world. After Gwynn had bathed his hands and face by candlelight, and put on a clean shirt, he ate a little of the food that was brought in and downed half a pitcher of *jaco*. Alayna stayed with him the entire time.

Whatever she said or did now, she must be mindful of his dignity. In his mind, his actions had been both honorable and necessary, despite ending in failure.

The world goes as it will, not as you or I would have it, ran the old proverb. And the world had not gone as she expected. Nor as he had, either.

"I don't know how to talk to you," she said.

"Nor I, you."

"Are you very angry with me? For coming here? Warning them?"

In answer, he held out an arm and drew her to him.

"I did not intend to betray you, you know," she said. "I truly believed that what you were doing would end in the deaths of my sister, her babes, and her husband. Your men. *You.* I didn't know what else to do. I thought that if I warned them, and their castle were shut up tight, you would give up and go home."

Gwynn's expression, which had softened somewhat, turned somber. "It would not have made any difference, whether you brought word of my intentions or not. One way or another, the invasion would have been discovered, and the results would have been the same. For all my plans and preparations, I did not count on Edric Aldaran possessing the Rockraven storm Gift. In my arrogance, I assumed that because he had spent so much time in a Tower, he was little better than a sandal-wearer. Weak, effete, bookish. He certainly gave no evidence of a martial bearing in Thendara. If anything, he treated me with such gentle courtesy, what else was I to conclude?"

"Perhaps that he wished to mend the quarrel of your fathers."

Gwynn shook his head. "You could have shouted it from the turrets of Thendara, and I would not have believed it." He sounded like he still could not quite encompass the notion. "When my men spotted a glider, I knew it had to be him. After all, who else at Aldaran had the *laran* to operate such a thing? I thought we had frightened him off, the coward. We pressed on, even more certain now that we could take the castle by ordinary means. And then . . ." His voice trailed away and he swallowed.

"And then he sent the storm."

"I have never witnessed anything like it," he said, his voice subdued. "Never *imagined* it. As if earth and sky, rock and rain, had all been overthrown, and chaos issued through the cracks in the world. Not even Aldones, Lord of Light, in all his glory, could sear the very air with lightning that way. Again and again—oh, gods!—until the ground beneath our feet turned into a smoking ruin, and the rain that rushed down on us from the sky stank of charred flesh. My men ... my men ..." He covered his eyes with his free hand, clinging even harder to her.

Alayna put her arms around him, feeling the tremors in his body, like sobbing that could not be expressed. "I'm so sorry, so very sorry."

How long they remained like that, she could not tell. At last, he took a shuddering breath and, pulling free, ran both hands over his face. He looked as if he had been weeping.

"And it has all been for nothing," he said. "Scathfell is just as vulnerable as ever. Aldaran wields powers that no ordinary man can withstand, and we have nothing to defend ourselves."

"But if Edric swore a pact of friendship, would that not set your mind at ease?"

"I have seen how little such promises are worth. And what is to prevent his sons from doing as they please, knowing we cannot mount even a token resistance? What good are spears and swords, and the bravest hearts in the world, against a thousand bolts of lightning?"

There must be another way, Alayna thought. *He is beaten in spirit now, but he will not remain so. His fears will eat away at him like the wolf in the old story, and he will entertain first this scheme and that. There will be no end to this feud.*

"I have wasted enough time on myself," Gwynn said. "I must see to the wounded among my men."

"They are in the Great Hall. I can take you there." Alayna moved toward the door.

"It is not fit for a gentle lady to see such things. Many of them were badly burned."

Alayna lifted her chin. "If you can look upon them, then so can I."

Gwynn allowed himself to be conducted down to the Great Hall. Along the way, they encountered a few guardsmen and women servants, all of whom greeted Alayna in a friendly manner. Gwynn looked surprised, as if he expected she would be treated with grudging politeness, nothing more.

He sees how welcome I am, but not that he is, too.

In the hours since the rescue party had returned, the Great Hall had been transformed into an infirmary. Pallets had been arranged in rows and covered with layers of blankets to serve as beds, leaving aisles for the free movement of those who were taking care of the patients. It seemed to Alayna that the entire castle household was at work here, except for Kyria and Edric. Some bustled up and down with arms full of towels and bandages and stoppered jars, or with trays carrying mugs of drinking water, bowls of soup, or basins of steaming water that gave off the aroma of pungent herbs. Others attended to the wounded, washing them, bandaging them, lifting them to drink, and comforting them as they cried out.

Renata came forward to greet them. She had covered her hair with a white kerchief, and wore a long, bibbed apron over her gown. "*Dom* Gwynn, you are looking much better. I'm glad to see Alayna has taken such good care of you."

"I had not expected—" With a gesture that encompassed the enormous room, Gwynn stumbled to a halt.

"This is not the first time I have dealt with numbers of wounded men. Right here, in this very castle. I had hoped such dreadful times were behind us and I would never need those skills again. Sadly, some of these injuries are beyond my help. Two of your men died of their burns soon after arriving. Another may not survive. I think it would ease his mind if you spoke to him. Come, I'll show you."

She led the way down a passage between rows of tables toward a corner. "We've separated the burn patients, and within that group, those with the worst cases. That makes it easier to administer numbweed salve and sleeping draughts, and to keep the area as clean as we can."

Alayna followed a pace behind, although she wanted to stop by every man she passed. Each one had a name, a history. A family. A reason for being in Gwynn's army. Some appeared to be asleep, at least that's what she hoped, but here and there others turned toward her as she approached.

"Lady Scathfell . . ." They murmured her name as if it were a talisman against pain.

Renata and Gwynn were getting ahead of her, but she could not pass by without a word. She turned back to the last man who had recognized her. His face brightened as she approached. She asked his name and where he was from, which turned out to be one of the herding villages in the hills surrounding the valley of Scathfell. He spoke of a wife and three children, and of hard times. She touched his hand and wished him a speedy recovery and safe journey home. From his look of surprise, she gathered that no one had told these men that they were not prisoners, that as soon as they had recovered, they were free to return home.

She reached Gwynn just as he was drawing a sheet over the face of the burned man. His jaw clenched, muscles visible through his stubble, and his eyes were bleak. Renata had withdrawn a short way and was attending a nearby patient. A man in dark, unadorned clothing sat on a stool beside the head of the table, a cane propped against one knee. When he glanced her way, she recognized Edric. He looked pale but alert. She saw then that he was in the process of tucking something small and radiantly blue into the front opening of his jacket.

"He held out long enough for me to—" Gwynn said in a voice she hardly recognized, it was so choked with emotion. "I don't know what good I did."

"You eased his passage with great kindness," Edric said. "To die with such words in one's ears . . . we cannot hope for better."

"Unless it is to die peacefully in our own beds," Gwynn said with a trace of bitterness.

He takes this upon himself as his fault. Alayna felt a surge of desire to assuage his guilt, but then paused. Why should she lessen the pain he ought rightly to feel, the consequence of his own choices? "The best way to honor this man's death is to make sure that no other suffers a similar fate needlessly," she said.

"I intended only to defend Scathfell, to protect its people," he protested. "You know that."

Renata glanced at them, her lips pursed. "Such conversations are best taken outside. The only thing that matters here is keeping these men alive. Blame and recrimination cannot do that."

"My words were ill-timed," Alayna admitted.

"As were mine," murmured Gwynn. "*Vai dom, vai leronis.*" With a half-bow, he took his leave of Renata and Edric, and the man for whom he could do nothing more. Together with Alayna he proceeded up one aisle and down the next, stopping at each bed. She was surprised at how many of the men he knew, their names and the places they had come from. Men whose faces had been contorted in pain smiled, and their eyes lit up. For the few moments Gwynn attended to each, their spirits lifted visibly.

This is what a lord ought to do, she thought, *go among his people and let them know his concern. Not recruit them for an army with no function except to drain food and resources from those who have little enough already. Not to send them off to be struck by a storm no man can stand against.*

Eventually they came to the end of the last row and thence to the door leading out to the central hallway. One glance at his face, however, told Alayna that he was too keyed up to rest. She slipped her hand into the crook of his elbow. "If you have had enough of the sick room, perhaps you would like to meet the rest of the family?"

"I have already made your sister's acquaintance, if that's what you mean."

"She is *your* sister now, and Edric is your brother," Alayna pointed out. "But I will not impose on you to be amicable toward him, not when the thunderstorm is so vivid in your mind. I meant your nephews. It's odd to say *kinsmen* when they have not yet got beyond thumb-sucking and creeping about, making purposeful but otherwise incomprehensible noises, but they too are your relatives."

"Lord Aldaran's get."

Alayna came to a halt, tightening her grip on her husband's arm. "Gwynn-Alar, you are not to refer to those little angels in such an odious manner! They are *babes*. The worst things in their experience are soiled breech clouts and having to share their favorite toys."

At this, he threw his head back and laughed, sounding younger and more carefree than he had in a long time. He had laughed in just this manner when they were first wed.

——— ✦ ———

At Alayna's tap, the door to the nursery swung open and, feeling she need not stand upon ceremony with her own sister, she went in. Gwynn followed a pace behind. Although night's chill had not yet settled fully into the stone walls and floor, a fire cast dancing orange reflections through the room, added to the soft light of the matched candelabra. An array of dishes on the sideboard gave off the delicious smells of roasted onions, herb-crusted poultry, and spiced apples. Alayna's stomach rumbled in response. She could not recall when she'd eaten last.

Kyria sat in the rocking chair, a lap robe tucked around her legs, playing with Donal. Pietro sat on the rug, the wooden ball between his chubby hands. When Pietro noticed Alayna, he dropped the ball. Laughing, she caught him in her arms and swung him up in the air. He shrieked in delight. Donal, noticing the attention his brother was receiving, let out a cry and held out his hands to Alayna.

"Wait your turn, little man," Alayna said. "There's only one of me."

Before Gwynn could protest, she thrust Pietro into his arms. Gwynn shifted the boy to a more comfortable position. Pietro snuggled close, laying his cheek against Gwynn's chest.

"You see, I do know something about children," Gwynn said.

"I can see that," Kyria told him, "and am heartily glad of it. I am without a nurse at the moment. She's down in the great hall, performing a different sort of nursing. Meanwhile, that lovely food has been sitting there, and every time I put these imps down, one or the other of them starts howling fit to wake the folk in Valeron, and then the other joins in. As a result, I'm famished." She went straight to the sideboard and began helping herself.

Alayna had heard that breastfeeding created an enormous appetite, but until she saw the size of the servings her sister took, she had not quite believed it. Kyria made up plates for her and Gwynn as well, and for a time, they took turns holding the children and eating. Plate loaded with second helpings, Kyria sat while Alayna curled up on the rug. At Kyria's insistence, Gwynn, still holding Pietro, took the rocking chair.

In between showing Donal how to pile up blocks—which he then took great delight in knocking down—Alayna watched her husband. He had the most peculiar, bemused, perhaps *bewitched* expression. It was the magic of babes, Alayna supposed, and most especially *these* babes.

She would have thought them enchanting even if they were not Kyria's. For a brief moment, he seemed to have forgotten the terrible events that had brought him to this place and time, even the farewell to the burned soldier.

Alayna glanced at her sister and wondered if she should mention having seen Edric in the great hall. Although Alayna knew little of *laran* healing, besides what it felt like to be on the receiving end, she suspected that was what he had been doing. Perhaps he felt obliged to make amends for the harm he had caused, even as Gwynn did.

As if summoned by her thoughts, Edric entered the nursery. He moved stiffly, leaning on his cane, but he did not seem to be otherwise impaired.

"Ah, there you are, love," Kyria said, in between mouthfuls of bread smeared with soft cheese. "We've left you a little food, although I'm afraid none of it is the usual for replenishment after *laran* work."

"I have already dropped by the kitchen," he said as he sank into a chair. "My mother has managed to use up a tenday's worth of honey pastries in a single night." He turned to Gwynn. "Lady Renata tells me you have recovered from your head wound."

"Thank you for your concern, but it was not as serious as it first appeared," Gwynn replied. Pietro, having given up on snuggling, took it upon himself to swat Gwynn's chin, despite Gwynn's attempts to get him to stop. When Pietro refused to desist, Gwynn attempted to continue speaking around the batting of little hands. The effect was not, Alayna thought, very warlike. "*Vai dom*, your lady wife has already accepted my surrender—"

"Blessed Cassilda," Kyria exclaimed. "You're not still harping on that nonsense."

"It is not nonsense, dear wife," Edric said. "These matters pertain to honor, and must be done in the proper manner."

"If you say so." Kyria returned to her spiced apple.

Edric shifted in his chair to face Gwynn directly. "I will of course accept your surrender if that is necessary, but I do so reluctantly. *Surrender* implies the forceful overthrow of one adversary by another, and I very much desire that we forge a different, more cordial relationship."

"You have defeated my army. My men and I are your prisoners, at your mercy. What other word do you have for it?" Gwynn was growing impatient with Pietro's antics now. Alayna glanced at her sister in mute appeal and Kyria, setting aside her plate, took the boy away.

"We have always been kin, and now we are brothers," Edric said. "That is how I would have us treat one another."

"Kin do not steal each other's promised brides," Gwynn pointed out.

Alayna's throat clenched. There it was, the twist of fate that could never be remedied. Gwynn resented having the wrong wife, the barren wife. That Kyria was so obviously in love with her own husband did not matter. When had the opinions and desires of women ever mattered?

"I believe the women have something to say about that," Edric remarked. "Kyria tells me that she had never laid eyes upon you when that contract was signed. Surely it is better to have a wife who knows and loves you? One willing to sacrifice her own happiness to keep you from harm?"

Alayna blushed at such praise. She had seen herself as desperate, not heroic. But Kyria was nodding, as if the truth was apparent to anyone who heard the tale.

"Other allegiances hold sway here," Edric went on. "We see two devoted sisters who were heartbroken at their separation. Seeing them now, in such accord, how can we who profess to love them do anything less than mend our differences?"

"Promises of peace are easily made, and just as easily broken," Gwynn said. "It is all very well to impose your idea of kinsmanlike relations upon a beaten man. But when these boys have grown to adulthood, assuming they have inherited the Rockraven storm Gift, what is to bind them to your fine words? What is to stop them from taking Scathfell for their own, knowing that neither I nor any heirs I may designate stand a chance against them?"

His words hung like fire in the room, and it seemed that Edric had no answer. For a long moment, for a handful of such moments, no one spoke. Even the babes fell still and silent, as if they sensed the gravity of Gwynn's question.

Kyria got to her feet, holding Pietro on one hip. Alayna looked at her through tear-filled eyes and barely recognized her, for she seemed taller and more powerful, capable of anything, as if a second figure overlay Kyria's: Evanda as the Eternal Mother? Blessed Cassilda cradling Hastur, son of Aldones, who was Lord of Light? *I hardly know this woman.*

But this was Kyria, after all, who'd wrestled with her brothers, gone out trapping against their father's wishes, stolen buns from the kitchen, gotten kidnapped by brigands, fought a banshee, snuck into Comyn Castle to see her ailing sister, birthed not one babe but two, and taken charge of the remnants of the Scathfell army as Lady Aldaran.

"Lord Scathfell has the right of it," Kyria said. They all looked at her in astonishment, but none more so than Gwynn himself. "It's easy to dismiss a feud as a relic of the past, something best forgotten. But for those who have lived all their lives with the stories of loss and grief, it is no simple thing to replace suspicion with trust. At the moment, Gwynn has no power to pursue what he sees as the only way to prevent another such tragedy. That does not mean all is well. Defeated men eventually recover, unless they are slaughtered outright, and no one is willing to propose *that* as a solution. Scathfell is not going to disappear. Neither is Aldaran. Someday, in our lifetimes or the next, the question will arise: how can the Lord of Scathfell make his lands and people safe?"

She paused as her words sank in. Gwynn bent his head, casting shadows across his face so that his expression was unreadable. Edric nodded, his features thoughtful. Alayna stared at her sister for a long moment, feeling as if she'd been caught in a landslide that had suddenly reversed direction. What surprised Alayna most was how well her sister had grasped the situation, and how fitting that Kyria should make such a speech while holding a child in her arms.

But what were they to do? Gwynn was guest and family; they couldn't imprison him or prevent him from returning home. And even if they could, it would not solve anything. It would only make the situation worse when whoever claimed Scathfell—doubtless it would be Nevin—took it upon himself to secure his realm.

"The heart of the matter is, I believe, the inequality in *laran*," Kyria went on. "A generation ago, the Rockraven Gift of controlling storms determined the battle. Scathfell had no such weapon then, and certainly not now, nor has Gwynn any prospect of introducing it into his line in the future." Her gaze flickered to Alayna. "Here at Aldaran,

Edric possesses the talent, and Lady Renata, who is a Tower-trained *leronis*, assures me that Donal and Pietro do, too."

"Fortunately, neither shows any sign of manifesting it yet, which gives us hope that their *laran* will emerge naturally, at the proper time, and in such a way that neither endangers their lives nor risks becoming uncontrollable," Edric said.

"If I understand you," Gwynn said, "Aldaran now has the advantage of not one but three storm-Gifted *leroni*. My people's future is thus made all the more bleak."

His voice all but broke Alayna's heart.

Kyria, however, was gazing at Gwynn with an expression of kindness. "There is only one solution, although it is not a perfect one. It is not possible to divide three into two parts, so you must allow my husband to remain whole, trusting to the extent you are able that he will honor his word to refrain from using his Gift against you and yours in the future."

Alayna permitted herself a glance at Gwynn. His expression seemed no less desolate, no less hopeless than before.

"What I propose is this," Kyria said, taking a step toward Gwynn, "assuming it is acceptable to all of us." She glanced at Edric, who gave her a small, encouraging smile. They seemed to be in communication, of the same mind. Then she crossed the remaining distance and placed Pietro back into Gwynn's arms.

"Here is your son, to hold and to raise. To teach love for Scathfell, its people and customs. To remain ever tied to Aldaran by bonds of brotherhood."

Alayna covered her mouth with her hands to keep from bursting into tears. Shudders passed through her body, part relief, part surprise, part wild rejoicing. She was to have a babe—Kyria's babe!—to love and nurture as her own!

"I don't understand," Gwynn said, even as he folded the boy close to him. "You mean for me to foster one of your sons?"

"Not foster," Edric said. "Adopt legitimately, so that the next Lord Scathfell will not only bear the Rockraven Gift you covet, but will share the strongest bonds with his twin brother here at Aldaran."

"You would do this for me—for us?" Gwynn asked, his gaze going to Alayna.

"There is a condition, however," Kyria said, and although her tone was severe, her eyes twinkled with merriment. "The boys are not to become strangers. They must grow up as brothers, with all that implies. I suspect their mothers will find many occasions to spend holidays together at your castle or ours."

"It might be prudent to have them receive training for their *laran* together," Edric said, "since it is likely to awaken in a similar time and manner. In the Towers, we say that an untrained telepath is a danger to himself and everyone around him. That may be doubly true for these two imps."

"Which is the elder?" Gwynn asked. "Which takes precedence by order of birth?"

"Neither you, nor Edric, nor the twins will ever be told," Kyria announced. "We shall treat them as equal in right and rank. And each must be taught to love the other as his younger—or older—brother."

"That is not possible," Gwynn protested.

"Nevertheless, those are my terms," Kyria said. "What do you say?"

"And we are to have Pietro? Why him and not Donal?"

Kyria, glancing at the way Pietro was snuggled against Gwynn's breast, rolled her eyes.

Alayna turned to Gwynn, feeling so giddy it was difficult to form words. "Say yes!"

"My Lord Aldaran, you are in agreement with this mad scheme?" Gwynn said.

"As if I had devised it myself. It will grieve me to be separated from Pietro for even a single day, let alone the months that will pass before I see him again. But it is the best, perhaps the *only* way both my sons—excuse me, *our* sons—can grow and thrive, and their sons as well."

"We shall just have to make sure the time between visits is not too long." Tenderly Alayna placed Donal in her sister's arms.

"You would trust me with your son?" Gwynn said to Kyria. "Not knowing me, or what little you do know being so ill?"

"I trust *my sister*, who is fierce enough to keep any five husbands in line. You see how wonderful she is with the boys. The only danger will be her spoiling Pietro."

"It will be some little while until you and your men are

recovered enough to make the homeward journey," Edric said to Gwynn. "That will give us all a chance to get to know one another across the dinner table and the dance floor instead of over castle walls and battlefields."

"Not to mention the process of weaning these two, for I do not think Pietro will agree so long as his brother enjoys the advantage," Kyria added.

"Do we have an agreement, then?" Edric levered himself to standing with the help of his cane and held out his free hand to Gwynn.

Still holding Pietro in one arm, Gwynn stretched out the other. "You have my hand and my word on it."

The hand clasp led to exclamations of relief and delight, occasionally verging on tears. The sisters embraced one another and vowed that they would fill the times of separation with many letters. In the midst of the celebration, Renata came in. To no one's surprise she, grandmother and telepath, had had a fair notion of how the situation might be resolved. Although she expressed regret at losing daily closeness with one grandson, she pronounced the other quite sufficient to keep everyone in the castle on their toes, even more so if he took after his father.

"I was not such a troublesome, wandering child as all that," Edric protested.

"You do not remember, but I do," Lady Renata assured him.

"Even if you were not," Alayna said, "I have it on good report that *Kyria* was. Adventuresome and disobedient, too."

"I was not!"

"Was too!"

"Who said so?"

"Not telling!"

With this, the party dissolved into laughter. It was not until much later that anyone remarked how peacefully Donal and Pietro had fallen asleep, each curled happily in a loving parent's arms.

DARKOVER®

Marion Zimmer Bradley's Classic Series

Now Collected in New Omnibus Editions!

Heritage and Exile   *978-0-7564-0065-1*
The Heritage of Hastur & Sharra's Exile

The Ages of Chaos   *978-0-7564-0072-9*
Stormqueen! & Hawkmistress!

Saga of the Renunciates   *978-0-7564-0092-9*
The Shattered Chain, Thendara House
& City of Sorcery

The Forbidden Circle   *978-0-7564-0094-1*
The Spell Sword & The Forbidden Tower

A World Divided   *978-0-7564-0167-2*
The Bloody Sun, The Winds of Darkover
& Star of Danger

Darkover: First Contact   *978-0-7564-0224-2*
Darkover Landfall & Two to Conquer

To Save a World   978-0-7564-0250-1
The World Wreckers & The Planet Savers

To Order Call: 1-800-788-6262
www.dawbooks.com

DAW

New novels of DARKOVER®
by Marion Zimmer Bradley & Deborah J. Ross

"[*The Alton Gift*] is a must for fans of the series, and reads as if Deborah has been channeling Marion's spirit."
—*Center City Weekly Press*

The Clingfire Trilogy

and

"Ross has fleshed out Bradley's encyclopedic vision of the Darkovian Dark Ages..."
—*Publishers Weekly* for *The Fall of Neskaya*

To Order Call: 1-800-788-6262
www.dawbooks.com

DAW 165

Deborah J. Ross
The Seven-Petaled Shield

An all-new high fantasy trilogy of magic, myth, and war—from a co-author of the Darkover novels!

THE SEVEN-PETALED SHIELD
978-0-7564-0621-9
SHANNIVAR
978-0-7564-0920-3
THE HEIR OF KHORED
978-0-7564-0921-0

To Order Call: 1-800-788-6262
www.dawbooks.com

MERCEDES LACKEY
The Valdemar Anthologies

In the ancient land of Valdemar, beset by war and internal conflict, justice is dispensed by an elite force—the legendary Heralds. These unusual men and women, "Chosen" from all corners of the kingdom by their mysterious horselike Companions, undergo rigorous training and follow a rigid code of honor. Bonded for life with their Companions, the Heralds endeavor to keep the peace and, when necessary, defend their country in the name of the monarch.

With stories by authors such as Tanya Huff, Michelle Sagara West, Sarah Hoyt, Judith Tarr, Mickey Zucker Reichert, Diana Paxson, Larry Dixon, and, of course... stories and novellas by Mercedes Lackey.

To Order Call: 1-800-788-6262
www.dawbooks.com